Pamela Morsi

JOVE BOOKS, NEW YORK

WILD OATS

A Jove Book / published by arrangement with
the author

PRINTING HISTORY
Jove special edition / February 1993

Jove Books are published by The Berkley Publishing Group,
200 Madison Avenue, New York, New York 10016.
The name "JOVE" and the "J" logo
are trademarks belonging to Jove Publications, Inc.

ISBN 0-515-11185-6

PRINTED IN THE UNITED STATES OF AMERICA

When the former local football star and hometown war hero ran off to marry the bootlegger's daughter, a divorced woman, everybody in town knew that it would never last.

Happy 45th Wedding Anniversary, Mom and Dad!

Chapter
One

A full hundred yards beyond the nearest house, the long, shiny black rig pulled discreetly into the anonymity of the trees. Isinglass shades were drawn down over the three open windows of the wagon, and black crepe bow curtains, hung with heavy fringed tassels, trembled lightly in the evening breeze. It was almost full dark, but it was still possible to read the words emblazoned in delicately arched gold letters above the windows: SPARROW MORTUARY. Beneath the name, in smaller, more elite script was the declaration "Modern Embalming," followed by the motto "Preservation and Sterilization."

The driver set the hand brake and glanced around nervously as he stepped to the ground, wrapping the lines around the pull. Uncertainly, he ran a young, strong hand through his blond hair and smoothed the sides that had grown a little too long and waved casually at the base of his neck. Retrieving his hat from the driver's bench, he placed it upon his head straightly, without even the slightest jaunt or angle.

Self-consciously he checked the cleanliness of his fingernails, the straightness of his tie, and the buttons on the front of his trousers. Warily he looked around him. Finding no prying eyes, he swallowed his nervousness and took a deep breath. Then he headed toward the house.

It wasn't a house, really. It was a cottage. A lovers' cottage, a newlyweds' cottage, a miniature of a larger, grander house across town. That grander house, however, gleamed with care and hospitality. This cottage sat faded with neglect and isolation on the edge of town. As he approached the back entrance, he noticed that a number of the once crisp four-foot pickets that surrounded the yard were bent or broken. Clearly attempts had been made to repair the damage, but from the looks of things the carpenter didn't know a hammer from a broadsword.

The young man mentally calculated the size and number of new pickets needed to do the repair. The cost would be minimal, he decided, and might be very appreciated.

With another guilty glance around the neighborhood, he stepped through the back gate, which creaked loudly as he passed through.

"That, too," he whispered aloud to himself. He'd grease the hinge on his next visit. That is, if there was a second visit.

Stepping up to the back door, he glanced through the screen to the tiny kitchen. It was clean and neat and there was a pleasant fresh smell of cooked greens. Beyond the kitchen there was a lamp lit in the parlor.

She was home.

A momentary flash of anxiety swept through him, but determinedly he raised his fist and knocked boldly at the door.

A long moment passed before he saw her puzzled face peek around the door frame. Clearly surprised, she hurried toward him.

She was tall, taller than he'd remembered, and full-bodied. He swallowed nervously at that observation. Her bosom was quite ample and her hips generously curved. The apron tied at her small waist enhanced those curves. The young man did not require such enhancement to find the woman attractive. Merely the *idea* of Cora Briggs set his blood racing.

With difficulty he forced his gaze to rise to her face. Behind a thin veil of dark brown lashes were a very ordinary pair of pale brown eyes that were curiously scrutinizing him.

"May I help you, sir?"

It was the first time he'd ever heard her speak. Her tone was proper, almost haughty, and her accent was well bred, educated, citified. It was the most exciting and exotic voice he'd ever heard. She was everything he wanted. *Make her say yes!* he prayed and then quickly reminded himself that his particular errand was not one a gentleman had a right to pray about.

Manners! he cautioned himself quickly. Haywood always said to "treat the whores like ladies and the ladies like whores." Jedwin couldn't agree with the latter, but he felt the former was certainly not unseemly advice.

Jerkily, he pulled his hat from his head.

"Evening, Mrs. Briggs," he blurted out too quickly. "I'm James Edwin Sparrow, Jr., ma'am. The undertaker." He paused momentarily to give her a chance to remember him.

She did. "Of course, you're young Jedwin," she said, relaxing slightly.

"Yes, ma'am." He smiled with gratitude. "We're related by marriage."

Jedwin watched her mouth thin into one prim line.

"I am no longer married, Mr. Sparrow."

A red flush stained Jedwin's cheek and he wanted desperately to kick himself. *Don't talk about marriage,* he admonished himself. *Don't mention family! Try not to be an idiot!*

"May I come in, Mrs. Briggs?" he asked. Gazing longingly into the parlor, he cast a nervous glance behind him. The cottage was on the edge of town and the nearest neighbor a good fifty yards away. Still, he'd rather not be spied standing on her back doorstep. "I have something I wish to discuss with you, ma'am."

Without hesitation, Cora Briggs turned the wooden latch on the screen door and led the young gentleman into her parlor.

She seated herself in a small sewing rocker and gestured to Jedwin to take a place on the divan.

The interior of the cottage was completely unlike the grand house on the other side of town. The Briggs mansion was graced with wide, high-ceilinged rooms and airy passageways. The cottage had only the parlor and the kitchen on the ground floor. A small foyer at the front door contained only a hatrack and a stairway. Up the stairs was, of course—Jedwin hesitated nervously with the thought—up the stairs was paradise.

Sitting on the edge of the worn piece of upholstered furniture, Jedwin fiddled nervously with his hat, carefully straightening the already straight brim and smoothing the already smooth band.

The warm yellow glow of the coal-oil lamp heightened and brightened the features of the woman across the room. Being alone with her was a fantasy Jedwin had savored for weeks. Now, he could hardly bear to look at her.

"So, Mr. Sparrow," Cora Briggs said finally. "If you've come to tell me that Maimie Briggs has finally gone on to her reward, believe me, I am uninterested."

Jedwin sat up immediately. *Of course she doesn't know why I'm here!* She sees the undertaker, of course she's going to assume someone's died.

"As of Sunday last, ma'am," he said reassuringly, "Miss Maimie enjoys perfect health."

"How pleasant for her," the young Mrs. Briggs replied with some amusement. Then a strange, sad, almost frightened look came across her face. "Is it Luther?"

Luther who? Jedwin almost asked, before he caught himself.

"No, ma'am," he assured her quickly. "No one has died. At least not since old Mr. Cravens from down by Frogeye Creek last Wednesday."

She nodded at him, apparently relieved.

The silence between them lengthened. She was obviously waiting for him to speak. But still he hesitated.

"Why are you here, Mr. Sparrow?" she asked finally.

Jedwin almost wondered the same thing.

If someone had told him a month ago that he'd be sitting, hat in hand, in the parlor of the infamous Cora Briggs, he'd not have believed it. He raised his eyes to face her question, but the sight of her stole his memory.

She sat primly in the rocker, her hands genteelly folded in her lap. Her eyes were wide with curiosity. The neatly tucked pleats of her bodice could not disguise the generous curves of her bosom. But the voluminous skirting of steel gray poplin completely obscured any suggestion of the nature of her lower body. Jedwin caught sight of one scuffed brown leather toe peeking out beneath her skirt. The sight entranced him, mesmerized him. In his mind he felt the supple smoothness of sleek brown leather, then moved on to the thin warmth of cotton stockings whose length would be topped by lacy garters leading enticingly to wicked ladies' underdrawers.

Jedwin's mouth was as dry as cotton as he stared at the decently covered woman before him and imagined . . . imagined . . . sin.

"Your purpose, Mr. Sparrow?"

Jedwin choked on his own desire, quickly covering it with a nervous cough as the town's most notorious woman sat so primly across from him in the sewing rocker.

His speech had been planned, rehearsed, revised, committed to memory, discarded, reworded, and relearned. He opened his mouth and waited for it to pour out. It didn't.

He cleared his throat and tried again.

"I'm James Edwin Sparrow, Jr.," he began.

"Yes, I know," she said.

Jedwin cleared his throat again.

"I'm the sole owner of Sparrow Mortuary, one of the most prosperous and growing businesses in Dead Dog."

Mrs. Briggs nodded. "Says something about the town, doesn't it?"

Jedwin missed her amused expression as he concentrated on watching his index finger methodically prick the grosgrain on his hatband. "It seems obvious to even the most casual observer, such as myself, that in the eight years since your divorce from Luther Briggs, your situation here has become increasingly untenable."

Mrs. Briggs's eyebrow furrowed in concern. "If some civic group has asked you to suggest I leave town, Mr. Sparrow," she said with a quiet firmness, "I will have to tell you that you are not the first to make such a request. I, however, have no intention of leaving."

Jedwin looked up at her. "Oh no, ma'am," he said hastily, discarding his speech. "I don't want you to leave at all!"

Mrs. Briggs tilted her head with a puzzled expression. Her richly colored lips were slightly parted and Jedwin could see her straight white teeth, so bright that the contrast made her lips appear unusually flush. Her face was a long, almost bookish oval and there was nothing about her that would have been described as tawdry or common. In fact she had more the look of a schoolmarm than a scarlet woman. But appearances could be deceiving, Jedwin knew, and the sordid truth about Cora Briggs was legend in Dead Dog.

Jedwin took a deep breath and began.

"The recent panic and depressed farm prices have hurt all of us, Mrs. Briggs," he said. "One can't help but notice that your house is in need of some repair and the paint is peeling so badly that whitewash can no longer suffice."

Jedwin watched her blush with embarrassment. Being poor was not immoral or uncommon, but it was humiliating and especially so when pointed out by a visitor.

Jedwin attempted to soften the criticism. "I, of course, can have no knowledge of your arrangement with Luther Briggs."

He paused, giving her opportunity to speak if she wished. She did not.

"It appears, however, that he has not been overly generous and that you could benefit from some financial assistance."

"Financial assistance?"

"I am willing to provide you with a modest stipend for your discretionary use."

Cora Briggs was sitting stiffly in her chair staring at young Jedwin Sparrow as if he'd suddenly grown two heads.

"Why would you be willing to provide this 'modest stipend,' Mr. Sparrow?"

Jedwin's hands were damp, but he resisted wiping them on his trousers. This was what he'd come to say and say it he would. He was not Mama's good little boy anymore, he was a man. Men said what they liked and asked for what they wanted. Jedwin liked Cora Briggs and, oh, how he wanted her.

Determinedly he raised his chin. He would speak plainly and openly and she could accept or reject as she pleased.

"I would like you—" he began.

Her very ordinary brown eyes were narrowed on him.

"I would like you—to become my—if we could—perhaps we—I was thinking that—"

Jedwin froze up, unable to get the words out of his mouth.

"Mr. Sparrow." Her words were soft and cool as she looked him straight in the eye. "Are you offering me an indecent proposal?"

"Yes, ma'am, I am."

Chapter
Two

It was Haywood's fault, actually, Jedwin decided. That Haywood could put an idea in a person's head and for life itself you couldn't get away from it.

Haywood Puser was a master embalmer, a genuine human being, one heck of a nice man, and the best friend that Jedwin Sparrow had.

Almost three weeks previously Jedwin had complained to Haywood about his mother's stepped-up campaign to marry him to some respectable female.

"Don't let Old Mellie get you in a pickle," Haywood had said. They had laughed good-naturedly as they worked together in the back room. "Your mama just wants her boy to marry up. That's what all the mamas want for their boys."

"I am not a *boy* and I *don't* want to get married," Jedwin had stated emphatically.

"Never?" Haywood's look was speculative. "Your mama'd best not hear that, it'd give her apoplexy. And if the boys down at the pool hall hear it, they'll be saying worse."

"I've got nothing to prove to a bunch of billiard bums," Jedwin said. "Marriage and manhood are two entirely different things."

Haywood raised his hands in mock surrender. "Don't tell me what I already know. It's your mama who hasn't got a firm grasp on the obvious."

The two were scrubbing the embalming room, sleeves rolled up, lye soap and carbolic in their buckets. The faint smell of formaldehyde clung to the air, making Jedwin somewhat queasy. He hated the room. It had memories that tortured him, weakened him. It was Haywood's workroom now since Jedwin no longer practiced embalming. He could have avoided the smells, the sights, the memories altogether, but instead he forced himself to walk inside it every day. He gave Haywood assistance he neither wanted nor needed. He did it to prove to himself that he could.

"Marriage is not something one just jumps into," Jedwin explained unnecessarily. "There are more than just practical considerations. Finer feelings are to be considered."

Haywood nodded and offered a wicked chuckle. "Not to mention the fine feeling that comes rising up in your trousers when you least expect it."

"Connubial bliss is more than copulation," Jedwin replied high-mindedly.

Haywood met that with a grin. "And copulation is more bliss than connubial."

Jedwin began scrubbing the table harder than necessary. "I just haven't found the right woman, that's all."

That statement evoked a disbelieving snort from Haywood.

"Ah now, this is me you're talking to. Admit it, Jedwin. You haven't found *any* woman."

Jedwin glared up at him. "Dead Dog isn't exactly Paris, France. I can hardly give a good look to a girl in this town before her mama and mine have got their heads together."

Haywood smiled and offered a sympathetic nod. In some ways, Jedwin Sparrow was the most eligible bachelor in Dead Dog. In others, he was the most unmarriageable man in town.

"Don't bother looking at those girls if you aren't thinking marriage," Haywood advised. "And you don't need to be thinking marriage, at least not yet. But sowing a few wild oats might surely take the edge off your disposition."

Jedwin shook his head. "In this town, the only oats are those I grow on Pratt farm!"

"There are women aplenty if you just keep your eyes open."

Jedwin shook his head. "Not for me, Haywood. Most of the women at those fancy houses in Guthrie are toothless and ancient, and even the pretty ones don't smell exactly clean."

Haywood's eyes widened in surprise. "Stay away from those places, son," he said with genuine concern. "If I'da thought you were thinking of such a thing I'da knocked some brains into that fool head of yours."

Jedwin's eyes widened.

"I've seen too many bodies eaten up with venerealia," Haywood told him. "Whorehouses are putrefaction in human form."

"You're contradicting yourself. First you tell me to get myself a woman, then you warn me of the dangers waiting in the fleshpots."

"I told you to look around," Haywood said. "There are decent women, clean women, that just need the slightest little push to go racing headlong off the straight-and-narrow."

Jedwin handed the scrubbed pine drying board to his companion and gave him a look. Haywood was nearing fifty, but he was still a handsome man. His thick, curly hair and beard had long since become more silver than black. His big blue eyes shone openly with the honest emotions of his heart, and the ladies seemed to be drawn to him like flies to honey. Jedwin wondered curiously which local woman Haywood was currently leading down the primrose lane.

"So," Jedwin said. "Are you going to introduce me?"

Haywood gave a howl of laughter. "Then your mama would have me out on my keyster!"

Jedwin frowned slightly. "The business belongs to me. You are in *my* employ. Even my mother understands that."

"Yes sir, Mr. Sparrow, sir," Haywood teased gently. "But Old Mellie's already near to driving you crazy now. Do you want to give her more reasons to bend your ear?"

Jedwin clearly had not. So he hadn't asked for suggestions of women willing to stray the path. He had followed his own judgment and decided on the sure thing. Tonight he'd sought out the most scandalous woman in Dead Dog, Oklahoma Territory, the infamous Cora Briggs, *divorcée.*

The infamous woman he had so determinedly sought out now sat staring wordlessly at the young man opposite her and wondered how in the world her life had become so muddled.

Jedwin Sparrow, a pleasant, hardworking young man and the bright, devoted, near-saintly son of that horrible harridan, Amelia Sparrow, was in her parlor making an indecent proposal.

She watched as he nervously slicked back the hair at his temples and waited for her reaction.

He was waiting for her reaction.

He was expecting a reaction.

The one that seemed most appropriate was for her to step across the room and box the young man's ears.

"Please leave my house, Mr. Sparrow."

She watched his face fall in disappointment. Did the young man actually think she'd be open to such a suggestion?

"Perhaps if you took more time to consider?" he asked quietly.

"Consider?"

"Mrs. Briggs, I am a generous man and very discreet. I am neither cruel nor unseemly. I'm sure, ma'am, that you could do worse."

The insolence of his speculation infuriated her.

"I'm old enough to be your mother!" Cora blurted out.

Jedwin seemed somewhat surprised. "I'm twenty-four," he said quietly. "I thought you weren't much past thirty."

"I am twenty-nine!"

Jedwin nodded without apology. "My mother was forty-three her last birthday."

"I *do* know your mother, Mr. Sparrow."

"It's a small town, Mrs. Briggs. Everybody knows everybody."

"Does your mother know you are here?"

Jedwin's mouth dropped open in disbelief. "She certainly does not."

"Perhaps she would be interested to know that you have come to visit me?"

Jedwin raised his chin. "I'm sure she'd be interested to know that you invited me in."

Cora gasped. "You said you wished to speak with me about business! I thought that—" She hesitated. No amount of explanation could ever correct a well-seasoned rumor. "Your mother would believe anything of me," Cora admitted honestly. "Unlike yourself, I have no reputation to lose."

Jedwin smiled. "For a gentleman, *reputation* can be all for the gain."

Cora opened her mouth to argue, but knew it to be absolutely true. That fact made her furious. If a woman made the slightest misstep, she was ruined for life. A man could virtually wallow in sin, scandal, and immoral turpitude, and the worst that would happen was a bit of tittering behind black lace fans. It was a lesson Cora had learned the hard way, but one she'd never forgotten.

That was behind her now, she reminded herself. Eight years behind her. Every day it seemed that she had to remind herself that all that was behind her. Apparently she was still the only person who believed it.

"Mr. Sparrow," she began coldly. "I find your suggestion highly unflattering."

"I meant no insult, Mrs. Briggs," he answered honestly. "I *am* younger than you. For most young men, there comes a time when one wishes to experiment a bit. To sow his wild oats, as they say."

Cora watched as he compulsively bent the hat brim he'd been so carefully straightening earlier.

"I find you extremely . . . attractive, Mrs. Briggs. And I hoped that perhaps you might consider a . . . liaison between us as beneficial."

Cora straightened her shoulders and adjusted her cuffs righteously. "I am no trollop to be purchased with ribbons and geegaws!"

"Certainly not!" Jedwin said quickly. "There are improvements I could make on your property. Paint and lumber can't be bartered with eggs and garden goods. I could provide cash money for such. And dress goods, Mrs. Briggs, I know you don't go out much, but surely you'd like a new dress? Maybe I could take you to Guthrie? A new dress and an evening at a play and dinner?" Jedwin seemed to be warming up to the idea. "And your future, ma'am. Everyone needs to save for their later years."

"A pension for promiscuity, Mr. Sparrow?"

Jedwin cleared his throat.

"Whatever you want, Mrs. Briggs."

"What I want, Mr. Sparrow"—Cora's words were crisp enough to cut shoe leather—"is for you to take your illicit propositions and immoral suggestions out of my house and never come back!"

Rising to his feet, he bowed stiffly to her as if to take leave. "I meant no offense, Mrs. Briggs, and I am infinitely sorry to have troubled you." The handsome young man's obvious dismay placated Cora somewhat. "Please be assured," he said, "that I shall never reveal my foolish and inopportune overture."

Jedwin's hands seemed to shake as he placed his proper black hat on his head.

Served him right! Cora told herself. The boorish little oaf propositioning her like some sort of Saint Louis fancy piece. She wondered, irrationally, if his mother had put him up to this, then immediately discarded the idea. Amelia Sparrow loathed Cora. She would die a thousand deaths if she even dreamed her precious only son had breathed the same air as the notorious Cora Briggs.

Suddenly—full-blown, a terrible, horrible, *wonderful,* idea came to Cora's mind. She watched the broad young shoulders impressively covered in fine black and gray cassimere retreating through the kitchen and an inexplicable smile twitched at the corner of her mouth.

"Mr. Sparrow!" She stopped him as his hand reached for the back-door screen.

"Mrs. Briggs?" She now was the one somewhat at a loss for words. She twisted her hands nervously and then smiled in what she hoped was an inviting fashion.

"Perhaps I've been hasty."

"Ma'am?"

Cora blushed honestly and then gave a fair imitation of a flutter. "All this talk about 'stipends' and 'benefits,' " she said, as if the words were unfamiliar to her. "Why, they just put a lady right off."

Jedwin swallowed. "Again, I apologize."

"When a gentleman comes to call," she said with feigned shyness, "he usually speaks of romance."

"*Romance?*" Jedwin spoke the word with such undisguised distaste that Cora almost laughed.

She looked up at him in a clearly flirtatious manner. Her eyes widened with feigned innocence and her lips curved into a clearly provocative smile. "Surely, Mr. Sparrow, you don't expect . . . well . . . what do you expect?"

Jedwin looked at her mutely, clearly beyond expectations of any kind. Her sudden change of mind confounded him. Her sudden nearness excited him. His sudden reaction embarrassed him.

Cora reached for his arm. "Come back into the parlor, Mr. Sparrow," she said, her fingers touching his upper arm which, though decently covered in fine, store-bought cloth, was firm and clearly strong. "Or perhaps I should call you Jedwin?" Her foolish little giggle sounded strangely foreign to her, and Jedwin wondered if she was the same woman of a few moments earlier.

"Dear dear Jedwin," she said as she led him back to the divan. "Sit right here and let me take your hat."

Woodenly he handed it to her and Cora took the somewhat battered hat to the foyer where she hung it on the rack.

Jedwin's eyes followed her curiously as she returned to the rocker and perched herself upon it nervously. She looked down at her hands for a moment and then hurriedly, as if just remembering his presence, raised her eyes to his. She smiled broadly.

Jedwin smiled back, but she got only a brief glimpse of it as she immediately dropped her eyes again.

If the previous conversation between them had been awkward, this nonconversation was positively maladroit. Jedwin was uncomfortable, but the possibility that she'd changed her mind kept him seated.

"What did you mean about being too hasty?" he asked finally. "And what about . . . about romance?"

Cora raised her chin to look him bravely in the eye. He had the look of Amelia Sparrow, she thought. That same yellow blond hair of which Amelia was so proud hung a little too long at Jedwin's nape in neat little curls. His features were well formed, with high cheekbones and a graceful jawline that seemed to accentuate the pink curve of his lips. He was almost too finely attractive, but something about his eyes, his intense and watchful maple brown eyes, saved him from prettiness.

Cora allowed her gaze to stray from his face to the width of his shoulders and the long, solid length of his arms. The hands he clasped loosely together at his knees were large, strong, workingman's hands. The kind of hands that could draw a woman's gaze from a pretty face.

"Romance?" Cora asked hastily and then recalled the game she wished to play. "Surely you know what I mean by romance." She smoothed the hair back from her temples and adjusted her hairpins as she smiled warmly. "Romance is flowers and poetry, sweet quiet moments and longing looks."

Jedwin swallowed. Carefully, he chose his words, trying not to offend.

"I thought *romance* was . . . ah . . . usually reserved for . . . ah . . . for honorable intentions," he managed finally.

Cora's eyes widened and her smile was playful. "And your intentions are not honorable, Mr. Sparrow?"

Jedwin raised his chin and spoke gruffly. "No, ma'am," he said. "They are not."

After a moment's hesitation, a small, light giggle escaped Cora's lips. "I admire honesty in a man, Mr. Sparrow," she said. "Perhaps you should try to remember that as our acquaintance progresses."

"Our acquaintance?" Jedwin's question was wary.

"Yes, our acquaintance," Cora answered. Her tone was almost businesslike. "I do find you rather attractive, Mr. Sparrow. With that curly blond hair and those brown eyes, I'm sure you turn the girls' heads at all the church socials."

Jedwin opened his mouth to deny it, but Cora didn't let him speak.

"As you said yourself, I rarely go out. For all my wicked reputation, I can assure you that I find life in Dead Dog infinitely boring."

Leaning back in her rocker, Cora crossed her legs, deliberately revealing a good three inches of leather-shod ankle. Jedwin's gaze was immediately drawn to the sight. When she casually traced her toe along the floor, his throat became as dry as the inside of a cotton gin.

"I would imagine that a dalliance with a strong, handsome young man like yourself could prove . . . amusing," she said.

Jedwin was almost stunned speechless by his good luck. Her smile was open, welcome, inviting. "You . . . want me . . . well . . . ?"

"My dear Jedwin," Cora answered softly. "I intend to allow you the honor of attempting to win me."

"Win you?"

"Win me, woo me—" Cora hesitated momentarily. "Seduce me. Is that what you have in mind, Jedwin?"

Pulling uncomfortably at his blue print neckerchief, Jedwin found it suddenly quite warm and airless in the tiny cottage.

She said yes. At least, that's what he'd thought she'd said. His wild dream had come true. She was going to let him touch her and kiss her, and eventually seduce her!

He stared at her now, imagining. What would that thick sorrel hair look like draped about her shoulders? Was that generous bosom mostly ruffles or mostly woman? Would her pale skin feel as soft as it looked? And when would she let him touch her?

Cora's eyes met his, and her heart caught in her throat. The intensity of his gaze was focused on her now and she was suddenly afraid of the risky game she played.

She'd thought of him as a boy, but in that instant Cora realized that young Jedwin Sparrow was a man, very much a man, and toying with him was surely foolhardy if not dangerous.

"Would you care for tea, Mr. Sparrow?" she said suddenly.

"Tea?" Jedwin repeated as if it were some strange foreign phrase.

Clearing her throat, Cora raised her eyebrows assessingly. "Tea, Mr. Sparrow, is a civilized drink that a gentleman and his lady friend might share as they become acquainted."

Jedwin nodded mutely. But in his mind he was coming to some conclusions. Easy now, he cautioned himself. She wasn't ready to let him touch her yet. She wanted to dress it up a little, make it seem more like courting and less like sin. He understood that.

Be calm, be polite, play along, Jedwin admonished himself. In another hour they'd be alone upstairs.

"Please, Mrs. Briggs," he said with his most sincere undertaker's tone. "I would love to take tea with you."

Cora sighed with genuine relief.

"Fine. I'll see you tomorrow at four then."

"Excuse me?"

"Tomorrow at four," she said. Her smile was uncompromising. "You may come for tea tomorrow, at four."

Chapter
Three

"James Edwin! Come into this parlor this minute!" The stern voice rang out the minute Jedwin opened his front door.

"Yes, Mama," he answered as he hung his hat on the rack. His steps were leisurely and unhurried despite the pique in his mother's voice.

The "family parlor" was in the back of the imposing red-brick house, which the sign over the entrance described as SPARROW MORTUARY AND FUNERAL PARLOR. His mother had designed the place herself with the most modern of funeral-home architecture in mind.

"Where on this earth have you been all evening?" she asked tartly as he stepped across the threshold.

Jedwin smiled.

Amelia Pratt Sparrow sat like a queen on a throne in the richly carved oak divan with blue damask upholstery. Although she was officially in "lavender mourning," the dress she wore was a deep rich color, almost purple, which showed her blond curls, pulled into a gentle matron's knot, to best advantage.

"I've been out with friends, Mama," Jedwin answered easily as he stepped across the room to place a gentle kiss on her forehead. "I left a message that you shouldn't wait up."

"That I shouldn't wait up?" His mother's words were as incredulous as they were dramatic. "That silly hired girl tells me that my *only* son has gone out somewhere I don't know, to see someone I don't know, for some purpose I couldn't guess, and that *I* am not supposed to wait up?" She gave a glance to heaven and a gesture of helplessness.

"I'm sorry, Mama," Jedwin said automatically and with very little apology. "Next time I will tell you in person. But you really shouldn't wait up."

Amelia hated it when she couldn't make him feel guilty. She tried another tactic, dabbing daintily at the nonexistent tears in her eyes with a lacy black hanky.

"Precious, you know how I worry," she whined in a much too girlish tone.

Jedwin very well knew. His mother had hovered over him like a shadow for as long as he could remember. Even when his father was still alive, Mama had always been there, always between them. Always taking Jedwin's side against his father and then making Jedwin do what *she* thought was best.

"There is nothing to worry about," Jedwin said calmly. "I'm a grown man, Mama. I can take very good care of myself."

Amelia gave a little sigh, followed by a pout that had been her trademark since girlhood. "I know you can, James Edwin, but Mama gets so lonely in this big house without you." Her expression sought pity. "If only you had a wife and children to give me some comfort when you are away."

Jedwin looked at his mother and sighed in defeat. There was nothing he wanted more than to go up to his own room, lie in the darkness of his own bed, and relive the last hour with Cora Briggs. The excitement, the disappointment, the anticipation all ricocheted through his brain like an explosion at a munitions factory. He wanted to examine each thought and feeling, savor each fear and fantasy.

But Mama wanted to talk to him. And, as so often with Mama, it was easiest to give in. Pushing back his own wishes, Jedwin seated himself comfortably in his armchair. Mama was alone in the world, except for himself; a fact she reminded him of almost on a daily basis. Although Jedwin loved his mother, her love was sometimes a burden.

Leaning back in his chair, he crossed his legs, laying one booted ankle on his knee. "I'll be marrying one of these days, Mama," he promised. "I even have a young lady in mind."

Amelia's eyes widened with delight. "Who is it?"

"It's someone of whom you will approve," he assured her. "But she is too young to speak with as yet. She has some growing up to do and it would be imprudent of me to name her." Jedwin smiled reassuringly. "Don't worry, Mama. You'll have your daughter-in-law and grandchildren in due time."

Pursing her mouth in vexation, Amelia wasn't totally satisfied. "Well, I certainly hope that I live long enough to see that day."

Jedwin ignored this guileful threat. "You need to socialize more, Mama."

"How can I socialize?" Amelia sighed with exasperation. "You know the whole town is waiting to see if Miss Maimie is going to claim us. None of the better people would dare befriend me without her approval."

Jedwin shrugged. "Then make other friends."

"And totally ruin our chances!" Amelia's voice was almost hysterically shrill. "James Edwin, I sometimes worry if you've got good sense. If we are ever to take our rightful position in this town, we will have to do it as members of the Briggs family." Shaking her head in dismay, Amelia spoke to her son as if he weren't at all bright. "All your father's money couldn't buy us a place. Not even your fine Eastern education has helped us."

Jedwin casually studied his fingernails. "Mama, I don't have a fine Eastern education. I have an embalming certificate from Toledo Correspondence School of Mortuary Practice."

Amelia ignored him. "I thank heaven every day that Grandpa Pratt married that horrible Matilda Copper after she was widowed. It was the only intelligent thing that old man ever did. Why, if she hadn't been a second cousin to Miss Maimie we would never amount to anything."

Jedwin shook his head and stifled a smile. If there was one thing in the world that Amelia Sparrow was sure about, it was the need to tighten up her loose family ties.

Allowing her to vent her spleen, Jedwin lounged comfortably in his chair and attempted to give the appearance of listening. He had heard it all before.

"You just don't know what it was like for me," Amelia continued. "Working myself near to death on that awful pig farm." She actually shuddered from the memory. "And me, the prettiest girl in Dead Dog, probably the prettiest in the whole territory, if the truth be known," she said with typical immodesty. "Do you think I wanted to marry your father?"

Jedwin knew better but his mother didn't give him a chance to answer.

"That awful old gray beard, with his cold hands," Amelia said, shuddering as she covered her forehead with a dainty hand. Then with an aggrieved sigh she straightened her shoulders. "Of course, you know that I came to be quite fond of your father," she admitted with soulful generosity before pointing an accusing finger at Jedwin. "I was a dutiful and loving wife to the old man until the day he died."

"Yes, Mama."

"And do you know why?"

"Yes, Mama."

"I did it for you, James Edwin," she said with a self-righteous sniff. "No son of mine will have to spend his life nursemaiding some filthy hogs! I made sure of that."

Actually Jedwin preferred hogs to coffins, but he'd learned better than to voice that opinion. He often wondered what his mother would say if he pointed out that had she not married Old Jim Sparrow, she wouldn't have had a son, to raise pigs or not.

However, discretion being the better part of valor, Jedwin held his peace and let his mother continue her familiar tirade.

Amelia's father had raised Duroc Hogs. It was a heritage the ambitious young woman hoped to outlive. At sixteen she'd married Jim Sparrow, the aging, withered undertaker. People talked. He was more than three times her age, but he had more than three times her money. She had assumed that marriage and money would give her a degree of respectability. To her distress, social status continued to elude her.

Having felt the stain of being a social outsider only vicariously, Jedwin found her distress difficult to understand. He hated it when she talked as if her life were over and somehow it was *his* fault.

His mouth thinned into a disagreeable line that had his mother immediately recanting.

"Not that I regret it for one minute," Amelia assured him as she turned her most gracious and long-suffering smile on him. "I only did what was expected of any normal, loving, Christian mother."

"I know, Mama," Jedwin said with only the tiniest trace of sarcastic humor. "You always do exactly what is expected of you, when you want to."

Jedwin's cynical reply went right over his mother's head as she immediately continued her conversation. Amelia Sparrow enjoyed her own talk more than anyone else's.

He did not disparage her. In fact, Jedwin admired his mother, but had few illusions about her. One advantage of growing up among the dead was knowing that rich or poor, illiterate or educated, human beings were pretty much flesh and bone and only careful and complete embalming kept them from going straight back to dust.

Jedwin had long since learned to take his fellow beings at face value. He could see faults and foibles, but rarely thought to censure.

He believed that people should be accepted as people. The fact that they were not, seemed only a strange social curiosity.

"So I realized that they would never choose a county seat named Dead Dog."

His mother's words caught Jedwin's attention.

"What are you talking about?"

Amelia puffed in exasperation. "You never listen to a word I say!"

"Yes I do," Jedwin assured her. "I just didn't hear this last."

Amelia gave a disgruntled hummph. "I've half a mind not to tell you at all."

Jedwin gave her an apologetic shrug.

She held her disapproval for a full minute before relaunching her explanation with vigor.

"It's the most perfect idea I've ever come up with," she said. "Maimie Briggs will be grateful to me till her last breath."

"Why, after all these years, would she be grateful?"

Amelia sighed with delight. "Because I'm naming the town after her."

"What?"

"I'm naming the town after her," Amelia said. "After her family—that is, after *our* family."

"What are you talking about?"

"Briggston."

"Briggston?"

Amelia's smile was dimpled with mischief. "Everyone in town is talking about what statehood is going to mean."

Jedwin couldn't deny that. Even as the U.S. Congress considered the Enabling Act, all gossip in the Twin Territories seemed to center on when and how statehood would come about and what it would change in the territory.

"You know how much Maimie wants Dead Dog to be named a county seat," Amelia said. "Well, as sure as I am living, no Washington congressman is going to consider a town for county seat that hasn't any more couth than to call itself Dead Dog."

"Mama, you can't just change a town's name," Jedwin protested.

"Well, I certainly don't know why not. It's a silly name if ever I heard one."

"The old trapper, Briggs, named it in honor of his loyal hunting animal."

"Poo!" Amelia disagreed. "Mr. Briggs should have named it for himself, not his dog."

Jedwin chuckled. "Actually, old man Briggs didn't really name the town. Maimie Briggs made up that tale for schoolchildren."

Amelia looked personally insulted. "How can you even suggest such a thing?" she asked.

Jedwin grinned. "Mama, Grandpa Pratt told me the truth years ago."

"How would he have known?"

"'Cause he was already here," Jedwin answered. "Old Henry Briggs was coming through this area trading whiskey with the Indians. He was drunk as a skunk that day. Which, according to Grandpa Pratt, was as common with him as head lice."

Amelia shuddered at the idea.

"Grandpa said that Briggs was so drunk he tripped over an old dog that was sleeping in a shady spot on the trail. Henry Briggs fell and broke his leg. He had a violent temper even when sober and, well, breaking his leg, it made him so mad that he shot that dog five times!"

Amelia gave a startled sound of disapproval.

Jedwin hooted with laughter.

"Grandpa Pratt told me that old man would still be shooting if he hadn't run out of bullets!"

Carefully adjusting the cuffs on her sleeves, Amelia gave her son a vivid expression of consternation.

"It was a Shawnee hunting party traveling through that heard the gunfire and came over to set the old man's leg and carry him out to the Pratt farm. *They* called this place Dead Dog for the carcass of that unfortunate animal. And the name just stuck."

"That is a horrible story," Amelia told him, but couldn't quite control the giggle that lurked in her smile.

Jedwin made no attempt to control his laughter. "Does Maimie Briggs know the true story, I wonder?"

Amelia blanched. "Don't you ever breathe a word of this, James Edwin! If Maimie had any idea that we know any of the family secrets, we'd be beyond the pale before morning."

Jedwin held up a hand as a vow to silence. "But if you don't intend to tell anyone the truth," he asked, "how are you going to get the name changed?"

"You don't have to show your laundry around town to wash it," Amelia insisted. "I'm going to appeal to the urbanity and sophistication of the townsfolk."

Jedwin looked at her skeptically. "I hope you aren't thinking of the townsfolk of Dead Dog. Urbanity and sophistication are not our strong points."

"You are such a gloomy Gus!" his mother said with characteristically coquettish pique. "Why, there is nothing really to change, just that sign at the railroad station and a few letters on a map."

"Mama, you don't have any idea what's required to change the name of a town."

Amelia shrugged unconcernedly. "Well, you *are* going to find out for me, aren't you?"

Cora Briggs placed the flat-brimmed straw hat on her head and secured it carefully with two long steel hatpins. She tested its position to assure herself it was properly anchored and then, with one last, hasty glance in her mirror, she stepped out her back door.

Her bicycle, a Hawthorne Safety with a duplex drop-frame designed especially for ladies, leaned against the house. She grasped the handlebars and walked it through the front gate to the road. The bicycle's once shiny frame now showed signs of rust and its tires were more patches than rubber these days. The bicycle had been a gift from Luther Briggs in the early days of their marriage.

Luther had given her what she wanted, she thought to herself. She'd asked for a house of her own and a personal mode of transportation. Both represented freedom and security, and at the time that was what she'd most desired. Some might say she now had more of both than she needed.

She mounted her bicycle, carefully arranging her skirts to keep them out of the chain or spokes.

Slowly, sedately, she rode through the Main Street of Dead Dog. Her back extremely straight and her head high, she looked neither to the right nor the left as she passed through town. As always, she felt eyes on her. Few of the local tradesmen missed the opportunity to see the notorious Mrs. Briggs taking her morning ride.

When she reached the railroad tracks, she dismounted and walked her bike over the crossing. Across the tracks was the area known as Low Town. Here were the homes of the town's few blacks, several families of Indians, and the dregs of the white community. As she cycled down the hill she picked up speed. By the time she passed the entrance to Moses Pratt's deserted pig farm, she was nearly flying, her skirt twirling unseemingly in the wind.

Unlike the calf-length, modish bloomers sported by many ladies back East,

Cora's cycling costume consisted of a long and very full bustleless skirt of nondescript navy, a neat press-pleated blouse of creamy white, and a short navy jacket that buttoned nearly to the collar. It was attractive but certainly modest attire.

But the fact that she bicycled at all was scandal enough for the small town. It was thought by some, including Reverend Philemon Bruder of Dead Dog's only church, that bicycling could stir unhealthy passions in women. The minister had warned Luther Briggs when he'd purchased the bicycle for Cora. And it was the preacher's opinion that the Briggs divorce could be traced directly to Cora's love for cycling.

That amused Cora. However, the reverend's disapproval was nothing humorous and she was careful not to purposely draw attention to herself. If he took it upon himself to do so, Reverend Bruder could have her run out of town. With no family, no friends, and nowhere to go, Cora walked a tightrope in Dead Dog. Unable to regain her reputation, she nevertheless could not afford to further antagonize the townsfolk.

That was why she was so concerned this morning about her impetuous plan. Yesterday it had seemed a fine and just revenge to pretend to be having an affair with young Sparrow. The snooty Mrs. Amelia Sparrow deserved to have her nose tweaked a bit, Cora was certain. And it seemed her son was cut from the same mold. But it could be dangerous. For Amelia to suspect an illicit relationship, the whole town would have to suspect, too. And what might that mean? Could Philemon Bruder accuse her of despoiling the town's youth?

It was a real possibility.

As Cora raced the rusty duplex drop-frame along the sandy road through the muted browns, yellows, and greens of the early autumn prairie around her, she contemplated her future.

As Jedwin had suggested, her financial situation was becoming desperate. Luther never sent her a penny, and Cora wouldn't have accepted his money if he did. She alone was aware of his difficult financial situation. No one else in town knew that Maimie had cut him off without a cent. Still, she was a woman on her own and assured herself that she neither needed nor wanted any contact with Luther Briggs. And as for accepting money from Jedwin Sparrow, well, that was impossible.

The house was hers, free and clear, and sometimes she almost felt guilty that it was hers instead of Luther's. Determinedly she pushed that thought away. Luther's troubles were of his own making. She had enough worries of her own without borrowing his.

The incline that led to the river bluff was steep and Cora slowed considerably. For the last several yards she was forced to stand on the pedals to make the top of the hill. Reaching the summit, slightly breathless, she dismounted and retrieved the contents of her basket before laying the bicycle gently on its side.

The highest spot for miles, this overlook of the winding, red, muddy Cimarron was Cora's own personal, private thinking place. She came here daily to restore her soul and refresh her health.

Carefully she laid out a worn quilt on the trampled grass and gently set her very tattered copy of Daisy Millenbutter's *A Ladies' Guide to Good Health, Fine Posture, and Spiritual Completeness* upon it. Removing her jacket and hat, she took a small flannel pouch containing a pound of marbles from her belongings and set it carefully on the top of her head like a beret. With precise, pointed-toe goose steps, Cora began to march back and forth across the knoll. With her chin high and her head held perfectly straight, the marbles did not roll and the pouch sat securely upon her head. According to Mrs. Millenbutter, fine posture and daily exercise were the keys to both good health and happiness.

Cora wasn't sure about that, but having been quite athletic all her life, she enjoyed fresh air and exercise. And perhaps it was not spiritual completeness, but Cora's outings helped relieve her troubles and lightened her burdens.

After several moments of posture exercise, Cora exchanged her marbles pouch for her Lewis wand. The hollow wooden pole, not quite four feet in length, could be adapted to sixty-eight different exercise activities. Cora started by turning it rapidly in one hand and then began twirling it wrist over wrist before her. Throwing the wand high in the air, she turned around rapidly before reaching up to catch it. The wand landed unceremoniously on the ground three feet in front of her. Placing her hands on her hips, Cora looked at the wooden instrument as if it were a traitor.

"I never miss!" she announced. Stalking over to the wand, she jerked it off the ground and began twirling again.

Today her lack of concentration was evident, but Cora couldn't seem to free her mind of her concerns.

"If you had any sense at all, you'd send that young man away the minute he shows up at your door," she told herself aloud. But she knew she had no intention of doing so. The opportunity for revenge against Amelia Sparrow was too priceless to pass up. Since the day Cora'd arrived in Dead Dog as Luther Briggs's bride, Mrs. Sparrow had done everything that she could to make her feel unwelcome. Certainly the fact that Maimie seemed to pit her daughter-in-law against Amelia didn't help much, either. Although Maimie, if she'd been reasonable, should have been content that her son had married a decent, healthy woman who appeared capable of bearing children and was a "real orphan" rather than some fallen woman's unlawful get, Maimie wasn't content at all. Cora's refusal to kowtow to Maimie and her determination to move into the cottage across town infuriated her even more.

Out of spite, Maimie turned her attention to Amelia, flaunting her preference for her distant cousin.

Then had come the divorce. She could easily have forgotten Amelia Sparrow as she'd forgotten the rest of her former so-called friends . . . except for the way Amelia handled the divorce. Maimie *knew* the truth behind the whole ugly mess, so she never said a word. She'd let Amelia Sparrow speak for her. And it was Amelia who spouted off lie after lie until the women in Dead Dog pulled their skirts out of Cora's way and the men declared open season on her virtue. Cora Briggs tried hard not to hate anyone. Hatred was a wasted emotion that fostered choler in the blood and acid in the stomach. For health reasons alone, Cora never hated anyone. But what she felt for Amelia Sparrow was about as far as one could get from friendship.

Again, Cora threw the wand high into the air. She swirled around in two neat turns and deftly caught the well-varnished piece of wood in her hand. Twirling it before her a couple of times, she leaned forward slightly and with her left hand tossed the wand right to left across the small of her back. Catching it with the right hand, still turning, she passed it to her left hand again and made the same movement across her neck. With one more orchestrated throw to heaven and a successful catch, Cora tossed the wand on the blanket and seated herself cross-legged for her deep breathing exercises.

Mrs. Millenbutter stressed the importance of freeing the mind of all thought. However, as Cora laid her hands open-palmed on her knees and closed her eyes, what she saw was not the oblivion of spiritual eternity, but the intense maple brown eyes of Jedwin Sparrow.

She shook her head.

Amelia Sparrow had hurt her more deeply than even Luther Briggs. At least Luther had had his reasons, such as they were. Amelia Sparrow hurt Cora just to please Miss Maimie. She deserved to be punished for that, and Cora deserved to be the one to do it.

But Jedwin Sparrow's eyes were not the pretty blue of Amelia's. They were his own eyes, a young man's eyes, eyes that appeared to have already seen too

much. Was it fair to use him for her instrument of revenge? No, it was not.
Cora knew that she must send the young man away. She would not play out
her vengeful plan. She would send him away today!

A wave of disappointment followed in the immediate wake of her decision.
In one sense she had told Jedwin the truth. Her life in Dead Dog *was* infinitely
boring.

With a sigh of defeat, she reconsidered. The young man might not be guilty
of slander as his mother was, but he was certainly guilty of uncouth behavior.
Thinking that his grave-digging money could buy him whatever he wanted!
Well, he certainly deserved to be set down a peg.

Cora opened her eyes and stared sightlessly into the distance. She'd already
set him down a peg. This afternoon she'd let him make a complete fool of
himself!

Cora couldn't quite tamp down the smile that came to her face. This was
going to be the least boring winter in eight years.

Humming a cheery tune, her cheeks finely dusted with flour, Cora Briggs
spent virtually all of her afternoon preparing for her caller. She hadn't baked
Indian cookies for at least a half dozen years. Luther disliked them, calling
them "a very sorry excuse for dessert." But for some unexplained reason, this
afternoon she'd been compelled to bake some.

Her sterling-silver tea service had been sold in Guthrie two years ago, but
Cora picked through the best of her dishes and set the table for lavish high tea.
The house was immaculate and smelled wonderfully of apples and burnt
sugar. Beneath her apron, Cora wore a rusty brown walking skirt with a
pleated back drapery that accentuated the curve of her bustle. On most women
the color would have been drab, but it was an exact match to Cora's hair and
the pale peachy-brown of her blouse brought color to her cheeks.

She knew she looked attractive; she knew her house was inviting; and she
knew her refreshments would be tasty. What she did not know was if she was
really going to go through with this.

"We'll just have tea," she assured herself. "And I'll tell him that I've
changed my mind."

She recited that plan to herself repeatedly as the clock made its torturously
slow movement toward the appointed hour. However, she still managed to be
startled when at exactly four o'clock she heard the discreet knock on the back
door.

Hastily, she removed her apron and hurried to greet him. She would give him tea, she decided, and a few cookies and send him on his way.

"Mr. Sparrow," she said, with an unseemly warm welcome in her voice. "Do come in."

Jedwin, hat in hand, stepped into the kitchen. He cringed a bit at being called Mr. Sparrow. "Jedwin" sounded so much more intimate and he'd been looking forward to hearing his name on her lips.

"Good afternoon, Mrs. Briggs," he said politely. He was scrupulously groomed and impeccably dressed. His blond curls were slicked down with spicy-smelling pomade, but still managed to wave attractively. His shirt was definitely Sunday linen and his tie was pure silk.

Cora was impressed. She had thought him attractive yesterday. Today he was even more so. Her hands trembled slightly as she took his coat.

"Please have a seat," she said nervously. "I hope you like Indian cookies, Mr. Sparrow," she began, almost chattering. She indicated the dining table covered with her best lace tablecloth before turning her back to him.

"Jedwin."

"Pardon?" She glanced back at him.

"Please call me Jedwin, Mrs. Briggs," he said. "It's so much friendlier."

Jedwin smiled warmly. The next step would be for her to permit him to use *her* given name. Cora. He'd already practiced the name in his head a hundred times since last night, and he was anxious to speak it aloud.

"Very well, Jedwin," she said. "I hope you don't take cream in your tea because I have none."

He stared mutely at her for a moment. She had not taken the hint! When she continued to look at him curiously, he realized that she'd asked him a question.

"Cream?" he responded finally. "Oh no, cream is not necessary."

"That's fortunate." Cora brought the steeping teapot to the table. It was Fairy pattern French china decorated with a delicate blue forget-me-not spray and a gold-traced handle.

As Cora poured the tea into the plain bone china cups, Jedwin immediately noted the startling contrast between the fanciful teapot and the cheaper cups.

"What a lovely teapot," he said conversationally.

Cora raised her gaze to his and smiled. "It was a wedding present from your mother."

She set the pot between them, and Jedwin eyed it with displeasure.

As he sipped his tea, he wondered how he was doing. After last night, he

hadn't expected to be immediately invited to the bedroom, but he had hoped
to make some progress toward that end.

She looked beautiful in the daylight, he decided. Casually he sneaked a
glance at her bosom. It was said that you could tell the real thing from ruffles
by the degree of roundness and a distinct separation of the two mounds. It
definitely looked as if she had two separate hills. He was trying to make a
judgment when he caught her eye.

Her cheeks were fiery red. "Do have a cookie, Jedwin," Cora said, offering
the tray.

Jedwin took three and set them casually on the small white plate before
him. Mentally kicking himself for embarrassing her, he eagerly took a bite in
hopes of making up lost ground. The cookies were more tart than sweet and
Jedwin liked them immediately. He raised his chin to comment on the fact,
only to find himself staring at the teapot. She had moved it to sit directly in
front of her. His appetite immediately deserted him.

"So, Jedwin," Cora said with appropriate civility. "Tell me about your
work."

"My work?" Jedwin was flabbergasted.

"Yes," Cora explained calmly. "Gentlemen usually talk about their work
over tea."

Staring at her, Jedwin was sure that she knew of what she spoke. Probably
she'd had tea with dozens of men. Men who were far more refined and
debonair than himself. Undoubtedly bankers, farmers, perhaps even plumbers
could speak of their daily activities with a young woman like Mrs. Briggs with
wit and interest. Mortuary service, however, was not something one usually
discussed over food.

"I'd rather hear about you, Mrs. Briggs," he said.

Cora glanced up from her tea, startled. *All* men wanted to talk about
themselves. In fact, it was her experience that it was almost the *only* thing they
wanted to talk about. Why would this man want to know about her? An
unpleasant answer came to her. He wanted the details.

"Myself? Jedwin, surely you already know everything about me." More
bitterly she added, "The whole town knows about me."

Jedwin remonstrated himself again for his clumsiness. He knew exactly the
appropriate things to say to families of the dead, but he had no idea how to talk
to a beautiful woman so full of life.

Occasionally he'd walked out with one of the local girls. They'd mostly
done the talking, cooing over some new geegaw or spreading stories about

their best friends. Jedwin had paid little attention. His main concern was that their time alone be long enough to show that he was courting and short enough so that the girl's parents wouldn't think his intentions were serious.

If he spoke at all, it would be about mutual friends or activities in the town. He and Mrs. Briggs had no mutual friends and she was not welcome at town activities. Jedwin frantically searched his brain for a conversation topic.

"I saw you ride out on your bicycle this morning," he tried finally.

"Oh?"

Jedwin warmed to the subject. "That's usually the time that I take a few moments for myself. I see you go by almost every day."

"Oh." Cora was aware that men watched her. Somehow it bothered her that he was one of those men.

"Where do you go?" Jedwin asked.

"Where do you think I go?" Cora's tart words were defensive.

Jedwin was surprised at her pique. "Why, I don't know," he admitted. "I guess I never thought about it."

Cora looked at the young man across the table and saw only sincerity in his eyes. She knew that rumors in town ranged from selling her body in Low Town to meeting Guthrie businessmen for a quick tumble on the seat of a fancy city rig.

"Actually I ride up to the river bluff," Cora heard herself telling him.

"That far?" Jedwin was clearly impressed.

"It's only five miles." Cora took a sip of her tea. She realized that she sincerely wanted to talk about her life. It had been years since she'd had a discussion of any kind with anyone. Jedwin Sparrow might have dishonorable intentions, but at the moment he was a captive audience.

"I am a great believer in the benefits of regular exercise."

"Oh, really," Jedwin replied politely, but with little interest.

"I've read most of the major thinkers on the subject, and find the philosophy of Mrs. Daisy Millenbutter follows most closely with my own."

Jedwin nodded. "I'm unfamiliar with Mrs. Millenbutter," he said.

"Perhaps I can lend you her book. She is truly most modern in her concepts of corporeality and spirituality as coexistent. The physical body is actually a proportionate blend of matter and energy," she explained. "Those two must remain in perfect balance for consummate human functioning."

Jedwin raised his eyebrows in surprise. He'd never heard such an idea. And couldn't imagine a woman having one. But then Cora Briggs was no ordinary woman.

Until eight years ago, Cora Briggs had been a decent, church-going woman. Reared in a Methodist orphanage and decently married to the town's leading citizen, no one suspected she would fall from grace. Jedwin could hardly remember her from that time. With his father still alive and his own demons to fight, teenage Jedwin had hardly been aware of Luther Briggs's marriage. His mother had talked of nothing else, worrying that the "little nobody" was not doing what Maimie wanted.

Her divorce, however, was the stuff of schoolyard legend. Divorce was not rare in the territory. In fact, with its progressive divorce laws, Guthrie was considered a haven of sorts for people all over the nation to get a quick sundering from an unwanted partner. Those divorces, however, involved strangers. Luther and Cora Briggs were not strangers in Dead Dog. And the cause of their breakup was mysterious enough to capture the imagination of every youth at school.

"She divorced him for desertion," Titus Penny had announced during a break from stickball. "But he didn't leave until she filed for divorce. So that's a damn lie for sure."

His news, which was undoubtedly accurate since his father had the Guthrie paper delivered twice a week, brought immediate speculation.

"My dad says that most divorced women are whores," Clyde Avery said. "A decent woman would stay with her man, no matter what."

Clyde's use of the word *whore* was almost as exciting as his father's declaration. A real whore in Dead Dog! It was almost more than the pack of fifteen-year-olds could contemplate.

Jedwin had made a point to get a good look at her. After he'd finished his chores the next day he'd sneaked down to the cottage and hidden in the shrubbery near the fence. He'd waited for what seemed like hours for the divorced Mrs. Briggs to appear.

Finally she'd walked out to take some sheets from the line. Jedwin's eyes had immediately taken in her womanly shape and handsome profile. When she'd raised her arms to the sheets, his gaze had been immediately drawn to the roundness of her bosom.

His physical reaction had been exactly what was to be expected of a youth of his age. Cora Briggs had been the first woman to make him experience desire. And his desire for her had colored all his dreams and expectations of women, both decent and indecent, from that day forward . . .

"Now matter," Cora continued patiently across from him at the kitchen table, "is more or less constant. But energy tends to build up within the nervous system. If that energy is not released on a regular basis, it begins to outbalance matter." Cora shook her head with dismay. "You can imagine the result."

"I can imagine," Jedwin lied. He'd allowed his thoughts to roam to the past and had lost the thread of the conversation.

"The result," Cora said, "is improper bodily functioning, ill health, and ultimately waste and death." Cora's declaration was adamant and her tone solemn.

Jedwin was puzzled by her strange words. What on earth could the woman be speaking of? Women were only interested in gossip, clothing, houses, and men. Usually in that order. Why on earth would a woman speak of energy and exercise?

As if a devil had alighted on his shoulder, Jedwin suddenly understood what he thought she was saying.

Haywood Puser had a similar philosophy.

A man's got to have a woman from time to time, Haywood frequently told him. All that wanting just builds up inside a man and he's got to have a woman or die trying.

Jedwin stifled a smile. Apparently, Cora was saying that she also had needs that she had to "get out or die trying." He'd heard his mother's horrified whispers with Maimie about the unhealthy indecency of a woman *straddling* a bicycle. If Cora Briggs was riding her bicycle daily, she must be needing him as much as he needed her.

"I've had similar thoughts myself, Mrs. Briggs," he said. Casually he stretched out his left leg and as if by accident pressed the toe of his foot against Mrs. Briggs's instep.

Cora immediately moved her foot.

"There is no question," Cora continued, "if you read the work of Sargent or Gulick, that internal cleanliness can only be achieved by external stimuli."

Jedwin took that as an open invitation.

Rising to his feet, he grabbed up the teapot that sat like his own mother between them and put it on the kitchen cupboard. Moving his chair around the table, he sat down beside Cora.

She seemed startled by his movement, and he gave her a reassuring wink.

With his elbows on the table, Jedwin leaned toward her. His smile was enticing, masculine. And totally devastating.

"There's no question about it." His words were a low purr. "That energy just builds and builds until we've got to get it out, don't we?"

Cora was totally baffled and more than a little flustered by the warmth of closeness and the temptation of his smile.

"Why . . . why, uh . . . yes, exactly," she stuttered. "I was not aware that you were a proponent of physical culture."

Jedwin brought one long masculine finger to her chin, touching her for the first time and bringing her gaze up to his. "I'd thought, Mrs. Briggs, that I'd made myself very clear that I am extremely interested in anything physical that involves you."

Turning his head slightly, Jedwin closed those intense maple brown eyes and lowered his lips toward Cora. He could almost taste her already. His heart was pounding. His brain was numb. Desire rushed through him.

The warm touch of his hand on her jaw, the masculine scent of his nearness, and the tingling anticipation of the moment almost paralyzed Cora. It was so warm, so sweet, her heart suddenly ached for something she did not understand, something unknown. Inhaling the essence of him only a hairsbreadth away, she was almost mesmerized.

He is going to kiss me! her brain finally screamed and she jumped as if there had been an actual shout.

Her chair clattered to the floor.

"Cora?" Jedwin hurried toward her, only to see her flatten herself more fearfully against the wall. "Cora, I—"

"You will refer to me as Mrs. Briggs!" Cora hissed defensively. "Now leave my house!"

Jedwin was stunned by her reaction. He reached out to comfort her.

She flinched.

Jedwin held his hands in the air beside him in a gesture to assure her she had nothing to fear.

"Please, Mrs. Briggs," he began.

"Leave my house." Her words were adamant, but Jedwin saw her swallow compulsively.

"Mrs. Briggs, forgive me," Jedwin said quietly. "Please don't make me leave. I do want to stay."

"I *know* what you want, Jedwin Sparrow. You told me yesterday, you want to sow your wild oats. Well sir, you will not sow them here!"

"Mrs. Briggs, I—"

"I am not some fancy woman that you can buy off with a few trinkets, Mr. Sparrow. I had every intention of telling you that you would *not* be allowed to call on me. Now I am more sure than ever that it is impossible."

"I'm sorry, Mrs. Briggs," Jedwin pleaded. "I thought—well, never mind what I thought. Nothing has happened, Mrs. Briggs, and I can promise you that nothing will happen between us until you are ready."

"Until *I* am ready?" Cora raised her chin haughtily. "I hate to shatter your fantasies, young man, but you will be wearing a long gray beard before *I* am ever ready for anything to happen between us!"

Jedwin stared at her silently for several minutes. The tension between them was tangible as he watched the agitated rise and fall of her breast. His eyes focused on her so intently, Cora felt like a specimen under a microscope. She was no longer frightened. She was embarrassed. She was humiliated at her own behavior.

"I have apologized, Mrs. Briggs," Jedwin said quietly. "I believe I deserve another chance."

Cora swallowed bravely and looked him straight in the eye. "Mr. Sparrow," she said. "I don't believe that our continued acquaintance can be worthwhile for either of us."

Jedwin folded his arms in front of him and gazed at her thoughtfully. She was, he decided, without doubt the most exciting, enticing woman he had ever seen. He wondered briefly about Luther Briggs's sanity. If Jedwin had a wife like Cora Briggs, there would be nothing she could do to make him want to leave her.

An almost physical catch jerked in his chest. He stood looking at the woman he'd dreamed about for so long. She was only a few feet away from him. And she needed him, he was sure. Jedwin decided, right there, that he'd sow his wild oats with Cora, or he'd not sow them at all.

"On the contrary, Mrs. Briggs," he said, his tone firm and decisive. "I believe our continued acquaintance could be worthwhile for both of us."

"No," she assured him, shaking her head and nervously studying her hands. "It can't. I know that yesterday I . . . please try to forget yesterday, Mr. Sparrow. I was not myself."

Jedwin raised a curious eyebrow and smiled. "Who were you? Can we get her back?"

Cora looked up shocked, until she saw his playful grin.

Jedwin took a step toward her and leaned an elbow against the wall. He was not touching her in any way, but he was very near.

"Please, Mr. Sparrow—" she began.

"I understand, Mrs. Briggs," he told her quietly, coaxingly. "I forgot the rules, didn't I?"

"Rules?"

His smile died and he let his gaze drift over her face. The smoothness of her forehead, the curve of her brows, the sweet, ordinary brown eyes and the flushed cheeks that narrowed to the fine, feminine oval of her jaw; he explored it all slowly, leisurely. When his eyes focused on her lips, they parted and she heard his involuntary indrawn breath.

"Wild oats is not what we agreed upon, was it, Mrs. Briggs?" he whispered. "We agreed upon romance."

"No," Cora insisted nervously. "We agreed upon nothing."

"Have you so quickly forgotten?" he asked. "You granted the honor of allowing me to try to win you."

"Mr. Sparrow, I—"

"Mrs. Briggs, I admit to being inexperienced, but I think I understand what you want. I am not giving up."

"What do you mean?"

"I intend to give you what you want," he said.

"Mr. Sparrow," Cora replied with the tone of a prickly schoolmarm. "You can't possibly know what I want."

"Of course I do, Mrs. Briggs, you told me yesterday," he said. "You want flowers and poetry; sweet, quiet moments and longing looks."

"What on earth do you mean?"

"I mean, Mrs. Briggs, that I intend to give you a romance."

Chapter
Four

"You're not wearing that?" Jedwin's words were more a sigh of resignation than a question.

"What's wrong with it?" Haywood Puser asked as he glanced down and straightened the short gray and brown checked jacket of his sack suit.

Jedwin shook his head. "If Mama sees you headed to a bereaved patron's home without a mourning coat she'll be furious."

Haywood smiled broadly, his perfect white teeth cheerfully framed by his smooth thick beard. "I don't mind sending Old Mellie on a conniption," he assured Jedwin. "Besides, that damn mourning coat is pure wool and hotter than a stovepipe."

With a sigh, Jedwin nodded. "Just get out the back door before she gets a look at you." He stopped in front of the mirror and examined his appearance. Stepping closer, he bent his head slightly and began fingering the thinning hair on the top of his head. After a moment's assessment, he reached into the bottom cupboard next to him and pulled out a big yellow onion from a sack he'd placed there. Taking a cleaver from the drawer, Jedwin halved the onion cleanly. With one half in hand, he stepped back to the mirror.

"Whew!" Haywood complained, waving a disgruntled hand before his face. "You're not still on that baldness cure?"

"It's working!" Jedwin claimed as he began rubbing the top of his head with the smelly yellow onion. I'm sure there's more hair up there today than there was yesterday."

Haywood shook his head. "You still got plenty of hair, but no onion is going to stop the hands of time. For a fellow like you, baldness is as inevitable as death."

"And I'm willing to accept both," Jedwin said. "I'd just like to wait till I'm an old man to experience them."

Haywood chuckled and Jedwin began smiling himself. "I'll be down in the basement if you need me. I want to see how the flowers are doing."

Haywood smiled at the retreating back of the young man he had so come to like and admire. He'd been working for Sparrow Mortuary since shortly after old Jedwin's father had passed on. He'd never known the old man, but he thought Big Jim very lucky. If Haywood's son had lived, he would have liked him to be like Jedwin.

Returning to his work, Haywood gathered the necessary equipment. Needa Willoughby's oldest daughter, Nadine, had passed away the night before. Haywood gave a slight sigh of sadness. Death was a part of life and the basis of his work, but it didn't make the loss of a blossoming young girl any easier.

Since it was still quite warm for fall, Haywood intended to suggest embalming rather than ice for preserving the remains for the funeral. Along with a portable cooling board, Haywood checked his dressing case for the pump, arterial tubes, a trocar, needles, forceps, scalpel, scissors, and eye caps. A length of surgeon's silk, a piece of oiled muslin, and a package of court-plaster were added to the case. The embalming cabinet contained two empty gallon bottles which were used for mixing, as well as several bottles of concentrated embalming fluid. A cotton sheet, a paper of pins, and a whisk broom finished up his mortuary needs. An assortment of door badges were the only trappings he took with him.

Jedwin would be meeting with the family later to plan the funeral and decorate the house for mourning. Jedwin could handle that without much trouble. He was good with people. He liked them. He just didn't like the mortuary business. Haywood understood that. Unfortunately, no one else did.

"Where is Mr. Sparrow this morning?" The voice from the doorway was sharp and shrewish.

Haywood finished his task before glancing up. "And good morning to you, too, Mellie," he said with a lazy smile.

Amelia Sparrow was dressed for mourning, but her gown was a far cry from sackcloth and ashes. The expensive black silk was cut in the latest hourglass fashion, emphasizing her generous bosom and youthfully cinched waistline. Giving her a thorough appraisal, Haywood noted privately that she was a little bit broad in the beam. However, he liked a woman with a good-sized backside on her. And he definitely liked the backside on Mrs. Amelia Pratt Sparrow.

"Pretty day for a funeral, wouldn't you say?"

Amelia Sparrow purposely ignored his good humor. Her bad tooth was positively throbbing this morning, and she was in no mood for pleasant conversation. "Where is my son, Mr. Puser?"

"Jedwin? Oh, he's down in the basement looking through the flowers."

Amelia nodded. "Very good. At least he's begun work on the Willoughby funeral."

Haywood shrugged. It was just like the woman, he thought, to check up on Jedwin as if he couldn't handle things for himself. She hovered too much and sure enough henpecked her son. To Haywood's mind it was only Jedwin's own strength of character that had kept him from being a Mama's boy. He was determined to do what he could to grease the way for the young man.

"I'm headed over there in just a few minutes to take care of the body," he told Amelia. "You can rest your mind about it, Jedwin's got everything under control."

Folding her arms across her chest, Amelia eyed her son's employee disdainfully. "Needa Willoughby is a dear friend of mine, Mr. Puser," she said sternly. "There is no need for you to trouble yourself, James Edwin will do the embalming."

Haywood glanced up, his face expressionless. But disapproval sparked like electricity in the air.

"Ain't no call for that," he said as he picked up the dressing case and headed to the back door.

Amelia's jaw set angrily as he walked away from her before being dismissed. She followed him and watched, temper rising, as he began loading the plain black dray.

"*You* are not dressed for mourning, Mr. Puser. Once you prepare the wagon, James Edwin will take it."

Haywood continued loading his equipment. "I'm doing the job," he said.

"I think not."

Haywood took a deep breath with a prayer for patience and turned to her. "You needn't worry about young Miss Willoughby," he told her calmly. "I'll have that poor little sick gal prettier in death than she ever was in life. Jedwin prefers for me to do it, and I'm going to do it. I am very good."

Amelia was not placated. "I am sure, Mr. Puser, that your skills are quite adequate. However, as a friend of the family, James Edwin owes it to the Willoughbys to do the job himself."

Haywood's jaw hardened. "Jedwin doesn't *owe* anybody anything. He downright hates embalming and if you had any sense at all you'd see that, Mellie."

Amelia's jaw dropped in shock and her eyes were shooting daggers. Raising her nose as high as humanly possible without falling over backward, Amelia's tone was deliberately haughty. "I am not the one lacking sense here," she said sternly. "You, Mr. Puser, forget yourself. I am your employer and my name is *Mrs. Sparrow!*"

Haywood carefully loaded the cabinet into the back of the dray and secured the door. "I know who you are, and as to who I work for—" His grin was humorless. "You'd best take that up with your son, Mellie. He says that I work for him."

With an insultingly slight tip of his hat, Haywood stepped around Amelia and headed to the front of the wagon.

She followed after him, angrily. "Mr. Puser! You will not walk away when I am speaking to you."

Haywood glanced back, raising his eyebrows in a feigned gesture of innocence before climbing up into the driver's seat. Looking down at the furious woman standing with arms akimbo on the ground beside him, Haywood noted her high color. In any man's estimation, Mellie Sparrow was a fine-looking woman. And she was one of the ones that looked beautiful when angry. It was a good thing, Haywood thought, since she was angry most of the time.

"I'm not walking away, Mellie," he said. "I'm driving."

With a full belly laugh, Haywood gave a flick to the reins and the chestnut dray took off at a sharp clip. Leaving Amelia Sparrow standing alone and furious in the yard.

Since Mrs. Briggs had stated unequivocally that romance meant flowers, romance was definitely meant to be a springtime activity, Jedwin was sure. Stepping carefully amidst the darkness of the basement, he assessed his options. With a wry grin, Jedwin realized that as the funeral director, he was one of the few who could wage a romance in autumn.

While most cellars and basements boasted innumerable jars of preserves and winter's stores of potatoes and peas, his basement was crisscrossed with hundreds of feet of unbleached cotton cord. Hanging blossom down from these lines, stems attached by plain wooden clothespins, was every leftover flower of springtime and summer. In a dark, dry basement, the flowers dried naturally, losing only the most brilliant vibrancy of their color.

Slowly, Jedwin walked through the rows, admiring his handiwork. The Sparrow Mortuary was known as far away as Kingfisher for having flowers at every service, winter and summer. That was Jedwin's greatest contribution to the business. Actually it was his *only* contribution to the business. For years he'd sought some aspect that he could excel at, something that he could offer from himself, something that he could enjoy doing.

He'd seen the idea in magazines and had approached his father with it. The traditional yards of black crepe and mourning ribbons were so lifeless, so depressing, so sad. People were sad enough at the reality of death, Jedwin had insisted. They need to be reminded of life. Jim Sparrow hadn't forbidden his son's pursuit, but he'd been uninterested. Seeking to impress him, Jedwin arranged a beautiful floral tribute to set next to the open casket of Walter Patrick. His father had only shrugged in acknowledgment and probably wouldn't have said a further word.

But fate, in the form of Reverend Philemon Bruder, played into his hands. When the good reverend arrived, he was scandalized, and with hellfire-and-brimstone gravity he ordered the "pagan symbols" out of the house.

At this Jim Sparrow had balked like a jackass at a railroad crossing.

Jedwin smiled as he recalled the memory. He'd really hardly known his father. Living in a house with someone for sixteen years made them familiar, but not always understandable. But on that long-ago day, the Sparrow men, for the first and possibly the only time, stood together.

"My boy put those flowers together," his father had stated flatly. "I think they are downright pretty."

Even in his later years, Big Jim Sparrow was tall and formidably muscled. Although a religious man and a faithful churchgoer, he had an independent streak as wide as eternity and a mile long. He may have let his wife run roughshod over him, but there weren't many others who dared. "If you don't like the look of them, Philemon, don't feel you have to stay. That front door goes out as well as in."

The good reverend was mad enough to spit nails, but he held his peace. Jim Sparrow was a gentle fountain of strength for the grieving. Given a choice, most would prefer to see him over the preacher. So Philemon Bruder *allowed* flowers at the funeral service and from that day forward, Jim Sparrow *insisted* upon having them.

The heady fragrance of dried roses distracted Jedwin and he stopped momentarily to examine the blooms. Immortelles, they called them in the cities, dried flowers meant to retain the beauty of life for eternity. Roses lasted well, as did carnations and greenbrier. Calla lilies, the most favored of funeral flowers, did not last well at all. Mother had wanted calla lilies for his father's funeral. But there wasn't a one to be had in the dead of winter. He'd laid his father to rest with a nosegay of winter-dried immortelles.

Jedwin's expression darkened. Immortelles for a lady's bouquet? It wasn't quite the thing, he thought as he considered the roses.

"Yes, the roses will be perfect."

Jedwin jumped with a guilty start at his mother's words behind him.

"Ma'am?" he questioned.

"The roses are the best choice for the young lady, I'm sure," Amelia answered easily.

Jedwin paled. How had she found him out? By heaven, did his mother have a Pinkerton detective on his trail? He raised himself to full height and set his jaw with determination.

"This is no concern of yours, Mama," he said sternly. "I am my own man and I will not be led around by your apron strings."

Amelia's mouth dropped open in surprise. "I was only making a suggestion," she retorted. "If you prefer the mignonettes or the cacalia, it is certainly your choice."

"Do you think me obtuse, Mama? I know we are not talking about flowers."

Amelia's expression was momentarily puzzled then hardened to a stubbornly set chin and a pretty pout.

"I suppose you heard me arguing with that awful Mr. Puser." Turning away from Jedwin, she folded her arms obstinately. "That man has not a lick of manners. He is common as acorns in August and I just don't know why you keep him on. Do you know what he said to me?" she asked, turning back to Jedwin, her eyes wide with indignation. "He said that this was *your* business, as if I were just some poor relation preying upon your good nature." Amelia began to pace restlessly. "As if I were not the woman who gave you your very life and sacrificed her own hopes and happiness to insure your own! The man has absolutely no respect for my position. Do you know what he calls me? Not Widow Sparrow, or Mrs. Sparrow, or even"—she stopped momentarily to take an exasperated breath—"not even Miss Amelia. That loathsome, ordinary creature calls me Mellie!"

Amelia Sparrow's voice had risen to a near caterwaul of frustration. When she turned to find her son's face displaying a wide grin, it turned to fury.

"What are you smiling at?" she screeched.

Jedwin valiantly tried to sober his expression. His relief that he'd not been found out had been quickly followed by amusement at her pique. No one had the ability to nettle Amelia like Haywood. It was one of the things Jedwin liked best about him.

"Now, Mama," he coaxed. "Don't take on so. You know Haywood is from Arkansas and can't be expected to have any manners to speak of."

Amelia turned on her son. "And you send that mannerless hillbilly to represent us to the family of one of my nearest and dearest friends?"

"I am going to the Willoughbys later. I intend to conduct the funeral myself."

"But you're letting *him* do the embalming!"

"Yes."

"Yes?"

"Yes!"

"And is that the end of it?" Amelia asked, nearly choking on her own anger. "You think you are too fine to do the kind of work your father had you trained for, so you hire another man to do it. A man who is mannerless, uncouth, and totally lacking in sensibilities. And I am just supposed to accept that. You may not care if he ruins your business, but I do. I am no spring blossom, James Edwin. If your business fails, who will support me in my old age? Will I go to gathering rags? Or would you prefer me to simply beg on the streets?"

Jedwin felt his own temper rising. "I will support you, Mama."

"Like my daddy did?" she asked. "I swear, you are just like him, not a drop of me or Jim Sparrow at all!"

"Mama—" Jedwin's tone was stern and cold.

"I have no time to discuss this with you," his mother interrupted him haughtily. "Poor little Nadine Willoughby lies silent forever, I must go over and comfort my dear friend Needa. Having buried a husband of my own, I fear the memories of my own long-ago grief will haunt me. But I am one person in this family who understands duty."

With an exaggerated sigh, the Widow Sparrow turned her back on her unrepentant son and piously headed toward the doorway. "I suppose that I will need to walk."

"I will drive you," Jedwin ground out between clenched teeth.

Amelia nodded perfunctorily at her son. "I shall be ready in a quarter hour."

Cora shivered as she drew on her coat and gathered her bucket for the trip to the outdoor pump. Cold weather was approaching, and she was ill prepared. The kitchen pump had frozen up solid the previous winter, and she had hoped all summer to get a little cash money ahead to fix it.

Shuddering, she allowed herself only a tiny moment of self-pity. "Women have survived for thousands of years without running water in the house," she reminded herself sharply.

Pulling her heavy coat on over her gown and work boots, she headed for the yard pump. The grass crackled beneath her feet. Still partially green, it glistened in the morning sunshine with the first hard frost of the year. She glanced up at the pecan tree. It was heavy with bright green clusters of nuts. Gratefully she anticipated the beginning of shelling before the week was out.

She trudged across the small backyard and the garden, now turned for the silent sleep of winter. Stoically, she made her way to the back fence and the water trough that Luther had used for his horses.

Luther had loved fine horses. He'd kept a matched pair of bays for the surrey and a quarterbreed saddlehorse. Luther looked good with horses. The memories of him handling a team or riding hell-for-leather to some forgotten appointment were ones that could still make Cora smile. He was a handsome man. And never more so than with a fine horse.

There were no horses now, and the trough had grown scummy and dark with disuse. As Cora jiggled some life into the pump, the thin sheet of ice on the surface of the trough cracked into a design like a spindly spider web.

Raising the pump handle to its full height, Cora grasped it with both hands. Throwing all her weight against it, she *rode* it down. When she'd reached bottom, she let the pump handle retreat with a light hand. Forcing it back into the upright position would only delay the rise of water. Unlike the pitcher-spout pump in the kitchen, the non-freezing hand-force pump in the yard was made for tall masculine shoulders and strong muscular arms. It took Cora a half-dozen strong, steady pulls before the frigid, stubborn water began to flow. By the time it had, she was no longer cold. The exertion had broken sweat across her brow.

Her bucket filled, Cora stopped at the woodpile beside the empty stable to grab up an armful of pine. It was green, sappy wood—the cheapest she could buy. Careful not to slosh the water, she made slow progress to her back door.

Once inside, she unceremoniously dropped the pine into the wood box with a loud clatter. Flexing her arm against the strain on her muscles, she then grasped the bottom of the water pail and poured most of it into the heavy iron reservoir built into the side of the stove. She'd already emptied the warm water left from last night into her washbasin.

Retaining the last bit of the freshly drawn water for the tea kettle that she set at the right, she hung the pail on its hook.

Cora shrugged out of her coat before stoking the coals in the fire box. She noted with dismay that the ash pit was almost full again. Last time she'd emptied it, she'd managed to drop the entire contents on the kitchen floor, and it had taken the better part of a week to remove the thin layer of gray film from the rest of the house.

Maybe the next time she'd bring the wheelbarrow inside. Long ago she had learned that being on her own in the world meant that she would have to innovate. But then, she'd always been on her own.

Her parents had come west from Missouri for the Oklahoma land run. Her mother had still been frail from her last birthing, another blue baby. Cora no longer remembered how many dead sisters and brothers she'd helped bury. But it seemed her mother lost one nearly every year. Finally, that year of the run, she'd lost her mother, too. She'd felt so frightened. Her father seemed to have forgotten her existence; it was as if she were invisible to the world.

Young Cora had spent her every waking moment doing the things her mother had done. Using her mother's broom and scrubboard, ironing her mother's sheets, putting up food in her mother's canning jars.

Despondent over the loss of his wife, and in dire straits due to a bad crop, her father had taken to drinking and gambling. When he lost the farm to a Kansas City card sharp, Cora had cried all the way into town. They'd lived in a tent that winter, with her father working odd jobs and drinking corn liquor.

The fire in the stove grate glowed cherry red with warmth, but Cora shuddered with that remembered cold. Sometimes when her heart was heavy and she felt misused, she'd remember that last winter with her father. It made her troubles today look like trifles.

It was the pleurisy that had killed him. It had happened so fast, Cora had never even thought to find a doctor. Strangers had come to her aid; strangers had laid her father to rest. And strangers had sent her to live at the Methodist Home in Muskogee, with strangers.

Home was what it was called, but not what it had been. The people had tried to be kind; Cora did not fault them. But she had known that her life would begin again some other time, some other place. She had worked and prayed and obeyed. And she had waited. She hadn't known why, but she was sure that someday someone would somehow come to fetch her.

Someone had.

The water in the wash boiler was making little warm whispers against the sides of blackened iron.

Cora gave a hasty glance to insure that all the window shades were drawn tightly. It was undoubtedly the height of indecency for a woman to bathe in the kitchen. But after living alone for eight years, Cora no longer felt the need to follow any conventions but her own.

Slipping her nightgown down to her waist, Cora dipped a clean cotton rag in the warmed water in the washbasin and soaped it lightly with a bit of homemade lye. Mrs. Millenbutter recommended a tepid shower bath for good health. Flushing away the impurities of the skin was a weekly obligation, she claimed. Cora, however, had no shower bath available and preferred more traditional, but daily, ablutions.

Rinsing away the soap and drying her stomach and breasts with a well-worn towel, Cora slipped on her corset cover and buttoned it completely before allowing her nightgown to drop from her hips and continuing her bath. Mrs. Millenbutter might have modern opinions on the occasional necessity of nudity, but the lessons of the Methodist Home stayed with Cora. On no occasion should a female ever be completely unclothed.

The Methodist Home was strict with the young ladies and rigid in their expectations. Marriage was the pinnacle of success. Luther Briggs had brought her that success. And Luther Briggs had taken it away.

Cora shrugged off the dark thoughts as she slipped into her drawers. She had wanted a home and Luther had given her one. The little worn white cottage was cramped and it was beginning to get a bit frayed at the seams, but it was home to Cora Briggs.

With some paint and a few small repairs it would be as good as new, Cora assured herself. The question of where the paint and repairs might come from was not one that she normally allowed herself to dwell upon. Today, however, she did try to consider her options.

Single women were very limited in their ability to make money. A baked-goods shop or a millinery were about the only businesses a woman could run. Most made a living at home taking in sewing or tatting lace. None of those occupations were open to Cora. Any food or clothing touched by a divorced woman was tainted in the eyes of the good women of Dead Dog. If she'd attempted doing business on her own, Cora would have starved to death years ago.

"Thank goodness for Titus Penny," Cora whispered to herself as she twirled her hair into a casual knot and pinned it securely to the top of her head. Titus bought her jellies and jams, even her persimmon syrup, and sold them in his store. He told the good folks of Dead Dog that they were made by the Widow Martin. The good widow also sold goods at the store, but she was old and frail. She couldn't produce nearly as much as Cora could.

And of course, the widow's were more expensive. Titus Penny was no saint, and Cora was sure he'd come by the name "Penny" quite honestly. He offered Cora only a third of what he paid the Widow Martin for the same product.

"I'm doing you a favor, Cora," he'd said, grinning at her in that irritatingly familiar manner of his. "If I don't buy this from you, nobody will."

Cora said nothing and kept her face free of expression, as he twirled the ends of his waxy, reddish moustache.

"What'll it be, Cora honey?" he said. "A little money or none at all?"

She'd wanted to raise her chin in defiance and strut out the front door of his store in a huff. But he was right. She had no place else to go, and something was just a little better than nothing.

With her hat on straight, Cora grabbed up her marketing basket and opened the back pantry. There was little left to sell. Berries had been scarce last summer and the drought had kept her garden from flourishing. Placing the last three jars of watermelon pickles in her basket, she carefully hid them from sight with a dishcloth.

"I have to lie to my own wife about this," Titus had often warned her. "It'd ruin my business if folks suspected I was helping you."

Cora cared little about ruining Penny's business. But he was her only source of income.

She banked the fire in the stove and carried her jars out to her bicycle. She needed flour or cornmeal. Sugar would be nice, although she could always substitute molasses for sweetener, but there was no substitute for bread.

The morning air was brisk as Cora made her way down the street. With the heavy basket hung on the handlebars, she had to be especially careful of the slick spots and holes in the road. It wouldn't do to fall and break her last jars of watermelon pickles.

As usual she kept her eyes to the center of the street. But as she passed Sparrow Mortuary she couldn't prevent her gaze from straying to the mammoth red-brick edifice with the wide, white-trimmed porches.

For the last two days she had tried, without much success, to keep her thoughts away from Jedwin Sparrow. But for someone whose only excitement was wondering how soon poverty would turn into destitution, the thrill young Sparrow had brought into her life couldn't be ignored.

She would simply send him away the next time he showed up, she assured herself.

Her decision so distracted her that she failed to check whether there were patrons in Penny's store. She'd already opened the door when she saw two women.

Standing in the middle of the floor was Titus's wife Fanny talking to Mrs. Amelia Sparrow, herself.

Chapter Five

Surprised at her own blunder, Cora stared momentarily at the two women.

Equally stunned, Fanny and Amelia stared right back. Fanny was dressed in a bulky calico that was designed, not too cleverly, to camouflage the fact that she was nearly six months pregnant. Her coat was apparently suited to her usual wardrobe and the buttons would not meet in the front, so she allowed it to hang open sloppily. In contrast, Amelia's gray silk, trimmed smartly with tiny intricate bits of black lace, was the height of mourning fashion and enhanced the attractiveness of her fair complexion and pale blond hair.

Cora almost blurted out an apology for interrupting, before she reminded herself that she had every right in the world to come to town and to visit a store. It was one of the facts of her life that Cora avoided Amelia Sparrow. Most of the other ladies in town were disapproving, but Amelia sought open confrontation.

Setting her chin with as much defiance as she could muster, Cora gave the women a civil nod.

A tiny huff of air exploded from Fanny Penny's throat at the horror of practically being spoken to by *that* woman. She gave Amelia a hasty, nervous glance.

"Whatever is she doing here?" Amelia asked Fanny in a whisper just loud enough for Cora to hear.

Cora determinedly turned her attention to the selection of pot lids in the corner of the store. Her heart was pounding as if she'd just made the top of the river knoll on her bicycle. Deliberately she attempted to slow her breathing and ignore the other occupants of the store.

"She trades here sometimes," Fanny admitted with some embarrassment. "I told Titus never to allow her credit," she quickly offered as proof of her own innocence. "He says she always pays cash in advance."

"Cash money in advance?" Amelia huffed as if scandalized. "Heaven only knows how she comes by it." Her tone suggested that she had her suspicions.

Cora kept her gaze on the pot lids. Experience had taught her that when the flames weren't fanned the fire faded out. Although Amelia Sparrow, of course, could always be counted upon to fan her own flames.

"I swear," she said to Fanny with a soulful sigh. "That dear Maimie Briggs has more to bear than the good Lord should ever have cast upon her."

Both women gave a half glance in Cora's direction.

"Yes, dear soul," Fanny agreed.

"What with having her only son so far from her, and the scandal she's had to live down." Amelia tut-tutted sadly.

Fanny nodded in agreement.

"Why, I do declare that the woman is practically a saint."

"A saint," Fanny echoed, nodding.

"With all she's had to bear, it just seems like the town ought to do something special for her. Something to lift her spirit from the pit that some have dragged her into. Something to acknowledge that none of us hold her responsible for the sins of others. Something just to show how much the whole town really loves her."

"What do you have in mind?" Fanny asked.

Amelia smiled, quite proud of the ingenious way she'd managed to approach the subject that was quickly becoming close to her heart. "I think we should name the town after her."

"Name the town?" Fanny looked skeptical. "The town already has a name."

"Certainly not a very good one."

"I suppose not," Fanny admitted.

"And certainly not a name that sounds like a county seat," Amelia said. "With statehood coming, we need to be ready to take on whatever responsibilities are thrust our way."

"Yes, of course." Fanny was gaining enthusiasm for the idea. The only way for the Pennys' business to grow was for the town to grow. And being chosen county seat was a very certain way to do that. "Why, a more prestigious name could be a great boon to the community."

"It certainly would. And we don't want to call it some unpronounceable native word, or name it after someplace back East—Boston, Oklahoma, just will not do."

Fanny giggled in agreement. "Oh no, nothing like that."

"I feel that for all concerned, the community should be named after its first and finest family." Amelia sighed with pleasure. "We should call it Briggston."

Cora Briggs completely forgot her nonchalant pose and turned, mouth open and eyes horrified, to stare at Amelia Sparrow.

Amelia glanced at her sharply and raised a disapproving eyebrow. "I've heard that those who are wont to eavesdrop frequently hear ill of themselves," she said sweetly.

Cora's jaw snapped shut and her face flushed in anger. Words of fury flew through her brain, forcing themselves to her lips, but she bit them back.

Briggston! Her brain screamed the word. No, no, she just couldn't believe it. It was bad enough that she was ostracized by her community, but to have that community named for that evil old crone who had ruined her life was almost beyond bearing. She wanted to scream, cry, roar the building down, demand to know who was responsible. But then she knew who was responsible: Amelia Sparrow.

Vicious words formed in Cora's mind, but she was saved from resorting to fisticuffs, not to mention social impropriety, by the sound of a little girl's black leather shoes beating a hasty gallop from the back of the store.

"I want a red one! I want a red one!" A cotton-headed child of about five years hurried to the counter, which displayed large colorful jars of hard, brightly colored candies. She jumped up and down in excitement, her thick white blond curls dancing and bobbing around her head. "A red one! A red one!"

"Maybelle!" Fanny Penny crossed her arms impatiently. "I told you, no more sweets until after lunch."

The little girl gave her mother a quick, blue-eyed glance. "Daddy said yes," she said with complete confidence in the outcome and returned to her cheerful hopping. "A red one! A red one!"

"Titus?" Fanny called to her husband as he entered slowly from the stockroom in the back.

The proprietor of Penny's Grocery and Dry Goods waved away his wife's objection. "Oh, let her have the candy," he said easily as he slipped behind the counter and unscrewed the lid of one of the large glass jars. "She's been a good little girl this morning."

"You'll spoil her," Fanny objected.

Titus didn't even look up. "Daddy's pretty little blondy deserves to be spoiled. What kind do you want, Maybelle baby? The red or the white?"

"I want both!" Maybelle declared loudly.

"Titus—" Fanny's tone was threatening, but her husband paid no notice.

"Then both you shall have," Maybelle's father told her. "One for now and one for later."

As Titus Penny filled each of his daughter's small pudgy hands with candy, Fanny turned back to Amelia, shaking her head disapprovingly. "I just don't know what to do with Titus. He just thinks the sun rises and sets on Maybelle."

Having grown used to having his wife speak about him as if he weren't present, Titus paid no visible notice to the women's discussion. But, of course, he plainly heard every word.

"Men just have no sense about children," Amelia said as she nodded with understanding. "Dear Mr. Sparrow, God rest his soul, would have allowed Jedwin to follow his own nature if I hadn't put my foot down. Fathers just don't think as clearly about their children's future as mothers do."

Amelia looked at the happy child, her mouth stuffed with candy.

"Mr. Penny thinks only to make Maybelle smile today. It never occurs to him how difficult it will be to find someone to marry her if she becomes ill-favored and gluttonous."

"She don't have to marry a soul," Titus Penny interrupted with displeasure. "She can stay right here and work in the store till her dying day. I'd be happy if she'd just brighten the life of her daddy in his old age."

Turning his attention to Maybelle, Titus heightened his voice to a childish decibel. "You want to just stay home and take care of your daddy when you grow up?"

Her mouth still filled with candy, Maybelle couldn't reply but nodded her head enthusiastically.

Fanny and Amelia glanced at each other with understanding.

"I'd best take her home," Fanny said with a sigh. She reached for her daughter's hand. When the young girl grasped hers, Fanny made a disapproving sound. "You are always so sticky!"

Maybelle shrugged with unconcern and allowed herself to be led out the front door.

As he watched his wife and child leaving, Titus Penny turned his attention to Amelia. "Would you care for a piece of candy yourself, ma'am?"

Amelia wasn't even tempted. Her bad tooth was already aching this morning, and she'd learned from experience that hot drinks or sugar could make it painful enough to send her to bed.

"No thank you, Mr. Penny," she said. "I am not some child to be bribed by sweets."

Penny nodded, in unhappy agreement. "Here's that roll of white bunting you wanted."

Amelia walked to the counter and fingered the material, considering. A movement on the far side of the room caught Penny's attention. Seeing Cora Briggs, he started.

Amelia looked up at him curiously.

"Fanny said that you allow *her* to trade here," she whispered too quietly for anyone else to hear.

Titus flushed darkly. "I'm the only grocer in town. I can't turn her away and allow her to starve."

Amelia considered his words casually as she considered the bolt of white cloth. "Perhaps if she couldn't buy food, she'd move on."

Titus looked skeptical. "Where would she move, Miz Sparrow? She ain't got no folks that we know of, no money to speak of, and she owns that house of hers free and clear."

Eyeing him again, more critically, Amelia said, "She must have some money or she wouldn't be able to trade here."

Again Titus's face blazed with embarrassment. "I don't give her a nickel of credit," he hedged carefully.

"See that you don't," Amelia's tone was louder and as deceivingly pleasant as her words were threatening. "I'll take this bolt, Mr. Penny, and a half-dozen needles, if you please."

Titus hurriedly wrapped Amelia's parcels. Guiltily he glanced several times at Cora, who continued to browse through the store with feigned unconcern. When he'd tied Mrs. Sparrow's purchases together, he chivalrously escorted her to the door, conversing pleasantly about the weather.

When the door shut behind Amelia, his smile faded and he turned to Cora. "I've told you not to come in here when she's here."

Cora's eyes narrowed in annoyance. "I am not a criminal, Mr. Penny," she said with calm deliberation. "I can come and go in this town as I please. I do try to avoid Amelia Sparrow. However, it is not because I *should* avoid her, but because I *want* to."

Titus Penny, a man who was easily intimidated by the ruffled feathers of his female patrons, quickly backed down. "Yes, yes," he cajoled. "And I want you to avoid her, too. That woman can be pure poison when she sets her mind to it."

"You don't have to tell *me* that, sir." Cora was still reeling slightly from the notion of renaming the town after Maimie Briggs. As far as Cora was concerned, Amelia might be the town venom, but it was Maimie Briggs who was the head of the snake.

Titus Penny nodded at her solemnly. "I suspect you would know." With a guilty glance to the front door, he gestured for her to follow. "Let's step into the back, shall we?" he suggested. "I wouldn't want any other customers interrupting our business."

With a nod of agreement, Cora followed him to the small storage area crammed with goods. A small work desk sat in one corner next to a poor quality yellow glass window that did little more than allow a bit of light to spill into the room. Piled high upon his homemade, shaved plank work desk were account books, invoices, and bills of sale. More papers filled the chair beside it. Titus swept them untidily onto the floor and seated himself. Self-consciously he straightened his moustache and cleared his throat before leaning back slightly in the chair and smiling speculatively at Cora.

"Well, what have you got for me today, Cora honey?"

Ignoring the endearment, Cora stared right back at him. "I have the last of my watermelon pickles," she said calmly. "I will be needing a few things today, but I believe I can wait to purchase my winter stores until after the pecans are in." Her tone was calm, unconcerned, and businesslike. "I had a look at my best tree this morning, Mr. Penny, and it is plainly loaded with pecans."

Titus nodded assessingly. "Pecans is good, Cora, no doubt about it. But I can get bushels of them from the farmers around here for a pittance."

Cora's too-warm smile was clearly feigned. "But would the farmers bring them to you shelled, in perfect halves, and impeccably clean?" she asked, already knowing the answer. "They sold very well last year, sir, if you will recall."

Titus shrugged. "Every year is different, Cora honey," he said. "Sure, you know I'll buy them, but I cain't promise that it'll be enough to keep you in flour and meal for the winter."

She swallowed nervously but continued to smile. "Well, I just know that you will do the best you can for me, Mr. Penny."

Titus put a finger to his temple and gazed at her thoughtfully for a moment.

Cora was used to bargaining with him; she knew that he wouldn't give her a penny if he could get by with five mils. But she had confidence in her product. The ladies in town had scooped up her pecans last year. Native pecans were by far the best tasting, but the toughest to shell and prepare.

Finally as if reaching a decision, Penny smiled charmingly at Cora and leaned toward her. "Every year *is* different, Cora honey, just like I said. I don't know how much I'll be able to do for you with pecans this year."

He reached out with studied casualness and grasped the material at the edge of Cora's bicycling costume. Rubbing the cloth with his fingers, as if assessing its quality, he looked up at her, his eyes darker. "It's been a rough year for farmers, Cora honey. It's been a rough year for me."

"I'm sorry to hear that," Cora replied quietly as she surreptitiously moved backward, hoping that he would release her skirt. He did not.

"Don't get me wrong," he said, his eyes still locked with hers. "Business has been real fine. I'm a lucky man. And a happy one. But, well—" He hesitated and glanced away momentarily. "You saw my wife out there," he said finally and shook his head. "Big as a cow already and still three months to go."

Cora felt the blood rushing from her face.

"She says she don't feel well most of the time, and she's taken to sleeping with Maybelle." His eyes traveled to his fingers and the cloth he continued to stroke. His gaze held there for a long moment before rising to look Cora in the eye once more. "A man can get lonely when his woman is nesting."

He looked at Cora for signs of understanding. "That big old bed of mine down on the corner can get mighty cold of a night."

No sound came from Cora's throat. Fear, anger, loathing, and pity all warred together. She wanted to walk away and never return. She wanted to slap Titus Penny's face and call him an adulterer. She wanted to scream that she was divorced, not immoral. She could do none of those things.

Slowly, purposefully, she gained control of her emotions. She needed Titus Penny and she didn't dislike him. He wasn't an evil man: just a somewhat boring and stupid one. There were many times that she had thought him downright kind. This was not one of those times.

With cool determination she stepped back, calmly clasping her skirt and pulling it from his grasp. "I know just what you mean, Mr. Penny," she said with exaggerated pleasantness. "Living alone myself, I do understand how long and cold these winter nights can be."

Penny looked almost stunned at her reply.

"You know what I think you should do," she said without giving him an instant to respond. "You should get Mrs. Penny to sew you up a thick down quilt. I swear, there is nothing in this world like the proper bedclothes on a cold winter night. It's certainly all I need."

Reaching into her basket, she set the jars of watermelon pickles on the desk beside him. "I am late for my morning ride, Mr. Penny. If it's not too much trouble, could I pick up some flour and cornmeal?"

Titus Penny's face was bright red, but he immediately followed Cora to the front of the store and measured her some of each and a bit of sugar extra.

Later that day when Cora turned her bicycle into her front gate, she was panting as if she'd run a race with the devil and as tired as if she'd spent the day chopping cotton. After her awkward conversation with Titus Penny, she'd ridden at breakneck speed through Low Town and had kept up a strong enough pace on the road that she managed to top the knoll without hardly slowing. She'd thrown her wand higher and faster than she'd ever managed. And she'd pushed herself to feats she had never before attempted.

None of these things, however, had managed to take the sting out of the morning's events. She was still angry, embarrassed, and unhappy. The injustice she lived with stung as smartly today as on the day of her divorce. Nearly every day she told herself that things were better, that she didn't mind anymore. Sometimes she could actually believe it. Then Amelia Sparrow or Titus Penny or someone, anyone, would remind her that she could not deserve anonymity or contentment.

She leaned the bicycle against the house and removed her basket from the handlebars, automatically checking the contents to insure their safety. Funny, she hadn't worried about her flour and cornmeal when she went flying hell-for-leather down the river road. All she'd thought about was fleeing the present, fleeing the past, and fleeing herself.

She was on the first of the back steps when she saw it. Propped up against the corner of the door was a bouquet of dried flowers. Cora's eyes widened. Tiny sprigs of myrtle surrounded three red roses, their dried color dark and rich, their petals still smooth and perfect. They were wrapped in a half-length of fine white linen and encircled by a blue satin ribbon. Tucked into the ribbon on the right side was a piece of folded notepaper.

Cora picked up the bouquet as gently as if it were a newborn babe and gazed at it with confusion and pleasure. When her hand brushed against the stiff folded paper, she hurriedly opened the note. The script was not penman perfect, but rather a large masculine scrawl.

> You are as fragrant as sweet myrtle
> And fair as the roses
> I can be more romantic
> Than you would ever supposes

Staring at the awkward, impromptu poem in her hand, Cora felt the troubles of the morning melt from her shoulders like candles on a hot cookstove. A smile teased the corners of her mouth and then one tiny giggle escaped her throat. She quickly covered her mouth with her hand, but not before real mirth had taken over. In a couple of moments she was leaning against the door, laughing until the tears ran down the side of her face. Laughing as she had not in years.

"Dear Jedwin, dear, dear Jedwin," she whispered as she leaned her head against the door frame. Poetry was undoubtedly one of his conceptions of romance. Smiling, she thought that surely someone should have told him it was best to steal words from Lord Byron.

Still smiling, Cora stepped through the back door. Leaving her hat and coat on the rack, she carried her romantic floral offering to the parlor and placed it carefully on the tea table.

Stepping back, she assessed the placement. She considered a vase, but decided none of the few she had left were deserving enough. The flowers were lovely in their wrapping, they would just have to stay that way. She moved them slightly to the left, smiled down at them again, and then proceeded with her business. It was a good hour past noon, and Mrs. Millenbutter was a great believer in taking meals at precisely specified times.

Humming to herself, Cora walked purposefully to the kitchen, only glancing back a couple of times at her unexpected gift.

It had been a long time since anyone had given her flowers. The last time . . . she couldn't quite conjure the memory. Then suddenly it was bright before her. The last time she'd been given flowers was on her wedding day.

"Here is your bouquet, my Cory," Luther had said warmly as he handed her up into the buggy in front of the Federal Courthouse in Muskogee. The judge had pronounced them man and wife not five minutes before and Cora had clutched the flowers nervously. "I picked those out myself," he admitted. "Mama told me that lilies were not appropriate wedding flowers, but since she couldn't be here, well, I thought they suited you."

Cora had felt a thrill of joy in her heart as she smiled at the unusual bouquet. "They are lovely, Mr. Briggs," she whispered.

As he seated himself beside her in the seat, Cora gazed up at the fancily dressed man at her side. Four times he'd come to call on her. But she'd never expected that he would ask her to marry him. Certainly she hadn't expected it to happen so soon.

Luther smiled broadly at her and Cora almost sighed at the sight. The dazzling bright smile only enhanced the deep blue of his eyes, his thick, curly black hair, and that one rebellious curl that slithered with unruly persistence down his forehead. His strong masculine jawline was tempered by the long, teasing dimples in his cheeks.

Cora's heart was in her throat. He was the most beautiful man she had ever seen. She was his wife. And she loved him.

"They are so beautiful, but it wasn't necessary, Mr. Briggs," she told him shyly. "I hate for you to waste your money buying me trifles."

Luther chuckled lightly and chucked her under the chin. "Now, Mrs. Briggs," he said. "I'll be buying you whatever I like. I want you to be the happiest woman in the territory."

"I am."

He stared at her seriously for a long moment as if uncomfortable. "Good," Luther replied finally. The word was positive, but somehow his tone was not. "Mama is going to love you, I'm sure of it," he insisted to both of them.

Feeling an attack of nerves skitter through her, Cora was not as certain. "I do hope she likes me, Mr. Briggs. I promise to be as good to her as if I were her own daughter."

Luther gave the team a whistle and started off down the street. "Don't you worry a thing about Mama. When she sees you and talks to you, why, she's going to be as thrilled as if you were her long-lost daughter."

The city streets of Muskogee were crowded with milk carts and surreys, delivery wagons and drays. Although Cora had lived in Muskogee since her father's death, she'd rarely had opportunity to leave the orphanage and take in the sights.

"I do think I'm going to love living in the city," Cora told Luther as she smiled at the excitement and noise surrounding her.

"We won't be living here," he said as mildly as if he'd just suggested the possibility of rain.

"We won't be living here?"

"No, I decided we should move to Dead Dog in Oklahoma Territory. My mama's getting older and she needs me near."

Cora nodded, but her head was full of questions. "I thought your business was here in Muskogee?"

"It is," Luther answered, glancing at her but not really looking at her directly. "I've got a competent foreman to handle things on a daily basis, and of course I'll need to make frequent visits to check on things. But I think that it's best if we live with Mama."

"Oh." Cora had a strange sense of misgiving. "But haven't you built your own house here in town?"

"I'm renting it out."

Cora's curiosity was immediately sparked. Most rented lodgings in Muskogee were crowded and mean. If a man could afford a decent house, then he built his own.

"Who in heaven are you renting to?" she asked him.

He turned to look at Cora closely. His jaw was set tightly. "What does it matter? If we decide to live in Dead Dog, we don't need the house. That is, of course"—he paused slightly before he turned to Cora; his most devastating smile formed at his lips and was aimed full force upon her—"if such a plan suits my new bride."

Blushing, Cora giggled with pleasure. It would take some time, she decided, to understand her new husband. But then, she had the rest of their lives. "Your new bride is pleased with any plan you decide on, Mr. Briggs," she whispered demurely.

Luther chuckled and patted her knee in a husbandly, familiar manner. "That's what I figured, Cory. And why don't you just call me Luther?"

She grinned at him. "Is that permitted?"

Luther laughed out loud. "Oh yes, ma'am," he said. "Just follow my lead. One thing your husband can be trusted to know is what's permitted and what ain't."

Cora laughed with him, running a stray hand through her hair to assure herself that the loose chignon she'd forced her curls into still held. "So tell me, Luther, my husband, what is the next thing that it is permitted for a married couple to do?"

Luther raised an assessing eyebrow. "The next thing . . . well, I suspect the next thing for us to do is check into the Williams Hotel. It'll be sundown before we know it."

Her mouth dropping open in horror, Cora quickly attempted to recover herself and gave her husband a nervous smile.

"Oh yes, of course."

Luther reached between them and gave her hand an encouraging squeeze.

"Now don't go all newlywed-jitters on me, honey," he said, smiling. "Things are going to work out fine. Trust me, Cory."

And she had.

Now, eight years later as she stirred a batch of johnnycake for her solitary luncheon, she regretted that trust.

Chapter

Six

Cora awakened with a start. She'd heard noises. Someone was outside. Fear clutched momentarily at her heart and she could hear the blood pounding in her ears. Thoughts of ax murderers, wild Indians, and violent outlaws poured through her head like a flood of headlines from the newspaper. Alone. A woman alone was always vulnerable, always easy prey. A woman alone had to protect herself, because nobody else would. Clutching fearfully at the bedcovers and forcing herself to take long draughts of air, Cora attempted to gain control.

"I'm fine," she whispered aloud. "I am a strong and independent woman. I can take care of myself."

She didn't believe the litany fully, but it helped.

Slowly, silently, Cora drew the bright quilted cover away from her legs and climbed out of bed. The moonlight was vividly bright and shone into the bedroom, leaving a silvery path to the window. Surreptitiously, Cora made her way there.

The noise was growing louder. The distinct sounds of pounding could be heard. Was someone trying to break through the fence? That was absurd. Why not just walk through the gate? It had no latch. Or just climb over it. It was only three feet high!

Reaching the window, she crept to the side and slowly, carefully, with one trembling hand, pulled back the lace curtain. An old-fashioned open-top undertaker's wagon was parked in the grass next to her north fence. Before her mind had time to absorb the information, she caught the gleam of bright blond hair shining in the moonlight and spied a tall, broad-shouldered man pulling a worn picket out of her fence.

She threw open the window.

"Jedwin Sparrow, what are you doing?"

His face turned up to hers with a broad smile. "Evening, Mrs. Briggs," he called up to her. "I'm sorry. I didn't mean to wake you."

"What are you doing here?"

The young man ran a hand through his hair. "Well, ma'am—" he began, only to be interrupted by Cora.

"Shhhh!" She hushed him as she became aware of the stillness of the evening. "Be quiet, somebody will hear."

Jedwin looked around skeptically, then nodded his compliance. "Well, ma'am," he whispered. "Well, I—" Jedwin looked about him as if disgusted. Trying to yell quietly was not an easy assignment.

He glanced thoughtfully toward the house for a moment. To Cora's complete surprise, he walked over to the house directly below her. Before she could stop him, he got a toehold in the parlor-window ledge and was climbing up the side of the house.

"What are you doing!" Cora was frightened and appalled. A moment later two strong young hands were braced on the sill before her. With the strength of young muscles and the desire to impress, Jedwin chinned himself on Cora's bedroom window.

Rather than the sigh of awe he expected, Jedwin was nearly knocked down the side of the house when Cora grabbed frantically for his shoulders.

"Oh, my heavens! You're going to fall and kill yourself!"

Jedwin threw his elbow into the room to brace himself. "Not unless you push me."

Cora wasn't placated. "Get inside this room right now!" she ordered.

Struggling, Jedwin tried to get a foothold on the worn clapboards outside to pull himself into the room.

"I'm not sure that Romeo did it this way," he said as his legs flailed wildly on the outside of the house.

The more he wiggled and squirmed, the more certain Cora was that the young man would be falling to his death any moment.

With Cora's nervous encouragement, Jedwin determined that he could hoist himself up. Finally he managed to get his waist bent at the window frame. He was moving to bring his knee through the window and climb in when Cora became too impatient.

Leaning out over him with frantic urgency, she tried to get a hold on him to help pull him inside. The most obvious thing to grab was the seat of the young man's pants. Digging her fingers into the strong muscular curves of his buttocks, Cora pulled Jedwin forcefully into the room.

"Whoa!" he cried as he fell on the floor, bringing Cora down with him. He fell flat on top of her. They lay together momentarily stunned.

Jedwin raised himself up on his elbows and looked down into the startled white face beneath him.

"Mrs. Briggs, I—"

No further words came to mind. Jedwin could feel the warmth and softness of her body and the heat of her left him speechless.

"Oh my! Oh my!" Cora was at a loss herself. She began moving frantically, trying to wiggle out from under him.

Jedwin's heart caught in his throat as he felt the scantily clad woman squirming beneath him. Desire raced through him. With a regretful sigh he rolled away, hoping that she hadn't noticed anything amiss.

They both sat up abruptly and quickly began righting their clothes.

"I didn't mean to knock you down," Jedwin said hastily. "Are you all right, Mrs. Briggs?"

Still a bit flustered at suddenly having so intimately felt his body atop hers, Cora stuttered assurances that she was fine. Slowly the absurdity of the situation struck her and she began to giggle.

Jedwin, fidgeting to find a comfortable sitting position, stopped dead cold at the sound of her laughter. Had she recognized his response? Was he the cause of her laughter? He was a twenty-four-year-old who was so green, just the proximity of a female person made him randy! Was that what caused her laughter?

"What's so funny?" he asked.

Cora could no longer keep her hilarity down to delicate, feminine little giggles. She guffawed.

Nearly choking, she tried an explanation. "I thought you . . . and then your legs . . . and then I grabbed you . . . and then we fell and . . ." She couldn't go on. And her laughter filled her until she grabbed her sides.

Her hilarity was contagious, and Jedwin began to forget his own discomfiture and visualize the scene at the window. In his imagination he conjured the picture of his legs swinging wildly out of the side of the house, of Mrs. Briggs hauling him inside by the seat of his pants, and of him falling right on top of her in her own bedroom. Somehow it did not seem like a typical romantic assignation.

Jedwin's own laughter bubbled up in a booming baritone. Hearing him laugh made her laugh harder and the two sat inches apart in the silver stream of moonlight that flowed from the window as tears of mirth rolled down their cheeks.

Cora regained her composure first with the sudden realization that she was sitting with a man in her bedroom clad only in her nightdress. Her nightdress, she reasoned quickly, was quite modest. The Mother Hubbard style was not one usually favored by females of illicit propensities. Only the tiniest piece of lace adorned the high collar and the sleeves were buttoned down decently at the wrist. The only unacceptable showing of flesh was her bare feet peeking from the edge of the material. Bringing her knees to her chest, she tucked the flannel of her gown beneath her feet and assured herself that she was decently covered.

"You really shouldn't be in here." Cora stated the obvious sotto voce.

"I hadn't intended to actually come in, Mrs. Briggs. I'd just thought to come closer to your window so that we wouldn't have to shout."

Jedwin was trying very hard not to look at the lovely woman at his side. All his fantasies of Cora Briggs suddenly seemed to melt into one warm, sweet longing. All he wanted to do was wrap his arms around her waist and bury his face in the soft curve of her bosom.

"But what were you doing in the yard?" she asked him.

"I'm fixing your fence," he answered as if it were the most natural thing in the world. "It's a hunter's moon, Mrs. Briggs. It won't get any lighter than this at night. I didn't figure it would be too discreet, me fixing up your fence in broad daylight."

"I didn't *ask* you to fix my fence."

"I know you didn't, Mrs. Briggs," he said soberly. "You just asked for a bit of romancing. I'm doing my best, ma'am, I truly am, but I'm probably better at fence mending."

The confession was made with such sincerity that Cora could only stare at the young man wordlessly.

"Did you get my flowers?" he asked.

Cora smiled warmly. "Yes, and your lovely poem, also. I liked it very much."

Jedwin chuckled. "You actually liked it?" He shook his head in appropriate disbelief. "Well," he admitted, "it really was a big improvement over my first attempt."

"Your first attempt?"

"I wrote another one," he said. "It was even worse than the one I sent."

"I loved the one you sent!" Cora insisted.

Jedwin shook his head in disbelief, but gave up the argument.

"I want to hear your first attempt."

"Oh, Mrs. Briggs, it is quite bad."

"Nonsense, I want to hear it. How bad could it be?"

"Well," Jedwin began slowly. "It can be pretty bad. Are you sure you want to hear it?"

"Absolutely, Mr. Sparrow, I'm sure it is lovely, despite your protestations."

Jedwin wasn't so certain, but he cleared his voice bravely, and raising his chin displaying his profile in the moonlight, he commenced his recitation.

> "There was a young woman from Dead Dog,
> Whose swain was as dumb as a boar hog.
> He'd ne'er had a chance
> To learn of romance.
> So he sat like a knot on a pine log."

Cora kept her face totally void of expression. "That was nice," she insisted firmly. "It was . . . well, it was . . . well, I do like your other one better."

"It's the last line," Jedwin said gravely. "The last line just wasn't the thing."

"Well, perhaps—"

"Do you have any idea how difficult it is to find something that rhymes with dog and hog?" he asked her.

"I don't suppose I'd ever really thought about it."

"I suspect not."

The two were silent for a moment before a tiny giggle escaped Cora. "Whose swain was as dumb as a boar hog?" she asked.

Jedwin chuckled with her. "Didn't I just prove that, ma'am, by falling through your bedroom window?"

"Did you fall in? Or were you pulled?"

"A little of both, I guess."

"Are you my swain?" The question was asked quietly.

Jedwin leaned more closely to her and took one of her hands into his own. "I think I've made it evident, Mrs. Briggs, that I would truly treasure the chance to be your swain."

The words were almost quiet enough to be a whisper. Cora looked into his face. The moonlight obscured his eyes and softened the contours of his face. His was a handsome face, a young face.

"You really shouldn't be here," she said.

"Probably not," Jedwin whispered. He could feel the tension radiating from her. Did she think that he would grab her? Did she think that he would try to take advantage? Maybe other men of her acquaintance might try to exploit such unconventional circumstances, but not Jedwin, even though he very much wanted to do just that.

The air between them was thick with unspoken thoughts. Cora was nervous, he realized. But no more so than himself. Maybe some men could just grab up a woman and kiss her, but Jedwin knew he wouldn't. She'd have to meet him at least halfway.

"I would very much like to kiss you, Mrs. Briggs," he said.

Cora sat up straighter. She had not been married for almost a year without knowing what a kiss meant. The kiss was the beginning. If she allowed the kiss, then before she knew it roaming hands would be pulling up her nightdress. And Jedwin Sparrow would be rolling on top of her sweating and moaning the way Luther used to do. She certainly didn't want that to happen! However, just the thought of it skittered across her heart with unexpected fascination.

Nervously she swept back the fullness of her lush sorrel hair and attempted a look of condemnation. "I do not think, Jedwin, that such a request is exactly proper."

Jedwin, her hand still gently clasped in his, nodded gravely. Her fear was tangible; he could feel trembling across her skin. "This is my first time in a lady's bedroom," he said with a warm whisper. "I can't be expected to know all of the formalities."

Cora's eyes popped open in surprise. She was unsure whether he was being truthful or joking.

He brought the hand he held to his lips and gently placed a kiss upon her knuckles. Slowly, hesitantly, almost with reverence, he brought the kiss he placed on her hand to the softness of her cheek.

"Oh—" Her tiny, breathless exclamation surged through them both like the warmth of a stove on a chilly morning.

Cora shuddered, but Jedwin knew it was not from the cold. He wanted her. His body ached for the warmth he knew he could find in hers. But she wasn't sure. Despite her reputation and experience, Cora Briggs was not some round-heeled sow to be easily pushed to her back and enjoyed. She was a person. A very lovely person. A person Jedwin wanted to kiss and caress and roll in the bedclothes with all night. Maybe for a thousand nights. He didn't want to frighten her. He wanted her to relax with him. He wouldn't risk his thousand nights with clumsy haste. He'd make her trust him. He'd make her want him. He'd make her laugh.

"And I believe you might be right, Mrs. Briggs," he continued.

Cora glanced at him quizzically. "Right about what?"

"I think I was *pulled* in, ma'am. I can still feel the marks from your fingernails on my behind."

Cora gave a little choking sound of horror as Jedwin came to his feet. He stood before her, leisurely rubbing the affected area.

"Mrs. Briggs, I swear I don't think I'll ever wash my backside again."

Before she had a chance to react, Jedwin had thrown one leg over the windowsill and was letting himself out of the window with a good deal more grace than when he'd come in.

Cora scurried to the window just in time to see him touch the ground.

"Jedwin," she called to him.

Looking up, he saluted her smartly and then, as if it were broad daylight, began repairs on the fence.

Cora watched his fluid movements as he went about his work . . . the gleam of moonlight silver on his blond hair and the shadow of his lithe body moving so gracefully in the darkness.

Cora was chilled in the evening air and hurried back to her bed to grab a quilt. Wrapping it around her, she seated herself once more by the window and watched him work.

He was kind and funny, she thought. A good worker and a man of principles, no doubt. He would make some lucky girl a fine husband.

She thought of the indecency of having him alone with her in her bedroom. What would the people of the town think if they found out about that! For certain, they'd be thinking the worst, and she couldn't really blame them. A handsome man in the wicked Mrs. Briggs's own bedroom. It was a scandal, indeed.

The staccato hammer strokes were rhythmic and comforting. Cora yawned and leaned her head against the windowsill. She actually liked him, she decided. *He's never washing his backside again,* she thought as she drifted into sleep.

"Come on, Cory, that's it, come on." Cora heard Luther's words hot and breathy next to her ear. "That's it, move with me, Cory, move with me."

Cora's whole body was jittery and tense. The hairs on her arms stood straight up as if she were cold, hot, both.

"What is it, Luther?" she whispered. "What's happening?"

"Move with me, Cory. Get what you want," he said. "This is pleasure. It's here for the taking."

Cora *was* moving against him. She couldn't seem to stop herself. She heard the bedstead banging against the wall. She smelled the raw, rough scent that was Luther Briggs all around her. She opened her eyes to see him above her. His dark good looks were obscured by a grimace. His teeth were clenched as if in rage. Powerfully he thrust into her again and again. Pushing her toward that precipice, pushing her over.

"Oh!" Cora cried out as her private parts, clear up to her womb, tightened into a white-hot knot and then quivered as the spasms flowed through her.

"I'm sorry," she heard Luther cry as he found his own release.

She suspected, even then, that the apology was not meant for her.

Amelia Sparrow hummed to herself as she made her way up the front steps. The morning had gone beautifully, almost perfectly. She'd managed to speak with the wife of every businessman in town. "Briggston" was practically a reality already.

Smiling, Amelia remembered Cora Briggs and her slack-jawed stare at Penny's Grocery yesterday. Did that unrepentant floozy believe that she could keep the Briggs name in the gutter with her? Amelia gave a sigh of defiance. Not as long as she was a member of the family. And she *would* be a fully accepted member of the family soon. Once she got the town's name changed, why Maimie Briggs would welcome her with open arms.

Stepping into her front foyer, Amelia carefully set her parasol against the stand and slowly removed her gloves, being especially careful to neither stain nor tear them. Even after twenty years of relative affluence, pretty things were still too precious to be taken for granted.

"James Edwin," she called softly down the hallway. Living in a funeral parlor, she had adjusted to keeping her voice at a respectfully low level most of the time. "James Edwin!" she called more loudly when he did not respond.

Hearing movement in the casket display room, Amelia went to the door. "James Edwin?"

"It's just me, Mellie," Haywood answered, giving her a broad smile full of wicked insinuation. If Amelia had not been so familiar with him, she might have taken offense.

He was standing near the back of the room, inspecting a damaged hinge on a new casket. It was an expensive item with a see-through glass half-top. As usual Haywood Puser was clad in the most casual of clothes. The striped overalls made him appear more a farmer than a man of profession. His casual unconcern for formalities irritated Amelia. Not for the first time, she wished that he would shave that untidy beard so that she could get a good look at his face. It was hard to trust a man who was hiding behind a mask of whiskers. And there was something about Haywood Puser that made Amelia uneasy. There were things about him that she was sure he wasn't telling.

Nervously and without conscious thought, Amelia's hands went to her hair to straighten the nonexistent disarray there.

"Where is Mr. Sparrow?" she asked politely, trying to shake off the strange, tingly feeling that she often felt in Mr. Puser's presence.

Haywood shrugged. "Couldn't rightly say, Mellie. As far as I know, he ain't even stirred from his bed yet this morning."

"That's ridiculous," Amelia assured him firmly, ignoring the overly familiar nickname she loathed. "Perhaps my son is not as ambitious as he should be, but he has never been a slug-a-bed."

"No, he sure ain't," Haywood agreed easily. "And he's plenty ambitious enough, if you ask me."

"But, of course, I didn't ask you," Amelia said sweetly. "I would never need to ask *questions* about my own son."

Amelia saw it as no mystery that an employee would defend his boss. Once Jedwin took up his responsibilities again as embalmer, the services of Haywood Puser would be unnecessary and he could be on his way.

Haywood raised a skeptical eyebrow, but then shrugged as he moved around the side of the casket and casually continued examining the defective hinge. "Then I expect you know that he didn't come home last night till nearly dawn."

"What?" She was well aware Jedwin had gone to bed early the previous evening, claiming tiredness. "That's utter nonsense. My son was in his bed before nine o'clock."

"Maybe so," Haywood said and then offered a little tutting sound through his teeth. "But I got a charley horse in my leg last night and had to get up to walk it out. I must have made fifteen trips from my cottage to the carriage house. Then, just as the moon set and the first pink light was coming in from the east, here comes Jedwin driving in that old open-top before sunup. He looked as fag-tired as if he'd put in a full day's work."

"I don't believe you."

Haywood shrugged. "Why would I lie?"

Amelia couldn't answer that. "Where on earth had he been?"

"I got no idea," Haywood answered. "And of course, I didn't ask him, like you would have," he said easily.

He stepped closer to Amelia, close enough that he could look straight down into her eyes. Close enough that Amelia felt obliged to take a step backward.

Haywood rubbed his beard as he studied the pretty woman before him. There was a glimmer of fire in his bright blue eyes. "I figure Jedwin's a grown man, Mellie, he shouldn't have to tell anyone when he's coming or going."

"Well, he certainly should! He—"

Amelia suddenly recognized the statement for what it was: baiting. Haywood Puser openly disapproved of the way she handled Jedwin, and there was nothing he wouldn't do to try to get between them. But Jedwin was her son and no one else would ever know him like she did.

Sure, Haywood cared for him as a friend, she thought. But to Amelia, Jedwin was her life. And she certainly was not going to allow him to fritter it away on useless pursuits. Where in heaven's name could he have been all night?

Amelia glanced over at Haywood. He was poised, waiting. Just itching for a fight, she thought. But she didn't want to argue about anything today, especially about her son. Things were going to come out favorably with Maimie very soon, and as for Jedwin, she'd deal with him. She always had.

Deftly she changed the subject.

"What are you working on?" she asked.

Haywood was a little disappointed with her lack of spirit this morning. "The damnable peek-a-boo casket that came from Groillers," he answered.

"Oh!" Amelia's eyes were lit with excitement as she moved closer. "Is that the one James Edwin ordered for Maimie Briggs?"

Haywood raised an eyebrow and gave Amelia a skeptical look. "Jedwin said *you* were the one so dang set on getting this casket for Miz Maimie to look at."

"Well, I think perhaps I did suggest—" Amelia began.

"'Cause if it had just been Jedwin a-wanting to order it, I'da talked him out of it in a gnat's age."

Amelia's mouth dropped open in surprise. "Why? I realize that it's expensive, but if our patrons—"

"It don't have nothing to do with expensive," Haywood interrupted. "I believe as strongly as you do that folks ought to have the kind of funeral that they want, all frills or nary a one. What I don't approve is this kind of useless product being foisted off on the public."

"It's not useless, it's beautiful. You don't seem to understand, Mr. Puser, that mourning should be a time of beauty. The days when funerals meant somber black crepe and fear are over. We understand, now, that stepping into God's hands should be a peaceful and serene passing."

Haywood leaned casually against the wall and gave Mrs. Sparrow a long-suffering look. "I read *Modern Mortician Magazine*, too, Mellie," he said quietly. "And I ain't talking about philosophical differences. I'm talking about the practical. Now look at this thing." He gestured toward the shiny new casket.

Amelia stepped closer and ran her hand gently along the fine lines of the gleaming dark green painted metal. Already she was imagining how she would speak to Maimie about mint green silk for her funeral drape. It would be both aesthetically perfect and incredibly fashionable. "It's lovely," she told him honestly.

"Sure enough," Haywood agreed. "The casket is a fine quality. Groillers make some of the best, and the lines and color are pleasing to the eye."

Amelia's eyes widened, not only for his lack of argument, but for his unexpected appreciation.

"But what about this?" he asked her. With distinct distaste, Haywood thumped the glass oval in the casket lid.

Was it possible he didn't know what it was? With a look of exasperation, Amelia spoke to him as if he were a child.

"Mr. Puser, by having this glass, the family can actually *see* their loved one."

Haywood tolerated her condescension. Folding his arms stubbornly, he asked, "So if they want to *see*, why don't they just have an open casket at the service?"

"Well, of course they will," Amelia answered. "But this will give them another moment as the body is lowered into the ground." With a quiet but oft-used sigh she added, "I buried my husband, you know. Another moment can be a great deal."

There was a flicker of some emotion in Puser's eyes that Amelia didn't recognize. Before she could examine it, it was gone.

"It does mean a great deal," Haywood agreed softly. "But not enough."

"What do you mean?"

"You can't seal glass, Mellie," he said. "No matter how hard you try, air will get in. And with air you get decay and you get seepage. That means danger and disease." He shook his head with certainty. "Is one last look at a body whose soul is already gone worth maybe putting cholera or typhoid in some farmer's well water?"

"Well, of course not, but—"

"There *is* beauty in the sleep of death, Mellie. But it is the living we must plan for. All of this." He gestured to the trappings around him in black crepe and mourning purple. "All of this is for the living. To ease the hearts of those who go on. But we must plan for their physical health as well."

"Well, of course, but—"

"As a trained embalmer," Haywood continued, ignoring her interruption, "I possess knowledge of the process of disease and the nature of contagion that most of the public will never need to understand. As the keeper of those secrets, I have an obligation to use what I know to the benefit of my community."

Haywood shook his head disapprovingly at the see-through casket cover. "This is a danger to my health, your health, and the health of every man, woman, and child in Dead Dog. I don't think pandering to an old woman's vanity is worth that."

Amelia opened her mouth to protest, but couldn't think of a word to speak in defense. A flash of remembrance niggled at her brain. Big Jim had been like this, just as obstinate, just as unmovable, but only when he was certain that he was right. The memory didn't sit well with the image of her dead husband that she usually recalled. The truth was so unsettling that she was distracted from defending her argument.

"Of course, you are right," she told Haywood with a strange, eerie distance in her voice. "Send it back to Groillers on the next train."

She turned and walked away, leaving Haywood to stare after her in disbelief. He'd never imagined that mule-headed Mellie could be so down-right reasonable.

*   *   *

Cora awakened shivering. The morning sunlight shone down on her face, but the wind from the open window was cold. She was surprised to find herself sitting on the floor next to the window, wadded up like a used handkerchief. As memory returned she scooted anxiously to her knees, only to wince from her own stiff, unwilling muscles. Ignoring the pain, she looked eagerly outside the window.

Jedwin Sparrow was long gone, but the evidence of his visit was not. The worn broken fence that surrounded her sad little cottage now stood proud and strong. Gleaming in the morning sun, not with new whitewash, but with real, store-bought paint.

It was wonderful. But how could he have managed it? "He must have worked all night long," she whispered to herself.

In her mind she again saw his strong young back leaning into the task. His bright smile and those errant wisps of blond hair warmed her heart more in memory than they had at the time.

She closed her eyes, the better to visualize his face. A whiff of sweet evergreen caught the attention of her nostrils. Puzzled, she opened her eyes.

A bright green juniper branch had been tucked into the corner of the window shutter.

"Jedwin," she sighed with surprise. Had he climbed back up the side of the house, once more risking his life, or at least a good leg, to leave her a memento?

Cora gently pried the juniper from its firm housing between the louvers. The bright green branch was fragrant and accented by a scattering of tiny blue berries. Near the base, tied on securely with a length of blue carpenter's chalk string, was a piece of paper.

Cora unfolded it, already sure what it was going to be. In the broad sprawling hand she'd come to recognize, was Jedwin's latest ode.

> For sure it ain't diamonds,
> Nor neither 'tis pearls.
> Can a sturdy new fence
> Please this swain's girl?

Chapter
Seven

Maimie Briggs no longer attended Sunday church services. Feeling that, because of her advanced age, she should be excused from any obligation to visit the church, Sunday afternoons she expected the church to visit her.

After their customary hasty Sunday luncheon, Jedwin drove his mother to the Briggs home. It was the only residence on Luther Street, the wide thoroughfare that bisected Main. The Briggs mansion sat at the end of the road, surrounded by rather futile attempts at English gardening. Luther Street was the only boulevard in town that boasted a street sign. For years it had been called simply the house street, until Miss Maimie had renamed it for her son as a surprise for his eighteenth birthday, nearly twenty years before.

"Do I look all right?" Amelia asked her son as they turned the corner at Main and Luther and the house came into sight. "Do you think this dress is too bright?"

"The dress is perfect," Jedwin assured his mother without bothering to give her more than a cursory glance. He held back a yawn; he hadn't quite recovered from his all-night work marathon two days ago.

His mother had come charging up to his room to find out why he was still in bed in the middle of the morning. Although she expressed concern about his health, Jedwin could tell that she was insincere. He knew Haywood had seen him come in near daybreak, and Jedwin suspected that he'd passed on that information.

Rising out of bed reluctantly, Jedwin spent most of the day at his mother's beck and call. She'd quizzed him vaguely about secret evening appointments, but Jedwin pretended not to understand. If she wanted to ask him straight-out where he'd been, he decided, he'd tell her it was none of her business. His mother, apparently, didn't wish to risk such an answer, so she never asked the question.

But even with his mother's continued attention, Jedwin allowed himself flights of fancy. He composed more verses in his head. He thought of gifts that Cora might like: candy, a bolt of silk, or perhaps new tires for her bicycle. And he dreamed about when he would see her. The next time they spoke he would be bright and amusing and witty. She would nearly swoon with laughter from his clever conversation . . . Then the moment would change and he would look deep into her eyes and she would throw herself in his arms. She would beg him to hold her, to kiss her, to . . .

Jedwin sighed with pleasure.

"Now stop that, James Edwin." His mother's waspish tone pulled him back to reality. "I don't want to hear any groans from you about this visit. I have almost won Miss Maimie over, and I won't allow your selfish bad manners to put us in a bad light."

Jedwin didn't attempt to defend himself. Although he hadn't groaned in agony at the prospect of spending another Sunday afternoon at Miss Maimie's, he certainly could have.

"I shall be on my best behavior, Mama," he promised. "If someone finally breaks down and strangles Miss Maimie, I can assure you that it will not be me."

"Everyone *loves* Miss Maimie!" his mother insisted.

Jedwin looked at her doubtfully, but responded with a pleasant, "Oh, of course, Mama."

The end of the drive was already crowded with vehicles of every description, from Titus Penny's blue and white striped surrey to Reverend Bruder's jump-seat buggy. Jedwin pulled up underneath a cottonwood tree a good distance from the house.

"Perhaps we should have parked on Main Street," Amelia suggested dryly, as she eyed the two hundred yards between herself and the house.

"When it is time to leave," Jedwin explained. "I want to be the first one down the road."

Setting the brake and securing the lines to it, Jedwin jumped down from the shiny black cabriolet and then turned to offer his mother a hand.

"Now if Maimie asks you about the business," Amelia coached him, "simply tell her that you are slowly retaking the reins and that your stomach has ceased to trouble you."

"Both those things are bald-faced lies, Mama."

"You are taking control again, James Edwin," she answered. "I'm sure that's what you want. And you haven't had a bout of nausea in weeks."

The handsomely dressed couple made their way to the Briggs mansion with the easy grace of long custom.

"I haven't been near an embalming in weeks," Jedwin said easily. "That's the secret to my cure, Mama."

Amelia sighed with exasperation. "You are nearly a grown man, James Edwin. Please try to remember that grown men do not suffer from vapors or weak stomach."

"I am *already* a grown man, Mama," her son replied without undue concern. "And were I to attempt to embalm someone this afternoon, I would lose my luncheon just as surely as I have in the past."

"James Edwin Sparrow," Amelia huffed with disgust. "You simply *must* get over this. Who ever heard of a man being sickened by his chosen profession? You are a mortician and embalming is a part of that. For heaven's sake, what kind of man vomits every time he opens a body?"

"This kind of man does," Jedwin snapped with more than a tinge of anger. "I don't know what to say to you, Mama. You seem to think this is something I do just to annoy you. You say, 'get over it.' Don't you think I've tried to get over it? I've been trying to get over it for twenty years. Don't you think I know how ashamed Papa was of me?"

The stricken look on her son's face pained Amelia as if she had wounded him purposely. Consolingly, she patted his arm as they walked up the steps to the porch.

"I know you are trying to get better. And there isn't a doubt in my mind that you will succeed." She smiled at him in that warm, open manner that had once put all the beaux in Dead Dog at her feet. "Let's not think about it any more today. We don't want to spoil our afternoon."

Jedwin gave her a wry grin. "If we don't want to spoil the afternoon, we shouldn't have come to see Miss Maimie."

Conrad Ruggy, his once curly black hair now pure white, opened the door before Jedwin had opportunity to knock.

"'Afternoon, Mr. Jedwin, Miz Sparrow," he greeted them, with a half bow of courtesy. "Fine weather we're having."

"Yes indeed, Conrad," Jedwin replied easily. "Cool of a morning and fine by midday, couldn't ask for a prettier autumn. And how is your mother? Is she feeling better?"

"She's better, much better," Conrad assured him cheerfully. "I think just contemplating the cost of your burying bill is going to keep that woman alive. She's just plain too thrifty to die."

"Well, I certainly hope so," Jedwin answered. "And how is Miss Maimie?" Leaning forward conspiratorially, he whispered, "No chance I'll be measuring her for a coffin soon?"

Conrad laughed heartily. "You are bad, Mr. Jedwin," he said. "That old woman gonna live to see us both in our graves."

"I wouldn't doubt it," Jedwin agreed. "They do say that the good die young."

Conrad was still chuckling as Jedwin made his way into the great parlor. The place was already crowded with all the best, and want-to-be-the-best, people in Dead Dog. Moving through the crowd was Conrad's wife, Mattie, and his daughter Maud passing half-filled cups of the sour apple punch that comprised the sum total of Maimie Briggs's hospitality.

Jedwin glanced up to see his mother ahead of him. She gave him an exasperated look and he knew she was irritated by having to wait for him. Speaking to Miss Maimie was like taking a dose of a purgative physic: best to get it over with before losing your nerve.

"I'm right behind you," Jedwin assured his mother as the two, with smiles and greetings to all they passed, made their way through the crowd.

Miss Maimie sat in the center of the room in a high-backed Queen Anne chair, her feet propped up on the ottoman like an Eastern pasha. A fancy brass-tipped cane curved its hand grip around the arm of the chair. She was a tiny woman, made more so by the shrinking of age. Her pure white hair was still thick and curly and she wound it across her head in a braided coronet. She was cheerful and laughing and all those around her were smiling, too.

"Miss Maimie!" Amelia exclaimed, as delighted as if she hadn't seen the older woman in ages. "How are you, dear?"

Amelia offered her hand and the older woman grasped it tightly between her own. Maimie smiled up at her sweetly, her eyes sparkling with such pleasure that her worn old face shone with beauty.

"My darling Amelia," Miss Maimie answered. "Why, I feel just as fit as I

dare to be." She tittered at her own comment, and the crowd around her
chuckled with her. "Is that a new dress you're wearing?"

Amelia blushed with pleasure. "Yes, do you like it?"

Maimie nodded, still smiling. "What an unusual color and fabric. It must
have been expensive."

"I sent to Kansas City for it," Amelia admitted.

Patting Amelia's hand, Maimie sighed before turning to speak to the ladies
at her right. "What a dear Amelia is," she said. "Just as fine a woman as
you'll find anywhere."

"Why, thank you, Miss Maimie."

The older woman was still smiling cheerily. "And coming from that pig
farm like you did." Maimie shuddered with distaste. "Old man Pratt was as
useless a farmer as I ever knew. Why, none of us can fault you for one minute
for your lack of good taste. Amelia dear, please be assured that we all just
treasure you, despite everything."

Miss Maimie's smile was so warm and open, Amelia heard herself
muttering a grateful, "Thank you."

As Amelia moved back, attempting to lose herself, and her tasteless new
dress, in the crowd, Jedwin was forced to step forward. Leaning over, he
politely kissed the old woman on her weathered cheek.

"Good afternoon, Miss Maimie," he said.

"Dear Jedwin, you grow more handsome every day. How is that weak
stomach of yours?"

"I'm doing well, thank you, Miss Maimie."

"Such a burden ill health can be. Especially for a man. My dear husband,
God rest his soul, never had a sick day in his life. I swear the man was strong
as an ox and ne'er suffered an ache or pain in all his days."

Jedwin nodded in agreement and smiled wryly. "Yes, ma'am, I understand
that he was quite a healthy man. Right up until he dropped dead at the age of
forty-one."

Maimie's eyes widened, and she demurred slightly. "Well, yes,
ah . . . Mattie, can you bring me some punch? I swear my throat is as dry
as a cotton patch in August."

The aging black woman quickly brought the drink and Maimie took it
without acknowledgment or thanks. Maimie Barlow Briggs had grown up in
those Southern cotton fields. She pretended a past "before the war" of
gentility and grace. The truth, which Jedwin had learned from his grandfather,
was that Maimie's father had been a struggling Alabama cracker with twenty

rocky acres of mealy cotton. The only slaves he'd "owned" were his wife and nine children. None of these facts, however, prevented Maimie Briggs from espousing the superior attitudes of lofty ancestors she'd never had.

"Oh, that has quite refreshed me," she assured her circle of admirers before turning her attention once more to Jedwin. "Who are you calling on these days, young man?"

A guilty flush flooded Jedwin's face.

"Well, I'll swanny. Look at him a-blushing." Maimie actually giggled as she looked around at the crowd. "This young man is sparking someone on the sly!"

"No, Miss Maimie," Jedwin said immediately. "I'm far too busy to take to courting these days."

Maimie shook her head and wagged a finger at him. "I never in my life heard of a gentleman who was too busy for courting."

With laughter all around, the friends and family obviously agreed. "You'd best be staking your claim on one of these little pretties coming out of the schoolroom," she suggested. "You aren't getting any younger."

"I'm only twenty-four, Miss Maimie."

"Only twenty-four, my heavens!" she exclaimed. "And already your hair is that thin on the top." She gave him a look of sincere consolation. "Now just don't fret about it, Jedwin, it's one of those things that just can't be helped. It happens to blond men more than is fair. They just go as bald as a turnip before they are even in their prime. Now, my son, Luther, he's got the thickest head of jet black hair you ever did see."

"Yes, ma'am," Jedwin agreed, taking a convulsive swallow. "Could you excuse me, I think I'm needing a little refreshment myself."

His smile strictly window dressing, Jedwin moved through the crowd, joking and talking with first one person and then another.

"Mrs. Maitland. What a becoming hat you're wearing," he commented to the plain, rather timid wife of the local farrier.

"Mrs. Avery," he greeted a younger matron. "I saw young Jasper rolling his hoop down Church Street last week. What a handful he's getting to be."

"'Afternoon, Titus," he said with a nod to the grocer. "Have you been out hunting yet this season?"

"I've bagged a few quail," he admitted. "But Fanny hasn't let me out at night to chase down coons."

Jedwin's teasing grin was an echo of their shared childhood. "Yes, I saw

Fanny when I came in. She does *look* like she's been keeping you busy of a
night."

Titus shoved an elbow into Jedwin's midriff, but couldn't keep the sound of
pride out of his feigned anger. "I'm hoping for a boy this time."

"A son would be a good thing," Jedwin agreed. "But the way I've seen it,
you sure set store by that little gal of yours."

Chuckling, Titus agreed. "That Maybelle, I swear I never dreamed I'd be
a father to someone so downright pretty."

Jedwin glanced over at the curly-haired blond child who was unconcernedly
running wild through the hallways. "In just a few years, you're going to be
beating the boys off with a stick."

At that exact moment, Maybelle slipped on a hundred-year-old carpet
runner in the hall. Falling to her knees, the spoiled little beauty gave out a
howl that captured the attention of the entire houseful of guests.

Titus was at his daughter's side in a moment. Pulling the little girl into his
arms and gently cuddling her, he tried to tempt her from crying with the
promise of jellycake.

"That child will grow up unfit for company." Jedwin heard the whispered
proclamation behind him. He turned to find Constance Bruder, the reverend's
wife, speaking to his mother.

Amelia gave a charming little laugh of agreement. "How right you are. I
swear, I was in the store just the other day and witnessed worse myself."

"He just dotes on the child too much," Mrs. Bruder said.

"Fanny tries her best. But when a man is set on ruining the disposition of
his own children, why there is just not a thing a mother can do."

Jedwin turned his back to the women, pretending not to listen. His
expression, however, was wry. If anyone knew how to get between a father
and child, it was Amelia Sparrow.

"It's a fact," Constance Bruder agreed. "It's the same for me and my Tulsa
May."

Amelia tutted sympathetically.

"It's sad enough that the girl is so . . . well, so ill-favored," Mrs. Bruder
said bitterly. "But the reverend seems to go out of his way to fill her head with
stories and nonsense. The two of them got their heads together and decided
they were going to try to learn to read Greek."

"No!"

"Have you ever heard of such foolishness in your life?"

"Oh, you poor dear," Amelia commiserated.

"If Tulsa May doesn't have her nose in a book then she's got her head in the clouds. That girl can sit and stare out the window for half a day."

"Whatever could she be thinking about?"

Constance Bruder threw up her hands dramatically. "The good Lord only knows! I just don't know what I'm going to do. I've told her straight-out that she's not a bit pretty, and if she's ever going to get a husband she's going to have to be able to clean and cook better than any woman in town."

"What did she say?" Amelia asked.

"Nothing, not one solitary word. She just walked away from me as if I hadn't spoken."

"Mrs. Sparrow?" a voice called from farther behind the women. Jedwin didn't bother to turn to see who had approached, but began making his way to the other side of the room, with no clear destination in mind.

Smiling, talking, a joke here, a question there, Jedwin made his way through the company. From the window he spied a group of men having a smoke on the porch. Although Jedwin disliked tobacco, he thought a change of company and a bit of fresh air would be refreshing.

As he stepped into the hall, from the corner of his eye he caught sight of a bright vision in pink and orange. Nearly blinded, he turned to look. Sitting alone in the corner of Miss Maimie's family parlor was a young girl of about fourteen years. Although she was taller than many grown women, she was dressed in the ribboned fashion of a much younger girl. The bright pink gown was pretty on its own, but truly lost some of its sparkle next to the girl's straight, stiffly coiffed carrot red hair.

She hadn't noticed Jedwin and he could have easily made his way outside without speaking, but he turned and walked toward her.

"Hello there," he called as he stepped into the room.

Her eyes immediately turned to him. They were brown as copper pennies and glowing with depth and intelligence. At the sight of her visitor, the young girl broke into a delighted grin.

"Afternoon, Mr. Sparrow." Her smile was warm and welcoming, but less than attractive. Her straight white teeth were as young and healthy as herself, but the gap between the two front ones was nearly big enough to drive a mule through.

"What are you doing in here all by yourself, Tulsa May?" he asked her. "I suspect all the other midlings are out in the yard playing handkerchiefs."

She shrugged. "I don't feel much like playing. I was just looking at the trees."

Jedwin squatted down next to the chair and gazed out the window as if trying to discover her interest there. The woods at the side of the house were definitely ready for winter. The ground was a carpet of fading leaves and the trees themselves were almost completely bare.

"They look pretty bleak this time of year," Jedwin said.

"I like them that way," Tulsa May said quietly. "Winter is my favorite time of year."

"Winter?"

She grinned in embarrassment. "I know it's foolish. Everyone either loves beautiful springs, warm lazy summers, or the colors of autumn. I like winter best."

"Winter's nice," Jedwin agreed. "Especially if there's snow. A winter snow is very pretty."

"I don't like snow. I like the trees in winter. I like them to be dark and gray with no leaves on them."

Tulsa May twisted her hands in her lap as if she were sorry she'd shared this personal bit of foolishness.

"Why?" Jedwin asked simply.

She looked up at him for a long moment, as if gauging his sincerity. She turned to gaze out of the window as she spoke.

"When you look out most of the year," she began, "you don't see the trees. You see the leaves and the blossoms and the grass growing up around them. In winter you can see the truth. All the glamour and dress of the rest of the year is missing. There is nothing left but the truth."

She raised her eyes nervously to his, as if she expected amusement or scorn.

There was no derision in Jedwin's smile. Quizzically, he looked past her to the truthful trees outside the window. He gazed at them for a long moment before turning his eyes back to the sparkling bright ones of the girl beside him.

"You're right," he whispered.

She sighed with relief and then the two laughed together in a moment of conspiracy.

"Tulsa May, you are a poet," Jedwin said.

Putting a warning finger to her lips, she hushed him with feigned horror. "Don't let my mother find out. She'll have a conniption. The shame of it. A poet right here in Dead Dog."

Jedwin laughed. "Maybe not the only one. I've been writing a verse or two myself lately."

Tulsa May's grin widened. "I won't tell your mama if you won't tell mine."

*   *   *

It was nearly an hour later when Jedwin finally made it to the porch. By that time there was still a small circle of admirers around Miss Maimie, but most folks had already paid their respects and taken their lumps.

Jedwin had just edged up to an animated group when he recognized his mother's voice.

"If our community wants a voice in this new state, we are going to have to make an impression," she said.

Carlisle Bowman, a prosperous wheat farmer, chuckled. "We've already made an impression. What other town would have the guts to call itself Dead Dog?"

Amelia glanced at him haughtily. "I don't believe that *audacity* is the impression that we wish to make."

"Of course it's not," Fanny Penny agreed. "If we want the town to grow, we've got to think about attracting people and business. A county seat could do that."

"Who says that we want to grow?" Bowman asked. "Beulah and I were in Guthrie just last week. Those folks think that being a state capital is going to make that town heaven on earth."

"Have you seen that new cable-car system?" Osgold Panek asked excitedly. "If I was to imagine heaven, it'd have cable cars just like them."

"Don't you be blaspheming!" Mrs. Panek warned him with a shaking finger.

"If you ask me," Carlisle said, "I'd say them cable cars are more likely in hell. The darn place looks like New York City!"

"How would you know?" Beulah Bowman challenged. "You haven't ever been east of Joplin."

A burst of laughter erupted from the crowd at Mrs. Bowman's defection. Jedwin chuckled also but used the distraction to edge away from the group. In the last few days, Jedwin had learned much more of his mother's "Briggston" scheme than he cared to know.

A group of men stood under the cottonwood tree several yards from the house. Jedwin thought them only a smokers' quorum until he noticed Reverend Bruder. The good reverend disapproved of tobacco and no man in town dared light up in his presence for fear of having his ears burned with verbal fire and brimstone.

The sound of laughter caught his ears and Jedwin made his way out to the cottonwood, a friendly smile upon his face. A little lighthearted company was definitely in order.

Barely a minute later, Jedwin's smile faded and he would have turned and walked away would it not have been so noticeable. Several of the men nodded to him, but the conversation didn't pause.

Reverend Bruder was clearly outraged. "I can't believe a word of it, but I assure you I will find out what is going on and put a stop to it."

Although the good reverend was the moral leader of the community and a stickler for propriety, his philosophical tendencies prevented him from being a reactionary.

"Now, Preacher," Clyde Avery said, trying to placate him. "There is no law, neither man's nor God's, against repairing and painting a fence."

Jedwin's face paled visibly and he choked on his horrible cup of sour apple punch. Mort Humley graciously pounded him on the back until he could catch his breath.

"We are not talking about the painting of the fence," Jedwin heard Reverend Bruder insist. "We are talking about *why* and by whom that fence got painted."

Murmurs went through the small circle. Jedwin looked at the faces around him. The men were mostly rolling their eyes in delighted speculation. Clearly they found the subject more entertaining than horrifying.

"Perhaps Mrs. Briggs hired someone to repair her fence," Clyde suggested. "Certainly a woman alone shouldn't be expected to do her own carpentry work."

"But where'd she get the money?" Titus Penny asked. "It'd cost plenty to have that done."

Reverend Bruder looked at him curiously. "I thought you always said she had lots of money and paid with cash."

His face flaming, Titus stuttered out an explanation. "I . . . She does! I . . . she does pay with cash, I don't know where she gets it."

"It is certainly none of our business where she gets her money," Clyde assured them.

"Why, it certainly is!" the preacher said. "Can we let some Jezebel turn our community into Sodom and Gomorrah?"

"I wouldn't bet there was much of a chance of that," Jedwin heard Mort whisper with a sigh.

Several of the other men chuckled.

"Mort Humley." The reverend's voice was firmer now and clearly irritated. "I heard that!"

Feeling a clear responsibility to stop the discussion, Jedwin bravely took on the preacher.

"Reverend Bruder, I believe you are jumping to some irrational conclusions. What possible reason could you have for believing that there is something amiss with the work recently completed on Mrs. Briggs's cottage?"

The reverend raised his chin and took a slow, dramatic perusal of the crowd. Softly, with the attention of all, he turned to Ebner Wyse. "When did you notice the repairs on Mrs. Briggs's cottage, Mr. Wyse?"

The old man coughed slightly and then scratched his beard thoughtfully. "Why, it was Friday morning, Reverend." He hesitated for a moment. "Yep, it was Friday. I spotted it over there, bright as a penny, first thing in the morning when I was taking Old Gray in to be shod."

He glanced over at Kirby Maitland, the farrier. "It *was* Friday when I brought my horse by, weren't it?"

"Yes sir," Kirby agreed. "Ebner brought that old horse to me first thing Friday morning."

Reverend Bruder nodded. "John Auslander, didn't you and Lily come back from visiting your daughter's new baby on Thursday evening?"

"Ya," the man agreed. "You should see my grandson," he said proudly to the crowd. "Four months old and already he tries to stand."

Murmurs of congratulations filtered through the crowd.

"You drove right by Cora Briggs's cottage," the reverend said. "Did you notice any new paint or any repairs on the fence?"

The man screwed up his mouth and shook his head. "No, but I don't remember even taking a look."

"Well, I looked!" Reverend Bruder declared. "I looked straight at her house when I drove by. A woman like that, well, I just never know what might be going on," he explained to the crowd. "And that fence was the same ramshackle pile of rotted lumber that it's been for the last two years."

The men were silent.

"So?" Jedwin asked finally.

"So, you say that there is no evidence of anything amiss in Cora Briggs getting her fence fixed." The preacher again surveyed the crowd to assure himself that even the dullest thinkers were following him. "If there was nothing out of the ordinary, then tell me, Mr. Sparrow, why anyone would have a fence painted and repaired in the middle of the night?"

Chapter Eight

Jedwin knocked lightly on the back screen of the Briggs cottage just after dark.

"Mrs. Briggs," he whispered against the door. "It's me, Jedwin, could you let me in?"

Nervously he glanced around the area to assure himself that he was not being watched. He'd left his rig at home and had walked south out of town and then circled back to Cora's cottage at the far north end.

Her face flushed with pleasure, Cora opened the back door with a warm smile. That smile faded quickly as Jedwin pushed past her into the house. Without so much as a "howdy-do," Jedwin rushed into the parlor and began jerking down the shades.

"What is going on?" Cora asked. Her startled expression was neither quite anger nor humor.

"People are watching your house," Jedwin answered without turning to look at her.

"Watching my house?"

"Let's go into the kitchen," he suggested, taking her arm protectively. "It's all my fault."

"What's your fault? What are you talking about, Jedwin?"

He seated her at her own kitchen table and then turned to the stove. "I'll make us some tea," he said, grabbing up the kettle and taking it to the pump.

Cora's eye's widened with surprise. She'd never heard of a man who could make tea.

"The pump's froze up," Cora told him. "There's clean water in the reservoir."

Jedwin nodded and opened the gray enamel-lined tub built into the side of the stove. With the dipper that hung on a hook at the corner, he scooped out enough water to fill the kettle and then set it on one of the burners. With a quick glance into the fire box, Jedwin gave the coals an encouraging poke before turning to Cora.

"You make tea?" she asked.

Jedwin's grin widened. "I used to follow my mama around more faithfully than a shadow. I can *almost* do a lot of little household chores. But don't let the word get out. I wouldn't want the women after me."

Cora giggled, inexplicably pleased at his ease at admitting something that most men would try to hide. "So you enjoyed working alongside your mother?"

Jedwin shrugged and then shook his head negatively. "It wasn't that I *enjoyed* working with Mama, but more that I *hated* working with Pa."

The warm crooked grin had faded now and that intensity was back in Jedwin's brown eyes.

"You didn't get along with your father?"

"We got along fine," Jedwin said. "I admired that man . . . oh, how I admired him." Jedwin's attention was momentarily captured by some memory in the distant past. "I wanted him to be proud of me."

Cora nodded. "That's what everyone wants from their parents. And I'm sure that he was."

Raising his eyes to hers, Jedwin looked at her a long minute before he shook his head. "No," he said. "I was always a big disappointment to my father."

As if such a statement customarily brought an end to that discussion, Jedwin turned his back to Cora and began perusing the kitchen cupboards.

"Where are the teacups?" he asked casually.

"I'll get them," Cora said as she immediately rose to her feet. "This is still my kitchen, Mr. Sparrow. Sit down while I make the tea."

Jedwin did as bid. It was a pleasure watching Cora move about. When her back was turned he let his eyes wander the narrow curve of her waist and the wide flare of her hip. He remembered the thrilling feel of her fingernails on his backside. It would surely be a pleasure straight from heaven if he could return the favor. "I was at Penny's last week and I heard your mother saying she was going to have the town renamed."

Startled from his fantasy exploration of Cora's bottom, it took Jedwin a minute before her words penetrated his skull.

"Yes," he said finally. "She's determined to have the name changed to Briggston."

Setting the tea service in the middle of the table, Cora gave him an impatient look. "She told Fanny Penny that it would give the town a better chance at becoming the county seat."

Jedwin nodded. "It might at that, but that's not why she's doing it, of course."

"Why is she doing it?"

"To please Miss Maimie. It's been the goal of my mama's life to become Miss Maimie's social heir."

Jedwin chuckled, but Cora didn't find his words amusing.

"I believe the tea is ready," she said, picking up the pot. Cora poured him a generous portion and pushed the sugar bowl closer to him.

"I would think that your mother had already secured her place in Miss Maimie's affection," she said.

Shaking his head, Jedwin disagreed. "Oh no, Mrs. Briggs, Miss Maimie will keep Mama hanging until the very last possible minute. She doesn't grant her favor easily."

"I know."

The quiet anger in Cora's tone brought Jedwin a swift reminder of Cora's place in the Briggs family. Since she was the now removed daughter-in-law, discussion of the social legacy of Maimie Briggs might not be terribly tactful.

There was an uneasy silence between them for a few moments. Jedwin finally broke it by asking the question that had been bothering him.

"I know you and Miss Maimie have a lot of hard feelings," he said quietly. "Was it Miss Maimie who broke up you and Luther?"

Cora gave a humorless chuckle and then shook her head disdainfully. "Oh no. Miss Maimie didn't break us up. In a way you could say she got us together. If she had had her way, Luther and I would still be living happily ever after."

The bitterness in her tone came as a surprise to Jedwin. Somehow he'd imagined Mrs. Briggs was quite content with her life.

"Are you saying that Luther left you?"

Cora raised her head abruptly. "I divorced him," she said.

"For desertion."

"You can't desert if you never volunteered," Cora replied obtusely. "Incompatibility. That's what the divorce decree says. Thank God there is such a reason in the territory. That way, we never had to testify in court."

Jedwin was puzzled. "It was all over town that you'd sued him for desertion."

Cora smiled. "I know. Your mother spread it all over town that way." She folded her hands against her chin and looked at Jedwin challengingly. "Just because your mother said it, doesn't mean it was the truth."

"I'm sure my mother wouldn't deliberately lie—"

"She just did what Maimie told her to do," Cora interrupted easily. "If she had any mind of her own, I might really blame her!"

Silent for a moment, Jedwin stared at the woman across the table from him. Slowly a smile began to flicker at the corners of his mouth.

"I believe you are trying to start a fight with me, Mrs. Briggs."

Cora raised an assessing eyebrow. "Is it going to work?"

"No, I don't think so. I love my mama and I'd defend her to the death if need be. But she's a mite shy of perfect, and I suspect I know that better than anyone."

With an appreciative nod, Cora acknowledged Jedwin's point. "Your tea is getting cold."

Jedwin sipped. Cora watched him, and reflected on his steady, calm, and clear thinking. In her experience, men generally acted first and thought about it later. Jedwin Sparrow was clearly a young man with a good head on his shoulders.

"I can't imagine why you could ever think that your father was not proud of you," she said.

Momentarily startled, Jedwin glanced up from his tea. Cora's direct look was unsettling.

"I'm not a good undertaker," he blurted out.

"You're not?" Cora seemed genuinely surprised. "I don't believe I've ever heard a word against you."

He shrugged. "Then you are not talking to the right people, Mrs. Briggs," he answered. "I'm so bad at it, I had to hire Haywood Puser to do my job."

Puzzled, Cora wasn't quite sure what to believe. "But you still do all the undertaking business, don't you? I understood that Mr. Puser just took over the embalming."

"That's what my father wanted me to be," he explained. "A licensed embalmer. I have my license, but I can't embalm."

"Why not?" she asked.

Suddenly embarrassed at his revelation, Jedwin quickly threw off the question. "Never mind, Mrs. Briggs. It is a very old and very long story. Your concern should be about yourself. Do you know the people of this town are watching your house?"

Shaking her head with wry humor, Cora set the teapot on the table. "People in this town have been watching me for years," she said, smiling. "I just have the good manners not to watch them back."

Jedwin leaned forward in concern. "If they watched you before, *now* they are really watching. They suspect something."

Cora waved away his concern. "They always suspect something."

"It's the fence," Jedwin said finally. "They think they have evidence against you now because of the fence."

Her smile faded.

"Reverend Bruder figured out that the fence was painted at night." Jedwin shook his head in self-derision. "Nobody would repair a fence at night, unless there was something to hide."

Cora clasped her hands together under her chin and gazed at Jedwin thoughtfully.

Her perusal was nearly his undoing. "I wanted to do something nice for you, Mrs. Briggs," he told her softly. "But I guess I've set the hounds out after you."

"The hounds have always been after me," Cora answered easily with a wave of her hand. "I'm just glad to have my fence fixed."

"I swear, Mrs. Briggs," Jedwin confessed. "If I'd thought for a moment that my actions would have caused trouble for you—"

"Then you would have never shown up at my doorstep with your unchaste proposition?"

The question hung between them momentarily before Jedwin gave her an appeasing grin.

"Then I would never have painted the fence."

Cora actually giggled at his response. "As I have said before, Jedwin, I do admire an honest man."

"About the fence—" he began.

"Don't let's say another word about it," Cora interrupted. "It is spilled milk for sure. We will just have to take care to be more discreet in the future."

"The future?" Jedwin swallowed a little nervously. "Are you agreeing to have a . . . are you—"

"Jedwin, dear, why are you always stumbling over the words? I'm agreeing to allow you to call upon me, discreetly. That is, if you promise not to fix my fence again." Her eyes were bright with amusement and Jedwin couldn't help but smile back.

"Mrs. Briggs, I—" Jedwin looked at her longingly. She was the idealized hope of his youth, the dream he slept with and the thoughts of his every waking moment. A thousand times he'd relived that unconscionable and indescribable time alone with her upstairs. Had she really been wearing her nightclothes? Had her feet truly been naked beside his booted ones? Oh, heaven of fantasies, had she really grabbed his backside and pulled him on top of her? He reached across the table and clasped her warm hand in his. He needed to touch her, just to touch her, he promised himself. There was strength in his grasp, but his heart trembled all the same.

As he pulled Cora's hand toward him, it was clear he intended to bestow a gentle kiss on her knuckles, like the one he'd given her the other night. The immediate response of fluttering fireflies in her abdomen frightened Cora. Stiffly she withdrew her hand, but softened the rejection with a bright smile. "Do you think you could fix my pump, Jedwin?"

"Pump?"

"Yes, the kitchen pump," she said. "It's froze up."

He stared at her stupidly for a moment. It was a long jump in his mind from the wild imaginings of his dreams to the reality of Mrs. Briggs's kitchen.

"Oh, the pump!" he said finally. "Of course, of course." As he came too hastily to his feet, he knocked the kitchen chair over backward and then nearly tripped over it as he clumsily tried to right it again.

"The pump . . . right, the pump." Jedwin made his way to the painted gray cast-iron sink. He examined the handle fastenings before turning back to her. "You have some tools?"

Cora hurried past him to the pantry, where from its burial place deep in an obscure corner, she pulled out a well-worn potato sack that clanged with the sound of metal. She dragged it toward him.

Jedwin squatted down and opened the bag, examining the strange variety of worn and rusty tools that it contained. He pulled out a harness bracket, several (but not all) of the pieces to a carriage jack, a claw-head hammer that was broken at the butt, a copper bit burnisher, and an iron hoof pick.

Glancing up, he saw Cora looking down at him hopefully. "Do you think you can fix it?"

He smiled with guarded confidence. "Do you have any other tools, Mrs. Briggs? Maybe a pipe wrench or a pair of pliers?"

Cora shook her head thoughtfully. "I've some gardening tools out in the shed," she told him helpfully. "A couple of rakes and a hoe."

Jedwin stared at her for a moment in quiet disbelief and then spoke gently, determined to keep any humor or condescension out of his tone. "I don't believe I'll be able to fix it with a rake, Mrs. Briggs."

Of course he couldn't fix it with a rake, Cora thought to herself, fuming at her own stupidity. The problem was she didn't know how to fix it, or she would have done it long before now.

"Oh, I've got a combination tool," she told him excitedly as she hurried to the flatware box. Rifling through the terrapin forks, salt spoons, and asparagus servers, Cora found what she was looking for. "Here it is," she said, pulling out a queer-looking instrument of wrought iron.

Jedwin examined it momentarily.

"It's pliers, wire cutter, nutcracker, can opener, knife sharpener, corkscrew, and glass cutter all in one," Cora told him grandly. "I bought it from a peddler before I married; he said it was the one household tool every woman should own."

Nodding vaguely, Jedwin gave Cora a hopeful smile and opened the contraption with the intention of taking the bolts off the pump handle. With the pliers open to their widest point, the corkscrew stabbed Jedwin solidly in the palm of his hand. The spurt of blood that ensued was more dramatic than it was painful.

"You're injured!" Cora cried breathlessly. She rushed to his side. Dropping to the floor beside him, she grabbed up the bleeding palm and brought it to her lips to stop the bleeding.

Jedwin's startled intake of breath was greater from the touch of her lips than the prick of the corkscrew. The sight of her tender and intimate ministrations had him setting his teeth determinedly against the sudden surge of pounding blood that curled low in his stomach.

Cora saw his grimace. "It must hurt."

"It's nothing," Jedwin said quickly.

Cora reached into the cabinet behind her and pulled out a clean rag with which she attempted to bind up the wound.

Jedwin gazed at her dark head, bent so tenderly over his hand, and a strange warmth surged through him. She'd made no jokes about his clumsiness or complaints about the trouble. She had touched his body with familiarity, as if it were her own, and now bound his wound with a gentle caring that nearly unmanned him.

"It's fine," he said gruffly. "Don't fuss."

"I just want to make sure you are all right," she said, looking at him, worried.

Jedwin's eyes were drawn to her lips and then lower to the pale flesh of her throat visible above her collar. This was a woman who could ease a lot of hurts, he thought to himself. Determinedly, he pushed the thought away.

Those warm brown eyes pinned Cora to the floor, and she let go of his hand. Nervously she rose to her feet.

"I think you will be all right, Jedwin," she said. "It's not a deep wound, though it may be sore for a day or two."

He shrugged with unconcern. "I won't be able to fix the pump, I guess," he said. "Maybe another time."

"It doesn't matter," she told him quickly. "I've been living with it broken for almost a year now. I'm really quite used to it. Thank you for trying."

Cora looked down at him. He was kneeling before her. The position was one of subservience, but as those intense brown eyes gazed up at her, Cora trembled. He was at her feet, and the power of his humility coursed through her like a fire. Her breathing quickened and her hands ached to trace the strength of his jaw. It had been so long, so very long. She just needed to touch him, to feel the warmth of another human being. She needed to be held in his arms. Was a little closeness too much to ask of life? Why should she deny herself what little comfort that was offered? Her lips parted and as she reached a tentative hand toward him, she saw his eyes widen in pleasure.

Catching herself, Cora jerked back her hand and looked away hastily.

Jedwin calmly began refilling the potato sack with its useless bits of rusting metal as if nothing had happened. "I'll bring some tools tomorrow and fix it," he said.

Cora felt shy. "There is no need for you to do that," she insisted.

Jedwin smiled at her warmly, too warmly. "I want to do it," he said softly. "It's some way I can please you that your neighbors won't be gawking at."

Making her way to the table, Cora nervously began fussing with the dishes. "You don't have to please me, Jedwin."

"I don't?" Jedwin asked. There was a hint of humor in his voice. "I thought that was what romances were all about."

Cora's mood turned peevish. "And you should stop talking all this nonsense about romance," she snapped. "I know full well that it is not romance you are interested in, but something entirely different."

"And what is that?"

He was standing next to her, his hands on his hips and a grin on his face. Cora raised her chin bravely. "You want to have passion and excitement and . . . and marital relations without benefit of marriage."

Jedwin's bravado faded slightly, but he held his chin high.

"I suspect I could be talked into that, Mrs. Briggs," he said with a lighthearted bravado that tempted Cora to kick him. "But what I'd really like right now is a kiss."

"A kiss?" Cora shook her head adamantly. "A kiss is all you want, Jedwin? You've been hanging around here trying to garner my favor because you want a kiss?" Cora's mouth narrowed into a thin line of displeasure. "I thought you were determined to be honest?"

"I honestly want a kiss."

"There are girls all over this town who would be willing to chance a kiss with you. I suspect a number of them already have."

"I've kissed a few," he admitted.

"So, there."

"But I've never kissed one the way I wanted to. I've never kissed anyone the way I want to kiss you."

He took a step forward, and Cora stepped away from him. Finding the back of her knees against the seat of the chair, she simply sat down. She assumed that he would seat himself as well, out of politeness. He did not. Instead Cora found herself at eye level with the buttons on his trousers.

With a shocked intake of breath at her desire to loosen those buttons, Cora attempted to rise once again to her feet. A pair of strong, masculine hands stayed her.

She looked up at his eyes now, fearful. The long straight arms that held her in place were heavily muscled and masculine. Men could sometimes lose control, she knew. He was bigger and stronger than she, and if he chose he could take what he wanted. That's why there were rules about unmarried couples being alone, reason reminded her. The rules of society were for a purpose. But Cora was a fallen woman, a divorced woman. The rules no longer applied to her, and therefore neither did the protection.

"Please don't hurt me, Jedwin."

The intensity of Jedwin's brown eyes darkened as a puzzled look came over his face. "Hurt you?" He shook his head slowly and then squatted down beside her chair. "I would never hurt you, Mrs. Briggs. I would hope that you knew that about me already."

Cora could look straight into his eyes now and she relaxed a little. His visage was young and strong, but there was no evil in it, no hatred or corruption.

He moved closer to her. The tiny niggling fear she still held quivered inside her, but didn't spark to fright.

"Please let me kiss you, Mrs. Briggs," he whispered only inches from her lips. "I am no expert, but I promise it will not hurt at all."

Cora didn't answer. But she didn't pull away, either. Slowly, hesitantly, Jedwin brought his mouth to hers. He was barely an inch away when he stopped and nervously swallowed. Cora watched him bite his lip for courage and then turn his head slightly before bringing his lips to her own.

The touch of his mouth on hers was warm and soft as a whisper, but Cora immediately laid a soft hand on his jaw and pushed him back gently.

"You are supposed to shut your eyes," she whispered.

He pressed his cheek more firmly into her palm, reveling in her touch. "If I close my eyes, Mrs. Briggs, then I won't be able to look at you. And looking at you is one of the sweetest pleasures of my life."

Cora smiled. He was so close. The heady feel of his admiration coupled with his warm masculine smell and the sincerity of his words, seduced her as no gallant poem ever could.

"Close your eyes, Jedwin," she told him. "And open your mouth. Isn't that how you really want to kiss?"

Jedwin didn't bother to answer. A heavy fringe of pale blond lashes lowered over his eyes and his lips parted—eager to taste her.

Cora met his kiss more willingly than she would have ever admitted. Kissing was wonderful. It was the same warm, tender sweetness she remembered. And as she let her hand steal from his jaw to curve around his neck and bury her fingers into the hair at his nape, a sigh of pleasure escaped from the depths of her throat. It had been so long.

He answered her sigh with a moan of desire. He wrapped his arms around her and deepened the kiss. His mouth was hot and questing. There was the tenderness Cora remembered, but there was more. Something hot and wild and infinitely frightening. This was not Luther Briggs.

With a tiny fearful cry, Cora pulled away. Jedwin still held his arms tight around her, but as he saw her frightened expression he reluctantly loosened his grasp. He was breathing rapidly and the wildness that she'd felt in his arms was now visible in his eyes.

"Didn't I get it right that time, Mrs. Briggs?" he asked.

"No," she answered without thinking and then at his puzzled expression she said, "I mean yes, yes, it was fine."

Could she tell a young man that his kiss was too passionate? She supposed not. Her only experience in kissing, first kiss to last, had been with Luther Briggs. Luther's kisses were always respectful preludes to the exercise of marital rights. They had certainly never made her as jittery as Jedwin's just had. Nor had her lips ever tingled in the aftermath.

And they definitely tingled now. Obviously a man didn't kiss a wife the way that he would a woman of dubious reputation. The ignoble thought flittered through her brain that here at last was an advantage to being a fallen woman.

"Was it all right or not?" Jedwin asked. "For me, it was wonderful, but I want to please you."

"Oh, it was fine," Cora answered hurriedly. "It was quite good in fact. You do that rather well."

Jedwin stared at her quizzically for a moment and then shook his head and offered a deep masculine chuckle. "You speak as if I'd just made a splendid croquet shot."

Cora blushed and lowered her eyes. "It was a very pleasant kiss, Mr. Sparrow. Are you seeking compliments?"

Jedwin shrugged. "No, not necessarily. But I might be seeking another kiss if you are interested."

As she raised her head quickly, she had it on the tip of her tongue to agree. But Jedwin's face was so close and the taste on her lips still so fresh and frightening that she shook her head.

"I believe we've had enough romance for tonight."

Jedwin smiled broadly as he teased her. "Romance, Mrs. Briggs? Or passion?"

Before Cora could think of a witty reply, Jedwin had risen to his feet. As he took her hand in his, Cora thought for a moment that he would kiss it too, but he did not. He only gave it a warm slight squeeze and then gently released it.

Reaching for his hat and coat on the hook, he helped himself as if he were at home rather than merely a guest. It was a good thing, as Cora was still slightly befuddled.

Jedwin shrugged into his coat and hooked the top button before smoothing the hair on the top of his head and donning his hat. He kept his gaze on Cora, who seemed frozen in place, still seated in her chair. Smiling at her warmly, he placed his hand on the doorknob before bidding her farewell. "I'll try to come tomorrow and bring some tools to fix your pump," he told her.

"You really don't have to do that, Jedwin," Cora insisted.

"I know that I don't, Mrs. Briggs. But it seems a perfectly good excuse to get another kissing lesson."

She wasn't sure if he meant for himself or her.

Chapter Nine

====

Amelia Sparrow stepped into the embalming room with an angry and impatient look upon her face. Absently she rubbed her jaw, as if that would ease the pain there.

"Jedwin's not here, Mellie," the man standing by the table said without looking up. "I would have thought you'd have known that by now."

Amelia took a step closer and looked down on the young man lying pale and still on the table. "Who is he?" she asked.

Haywood glanced up momentarily. "His name's Whitlow. That's all I know. Nobody's sure where he's from or if he's got family. He'd been living in Low Town for about six months. Ross Crenshaw is trying to locate some folks that know him."

"How did he die?"

"Doc Perkins says asthma," he answered with a sad shake of his head. "I say diphtheria."

"Diphtheria!"

Haywood nodded. "There's an epidemic of it in Indian Territory. Just because we haven't seen it, doesn't mean it isn't here."

"Doesn't the doctor know about the epidemic?"

"Of course he does, but the truth is he ain't much of a doctor. He's one of those blamed hydropaths, Mellie. If you can't wash it away, he don't know nothing about it."

"But diphtheria," Amelia whispered. "How can you be sure?"

"I'm not *sure*," Haywood answered. "But I took a good look in his mouth. He's got a gray veil over his throat. I never heard of an asthma that would do that."

Mrs. Sparrow nodded agreement.

"That's why I volunteered to embalm him."

Amelia complete forgot her fear of contagion as she huffed with disapproval. "They should have just buried him. We'll never recoup a penny for the embalming."

Haywood gave her a look of displeasure. "Embalming fluid costs very little and I'm donating my time."

"Well, it's certainly easy for you to do that," she complained. "After all, we pay for it."

"Oh hush up," Haywood snapped. "Look at him, Mellie. He's about Jedwin's age, I think."

Quieting immediately, Amelia came closer and looked down at the pale stiff features of the young man on the table.

"It's such a shame," Haywood said softly. "His whole life before him and it ends too soon. He hadn't yet started to live before he died."

Amelia reached up and straightened a reddish brown curl that had strayed to the young man's forehead. "He does look to be about the size of James Edwin. Maybe we should give him that old gray suit he doesn't wear anymore."

Haywood's deep blue eyes studied Amelia for a moment before he nodded approval. "That would be real nice of you, Mellie," he said.

Amelia felt a strange and unexpected sense of comradery. Without understanding it, she hastily pushed the feeling away, uncomfortable with it. She watched silently as Haywood made a slight incision in the side of the young man's arm. With a trocar, Haywood carefully raised a large artery at the border of his muscle about an inch outside of the wound. There was no bleeding to speak of, but still Haywood wiped the area with a damp cloth. Using a pair of scissors, he cut the vein straight across and inserted a tube into the artery, securing it by the tying of two small threads.

Amelia watched, fascinated, as he attached the other end of the tube to the bottle of embalming fluid and began to slowly infuse the fluid into the body.

"How do you know which vein to use?" she asked him.

Haywood was momentarily startled by the question. He'd always figured that a woman with a husband and son who were undertakers would already know the basics of embalming.

"We don't use veins, Mellie," he answered easily. "No excuse for that. The veins will collapse on you. It's always best to use a good, strong artery. It doesn't matter which one."

Amelia peered curiously into the small cut in the man's arm. The web of vessels was fascinating. "How do you know which ones are arteries?"

Haywood took his thumb and forefinger and widened the incision ever so slightly so that Amelia could see inside. "The arteries are the white ones," he said. "I usually pick a good-sized one so the tube will fit in easily. You want to flush the fluid back down the arteries and toward the heart." He gestured to the tube in the man's arm and then laid a hand gently on the still, silent chest.

Amelia nodded and continued her curious inspection of Haywood's work. She felt his eyes upon her and started slightly when she realized that she was standing so close and that he was looking right at her.

"This doesn't bother you at all, does it?" he asked.

"Of course not," Amelia replied adamantly. "If you were thinking that James Edwin got his squeamishness from *my* side of the family, well you can just think again!"

"I wasn't thinking about Jedwin's 'squeamishness' at all," he said with more than a hint of impatience. "I think that it is perfectly natural for anyone to be disturbed by the sight of death and to be overset by having to prepare bodies. Undertaking is not for everyone."

Amelia shook her head in disapproval. "There you go again, trying to make excuses for that boy." She sighed with disgust. "There just isn't any excuse. From the time he was big enough to walk, Mr. Sparrow brought him in here and tried to teach him the business. That boy wouldn't learn a thing. He was always choking and coughing and racing to the door to lose his breakfast."

"He doesn't like the smell of formaldehyde," Haywood said evenly. "It is not a pleasant smell. It makes a lot of people sick to their stomachs."

Amelia dismissed his excuse. "A lot of people don't own their own mortuary! It is just completely beyond my understanding. I spanked him until he was too big for it, scolded him until he was old enough to outreason me, and warned him that his father would never forgive him, but it didn't do any good. He never was a lick of help to his father in the business."

Walking away from the table, Amelia casually perused the contents of the shelves and cabinets. She occupied her eyes with the trivial as her mind stayed mired in her disappointment.

"I was so proud when he passed his embalming examination," she said quietly. "He had the highest grade of anyone who took the test that year. I could hardly wait to tell Mr. Sparrow. He was very pleased, too."

Shutting a glass-fronted cabinet quietly and turning back to look at Haywood, her expression was derisive. "That lasted three whole days. Then old Addie Macon died and Mr. Sparrow asked James Edwin to prepare her."

"And?"

Folding her hands across her chest, Amelia made her way back to the table. "I heard him from the upstairs window," she said. "He was heaving and vomiting like a drunkard with a batch of bad brew."

"Just because he knows exactly *how* to do it," Haywood said, "doesn't mean that he might not still be sickened by doing it."

Amelia nodded. "That's what we discovered. I swear it nearly broke his daddy's heart. All he wanted to do was leave his business to his son, and no matter how much he tried, his son didn't want it."

Haywood glanced down at his work. "Did his daddy ever forgive him?"

Amelia shrugged. "Oh, I suspect so. He didn't ask him to work in the embalming room much after that. And he seemed to take some pleasure in James Edwin's interest in the flowers." She shook her head.

"I'm sure your husband forgave him," Haywood said.

Amelia looked up, surprised. "Why do you think that? You didn't even know him."

He shrugged. "I guess because he was an undertaker like me."

"And undertakers don't want their sons to follow in their footsteps?" she asked.

Haywood shook his head. "Some people think that undertaking is a trade," he said. "Like carpentry or shoemaking. But Mellie, it's not like that at all. Caring for the dead is not something that just anybody can do. I think it's a lot like preaching. It's more a calling that it is a profession." Haywood nodded, sure of himself. "Your husband *had* to understand that. I don't believe that he'd blame his son for something that was just not in his nature."

Amelia huffed in disbelief. "I just can't agree with that. If somebody leaves you an undertaking business, you had just better change your nature to suit. I told Mr. Sparrow myself, that I was just sure it was some foolish boyhood nonsense and that he would grow out of it. It just breaks my heart that he hasn't."

"What difference does it make, Mellie?" Haywood asked her.

"What difference?" She looked at him as if he were a complete fool. "Why, the difference is your wages, Mr. Puser. If James Edwin would take on his own responsibilities, we wouldn't have to pay an outsider to do our business."

To Amelia's extreme displeasure, Haywood found something quite amusing about that and chuckled heartily. He began washing down the instruments on the surgical tray. "Now Mellie, you don't pay me enough to worry yourself about."

"The fact that I have to pay you at all is infuriating. James Edwin should be doing this. I've done everything a mother could do for a son. You can't know how much I've sacrificed. And this is how he repays me. By being such a coward he can't even face a dead body."

With a deafening wham Haywood slammed a trocar onto the tray. "Damn it, Mellie! Sometimes I'm tempted to take a switch to you. Are you so full of yourself that you can't see Jedwin at all?"

"How dare you talk to me that way!"

"How dare I? Damn it, woman, it's high time that somebody did," he hollered right back. "You love Jedwin, don't you?"

"Well, of course I do! What kind of question is that?"

"It's the kind of question you ought to be asking yourself."

"My whole life has been sacrificed for that boy."

"You've said that already, at least a million times if I haven't lost count, and he's not a boy. He's a man. If you'd quit 'sacrificing' yourself and let him have his own life, you'd both be a lot better off."

"You, sir, know absolutely nothing of which you speak."

"I know a damn sight more about what I speak than you do, because you won't come down off your high horse to see anything."

"I only want what's best for James Edwin."

"And you think you know what's best?"

"I certainly do. We all have our demons to face, Mr. Puser. The only way to deal with them is to raise our chins and confront our fears head-on. It's what I do and it's exactly what my son would do if he weren't such a coward."

"A coward!" Haywood shouted. He took a deep, cleansing breath. "A coward?" he asked more quietly.

"Yes," Amelia said firmly. "There is no reason not to speak plainly."

"A coward," Haywood said softly and then shook his head. "Mellie, do you remember when your husband died?"

Momentarily distracted by the abrupt change of subject, Amelia hesitated.

"Why . . . yes, of course I remember. The loss of one's husband is not something a widow is likely to forget."

"Do you remember the funeral?"

"Yes, of course."

"How much of it do you remember?"

"I remember all of it. What are you getting at? Do you think you know something about the funeral that I don't? You weren't even here in town back then."

"Was your husband embalmed for the funeral?"

"What?"

"Was your husband embalmed?"

"Why, yes, I mean I think so." Amelia hesitated. "Yes, of course he was embalmed."

"And who embalmed him, Mellie?"

There was silence between them for a moment.

"I guess James Edwin did," she said.

Haywood nodded. "Yes, I guess Jedwin did."

Amelia looked down at the young man on the table. Cold and silent, he was a very sad sight. He was someone she didn't know.

"Can you imagine what it was like in here that day, Mellie?" Haywood's words were soft, sorrowful. "Jedwin's hands tremble every time he has to come into this room. Can you imagine the day that his own father lay here?"

"I don't want to talk about it."

Haywood ignored her. "The smell would have soured in his stomach before he got much past the door."

"Mr. Puser, please."

"Can you feel him choking on the stench of formaldehyde? Can you see him flinching as he cut the flesh of the man who gave him his life?"

"Don't."

"Can you see the tears running down his cheeks as he begs forgiveness for not being the man his father wanted him to be? Can you see it, Mellie? Can you see it and still call him a coward?"

"Stop it!" Amelia turned away, a hand covering her mouth and her eyes squeezed tightly shut as she desperately tried to still the vivid images that Haywood had conjured up. And unwilling to let him see the tears that she could not hold back.

Haywood turned again to his work. His own eyes had filled with sorrow. He was a man who had seen too much of the world, but he was still able to cry.

The silence lengthened between them and Haywood began to regret his words. He had a grudging admiration for Mellie. There was no excuse for deliberately hurting her. He just wanted her to know what a fine son she really had.

"You are right, Mr. Puser. My son is no coward." He heard the quiet words and he turned to look at Amelia Sparrow. She attempted a smile, but it was somewhat wan. "My father always told me that I wasn't cut out to be a mother."

Haywood smiled warmly. "Then being wrong about one's children must run in the family. I wouldn't fault you as a mother, Mellie. You've raised a very fine man."

"Thank you."

"I buried my own son twenty years ago," Haywood said evenly as he checked the lines on the infusion. "I like to imagine he would have grown up to be like your Jedwin."

"You had a son?" Amelia was astounded.

"Yes, ma'am. And a pretty little daughter, too." Leaning forward as if relaying a frightening secret, he added, "I even had a full-time wife, once upon a time."

His joking eased the tension between them, but not Amelia's curiosity. "What happened to them?"

"Cholera," he answered simply. "Cholera happened to them."

"I'm sorry." She felt very uncomfortable. She'd spent most of her life dealing with grieving families, but in this instance, somehow the usual platitudes seemed pale. "I didn't know, I—"

"You didn't know," Haywood explained, "because there was no reason to tell you. It's been a long time now. I miss Abby sometimes. I think about her and the children. But I'm not a man to grieve forever. One thing about working with the dead is you learn right away that life is for the living."

"Yes, of course you are right," Amelia agreed.

Haywood gave her a curious squint. "What's wrong with your jaw?"

"My jaw?" Amelia realized that she'd been rubbing at the pain in her mouth.

"It's nothing," she said. "I've just got a sore tooth."

Haywood turned to the washbasin and began cleaning his hands. "You want me to have a look at it? I've got some experience in dentistry."

"Certainly not!" Amelia was absolutely horrified at the idea.

Haywood chuckled. "I was asking to have a look in your mouth, Mellie, not up your dress."

The Lewis wand swirled high in the clear blue sky over the river knoll. It came back to earth at precisely the expected place and exactly parallel to the earth when it reached six feet from the ground. A very easy catch.

Cora missed it.

Giving the perfectly innocent wand an evil glance, Cora jerked it out of the grass and tossed it on the picnic cloth.

With self-disgust she followed its example and seated herself abruptly. Concentration. That was what was needed for healthy exercise. And healthy exercise was needed for spiritual completeness. This morning Cora felt she suffered a distinct shortage of both.

Dutifully she picked up Mrs. Millenbutter's book and leafed through it, trying to find a passage that would help relieve her current emotional upheaval. Mrs. Millenbutter seemed to see great value in the release of tension. Surely she would have some solutions for the tension that had been building inside Cora since Jedwin Sparrow gave her a sweet and simple kiss in her kitchen the night before.

She should never have allowed Jedwin to pursue her, Cora thought. She no longer harbored any foolish notions of visiting revenge on Amelia Sparrow but that had been nothing in comparison to the confusion she was now confronting.

Cora slammed the book closed and tossed it next to the wand. Apparently Mrs. Millenbutter was as ignorant of the ways of wicked women as Cora was herself.

With near disbelief, she ran a gentle hand across her lips. She had worried that even a gentleman might lose control. She had worried that perhaps Jedwin Sparrow was no gentleman. But she had never considered the fact that perhaps he could make *her* want him. Living without a man had been so easy.

"You just go behind the screen there and change into your nightgown," Luther had directed that first night in the Williams Hotel. "I'll just be waiting here in the bed for you."

Cora blushed even now, nearly a decade later, at the embarrassment she'd felt on that first night of her marriage.

"Turn the light off, Mr. Briggs," she called from behind the screen a few moments later. "I'm not coming out without that light off."

"Call me Luther, my Cory," he answered. "You call me Luther, and I'll turn the light out."

Trembling, Cora found it difficult to speak at all. "Please Luther, turn out the light."

She heard him fumbling around a bit as he got out of bed and then the gaslight faded down to darkness.

Cora took a deep breath for courage and stepped from behind the screen, only to run smack-dab into Luther's chest.

"Oh!"

"I thought I'd come and get you," he said. "I didn't want you to stub your toe or something running around in the dark like this."

"Thank you," she answered. He was wearing only the drawers of his union suit and Cora was grateful for the darkness that obscured what seemed to be a huge hairy body.

Luther snaked his arm around her waist and walked her to the bed. "There just ain't no call for you to be afraid of this lovemaking, Cory. Why, every woman you know that's got a baby has done it and a lot of them that don't got a baby, too."

"I'm not afraid," Cora said bravely.

He pulled back the covers on the bed and Cora sat down and scooted far to the other side. Luther followed her.

"It hurts some the first time," he said. "I'm not going to lie to you about that. But only the first time. After that, why it don't feel bad at all."

Cora nodded.

"Some women even like it," Luther said. "I admit to having some experience in these things and I'll do my best to make it nice for you." He moved closer and pulled her into his arms. "But if you don't like it, Cory," he whispered, "that's all right. Truly it don't matter to me. I promised today for better or worse, so whichever, I'm here."

"I'm here, too, Luther," Cora said shyly. "I know a woman's got to do her duty to her husband and I'm willing."

He sunk his fingers into her hair as he gazed at her. "You are a good girl, Cory. To tell you the truth, I may not be the best husband you could have had. But honey, I'm going to try."

He'd kissed her then. It had been a lover's kiss, full of tricks and techniques and tongue. It was a kiss that distracted her while he pulled up her nightgown. It was a kiss that went on forever as his hands surveyed her bosom and searched the inside of her thighs. It was a kiss that was interspersed with sweet words against her lips. It was a kiss that ended only when he plunged himself into her for the first time.

But it was not a kiss that had tingled on her lips and stolen her sleep. Luther's kiss had not done that. But Jedwin's had. Jedwin's did.

Cora jumped once more to her feet. Grabbing up the wand, she casually twirled it from one hand to the other as she walked toward the edge of the knoll and gazed down at the river.

Her marriage bed had been no hated duty or painful humiliation. Luther had always treated her kindly and in fact she had come to like those warm, close moments when their bodies were joined.

But she had never thought to share those feelings again. She never imagined herself with another man. Another man was against the rules. She had promised to "keep herself only unto" Luther Briggs. Although her marriage had become a lie and a travesty, she'd meant those words when she'd spoken them. And for all these years, it had been no hardship to keep those vows.

Today, that ease of virtue was gone. Temptation was new and exciting. And she found Jedwin Sparrow to be very tempting indeed.

What could it hurt? she asked herself. Her reputation was already ruined, and the young man was going to sow his wild oats somewhere. A short, discreet fling wouldn't bother a soul and could be a very pleasant diversion, Cora told herself.

"Ouch!" Cora hollered. Somehow she'd managed to give her shin a good solid wallop with the wand. Grimacing painfully, she hopped on one leg as she rubbed the shin of the other. "So graceful, Cora dear," she mimicked snidely to herself. "Oh yes, do involve yourself immorally with this young man. You are so clumsy, you'll probably get a baby on the first try!"

Disgusted, Cora began gathering her things. Mrs. Millenbutter would not be proud of her today. But then Mrs. Millenbutter was probably never tempted to have an illicit relationship with a younger man.

Cora was tempted. She had to admit it to herself. She wanted Jedwin Sparrow as she'd never wanted a man before. A child was, of course, a real possibility, she reminded herself as she loaded her things on the bicycle. That consequence didn't bother her as much as it should have. She had told herself at least a thousand times how fortunate she was that her marriage to Luther was without issue. However being a mother was something she had always dreamed about, something she had always desired. Eight years ago she had shoved those dreams away. Once more she shoved bitterly at them.

"He won't be coming to your rescue with a hurry-up wedding," she warned herself aloud.

If she were to become pregnant, she would likely be run out of town. Amelia Sparrow would never allow an illegitimate grandson to grow up in her shadow. And Cora would be out on her own with nothing, except for a child to raise.

Maybe she could sell the house. It was not the first time such an idea had occurred to her. The lure of starting over had enticed her more than once. In another place where no one knew her, she could present herself as a widow, and if she didn't act untoward, no one would ever be the wiser.

But what about the child? She could barely support herself now. How would she manage to pay rent and feed a baby, too? And one day she would have to tell him, "Oh, your father was just a lusty young man who was sowing his wild oats." And then there was poor Jedwin. What would she say to him? Thank you, sir, for a pleasant diversion. I am taking your own flesh and blood away and you must never think of us or try to find us again. Cora shook her head disapprovingly.

Scooting off, she pushed her bicycle to begin its hurried descent down the steep knoll. With the wind in her hair and the sky bright blue above, Cora was able to rein in her wild speculation.

"You are not having a baby!" she reminded herself. For heaven's sake, she was with Luther for almost a year without even a hint of increasing. One unsanctioned coupling with young Sparrow would not make her the Old Woman in the Shoe.

Reaching the bottom of the hill, she put down a foot and stopped herself abruptly. Had she decided? she asked herself. Was she certain about what she was doing? Was she really going to sow grain in an unblessed field with Jedwin Sparrow?

Chapter Ten

Cora set the pecan, tip up, on the flattened rock before her. Holding her tongue just right, she raised the broken clawhammer about a foot above her target. Squinting slightly, she took aim. With a quick, jerky movement, she popped the pecan sharply, splitting it perfectly in the middle. Setting down the hammer, she carefully picked out the uninjured pecan halves and rubbed them casually to remove any remaining pieces of shell. She tossed them into the washpan beside her.

"You do that very well."

The unexpected voice behind her was startling, and Cora jumped slightly. "You scared the life out of me, Jedwin Sparrow!"

His smile was teasing. "That's my job, ma'am," he said with an exaggerated peddler's spiel. "How else can I expect my business to prosper if I just let people live as long as they would?"

He was wearing a pair of apron-front overalls and a pale blue calico shirt. The costume was in sharp contrast to his usual staid, dark clothing. The slightly long blond curls twirled carelessly at his collar and the pale color of his shirt seemed to accentuate the leftover warmth of summer color in his face. The effect was rather pleasing. He really was quite handsome, Cora thought.

Coming to her side, Jedwin laid out the mechanic's apron that he carried beside her on the bench. Squatting down, he slipped a fine steel hammer from its loop and held it out to her. "This won't be as hard to balance as that broken clawhead you're using," he said.

Cora took the heavy weight of his hammer in his hand. It was not new, but there was not a hint of rust or even a chip in the metal. She ran her hand along the smooth, polished blond hickory handle. Grasping it, she tested its balance in her hand. She smiled approvingly at Jedwin. "It just might make this a bit easier," she said. "May I borrow it?"

Jedwin took the hammer from her and looked down at it for a moment before he smiled. Holding it out to her like an offering, a look of long-suffering upon his features, his voice again mimicked an actor in a romantic melodrama. "My dear lady," he said with a bit of lisp. "Flowers pale next to your beauty and candy is not as sweet as your own pink lips. Take then this hammer as my gift to you . . . that when you look upon it, you will always be reminded of me."

Cora jerked it out of his hand. "I'm tempted to hit you on the head with it."

Jedwin laughed. "Please keep it, Mrs. Briggs," he said, glancing into the washpan. "I'll consider a warm pecan pie in payment."

"Done," she answered as she raised the hammer and used it to crack its first pecan. "So what are you doing here in broad daylight, young man? Are you trying to ruin my reputation?"

Cora spoke the words as a joke, but Jedwin faltered momentarily before he answered.

"I believe I promised to fix your pump," he said honestly. "I got to thinking that people are probably not nearly as nosy about what goes on in your house in the daytime as they would be at night. I decided that it was safe to be here."

Cora nodded with a chuckle. "You are right there. One thing we have around here is a shortage of people when there is work to be done."

Jedwin grinned and took up his apron. Slipping the neckpiece over his head, he fastened the ties at his slim waist. "Not another word, Mrs. Briggs," he said. "I'm no shirker. You stay here and shell enough pecans to make me a pie, while I make an attempt to earn the eating of it."

As he turned to walk toward the back door, Cora called back to him. "Don't you make a mess of my kitchen floor or you'll go without your pecan pie for a good long spell."

"Yes, ma'am," Jedwin called back as he opened the screen.

It was strange to just walk into her house as if it were his own. Only a few weeks ago, he'd only dreamed of stepping inside, and now he came and went as comfortably as a boarder.

No, not a boarder, he decided. Like a secret lover. That thought brought a smile to his face.

Cora had kept the door shut against the coolness of the fall afternoon, but Jedwin determinedly propped it open. If she asked, he would tell her that pump fixing was hot work. But in fact, he just wanted to be able to hear her and maybe glance out at her. He wanted to be close to her even when they were apart. She had become a constant presence in his mind. It seemed that no matter what task he set himself, or to whomever he might be speaking, it was Cora whose face he saw before him, it was Cora whose words he heard.

He smiled to himself and shook his head. This had to be a kind of craziness. But it was an insanity Jedwin liked.

He began to whistle as he latched the adjustable farmer's wrench onto the head of the pitcher pump. By the time the head was off and he was inspecting the rods in the tubing, his whistle had turned into a hum. He hardly noticed the tuneless ditty that came from his lips until it was joined from the backyard by a high breathy soprano.

> "Hello my baby, hello my honey,
> Hello my ragtime gal.
> Send me a kiss by wire
> Honey, my heart's on fire."

Jedwin grinned both at being caught in such a good mood and at the pleasure of sharing a song with Cora.

Leaning out the door, he called sternly, "Mrs. Briggs, I do believe that beer-garden music is quite inappropriate for our little town." His voice eerily mimicked Reverend Philemon Bruder's. "Such frolic can only lead to modern thinking, unseemly behaviors, and the world of sin."

Cora turned to him, her eyes bright with amusement. "Do you think it will lead to the world of sin, itself?"

Jedwin grinned broadly and raised both eyebrows in wicked devilment. "Oh, I certainly hope so!"

Giggling, Cora pointed at the pump before continuing her pecan shelling.

Jedwin resumed his work, but along with it he hummed a very loud and slightly off-key rendition of "A Hot Time in the Old Town Tonight."

For better than a half hour they worked separately, but together, before Jedwin gathered up a handful of pump pieces and headed out the back door. He came over to the bench and seated himself on the grass before her.

"Did you fix the pump?"

"Not yet," he answered. "But I can." He held up a thin, curved piece of metal. "You've got a faulty foot valve. The water's been seeping through it back down the rods. Without a good steady pressure, that pump just can't pump."

"But you can fix it," she said.

Jedwin nodded. "I'll need to get a new valve for it. And while it's torn up, I might as well replace the leathers."

"Leathers?"

He held one up before her. "They are little leather cups that scoop the water and bring it to the surface," he said. "Since these have been dry for nearly a year, I suspect that they are right ready to crack. So I'll just replace them."

"How much is it going to cost?" she asked.

"How about a kiss?" he asked.

Cora raised a censoring brow. "How about another pie?"

Jedwin grinned and glanced at the washbasin that was considerably fuller than before. "I'm not sure how many pies I can eat, Mrs. Briggs."

Cora shook her head. "You won't get another, sir. This is my cash crop you've set your greedy eyes on."

"Your cash crop?"

Blushing, Cora momentarily regretted her hasty reply. "You are not to say a word," she admonished Jedwin. "Titus Penny buys my pecans for his store."

Jedwin's eyes widened in surprise.

"He tells everyone that they come from the Widow Martin."

He stared at her for a long moment and then chuckled. "And I was thinking that old blind widow had to be the most industrious female in the territory."

"Don't say anything," Cora said. "If Fanny found out, I'm sure she wouldn't let Titus buy from me, and I really need the money."

"I won't breathe a word," Jedwin assured her. "What else do you sell down there?"

"Whatever I can. I grow a big garden in the summer, as much as I can manage," she said. "What I can't sell fresh, I put by to sell in the winter."

Leaning back on his elbows, Jedwin crossed his long legs at the ankles and laughed. "Now I know why poor Titus got all tongue-tied when the preacher asked him if you always paid cash."

Cora sat watching Jedwin as he continued to chuckle. There was a strange expression on her face that finally caught Jedwin's attention.

"What is it?"

She shrugged and shook her head. "Nothing . . . no, something . . ." She gestured absently at her own foolishness. "You are very different than I thought."

Jedwin raised a curious eyebrow before rising to a sitting position, legs crossed Indian-style. "In what way?"

Hesitating, Cora collected her thoughts. "Well . . . I always thought you were a quiet and reserved young man," she said. "But when you smile . . ." She hesitated again, this time blushing. "When you smile, you are very nice looking."

Jedwin raised his chin with an exaggerated preen. "All us swains are handsome devils."

"That, too," Cora said, giggling.

"What?"

"I just never expected you to be so funny," she said. "You, making jokes, it's not what I thought of Jedwin Sparrow."

The young man shrugged, but from his expression, he was taking her comments seriously. "I'm an undertaker, Mrs. Briggs. It wouldn't do for me to walk around laughing and cutting up all the time."

"I guess not," she said. "It does seem that smiling comes more natural to you."

Jedwin laughed a little, pleasantly embarrassed. "I don't think it ever has before," he admitted. "You make me smile, Mrs. Briggs. I think about you all day long and just find myself smiling."

"Oh?" Cora began to fuss with her pecans again.

Jedwin leaned forward hugging his knees, feasting on the sight of her shy blush and her pretty agitation. "You are different than I had thought, too," he said.

"Really?" Cora smiled. Then her happy expression darkened abruptly. "I suspect you thought me no better than a soiled dove from Wichita."

Jedwin sat up straight, clearly displeased. "Mrs. Briggs, that is not what I thought at all."

Cora raised a brave, proud chin. She had faced the gawking and censure of the whole town, she was ready to face his.

The intense brown eyes that had become so familiar to her now showed deep down to the young man's soul. And there was no malice.

"Are you sure?" she asked, still uncertain.

"I never thought you were a harlot, Mrs. Briggs," he said quietly.

Jedwin looked her straight in the eyes. His expression was warm and vital and held some emotion she did not yet recognize. But Cora could not doubt his sincerity.

When she gave a slight nod of acceptance, Jedwin's expression warmed to a teasing grin. "But," he continued, his intense brown eyes narrowing in mischief. "I did *hope* that you were a bit more wicked than you've proved to be."

Cora stared at him, momentarily stunned. "Why you—you—"

Jedwin couldn't hold his mirth back another minute. He hooted with laughter, pointing toward her. "If you could see your expression—" he began before hilarity took over.

"How dare you laugh at me!" Cora screeched in exasperation.

That set Jedwin off even worse. Falling back on the cool grass, he howled with laughter.

"Oh you—" Cora began again, but again words failed her. Snatching up the bucket of unshelled pecans, she tossed them at him in impotent fury.

The rain of pecans amused Jedwin also. But his laughter began to quiet when she threw the pail at him, too.

"Mrs. Briggs!" He raised his hands just quickly enough to fend off the bucket aimed at his head, still laughing. "You've got me worrying for my life. Don't kill me, ma'am," he teased. "Don't kill me."

As if his taunting plea had given her an idea, she gripped the fine hickory hammer in her fist. He grinned hopefully and then scrutinized her black expression. He couldn't tell if she was truly angry or not. He leapt to his feet. "It was a joke, Mrs. Briggs," he assured her quickly as he began backing away. "It was just a joke."

Cora jumped to her feet, her eyes wide and the hammer held up before her like an avenging tomahawk.

When Jedwin started to run, she was right behind him.

"It was a joke!" he hollered as he raced around the side of the tree. He was up to the porch and down off the other side in an instant, but she was right behind him. "I didn't mean it!" he assured her as he raced to the backyard, amazed at how fast the woman was on her feet. "I swear I will never joke about such a thing again!" he promised as his path led him full circle and he leapt over the bench she'd been sitting on all afternoon.

He started around the right side of the tree once more, deciding that he'd let her chase him around the house again. Surely he had stamina on his side. To his dismay, Jedwin found that he'd underestimated the woman's mental abilities. He might have stamina, but Mrs. Briggs was crafty. Cora had run around the left side of the tree, opposite Jedwin, and met him, her hammer raised like Lizzy Borden's hatchet.

Turning, Jedwin saw that behind him was the corner of the picket fence, largely overgrown with forsythia. The shrub was too tall to jump over and too wide to climb around.

Cornered, Jedwin turned back to Cora, his hands raised before him like a surrendering criminal.

"Please, Mrs. Briggs," he said softly. "Don't throw the hammer. I know you are angry. I can assure you I was only teasing and will not do so ever again." Slowly he backed farther and farther away, but she followed him step by step.

Although Jedwin could have easily twisted the hammer out of her hand, he didn't want to overpower her. A gentleman never used physical force against a lady. However, an angry woman with a dangerous weapon in her hand called for very careful handling.

"Now, ma'am." His voice was calm and determinedly rational. "You could seriously injure me with that hammer, and I know that you would regret it. I have sincerely apologized for my little joke. Clearly, I never meant to hurt you or upset you in any way." Jedwin took a tentative step forward. "Please, Mrs. Briggs, don't throw that hammer."

There was silence between them.

Slowly, Cora lowered the hammer until she held it before her, staring at it. She raised her eyes to Jedwin and spoke. Her voice was as cold as it was smooth. "I will throw this hammer if I choose!"

"No!" Jedwin hollered as he saw it fly out of her hand.

The hammer, tossed, went straight up to heaven. Jedwin watched as it spun end over end a half-dozen times. In amazement he watched as Cora, her eyes heavenward on the twirling hammer, spun around twice, as graceful as a dancer, before raising her right hand to neatly catch the polished hickory handle.

Jedwin gaped. Cora smiled brightly, held the hammer before her daintily, and bent in a deep and graceful curtsy.

"Did you honestly think I would risk breaking my brand-new hammer on your thick skull?" she asked sweetly.

He looked so dumbstruck that Cora burst out laughing and pointed her finger at him in just the same manner in which he'd pointed at her earlier.

Jedwin stood frozen in place for only a moment. At his first movement, Cora squealed like a naughty child, dropped the hammer, and took off running.

He was right behind her. They followed the same route as before. This time, however, their breathing was hampered by their laughter.

When Cora scampered across the porch, rushed headlong to the backyard, and came back to the south side of the house, Jedwin was at her heels. Seeing the bench before her, she hesitated only slightly. She'd hadn't tried to jump anything in twenty years. *You can do it,* she admonished herself. But it was too late to try. Her hesitation was her undoing. Jedwin's arm snaked around her waist. Laughingly, he pulled her feet right off the ground.

"You little dickens," Jedwin complained. "You had me apologizing my heart out."

Cora struggled giggling in his arms. "I wish you could have seen your face."

Jedwin, quite appreciative of her squirming, turned her around and pressed her up against him. "I'd much rather see your face, Mrs. Briggs," he whispered. Leaning toward her, Jedwin pressed his lips gently against her temple.

Her laughter stopping abruptly, Cora was suddenly very aware of her new situation. A handsome man, with an expression that no longer displayed even a hint of humor, held her in his arms. His hands, at her waist, were caressing. Then gently he pressed her to him and she felt the evidence of his desire against her belly.

Cora's eyes widened.

"Jedwin," she whispered, scandalized, "it's daylight."

"Ma'am?"

Grabbing his wrists, she placed his hands at his sides firmly. "It's daylight," she repeated as she stepped away.

"Yes, Mrs. Briggs," he said. "I can see that."

She took another step backward and found herself unable to meet his eyes.

Jedwin cleared his throat, not sure exactly where to look, either. He knew she'd been able to feel his arousal. He didn't quite understand her reaction.

The uncomfortable moment lengthened. Jedwin glanced over at Cora. She was patting down her hair and nervously trying to straighten her disheveled state.

From the corner of his eye, Jedwin spotted the hammer and casually walked over to it. He picked it up, unconsciously weighing it in his hand. Shaking his head, he marveled at how she'd made it spin in the air and then caught it like some circus performer. This woman was really something.

"Here, Mrs. Briggs," he said, holding the hammer out to her.

"Thank you," she answered, still clearly embarrassed.

"You'd better keep it close," Jedwin suggested. "You never know when some adoring swain is going to try to kiss you in broad daylight."

"Kiss?" She blurted out the word, then would have given her new hammer to have it back.

Jedwin raised a quizzical eyebrow. "Yes, kiss," he said. "That was all I was asking for, Mrs. Briggs. Just a kiss."

Cora's cheeks flamed. How was she supposed to know that a kiss was all he wanted? Whenever Luther had pulled her close and she'd felt him swollen like that, he'd expected her panties off in five minutes.

"I—" Cora began, but stopped abruptly. She would not apologize. No other words, however, came to mind. Quickly, without giving herself time to question her actions, Cora rose up on her toes and briefly pressed her lips against his. "If you want a kiss, Jedwin," she said with feigned worldliness, "you will simply have to say so."

She turned to walk away.

Jedwin stared after her. He could still feel the warm touch of her lips against his. *If he wanted a kiss all he had to do was say so?* Jedwin mused. Then he shook his head. He knew that it was not as easy as the lady made out.

Cora retrieved the bucket and began picking up the pecans that had scattered across the grass. For a moment Jedwin watched her with pleasure before helping. As they searched the long grass, occasionally they gave each other shy glances. When the weight of the pecan bucket grew heavier, Jedwin wordlessly took it from Cora's hand and began to tote it himself.

"Is this really your cash crop?"

Cora was noncommittal. "I sell whatever I can. If the pecans do well, I sell pecans. This year that tree has decided to put bread on my table."

Jedwin found himself wishing she could be as grateful to him as she was to the tree.

"You know there are still a lot of pecans up there," he commented as they finished gathering up all that had been spilled.

Cora glanced up. The topmost branches were heavy with clusters of pecans, still cloaked in their dark green overshells. "There are plenty up there," she said. "But they are up there, and we are down here. We'll just have to wait for them to fall."

Jedwin put his hands on his hips in a challenging stance. "So you are a believer in the 'take 'em as the Lord sends 'em' philosophy."

Cora giggled at the way he managed the old saw. "I shake the lower branches," she admitted. "But those high ones, well . . . I just have to wait."

"Squirrels will get most of them."

Cora nodded agreement. "Can't be helped."

Jedwin gazed up at the treetop another minute. "Did you say you've got a rake in the shed?"

"Yes."

"Go get it."

Cora assumed he intended to use the rake to shake the tree a bit higher than she had. It was a good idea, actually. He was taller than her by nearly a head, and with the rake, he'd be able to reach nearly halfway up the tree.

The rake was hanging on its designated nail in the shed and Cora quickly retrieved it. When she returned to the yard, however, Jedwin was out of sight.

Had he gone back into the house? Surely he hadn't just left. She was looking around curiously when she heard him call. "Mrs. Briggs!"

Looking up, Cora's mouth formed a little O of surprise. "What are you doing up there?"

Jedwin stood on the second, rather large branch of the pecan tree. Barefoot, with his sleeves rolled up, he looked more like Huck Finn than the local undertaker.

"You are going to break your neck!"

Grinning as if she'd issued a challenge, Jedwin leaned a hand down to her. "Give me the rake, ma'am, and I'll shake the come-and-get-'em out of this tree."

Cora handed up the rake. "Be careful." Jedwin nodded, but never actually agreed.

Rake in hand, Jedwin propped himself solidly against the tree trunk and reached to a distant limb. Capturing a clump of leafy branches in the rake tines, Jedwin began to pull on the limb with quick jerky motions. Pecans fell, rattling against the ground like a hailstorm.

"These are right ready to fall," Jedwin called down to Cora. "One good stiff wind and you'd have gotten most of them."

Cora was delighted with the windless fall, but continued to keep a wary eye on Jedwin as he moved the rake from branch to branch. When Cora saw that he'd shaken all the limbs he could reach, she called up her thanks. "This is wonderful. Though the poor squirrels will probably starve to death this winter," she joked.

"There are plenty more up higher," Jedwin answered. "There's no reason to leave them."

When Jedwin secured the rake into a limb above him and began to climb higher in the tree, Cora's breath caught in her throat. "Be careful, Jedwin."

She was sure he must have heard, but still he ignored her, climbing even higher in the tree.

"Jedwin!" she protested.

Finally he stopped at what looked to be the highest branch that would support his weight. He smiled down at her reassuringly. "I might as well get all that are ready," he explained as he reached for his rake again.

Cora listened to the mad rustle of leaves and the patter of falling pecans for a good ten minutes before the fruitful rain began to taper off.

"Stand back," he called. Then he tossed down the rake. Cora hurriedly retrieved it and carried it back to the shed.

She'd surely make enough on her pecans now to last her through the winter, she thought. And at least Jedwin had managed not to break his neck.

The thought had hardly time to pass through her head when she heard the loud crack of a breaking branch. Cora couldn't even see Jedwin in the tree, all she saw was the too-quick rustle of the leaves and then Jedwin Sparrow dropped flat on his back in her yard.

"Jedwin!"

Cora had no time to think as she ran. One moment he was across the yard from her, the next she was kneeling at his side. His eyes were closed and he groaned.

"Jedwin? Oh, Jedwin? Are you all right?" She ran her hands nervously across his body, searching for bloody wounds or broken bones. His arms were straight, his ribs seemed intact, his legs were uninjured.

"Jedwin, darling, speak to me. Tell me you are okay."

He opened his eyes and looked straight into her own. "Is that you, Cora?"

"It's me, Jedwin. Where does it hurt? What can I do?"

He whispered a word as if speaking was painful in itself. Again Cora ran her hand along his chest, seeking a rib that might be stabbing his lung.

"What is it? What is it, darling?" she pleaded.

"Closer." The word was said harshly.

Cora's face was only inches from his, her fear furrowed across her brow, as she gazed at the young man she had come to care for so much.

"What can I do, Jedwin?" she whispered close to his face.

"Kiss me," was his breathless answer.

"What?"

"You said all I had to do was ask."

Cora looked at him, puzzled. His eyes were closed again. Did he think he was dying? Was he dying? Did he want to step out of this world with the taste of her on his lips?

"Of course, my sweetheart," she said, bringing her lips to his, warm and open.

His lack of initial response frightened Cora. Was he closer to the end than she thought? Gently, lovingly, she deepened the kiss and broadened it to include his chin, his upper lip, his cheekbones.

He moaned and she moved back. "Did I hurt you? Oh Jedwin, promise me you aren't going to die?"

His eyes opened and the deep brown intensity of them was directed straight at her. "I think I already have, Mrs. Briggs," he said softly. "You are absolutely heaven."

Wrapping his arms around her, he pulled her on top of him and raised his head to meet her own.

"Jedwin?" Questions sprang to Cora's mind immediately, but as his mouth met hers and hot lush kisses caressed her lips and face and neck, Cora forgot every one. It was her moans that broke the silence in the yard now as the tender touch of his mouth seduced her.

He rolled her on her back and raised himself up to look into her face.

"You are not hurt, are you." She stated the obvious with a bit of pique.

Jedwin gave her a half grin. "Only my pride, Mrs. Briggs. And I think you've already restored that."

"You should be ashamed—"

"Oh I am, Mrs. Briggs," he whispered against her neck. "I truly am."

His lips gently touched the tender flesh of her throat and then he buried his face in her hair. Cora moved against him to give him better access. This action arched her back, pressing her bosom, which felt strangely taut, more firmly against his chest.

"Heaven," he whispered close to her ear, and the warm breath sent a furrow deep down inside her.

Cora should have reprimanded him, spurned him, fought him. Instead, she wrapped her arms around his neck and pulled him closer. He was so warm, so strong in her arms. She needed warmth. She needed strength. At that moment she knew that she needed Jedwin Sparrow.

"Oh my sweetheart—" she whispered, before he clamped his hand over her mouth and went dead-still.

Startled, she opened her eyes to see the warning in his. It was then that she heard the faint hum of a man's crusty baritone.

> "Rescue the perishing, duty demands it;
> Strength for thy labor the Lord will provide;
> Back to the narrow way, patiently win them;
> *Dum* da de *dum* da, de *dum* da de *dum*!"

Cora raised her head slightly, her eyes wide in fear and her mouth still covered by Jedwin's strong tanned hand. Reverend Philemon Bruder had stopped before her front gate and from the sound of it was working the latch.

She had hardly time to take in the full ramifications of this horror when Jedwin grasped her firmly and rolled over on his back pulling her with him. She was on top, then on bottom, then on top again when he stopped. Having propelled the two of them beneath the overgrown forsythia bush, Jedwin quietly spread the vine around them like a curtain to secure their hiding place. He put a silencing finger to his lips. But his warning was unnecessary. Cora was so scared, she could not have made a sound if she'd wished.

A smart tapping on wood brought her attention back to the reverend. He was standing on her porch, glancing around curiously as if assessing the area. He was a very tall man and quite sparse of flesh. As a result his face seemed at least a decade older than his forty-five years, and his attitudes even older than that. His arms were stubbornly folded across his chest, and carefully tucked next to his heart was his black calf-lined morocco leather Bible.

He waited several moments before tapping again, this time more impatiently. "Mrs. Briggs," he called out. "It's Reverend Bruder."

When he still didn't receive an answer, Cora saw him walk to the end of the porch and look out on the side yard.

"Mrs. Briggs!" he called again, before stepping down off the porch to investigate the area. He walked to her workbench, casually picking up the bucket of pecans. The washpan, more than half full with shelled pecans, received only a casual glance. His eyes seemed to be drawn to some other object on the ground.

Cora almost groaned aloud when the preacher took a couple of steps from the workbench and leaned down to pick up a man's heavy, gray, bib-front mechanic's apron, complete with tools. He bent down to examine the pieces of the dismantled pitcher pump. Holding the worn leather cups in his hand for a minute, he slowly allowed his gaze to wander across the area.

Cora could sense that he knew someone was hiding. She expected any moment that he would go ripping open the shed door, flushing out whoever had taken refuge in the stable and batting the bushes in search of sinners.

The reverend did not. Rising to his feet, the gentleman addressed the air as if speaking to a ghost. "I see, Mrs. Briggs, that I have come at an inconvenient time. I will return to speak with you tomorrow."

Chapter Eleven

Amelia found herself making unexpected excuses to go to the business portion of the house. Since the day Haywood had shown her the young man dead of diphtheria, she'd found herself thinking of her son's assistant on the most unexpected occasions. He was a fine-looking man and an entertaining conversationalist, Amelia thought. It was not that she *liked* Puser any better than before, she assured herself. It was simply that she was getting lonely. And Mr. Puser certainly had a way with lonely ladies, she decided ruefully.

Lately, it seemed Jedwin hardly had a moment to speak with her. He left early and came in late. Even when he did have time to visit with his mother, he seemed to avoid her. If she didn't know better, she'd have thought he was up to some scampish adventure. But Jedwin had matured greatly since his father's death, and despite his failings, he had proved himself to be responsible and serious-minded.

"Mr. Puser," she called from the doorway. "Is James Edwin with you today?" she asked, already knowing the answer.

Haywood looked up from the cabinet that he was inventorying. "Jedwin hasn't been here all week," he said. "He's still trying to harvest his oats out at your daddy's farm."

Amelia shook her head and came closer. Her manner was almost coquettish.

"Still? My heavens, he's been working at that for over a week. It never took him so long before."

Stepping into the room and walking casually toward Haywood, Amelia sighed. "I don't know what I'm going to do with that boy," she said. "I've been trying to get rid of that nasty old farm for years, but he holds on to it like a lifeline." She shook her head. "I can't imagine why; it barely produces enough hay and oats to feed our horses. Of course, that huge flower garden is helpful, but he could manage something more easily here in town."

Haywood shrugged. "He's not got much of that farm planted. And with all the things you expect him to do around here, he doesn't get a whole lot of time to spend out there."

Amelia frowned. "I should know that you would, of course, take his side."

Haywood chuckled. Rising to his feet, he surveyed the mother of his employer. "That I would, Mellie, if I was taking sides. But I'm not taking sides, just stating facts."

"Oh? And just what are the facts?"

Haywood smiled, clearly delighted at the chance to spar with her. "The facts are that Jedwin likes outside work, he likes farming, and he'd devote himself to it wholly if you'd let him. But you've got your heart set on making him into something he's not. And he's doing his best to be a good son to you."

Amelia raised her nose disdainfully. "I will not have a son of mine scratching in the dirt for a living like a hog or a chicken!"

Haywood laughed out loud. "You better keep your voice down when you say that, Mellie. Half the folks in this town fall into either the hog or chicken categories."

She couldn't help but be amused, but rather than give in to his argument, Amelia deftly changed the subject.

"Have you seen any more of Doc Perkins's 'asthma' victims?" she asked.

Haywood's expression sobered. "Two more," he replied. "A young woman and her baby. Conrad Ruggy brought them in last night, says they are shirttail kin of his. I did them right away. They put them to ground together this morning."

Amelia nodded gravely.

"What does Conrad say? Is there much 'asthma' in Low Town?"

"Seems so," Haywood answered. "I told Conrad to keep the healthy separate from the sick and call me to get the dead right away. Folks live close down there. The diphtheria will be spreading like a prairie fire."

She knew he was right. "James Edwin should be here to help you," she said sharply.

"I don't want him here."

Amelia looked up at him with consternation.

"I'm planning for the worst. I'll send Jedwin to Guthrie for chemicals, but I don't want him in here."

Folding her arms stubbornly, Amelia was clearly piqued. "You'll *send* him for supplies. You don't *want* him in here. Have you forgotten whose mortuary this is, Mr. Puser?"

"No," he answered easily. "But Jedwin don't mind me telling him what to do. And you, Mellie, ain't big enough to stop me."

"Why you—"

"How's that tooth?"

"What?"

"Your bad tooth. Is it still bothering you?"

Amelia was slightly befuddled by his abrupt change of subject. "My mouth, Mr. Puser, is no concern of yours."

Haywood grinned. "I can't help but be concerned about your mouth, Mellie. It seems to always be spouting off at me."

He reached over and grabbed her by the chin. "Open up and let me have a look. I know as much about dentistry as I do about everything else."

"Whith ith pwatically nuffing!" Amelia attempted to retort haughtily as he held her jaw firmly.

Haywood pulled her forward until she was nearer the lamp and peered down into her mouth. "Well, Mellie, your teeth ain't as old as you are. But that school-days molar is going to have to come out."

Forcefully, Amelia jerked her chin out of his grasp. "Nothing is going to come out!"

"Now, Mellie," Haywood cajoled. "We all lose a tooth or two. It don't mean we are over the hill. As I said, your teeth look pretty good. But that bad one is like a rotten apple. You keep it in there and you end up losing everything you chew with."

"It is certainly none of your concern, sir."

"It is," Haywood insisted. "If you get where you can't chew, well, don't forget I have to eat here and I'd prefer a little something for my meals besides mush and soup."

"Oh!" Amelia was insulted to the tips of her toes. She slammed out of the room in a huff, but she could hear his laughter behind her. Why had she ever thought she enjoyed conversing with that man!

Cora Briggs headed out of town right on schedule. Her bicycle ride was such a predictable event, the folks in Dead Dog could almost set their watches. She kept up her usual sedate pace and followed her ordinary route, so no one suspected anything amiss. But then no one in town knew that Mrs. Millenbutter's book, the marbles bag, and the Lewis wand were no longer in Cora's basket. Instead, she carried a fried chicken, some potato pancakes, a large jar of barley broth, pickled beets, a loaf of white bread, and a pecan pie.

The chicken had arrived on her back-door step that morning, killed and cleaned and plucked. It was wrapped in a clean white dishtowel, surrounded by a wreath of dried herbs, and a note was pinned to the bird's chest.

> A swain who hungers for your kisses,
> A swain who hungers for your charm,
> A swain who hungers for fried chicken,
> Waits for you at Pratt farm.

Cora smiled as she crossed the railroad tracks, riding through Low Town at her usual downhill pace. But before the difficult climb up the hill, she stopped and looked in all directions and then turned into the overgrown entrance of Moses Pratt's old hog farm.

It was the third day she had had a secret rendezvous with Jedwin Sparrow. And after each one she had sworn to herself that she would never meet him again. It was something that could only come to no good, but she felt powerless to stop it. The sweet, handsome young man was becoming entirely too important to her and she should nip the situation in the bud. That was what she *should* do. But increasingly, she found herself doing rather what she *wanted* to do.

After Reverend Bruder had stalked out of her yard like the wrath of hell itself, the two had lain quietly together for a few moments.

"That was close," Jedwin had whispered quietly.

"Too close," Cora agreed. "Oh Jedwin, if the preacher had found out about you, I would have never forgiven myself."

"Found out about me?" Jedwin joked. "I told you the first day, Mrs. Briggs. A scandal only enhances a man's reputation."

Cora nodded. "But it would have hurt your mother."

"My mother?"

"Actually," she confessed. "That's why I decided to let you call on me in the first place. I *wanted* her to find out. I wanted the *whole town* to find out. I wanted to hurt and embarrass her the way she has hurt and embarrassed me."

Jedwin lay quietly absorbing her words. "That's why you've let me call?" he asked finally.

Cora nodded.

Glancing out toward the now empty porch, Jedwin said, "It seems that you have changed your mind." It was almost a question.

"I didn't expect to like you so much," she whispered.

She *hadn't* expected it. Hadn't wanted to. But now as she rode her bike around the twisting lane that skirted the front field of the farm, there was little she could do about it.

"Hullo!"

She heard the call and looked toward the field. Jedwin sat high upon an old and slightly rusty table reaper. He waved his arm in greeting and Cora waved back. Stopping the bike, she leaned it against a small blackjack tree next to the fence. Leaning casually against the tree, she watched him, his blond hair glistening in the sun and his shirt already damp with sweat, causing it to stick to the muscles of his chest.

Jedwin slowly drove the team in the general direction of Cora Briggs. He needed to keep his edge on the field and he needed to work as much as he could. Even though he would have preferred to pull the horses to a stop and spend time with her.

The reaper slowly moved across the sea of bright gold oats. The sharp blades cut down the plants at the bottom. As they fell upon the machine's sheaving table, a mechanical arm swept across each cut, pulling it into a bundle that was automatically tied with a piece of oats. When several sheaves were collected on the table, they were released to stand together in a shook. The tepee-shaped stack would help the oats resist the rain and cold while the grain dried enough to be put into the barn.

Jedwin's movements across the field were slow and sure. Cora thought he never looked so certain of himself as he had these last days here on the farm.

"Whoa!" he called to the team as he neared the fence. Casually, as if he had all the time in the world, Jedwin released the horses from the heavy burden of the reaper and allowed them to graze, in harness, in the tall grass near the fence.

"Good morning, Mrs. Briggs," Jedwin said conversationally as he walked toward her. "Nice day for a bicycle ride."

Cora grinned at him. "Yes, indeed," she said. "Beautiful weather that we're having, don't you think?"

Jedwin had removed his hat and was standing next to her, just on the other side of the split-rail fence. "Yes, it's mighty pretty, ma'am. But not nearly as pretty as you."

Cora laughed and Jedwin reached for her. Circling her waist, he pulled her as close to the fence, and himself, as possible. His lips met hers in a welcome that was at the same time both tender and ardent.

"I've missed you," he whispered next to her throat.

"You saw me just yesterday."

"It feels like a lifetime ago," he told her. "When you leave my sight it's as if you take the sunshine with you."

Cora pulled back from him and smiled, attempting to keep the tone light. "You *are* becoming quite the poet now, Jedwin."

"A woman like you will bring the poetry out of a man."

With a youthful spurt of energy, Jedwin vaulted the fence and took her arm, like a gentleman leading a lady out to a dance.

"I really have missed you, Mrs. Briggs," he told her as they began a slow walk toward the homestead. Cora's picnic basket was clasped neatly on her arm. "These days it seems like whenever I'm not with you, I'm thinking about you."

Cora felt the same way, but was much too cautious to say so.

Her silence made Jedwin a little unsure and he ran his hand restlessly through his thinning hair. "I need a haircut," he blurted out without thinking. Then he cursed himself when she turned her attention to his head, where the cure of raw onions was not particularly working.

Cora reached up and caressed the fall of pale blond curls at his nape. "Oh, don't cut it yet, Jedwin. I think your hair is beautiful."

"What's left of it."

Stepping back slightly, Cora assessed his appearance. "It saves you from looking boyish, you know."

"What?"

"The bit of hair you've lost. Your features are so fine that I'm afraid with a full head of hair you would look downright pretty."

"You're being kind."

"No," Cora answered, looking him straight in the eye. "I'm being honest. I like your looks just as they are."

Jedwin looked at her closely, not quite believing. "Miss Maimie says that Luther has the thickest head of black hair she's ever seen."

Cora paused momentarily, surprised. "Yes," she said finally. "I suppose that he does. Luther Briggs is a very handsome man."

They walked together silently for a moment.

"Are you jealous of Luther, Jedwin?"

He hesitated only a few seconds. "Yes, Mrs. Briggs, I suspect that I am."

"Because he had a full head of hair?" There was clearly humor in her question.

But Jedwin's expression was serious. "Because he's been your husband."

There was no reply to that. After a moment, she took her hand from its rather formal position in the crook of his elbow and wrapped her arm around his waist. He returned the gesture and linked they walked up the slight incline to where the house, barn, and outbuildings stood, weathered and slightly forlorn.

"You love this farm, don't you?" she asked.

Jedwin nodded, grateful for the change of subject. "Yes," he said. "I do love it." He chuckled lightly. "When I was a boy and Grandpa Pratt was still alive, I used to run off a couple of times a week and come to help him."

"What did your parents think of that?"

Jedwin shrugged. "My father never said anything, he'd just come up here and fetch me. But Mama was always furious. She told me that Papa was very disappointed in me."

"She didn't want you to farm."

"She didn't want me to take after Grandpa Pratt!" Jedwin shook his head, smiling in remembrance. "She used to say that 'Grandpa Pratt was lazier than a rock.'" He made a face that resembled Amelia Sparrow almost perfectly.

Cora giggled. "Was she right?"

Jedwin considered the question. "Well, it's true that Grandpa Pratt didn't have a lot of ambition. He raised a few chickens and pigs and he only grew enough crops to feed himself." He gestured to the surrounding countryside. "We own everything from here to the riverside," he said. "Including that pretty knoll that you are so fond of. But Grandpa left nearly all of it fallow year in and year out."

Cora nodded. "What would you do with it, Jedwin?"

He looked at her curiously. "You mean if I had time to really work it?"

She nodded.

"Well," he said thoughtfully. "I'd put most of it in wheat, I think. Folks around here think that corn is the only crop, but I think this country is better suited to wheat. And it's the coming thing."

"So you would be a wheat farmer?"

"That would be my cash crop," he said. "At least at first. I have some other ideas."

"Such as?"

"Commercial floraculture," he answered simply without meeting her eye.

Cora's expression was puzzled. "What is 'commercial floraculture'?"

Jedwin allowed himself one uncertain glance before he shrugged out an answer. "It's flower farming."

Her eyes widened in surprise. "Flowers as a farm crop? Can you do that?"

"Are you asking if *I* can do it, or if it's being done?"

Cora gave a sigh of exasperation. "Of course I'm asking if it can be done."

"It's being done in some warmer climates already," he told her. "There are farmers making four thousand dollars an acre on floral and nursery plots."

"That much!" Cora was astounded.

"Of course, a farmer's got to establish a market first," he explained quickly. "I can't just walk out in this field and plant ten bushels of canna bulbs and expect to be rich by spring. But I think it can be done."

Cora gazed out over the fallow fields and her eyes widened in delight. "Whole fields of flowers! What a beautiful idea."

Her enthusiasm was contagious, and Jedwin found himself confessing his most wistful dreams.

"Over there," he said, indicating a treeless rocky ridge near the barn, "I could build a hothouse. With proper care, flowers will grow inside all winter long. And somewhere over this way"—he gestured toward the blackjack woods—"I could build a drying house."

"A drying house?"

"Like the ones they use for tobacco. I think I could use a shed like that for drying my excess summer crop and then market them mail order as immortelles."

Cora stopped walking and turned to look at him. "This is what you really want to do with your life, isn't it?" She didn't wait for an answer. "Why aren't you doing what you want?"

Jedwin took her hand and urged her to resume the walk. "Starting up will take money," he said. "And time, more time than I've got these days."

"But you are going to do it."

Cora's words were spoken with such conviction that Jedwin found himself suddenly determined to quit dreaming and start working.

"Yes, Mrs. Briggs," he said. "I am going to do it."

They gazed into each other's eyes for a moment, each gathering strength from the other, until the intimacy of the moment grew uncomfortable. Cora looked away first. Jedwin hurriedly brought a playful smile to his face.

"I'm nearly starved!" he exclaimed, leaning over as if to sneak a peek into the picnic basket. "What did you bring me, Mrs. Briggs, Indian cookies?"

"Fried chicken, just as your poem suggested," Cora assured him. "I can cook more than Indian cookies."

"I love your Indian cookies," Jedwin protested. They'd reached the barnyard fence and turned to lean against it as he pulled Cora into his arms. "I would eat mud pies, ma'am," he declared, "if they were made by your hand."

His arms wrapped around her waist and pulled her close, his mouth lightly brushing against hers.

Since the day he'd fallen out of the tree, Jedwin had taken every opportunity to kiss Cora Briggs. He felt comfortable doing that; she never objected or held back. But he had never pressed her for more. In his tortured nights he dreamed of caressing her bosom or lifting her skirts to touch the curve of her hip, but he never attempted either. When he was honest with himself, he knew it was not entirely because he thought that she might reject him, although she might.

Working the reaper gave him a lot of time to think. He'd decided that he understood the reason men wanted to marry virgins. If the man was clumsy and fumbling, a virtuous woman would be too ignorant to realize. It was a bit daunting that Mrs. Briggs could not be fooled. If he blundered she would be sure to know it.

For her part, Cora thought Jedwin's hesitation to press her for more intimacy was both considerate and endearing. Before she'd met Luther she'd never kissed a man. And Luther only kissed her as a prelude to the bed. Cora figured that she'd kissed Jedwin Sparrow more in the last four days than she'd kissed Luther in their entire year of marriage.

Jedwin was by turns tender and gentle and passionate. His lips had explored every inch of her face and neck, and even her hands and fingers had felt the hot caress of his lips. But he never frightened her or took advantage. Yesterday they had lain in each other's arms in the haymow. Talking and talking and kissing until Cora could feel the hardness in the front of his trousers through her skirts.

He'd stopped and moved back a little, surveying her as if trying to make a decision.

"Mrs. Briggs," he'd whispered quietly. "I've . . . well, I've heard that there is a kiss where the man puts his tongue in the woman's mouth."

Cora's eyes widened and her face flushed brightly. "Yes," she answered. "There is a kiss like that." In fact, she knew it well. Luther was always poking his tongue down her throat, nearly gagging her, frightening her. It didn't seem like a kiss at all. It seemed more an invasion of her privacy.

"I don't like that kind of kissing," Cora said a little too sharply.

"All right," Jedwin answered. Again he covered her lips with his own, gently, lovingly.

"That tongue kiss is not much of a kiss," Cora told him when their lips parted. "I never cared for it."

"All right," Jedwin said again and gently feathered his lips along her jawline.

"I know you are probably disappointed," Cora said.

Jedwin pulled back a little to look at her. "Nothing about you could disappoint me," he said. "If you don't like that kind of kissing, then we won't do it. That seems simple enough."

"But aren't *you* disappointed?" she asked. "You are here alone with a woman whose reputation is in shreds and she decides that she is finicky about what kind of kissing she wants. It doesn't seem fair."

He looked at her curiously. "Just having you close to me is more fairness than I could ever hope for."

Cora knew that it was true. And in a way, she wished he weren't so honorable. If he insisted on more, it would relinquish some of her responsibility for her own actions. Or maybe give her a real reason to call it all to an end.

"All right," Cora said, raising her chin bravely. "If you want to kiss me with your tongue, you may."

Jedwin chuckled humorlessly and shook his head. "Mrs. Briggs, if you don't like that, why would I want to do it?"

"Because you've never done it," Cora said tartly. "You are supposed to be sowing your wild oats. This is one of the things men get to do when they are sowing wild oats."

"The only oats I am sowing, Mrs. Briggs, are out there in that field. I find you extremely attractive and adore being with you. But I expect nothing."

"Well, perhaps you should begin to expect some things," Cora told him. "Come here," she whispered, pulling him closer.

Her mouth covered his and he felt the tip of her tongue along his teeth, begging entrance. When he opened wider, her tongue slipped inside his mouth, fluttering around like a butterfly caught in a Mason jar.

Desire curled deep within him and he startled and pulled slightly away. When Cora pulled back, his breathing was rapid and he swallowed convulsively.

"I like it!" was his whispered exclamation.

Cora giggled lightly. His enthusiasm had been coercing.

Now, after only one day of practice, Cora felt Jedwin's tongue gently asking for entry. She obliged him, knowing that the warm, sweet duel their mouths would play was nothing like the suffocating domination of Luther Briggs.

Jedwin held her close. There was as much teasing in his passion as awe. She felt safe and warm and beloved.

Slowly he pulled away, his fingers lingering on her jaw. His smile was lazy and languid. It thrilled her to the tips of her toes.

"Come along," he said softly. "I want you to see the house. I've been fixing it up."

Walking together, hands clasped and swinging between them, they were like two children on a school holiday. The house was set a little back from the barn. An ancient log structure, it was taller than it was wide, giving it a strange, slightly awkward appearance.

The house was set up on a foundation of local stone, though most of it had sunk down into the earth through the years. But there was still a large, flat piece of sandstone that served as the doorstep.

"It's still pretty messy," Jedwin warned her as he assisted her up the step and through the door. "I've used it for an overflow barn a couple of times. And, of course, just being empty and uncared for doesn't help a place."

As Cora looked around, she couldn't keep a delighted smile from her face. "Oh, Jedwin. It's wonderful."

The ground floor was only one room. A huge stone-and-mud fireplace was at one end and a set of incredibly narrow stairs at the other. The pine floors creaked beneath her feet as she moved around the room. Large windows had been cut in every wall. They were not fancy, city windows with glass panes.

Cora reached up and undid one of the rough-looking fire-bent latches. As she opened out the shutters, the room was suffused with light.

"It's beautiful," she said, looking out on the oat field with its bright gold shooks standing in precision file like palace guards.

She felt Jedwin's nearness before he wrapped his arms around her waist. "It's like Grandpa Pratt was trying to bring the outside inside," he said. "From the upstairs windows you get views of the river from three directions."

"Oh, let's see!"

Taking her hand, Jedwin led Cora to the narrow stairway, admonishing her to be careful of the old stairboards.

The second floor was divided into two rooms. Cora hurried to the nearest window and flung it open. In the distance the Cimarron River made its twisting curve back toward town.

"Look." Jedwin stood so close beside her that she could smell the hint of fresh-mown grain on his clothes and hair. He pointed to a distant landmark. "There is your knoll."

"Why it is! I always thought that up there I was completely out of sight. If you were in this room you could watch my every move!"

"I know."

Cora turned to him, her eyes wide in surprise. "Jedwin Sparrow! I am surprised at you!" But she laughed.

Jedwin showed her around the house, pointing out the hand-hewn woodwork and the tongue-in-groove window fittings.

"The story is," Jedwin told her, "that Grandma Pratt was a very difficult woman to please. She thought she was too good for this rough frontier and believed that she deserved far better than life here had to offer her." Jedwin hesitated. "Kind of like my mama, I suppose. Grandpa spent most of their first years here trying to build a home to her specifications."

"Well, he certainly did a beautiful job," Cora said. "Did she come to appreciate it?"

Jedwin shrugged. "She died the first year they lived in the house. That's why Grandpa never bothered with improvements. I suspect that's why he never bothered with much of anything."

As they made their way back down the stairs, Jedwin was thoughtful. "Even after he'd remarried, Grandpa used to talk about her nearly every day. I think he had kind of lost his own life when she died."

Cora thought of her own parents with a pang. She wished she remembered more good stories about them. "Do you want to have our picnic in here?" she suggested, wanting to dust away the melancholy shadows that had fallen around them.

Smiling, Jedwin readily agreed. "You want me to build up a little fire?"

"It's not really that cold," Cora said.

He nodded. "It isn't, but if I build a fire, we can open all the windows and invite the outside in."

Chapter Twelve

The crisp fall breeze poured through the open windows of the Pratt farmhouse as Jedwin and Cora sat on the tablecloth in front of the crackling fire.

"You sure you don't want some of this chicken?" Jedwin asked, holding out a bite to her.

Cora shook her head, looking down at her potato pancakes and barley broth. "Mrs. Millenbutter is fairly certain that meat of any kind is counter to spiritual completeness."

Jedwin raised an eyebrow. "Why would she think so?"

"It seems that there is a direct relationship between the physical body and the spiritual soul. They are like two parts of one whole."

Cora picked up a piece of bread and tore it in two. "You see that these are about the same size," she said, holding up the pieces of bread. "But you can see that the edges are ragged."

Jedwin nodded.

"That's how the body and soul are. Where one is a little too much," she said, pointing out a protruding jut on the bread's dissection, "the other has too little."

Jedwin took the piece of bread that had too little and, with a shrug, stuck it into his mouth.

"So," Cora concluded. "If you are unhealthy physically, your spirituality will overrun you. And if you are unhealthy spiritually, your body will have more meaning than was ever meant."

"Then you are supposed to be neither," Jedwin said.

"Balance," Cora explained. "Balance is the key to everything. That's why I do the exercises marching and with the wand. I try to perfect my sense of balance so that I can expand it to my entire life."

Jedwin eyed her curiously. "Eating only vegetables and no meat seems a little out of balance to me."

Cora shook her head. "The eating doesn't have to do with the balance exactly," she said. "It has to do with health. Mrs. Millenbutter finds meats difficult to digest."

Nodding sagely, Jedwin tore off a perfect bite of chicken. "It sounds to me as if Mrs. Millenbutter has gallbladder problems."

Cora stared at him, openmouthed and aghast for a moment. She'd been following Mrs. Millenbutter's advice for so long, she never questioned the author's logic.

Then Jedwin slowly waved a piece of chicken before her eyes. She began to giggle.

"Mrs. Briggs," he said in the monotone of a mesmerizer. "You will want chicken. You will seek to eat it. And it will not upset your balance because you don't have gallbladder problems."

Jedwin continued to move the chicken back and forth before her eyes like a metronome. "You will dream of fried chicken. You will not be satisfied until you taste it. The salty flavor of it will be on your tongue. You will no longer be able to live without it."

Cora was giggling near hysteria, but his hypnotic suggestion seemed to be working. Suddenly, it looked very delicious, and it had been a very long time since she'd had any. She lunged for the chicken. Jedwin pulled it out of her grasp.

"All right," she conceded. "I want to taste it!"

"Good!" Jedwin answered with his own mischievous laugh and then stuck one end of the beautiful piece of chicken into his mouth. Jutting out his chin he offered her the other end of the same piece.

"Come and get it," he teased through clenched teeth.

Giving him a look of playful exasperation, Cora shook her finger at him. "Shame on you. First you tempt me to chicken and then kisses to go with it!"

He grinned, the slab of chicken still held tightly between his teeth.

Cora tutted in disapproval. Then without warning she threw her arms around Jedwin's neck, nearly knocking him over and solidly bit off her half of the chicken.

She immediately pulled back away from him and began to chew. Jedwin, still a little stunned by her quick move and the light warmth of her lips lingering on his own, followed suit, grinning.

"How about some pickled beets?" he asked after he'd finished his bite of chicken.

Cora laughed. "I warn you, Jedwin, there is no way that you can hold those beets in your teeth long enough for me to bite off my half."

He nodded in agreement. "Well, perhaps you'll let me feed them to you."

He opened the jar, carefully, trying not to spill any of the bright purple juice that might stain Cora's dress. He fished out a beet on his spoon and with his hand cupped under it, offered it up to Cora to eat.

Cora's eyes widened. "Now you're trying to feed me? That's too big, you should cut it in half."

Jedwin brought the spoon to his mouth, bit off a good portion of the beet for himself and then raised the remainder to Cora's mouth once more.

There seemed to be something inexplicably wanton about being fed by a man.

Daringly, Cora opened her mouth and Jedwin slipped the spoon inside. When he pulled it out, the spoon was clean and shiny. But a remnant of pretty purple stained Cora's lips.

"How is it?" he asked.

Cora grinned at him wickedly, but spoke with a tone that feigned innocence. "It's the best pickled beet I've ever tasted."

Jedwin fed her another and watched as her pretty pink tongue, now lightly stained with purple, swept across her upper lip with libidinous efficiency. Then he handed her the spoon. "Feed me," he said.

She managed to alluringly feed him a couple of much appreciated pieces before the naughtiness of their actions overrode the sensual sparring. She giggled.

"Now, now," Jedwin cautioned. "No giggling. We are striving for balance here."

"What kind of balance is that?"

"The balance between what I am doing and what I would like to do," he answered with a chuckle. "My turn," he said, retrieving the spoon from her. Dipping deep into the jar, he brought out another beet.

"My dear Mrs. Briggs," he said in the tone of a lyrical swain. "A man could write poetry about your pearly white teeth so daintily chomping down on a crisp red vegetable."

Cora nearly choked with laughter and a piece of beet dropped from her mouth onto the clean white pleats of her cotton batiste shirtwaist. Skidding down, the beet left a bright purple trail from the bottom of her throat to the hillock of her right breast.

"Oh!" she exclaimed, looking quickly for a cloth.

"I'll get it," Jedwin said. To her total surprise, the young man leaned forward and, with his tongue and teeth, plucked the small spill from her bosom.

His touch had been so light, so delicate that Cora had hardly felt it. But as she looked up into his eyes, her nipples hardened with remembrance and her throat dried with rough desire.

"Jedwin, I—"

His expression was soft, but serious. He dipped a corner of his napkin into his water cup and brought the damp cloth to her bodice. "I'll have you cleaned up in just a minute, Mrs. Briggs," he whispered. "It was all my fault, I assure you. I take full responsibility for any damage done to your gown."

"Jedwin, I—"

His eyes had left her now and were focused on the growing damp spot on the front of her blouse. Cora, too, lowered her eyes to watch the long masculine fingers so delicately wipe away the pale purple stain.

"I believe that's got it," he whispered finally as he removed the napkin. He laid it to the side and looked up into Cora's eyes.

He swallowed, hard.

Cora trembled.

He raised his hand again. This time, unhampered by the thick cotton napkin, Jedwin laid his hand on Cora's breast.

"You are so soft," he said quietly.

Cora laid her own hand upon his and pressed his flesh against hers. Jedwin felt the hard point of her nipple in his palm. He tenderly squeezed her breast again, before allowing his fingers to cautiously explore the stiffened nub.

"So soft," he whispered. "And so hard."

Her breath caught in her throat, Cora could no longer think. She could only feel. And what she felt was the warmth of Jedwin's hand caressing her bosom. Strangely, she wanted to remove her confining clothing and feel his nakedness upon her own. But she was also quaking in fear that the awakening man before her was one whom she could not control.

Would he soon have her lying here on a dirty floor in an abandoned house?

"Jedwin—" she pleaded, fear quivering in her voice.

He heard her fear. With one last tender caress, Jedwin moved his hand up across her shoulder to rub her shoulder blade. Then he wrapped his arms around her. He edged her into his lap and rocked her as if she were a baby.

"Easy, easy, my sweetheart," he whispered. "I will never ask for more than you want to give."

Even as the strength of his arms and his tender words reassured her, Cora could feel the rigid evidence of his desire beneath her. Oh, how she wanted him. Oh, how she did not.

"You'd best let me up," Cora said, her common sense, carefully schooled by Mrs. Millenbutter, winning.

Once again she seated herself across from him and picked up a piece of bread from the tablecloth. She tore a delicate piece and placed it in her mouth, chewing purposefully. It tasted like sawdust.

A quietness fell between them.

"I'm sorry if I was crude, Mrs. Briggs," Jedwin said finally. "I acted on impulse and clearly I frightened you."

"You were not out of line, Jedwin," Cora answered with dignity. "Clearly, my meeting you in secret would lead you to believe that I am available to you. And I am."

Jedwin was quiet and swallowed nervously.

"What do you mean?"

"I mean that I do intend to allow you to bed me," she said bravely.

Stunned momentarily to silence, Jedwin searched his brain for an appropriate response. "Thank you," he said finally.

Cora waited. She had said that she would. Having spoken plainly, she was certain that Jedwin had understood. Yet he sat across from her. He made no attempt to touch her. He was not even looking at her.

To her amazement he rose to his feet and walked over to the fire, which he poked casually.

"Jedwin?"

He turned to look at her. His eyes were so wonderfully intense it nearly took her breath away.

"You do remember that I promised you a romance, Mrs. Briggs," he said.

He made a careless gesture to the sparsely furnished, dirty room. "This is no romantic bower."

Cora looked at him, a strange fluttering within her. He was neither rough nor demanding. He was as frightened of his feelings as was she. He was giving her time. Giving himself time, and she was grateful.

"It's a beautiful old house though," she said.

Jedwin smiled at her. "Yes," he said. "It is."

More at ease, the two began packing up the picnic things. Soon they were back to blander topics. Cora asked him about the reaping and he talked at length about the tonnage of oats he thought to get and how much hay he'd already put up.

"I'd better let you get at it," she said finally. "Although I am truly loathe to leave. It's a wonderful place. It's just like taking a step into the past."

"I've always loved it. I've tried to pretend that I lived here since I was a boy. All my daydreams about my future have always centered around this house."

They stepped outside.

"What did you imagine?" she asked him.

"Oh," he said casually. "I always thought I'd put on an addition and then run a wide porch around two sides."

They both turned to look as he pointed. "I would add a full modern kitchen to the back," he said. "And it would give the house itself some better proportions."

Cora nodded, able to visualize his conception.

Jedwin chuckled self-consciously. "I used to imagine myself coming in from a hot day in the fields and having a whole flock of little children come running down from that porch hollering for me to see what they made or tattling on each other."

"You like children?" she asked.

"Having been raised by myself," he said, "I've always wanted just a huge household to feed."

Cora was quiet for a moment. Sorrowful. It wasn't much for a man to want, and for him everything was possible. "You could have that if you truly want."

Jedwin nodded. Slowly they began to walk hand in hand down the lane. "I'm trying to give more and more of the business to Haywood. I wish he'd buy me out, but Mama would surely have a fit at that."

"And if he did buy you out, you would come to live here? You would come here and grow flowers?"

"Eventually," Jedwin answered. "Oats and wheat first, then acres of flowers. That's really what I have in mind for the future."

"Then you should do it," Cora said firmly.

"I am." Jedwin's words were decisive. "But I needn't rush. I've got lots of time."

"Time for what?"

"Well, the woman I'm thinking to marry is still quite young. It'll be six or eight years before we can wed and start a family."

Cora felt a tiny catch in the center of her being. But she kept her voice light. "You are betrothed?"

"Oh no!" Jedwin assured her quickly. "I've not made any kind of declaration. I just have sort of picked out the girl that I think is most likely to suit me."

"Does the young lady know of your affection?"

Jedwin laughed. "Now I doubt that very seriously. She treats me like an admired older brother."

Cora was shaking. She wasn't sure if it was with anger or jealousy.

"Who is she?" she asked finally.

"Tulsa May Bruder."

Stopping dead in her tracks, Cora stared at Jedwin as if she'd been poleaxed. "Reverend Bruder's daughter?"

"I know what you're thinking. The girl is worse than plain and downright odd sometimes. But I think she'll grow out of that."

"I wasn't thinking that at all," Cora said honestly.

"She's a very genuine kind of person," Jedwin continued. "She's kind and caring. I guess I feel like I understand her, because her mama is almost as disappointed in her as mine is in me." He gave a rueful chuckle. "Tulsa May is hardworking and cheerful. I think she'll make a loyal and dependable wife."

Cora reached her bicycle propped up against the blackjack tree. With more force than necessary, she jerked it away from the tree, loudly ripping the bark.

"What's wrong?" Jedwin asked, suddenly aware that Cora was angry.

"Absolutely nothing."

He put his hand on her wrist to stop her. "Are you angry about Tulsa May?" he asked. "I swear, Cora, I've never so much as passed a secret word with her. She's still a girl, for heaven's sake. Surely, you don't think I would . . . I would *call* on you if I were sparking someone else. There is no need to be jealous."

Cora jerked her hand from his grasp. "I am not jealous, Jedwin Sparrow," she snapped. "I am furious!"

"But?"

"Hardworking? Loyal? Dependable? How dare you choose a wife for those qualities! My heavens, what is wrong with the men of this world! What about love, Jedwin? Shouldn't a marriage be based on love?"

Jedwin's expression, at first confused, softened. The dark, secret intensity of his eyes focused on Cora and his words were as quiet as they were powerful.

"Mrs. Briggs," he said. "I don't intend to love more than one woman in this life. And I already love you."

Amelia Sparrow stepped through her front door and tiredly hung her coat on the rack. Slowly, lethargically, she made her way to the kitchen. A tub of lye and water stood just inside the door and she removed her apron and dropped it there. Stepping to the stove, she dipped out a basin of warm water from the reservoir and thoroughly washed her face and hands. She wanted a full bath, but she'd have to rest before she had the strength to draw and heat the water for one.

Taking a clean cotton cloth from the cupboard, she dampened it in the warm water and pressed it firmly against her sore jaw. It hurt terribly. Her whole face was hot. If she hadn't known for certain that she'd had diphtheria as a girl, she would have been worried.

Hearing a step behind her, she turned to see Haywood in the doorway.

"I heard you come in," he said, looking her over from head to toe. "You look pretty ragged, Mellie."

Amelia ran a hand haphazardly through her hair and gave him a look of disdain. "Thank you."

Haywood gave a shrug as apology. "You been down in Low Town all night?" he asked.

Amelia nodded.

"It don't seem much like you," he said. "Nursing the sick."

She glared at him coldly. "What am I supposed to do?" she asked. "Beulah Bowman, Grace Panek, and I are about the only women in town that have had the disease and aren't burdened with small children to tend. Somebody has to take care of those sick people."

Haywood nodded, a spark of admiration in his eye. "I'm just pleased to see it, Mellie. All these years you've had me thinking that there wasn't a spark of charity in your self-centered soul."

Amelia flung the damp cloth she held at him. It struck him square in the face. When Haywood peeled the wet rag from his skin, to Amelia's amazement he was smiling.

"I thought that might perk you right up," he said.

She gazed at him in fury for a full moment, not willing to soften. "Give me my cloth," she said finally. "My tooth is throbbing awfully."

"Let me look," Haywood said, coming closer.

"I don't want you to look at it," Amelia replied. But Haywood was standing over her holding her chin down and gazing into the deep recesses of her mouth.

"Oh Mellie," he said. "That's a bad one. I bet it hurts like the dickens."

She pulled away from him. "It will be fine in a little bit," she assured him. "A warm cloth will draw the ache out of it."

Haywood looked around the kitchen. "You got any sieve cotton?" he asked her.

"In the pantry," Amelia answered without interest.

Haywood opened the door and located what he wanted in a couple of moments. Taking the scissors from the hook, he cut a four-inch square.

"Where do you keep your tea?"

Amelia glanced up at him curiously. "In the can," she said, indicating a group of painted tin canisters on the shelf. "What are you up to?"

"I'm making a poultice for your tooth," he said.

Her interest perked up immediately. "Will it help?"

"You'll feel a hundred percent better by tomorrow at this time," he said. "I guarantee it."

Amelia watched him put a heaping teaspoon of good India tea in the middle of the sievecloth. He folded it up in a good-sized square and looked it over carefully.

"Just a couple of stitches to hold the thing together," he said. "Come on down to the workroom."

Amelia followed him. She watched as he threaded a piece of sterile thread into a needle he'd washed with carbolic. He placed a few careful stitches, forming the ball of tea and cloth into a neat little square.

"Lie down on the table," Haywood ordered.

"What?"

"Lie down here," he said. "Let your head hang off the end so that I can shine the lamp in your mouth and see what I'm doing."

Amelia, a little reluctantly, seated herself on the table. Careful to arrange her skirts with perfect modesty, she bravely lay down full-length with her head hanging off the end. She was glad she was a practical woman with no foolish fears about the purpose of the table. She just hoped his cure worked quickly.

"Perfect," he said as he began gathering up some other items from the cabinets.

"It's not very comfortable," she complained.

"It shouldn't take long," he assured her.

On the embalming case beside the table he placed a clean porcelain pan which contained the poultice, a polished piece of white pine about an inch wide and a half foot long, and a pair of pliers.

"All right, Mellie," Haywood said as he came to stand beside her. "Open wide." He placed a hand beneath her head to support it, and Amelia obediently opened. The tooth was so sore, she dreaded even having him touch it with the poultice, but anything was better than this constant throb. At least that's what she thought before she saw the shiny steel pliers in his hand.

"What!" she screamed as she tried to rise. "You said you were putting a *poultice* on it."

"I am," Haywood told her. "As soon as I get that rotten tooth out of there."

Amelia struggled to get to a sitting position, but Haywood easily pinned her. "Let me up!" she demanded.

"Now, Mellie," he said as he tried to force her back into position. "The only way you are going to feel well is to get that tooth out of there. Now I'm bigger than you and there's no need to try and fight me."

"I'll fight you with my last breath!" she declared furiously.

To Haywood's surprise, she proved to be a worthy opponent. Her kicking and struggling proved to be so effective, he was forced to lie down on top of her full-length on the table.

"Get off me!" she screeched.

With her arms and legs now both captured by the weight of his body, Haywood was not about to lose his advantage.

He pried her mouth open and wedged his fist in one side. She was still tossing her head violently and biting down on his hand with painful effect, but he managed to get the pliers around the sick, aching tooth.

When she felt the metal surround her tooth, Amelia stilled. Tears welled in her eyes, but Haywood coldly proceeded. With his palm braced against her forehead and the sweat beading upon his own, Haywood began wiggling the sick tooth out of its socket.

The woman beneath him made noises of fear and pain, but he held firm. Some things had to be done, no matter who they hurt or how much.

Amelia could feel the cold pliers seeming to rip out the side of her mouth. A sharp, stabbing pain like a white-hot knife shot through her jaw and to her throat. Tears sprang to her eyes. She could hear the sucking sound of flesh relinquishing bone and a wave of nausea swept through her. An unearthly buzzing and a sprinkling of stars before her eyes warned her of an impending swoon, but she fought against it.

"Breathe deep, Mellie," he whispered. "Stay with me, it's almost over."

Above her she heard him sigh heavily and the ringing plunk of a piece of bone and enamel on porcelain.

The pain was still there. Hot, fiery pain, but it no longer held itself to one achy tooth but spread itself generously throughout her mouth, her head, her whole body.

"Good girl," she heard Haywood tell her from what seemed like a far distance.

Blood rushed back to her head and he laid the pliers down and stuffed the tea poultice in the gaping hole in her mouth.

He set the white pine sideways in her mouth.

"Bite down," he ordered.

She did.

Moving back down the table slightly, he pulled Amelia with him until her head rested easily on the end.

"Now was that so bad?" he asked.

Her wits slowly returning, the fury in her eyes said "Yes," but with the wood brace in her mouth she could only mumble incomprehensibly.

Haywood looked down at her, his expression apologetic. "Sorry for the trick, Mellie," he said. "But I swear it was the only way. You let a tooth like that fester in your mouth, you're just asking for a lot of sickness and a hurry-up trip to the grave."

From Amelia's expression, she was not the least bit grateful.

Haywood started to move off her. Then, changing his mind, settled himself more comfortably on top of her.

"Now this is really something," he said. "I can't tell you how many times I wanted to shut that spiteful mouth of yours up and lie down right on top of you."

Amelia's eyes widened in shock and she recommenced her efforts to free herself.

He chuckled lightly as he shifted on top of her. "No need to defend your honor, Mellie. I'm going to let you up right now. You should probably take to your bed this afternoon after the work you put in last night and the blood you lost from that tooth."

As Haywood moved to rise, Amelia drew her knee up sharply between his legs, but he managed to catch it.

"Don't geld me, Mellie," he warned. "I'm thinking that would be something that we might both live to regret."

Chapter Thirteen

"I think changing the name of the town is a good idea. But couldn't we call it something better than Briggston?"

"Tulsa May, please don't interrupt your elders!" Constance Bruder's words were spoken sharply. The other adults who stood around the front door of Osgold Panek's Fine Shoes and Harness Emporium ignored her completely.

Osgold had moved his cutting table to the grass outside the store to take advantage of the sunlight, although the afternoon air still held quite a chill. All were bundled up warmly in hats and coats except for Osgold himself, who sat in his shirtsleeves and quietly cut dozens of leather soles without benefit of pattern or markings.

Tulsa May leaned over the table, watching him work while her mother was seated with Mrs. Panek and Nora Dix on the long wooden bench that was propped against the front of the building.

"Anything that brings more business to town would be very welcome to us," Grace Panek told Mrs. Bruder. "We are not as young as we used to be. If we had more work, Osgold could take on an apprentice. His eyes are not as good as they used to be," she whispered.

"But my hearing is just fine," Osgold snarled without bothering to look up from his work.

The three women exchanged looks of long-suffering exasperation.

"More business means more culture," Nora pointed out. "It is so dreary living in a virtual frontier when folks in Kansas City and Saint Louis reside amidst beauty. Once we are named county seat we can open an opera house, or build a bandstand for concerts in the park."

Constance nodded agreement. "Exactly. A true community needs a bandstand. A true community needs a park!"

"Perhaps Miss Maimie could donate some of her garden area to the public," Grace suggested. "Nothing near the house, of course. But all of Luther Street is vacant lots; it would make perfect sense to develop a town square of sorts near the center of town."

"And she might very well do it once the town has her name," Nora said.

Constance smiled wistfully at their collective daydream. "A new name for the town would mean progress and progress benefits all of us."

Osgold looked up from his work momentarily and gave a warm smile to Tulsa May before addressing her mother. "I'm a great believer in progress, myself," he said. His words were heavy with an Eastern European accent. "It's why I left Lublin when I was little more than a boy. I come to America, here to this place so far from home, and see," he said, gesturing toward the sign that hung over the front door of his shop. "In this new country, I own my own business. I work for no one."

"And you make wonderful shoes, too," Tulsa May told him quietly.

"Yes, yes, Osgold." Mrs. Panek ignored Tulsa May's words and shot her husband an exasperated look. "We are talking the future here, no one is interested in history."

The old shoemaker shrugged, but Tulsa May would not be still. "I'm interested in history. And all of you should be if you are thinking of naming a town. A name should have historical significance."

Nora Dix's expression was tolerant. "She uses such big words for such a little girl," she said to Constance before returning her attention to Tulsa May. "Briggston is a name with historical significance," she said. "Trapper Briggs was the first person in town."

Tulsa May's brow furrowed. "People say that. But the Indians were here long before Mr. Briggs. And I understand that the old trapper just wandered away one day and never returned. So he certainly never considered this place home."

"Tulsa May, please cease to prattle about things you know nothing about," Constance Bruder said. "No one knows what happened to the old trapper or where he might have died."

"That's my point," the young girl insisted. "What if he ran off to Arizona Territory and they are naming a town after him out there this very minute."

Mrs. Bruder's expression was not at all amiable.

"Well, it could happen," Tulsa May insisted with a glance for support in Osgold's direction.

Nora Dix tittered lightly and adjusted her gloves. "What kind of name would you choose, dear?" she asked.

Tulsa May screwed up her mouth in contemplation. She grasped one long orange braid in her hand and thoughtlessly flicked the tail of it repeatedly against her chin.

"Get your hair out of your mouth!"

Tulsa May immediately dropped the braid, and didn't even bother to defend herself against the unjust accusation.

"I think I would name the town for one of the Greek scholars," she said.

"What!"

"One of the Greek scholars, Socrates or Plato or Aristophanes."

The three women looked at her as if she had grown another head.

Nora smiled with feigned benevolence. "It is all well and good to understand the higher things in life, Miss Tulsa May. But"—she turned with wide eyes to the other women—"Aristophanes, Oklahoma?"

The women burst into laughter. Tulsa May's face flooded with embarrassment. She turned her attention to Mr. Panek as if the others were not even there.

"How do you know what size to cut the leather?" she asked.

Osgold smiled at her and gave a careless shrug. "I have cut so many shoes. It's something that I can do well. The truth is, I see a man walking half a mile away and know exactly what size will fit him."

Tulsa May smiled broadly at his words, displaying the wide gap in her two front teeth. "Someday, I want to do something well."

Osgold smiled at her strange words. "Someday? Silly girl, I'm sure you do many things well right now."

Tulsa May shook her head without self-pity. "Not that I can think of."

Osgold laughed in disbelief, but didn't offer any suggestions.

Picking up a small scrap of smooth brown cowhide, Tulsa May caressed it lightly before bringing the piece to her nose for a deep whiff of the fragrance. Casually, she rubbed the rough side of the leather against her cheek.

"You like it?" he asked.

"It's strange how it can appear so smooth and perfect on one side and be so rough and scarred on the other," she said.

Osgold looked at her strangely and then waved a hand at her. "You want a piece you take it, no charge."

"Oh, I couldn't."

"Sure that you can," he said. "I got more scraps than I need right now."

Tulsa May smiled her thanks as she held the small piece of leather against her heart like a treasure.

"Amelia is going to write to the railroad," Constance Bruder was saying to the women on the bench. "And we will have to circulate a petition to present to the governor."

Tulsa May determinedly ignored their conversation. "What do you usually do with the scraps?" she asked Osgold.

The old man looked up at her, pleased at her interest. "I make little things, belt loops, shoe strings," he said. "It depends on the size of the scrap and what people want made. I made a scabbard for a paring knife with something this size. Auslander wanted it for his grandson." He held up a wide piece of leather left from the insteps of two soles. "And these could be hinges for a toolbox, like your father has. This morning, Jedwin Sparrow had me to make new leather cups for a pump. I make most anything that people want to buy."

The young girl nodded gravely, her orange braids bobbing in agreement. "It's a good skill to take what you have and make it into something people want."

"Tulsa May!" Constance Bruder's voice was strident.

Glancing up, the young girl realized that Mrs. Dix had already left and that her mother was looking at her, both with impatience and disappointment.

"Thank you for the leather, Mr. Panek," she said hastily as she hurried after her mother. "Good day, Mrs. Panek. See you in church."

She had barely reached her mother's side when Constance Bruder looked down at her with tears in her eyes. "I have never been so humiliated in my life," she whispered dramatically. "Aristophanes, Oklahoma?"

There was a light tap on the back door. Cora smiled in recognition.

"Come in, Jedwin," she said evenly.

The night was blustery and bleak. Jedwin was wrapped warmly in a wool greatcoat of dark brown. The exact color of his eyes, Cora thought.

"Evening, Mrs. Briggs." He smiled at her a little uncertainly. Their leave-taking at the farm two days before had been strained. Jedwin was not exactly sure what he had done wrong, but he knew that talking about love had been a blunder. He hoped not to blunder now. "I've got the new foot valve and leathers for the pitcher pump," he explained. "If it's convenient for you, I'd be pleased to finish fixing it."

Cora nodded a little hesitantly. "All right."

They stood staring at each other, unsure. Jedwin shrugged out of his coat and donned his apron. He pulled the new pump parts out of his pockets and without further word he started to work.

Intending to ignore him, Cora stepped into the parlor and seated herself in her sewing rocker. Taking up her mending, she attempted to give new life to a shirtwaist that was more patches than fabric. Silently she assured herself that this was the correct behavior for the situation.

Jedwin's revelation about Tulsa May Bruder had felt like a physical blow, only partially from jealousy. Although she knew that she could never wed Jedwin herself, she hadn't really thought of the different paths their lives would take. Or that he'd already picked her successor. Or that he planned to shortchange the girl.

Now, like a can of worms that could never be contained again, the reality of the romantic game they played was laid bare before them. Jedwin had come to her, a scandalous female, to learn the ways of a woman's bed. She had teased and cajoled and lured him to romance her. And he claimed to have fallen in love with her.

Love, she thought bitterly. The last thing she wanted in this world was another lesson in *how men love.*

As if she were reliving it today, she felt a painful tightness in her chest, and she could almost hear Luther's voice.

"I can't help myself, Cory," he had said. "I tried to do what Mama wanted. I tried to make a life with you. But I already have the life I want."

"You told me you loved me!" Cora accused him, stunned.

Luther shook his head apologetically. "That's just sweet talk, Cory. A man is supposed to say that, even when he don't mean it."

Tears had welled up in her eyes, and after she had cried for days. But Cora's eyes were dry now as she contemplated the worn shirtwaist in her hand and searched the rag bag for a patch that would match well enough to be inconspicuous.

Luther had claimed to love her, but he hadn't. Jedwin had said that he loved her. And Cora believed that he was sincere. Not that he really loved her, but that he really believed that he did. Unlike Luther, Jedwin was too innocent in the ways of the world to separate wanting a woman in your bed and being in love with her.

Setting her sewing aside, Cora took a deep breath. Perhaps it was time to teach him the difference. To teach him that inequitable truth that men could choose to please themselves in this world, and then leave the women to pick up the pieces.

It would be no chore or great sacrifice, she admitted to herself honestly. She wanted Jedwin Sparrow as much as he wanted her. She needed to know warmth and affection from another human being. In her years as the scandalous Mrs. Briggs she had never allowed her own desires—even her desire for companionship—a moment of unrestraint. Unwaveringly she'd adhered to the rules of society more closely than the most pious paragon. But those days, she decided, had come to an end.

Rising to her feet, she stepped back into the kitchen. Jedwin was tightening the pump head down and smiled with pride.

"I think I've fixed it. All we need to do is prime it and see if it works."

"We will do that tomorrow," Cora said evenly. "Bring the lamp, Jedwin, and come upstairs."

Freezing in place, Jedwin looked at the pump for a long moment before turning his eyes to Cora.

"Come upstairs?" he asked quietly. His throat was unexpectedly dry and his voice sounded raspy.

She nodded. "I want you to spend the night."

Cora turned to go. Jedwin, still rooted to the floor, attempted to comprehend what was happening. He loosened the wrench on the pump and as it clattered loudly in the sink, he started. She had already reached the stairs and had not so much as glanced over her shoulder.

She was going up to her bed, and she'd invited him to join her. At that particular moment, Jedwin's desire was practically nil. Fear, cold, blank fear, flowed through his veins like a broken drainpipe.

He leaned his hands against the sink. Lowering his head, he took a deep, calming breath. This was it, he told himself sternly. This is what he had planned all along. Don't make a fool of yourself. Latch the door, get the lamp, go upstairs and crawl on top of her. At that moment, the first two seemed infinitely more pleasant than the third.

Slowly, Jedwin made his way to the stairs. He remembered the first night he'd been in her house. How he'd wanted to climb those stairs then. That night he'd been eager. Eager and ready to be a male stud to a handsome mare. Then it would have been impersonal. But now it was no pair of horses performing a functional act. It was Cora Briggs and Jedwin Sparrow. Two people with feelings and problems and fears. Mrs. Briggs had been hurt. He knew now that she was no lightskirt who'd been deservedly ostracized. She was a warm and loving woman who'd somehow allowed Luther Briggs to ruin her life. She deserved joy and love and happiness and a man who could give those to her. And he knew it couldn't be him.

There was a little hallway at the landing, but the door to Mrs. Briggs's bedroom was open. A pale yellow light glowed from the far side of the room.

Jedwin stepped inside and immediately set his lamp down on the highboy by the door, fearing that any minute he would nervously drop it to the floor and set the house on fire.

He didn't see Mrs. Briggs in the room until a movement captured his eye. Behind an oak-and-panel dressing screen, Jedwin saw a long shadow of movement and heard the rustle of clothing.

She was undressing.

Jedwin's hands began to tremble and he thrust them roughly into his pockets. And he waited.

Cora was waiting, too. Biting her lower lip, she was waiting for the courage to step out from behind the screen. The decision had seemed much easier downstairs. Downstairs, she was Mrs. Briggs and he was young Jedwin. Now, alone together in her bedroom, they were a man and a woman. And Cora found her composure slipping.

She glanced down forlornly at her nightgown. The faded flannel was nearly worn through at the elbows and hung upon her as unattractively as a lawn tent. Dismally she remembered the sheets on the bed. They were a patchwork of flour-sack cloth. Soft and sturdy but not fine enough for company. A first time deserved a new nightgown and good sheets, she thought to herself.

There was no help for it. Head high and with a bright smile plastered across her face, Cora stepped from behind the screen.

He stood near the doorway, hands in his pockets, looking almost as ill at ease as she felt.

"Jedwin," she whispered.

"Here, ma'am," he'd answered hurriedly, as if she were the teacher calling the roll.

Walking toward him, Cora could feel the cold pine boards beneath her feet.

"Would you like to slip out of your clothes, Jedwin?" she asked him as she reached the end of the bed and leaned gratefully against the sturdy oak bedstead for support.

For a long, very long moment, Jedwin said nothing.

She watched him take a nervous swallow.

He stared at her in the warm glow of the coal-oil lamps. The one in front of her showed the beauty of her face and the long fall of wavy sorrel brown hair, unbound by its usual restrictions. The lamp behind her shone through the thin cotton flannel she wore, defining her hips and thighs. His imagination took off, hell-bent, at the sight. He could almost see her parting those white thighs. He could almost feel the hot, hidden depths of her. His body hardened and he fought the urge to pull her toward him roughly.

"Jedwin?" His name was a soft question.

With tactless haste, Jedwin raised one foot in the air, grasping the heel and toe of his brown leather congress gaiter. He hopped a couple of times for balance before freeing his foot of the shoe. He threw it unthinking, where it banged loudly against the wall.

Startled by the noise, Cora moved back slightly.

The back of her legs touched the bed.

Jedwin breathed deeply as he sent his other shoe flying in the direction of the first. Pushing his suspenders from his shoulders, he pulled at his shirt. One button flew across the room. Finally, he dragged the shirt over his head.

His trousers fell to the floor and he stepped out of them without a backward glance. Wearing only his balbriggan underwear and beads of nervous perspiration on his upper lip, Jedwin took one more step. And he was standing right in front of her.

"Jedwin?" she asked again.

He could hardly concentrate over the screaming self-admonitions in his own brain. *Slowly, slowly,* he told himself. *Be gentle, be careful.* But the restraint of the past weeks and his long-frustrated need surged through him. Desire overwhelmed the last bit of good sense remaining.

He saw Cora's unchaste glance flicker downward. It was only a glance, but the skimming of her gaze felt to Jedwin like the touch of her hand. He was rigid with aching need.

Cora's trembling hands came up to touch the hard, muscled flesh of his shoulders and to stroke so gently along his arms and chest. Her encouraging touch had his heart beating loudly and sent hot surges of desire and anxiety within him. Passion overwhelming fear, Jedwin tilted his head slightly and with one finger raised her chin until his lips were next to her own.

It was a sweet, gentle kiss. So reminiscent of many others they had shared. But, the quaking of his body was a totally new and almost frightening sensation. He had to have her. He had to have her before he shattered into pieces.

Pulling his mouth from hers, he almost didn't have time to breathe before he slid an arm behind her knees and laid her beneath him, sprawling them both across the faded quilt on the bed.

"Jedwin!" her voice held a note of genuine apprehension.

"Oh, Mrs. Briggs, Mrs. Briggs," he murmured hotly against her neck. "It's just me, just Jedwin. Oh, Mrs. Briggs, you are heaven. I can't believe this. I must be dreaming."

His hands flew hurriedly across the generous curves of her body. He expected at any moment to lose permission to touch her, and he couldn't stop touching her, he would never be able to stop touching her. Jedwin could feel her fears easing, as he held his caress to tender touching that was enticing and familiar.

"I'm going to be gentle," he murmured. "I'm going to be gentle with you, Mrs. Briggs." His words were as much for his own reassurance as hers.

Helpfully Cora worked open the buttons on his undershirt and eased the heavy cotton from his shoulders. Temporarily the sleeves had him trapped with his arms behind him. Cora took that opportunity to lay her cheek against his breastbone and to slowly turn her head until her lips touched his skin.

"Ahhhh!" Jedwin's exclamation was as much pleasure as pain.

Tearing himself out of the undershirt, he reached down to the woman beneath him and pushed up her nightgown. His hands were there, smoothing as if enraptured by the soft, silky flesh of her inner thighs.

"Oh, Mrs. Briggs," he whispered in breathless awe.

His fingers delved in her forbidden warmth, his body trembled uncontrollably, like a man taken with fever. Never, never had he felt such sensation. Never, never had his body so controlled his actions.

"I love you, Mrs. Briggs!" he declared as he jerked down his briggans. "I love you so much!"

He parted the womanly flesh that was wet and warm beneath his hand and thrust himself inside her.

Cora hadn't time to emit even a cry of surprise before his body stiffened convulsively and he collapsed on top of her.

Both were stunned to complete silence.

Jedwin spoke at last in hard-won, groaning words. "Thank you, Mrs.

Briggs," he murmured. "Oh thank you so much, oh it was so good, it felt so good, oh thank you so much, oh I love you, oh—"

With a deep, masculine sigh of satisfaction, Jedwin snuggled against the feminine flesh. Pillowing his head against her ample bosom, he murmured more muffled gratitude against her breast for a moment before the smooth, even breathing told her that he had fallen fast asleep.

Cora Briggs lay staring at the ceiling for several minutes, quite unable to think or imagine or even grasp what had happened. Then she felt the warm breath of Jedwin Sparrow against her bosom. She looked down at him.

He was quite handsome, she thought. His mouth was partially open, and Cora was now sure that it was true that a man could fall asleep with a smile on his face. It was a young face. With his eyes closed, he could have been still a lad. But the prickly stubble that abraded her breast was clearly not a boy's peach fuzz. Jedwin Sparrow was a man, and Cora was glad.

He was still inside her and she could feel the tenseness of his invasion lessening as he softened. He had hurt her, some. She had been far from ready. But there was no great injury and she felt a strange comfort in this moment of closeness and in his eagerness. Lovemaking with Luther had always been something *he* did to *her*. Usually pleasant, sometimes shatteringly pleasurable, Luther controlled every moment, every movement of their mating. Seeing to Cora's satisfaction was taken up by him with as much sense of duty as providing for her shelter. Luther had been a demanding husband in bed, but never a selfish one.

Jedwin had clearly left her wanting, still she found herself inexplicably a bit pleased. Luther had always been so proud of his stamina. Jedwin had been carried away with his desire.

Tentatively Cora reached out a hand and caressed his hair. She suddenly felt the very inappropriate urge to giggle, but she managed to stifle it. She was finally a scarlet woman. But after waiting eight years, the sinful act had lasted less than a minute. Smiling, she leaned forward to feather a tiny kiss on the smooth brow of the man in her arms.

Strangely, she didn't feel sorry, or even that she should be. Guilt and recrimination could come tomorrow. Tonight she felt pleasantly warm and safe in this man's arms.

With a deep baritone moan, Jedwin came awake and opened his eyes. He stared at her in awe as if he were not entirely sure that she was real.

"Hello there," she whispered quietly with a smile.

"Hello yourself," he answered in a slightly hoarse voice. His grin was slow and languid as he looked up at her. "Thank you," he said again.

As if suddenly realizing that he lay full upon her like a two-hundred-pound sack of meal, Jedwin moved to rise. Cora wrapped her arms around him and stayed his retreat.

"I must be heavy."

"It feels good," she answered. Wiggling her pelvis provocatively, Cora felt him, half inside her, react. "Don't leave me," she said. "Not yet."

Jedwin's eyes widened and he pressed himself deeper within her. "You mean you want to do that again?" he asked.

Cora did giggle then. "No," she told him with warm laughter. "I hope we never quite do *that* again. Let's do something more fun."

He sighed, his expression sober. "I didn't please you very much."

Cora took his face in her hands and forced him to look at her. "It was a bit hurried, Jedwin," she told him. "But, you were gentle and I . . . I felt wanted." Her hesitation spoke her sincerity. "These things take practice, I think."

"I'm sorr—" Cora put her hand over his mouth.

"Don't apologize, Jedwin," she said with a wicked gleam in her eyes. "I fully intend that you to take this practicing quite seriously. You will just have to do this again and again until you get it right."

Her naughty grin was contagious. Jedwin shifted within her slightly. "I'm not sure how much practice one man can take."

Cora caressed his shoulder reassuringly. "You'll be ready again soon, I think." As if to insure that her statement become fact, she wiggled sensuously beneath him.

Jedwin's chin came up and he chuckled. "I wouldn't be surprised ma'am. I've been hard enough to hammer railroad spikes for a couple of weeks now."

Cora's mouth dropped open in surprise, then she laughed right along with him.

Jedwin's smile waned. "I'll try to make it better for you next time, Mrs. Briggs," he promised her quietly.

Cora ran her hand along his jawline, a loving touch. Her expression was tender, but serious. There was no amusement in her now. "Jedwin, I didn't choose to have loving with you because I thought you were a fancy Romeo who'd know all the tricks and all the moves. There are plenty of men in this town who would volunteer for that," she said. "I chose you because I wanted *you*, Jedwin. Just you, having loving with *me* and no pretense."

She raised her face to his invitingly and Jedwin's lips met hers. He took her lower lip between his teeth and sucked it gently. The sweetness warmed them both as his arms came around her and eased her more tightly against him. Kissing was something they had already practiced, and with leisurely remembrance he teased and coaxed her lips with his own. Tiny pecks and love bites were interspersed with hot, openmouthed kisses and an occasional slip of the tongue.

"This is nice," she whispered against his neck.

Encouraged, he let his lips travel across her face to her neck and throat.

The nightgown that he'd raised so hurriedly was uncomfortably bunched around her waist. Slowly, as if expecting to be refused, Jedwin raised the soft cotton flannel up around her neck, baring her before him.

"You are beautiful," he said breathlessly as he laid a kiss in the pale valley between her breasts.

Cora hadn't needed the words, she'd felt him stiffen inside her and rocked her pelvis against him. Reaching up, she pulled the nightgown over her head, reveling in the freedom of being naked beneath him.

His hands trembled as he laid them upon her bosom. He touched her as if she were fine spun glass, too delicate to caress. But her nipples tightened in response.

"I won't break," Cora assured him.

He smiled lightly, but still his touch was gentle. He brought his lips to the rosy crested peaks and a small sigh of pleasure escaped from Cora's throat.

"How does this feel?" he asked her.

She couldn't quite find the words. "Your mouth is so soft, your breath is so hot," she whispered. "It feels—" From the back of her throat a tiny moan escaped her. "It feels so sweet, so warm, so . . . oh Jedwin."

Her hands played lovingly through his hair and along his shoulders as he tested the taste and texture of her. She arched her back, fitting him more deeply inside her. They both moaned with pleasurable appreciation.

His hands traced every inch of her. He wanted to touch her everywhere at once . . . each touch more sure than the last.

Cora, too, wanted to touch him, to learn the secrets of his body. The hair on his chest was so pale that it was barely visible. But, as her fingers explored him, she was delighted to find the curly mat of blond to be surprisingly thick.

His back was long, and more muscled than she'd expected. She ran a caressing finger along the bumpy trail of his backbone. Her questing hands grasped the baby soft flesh of his buttocks. She sighed with delighted feminine power as the touch of her fingernail produced gooseflesh atop the masculine firmness.

Cora pulled him to her wantonly and was rewarded by the tightening of his body inside her and the groan of need he pressed against the tangle of her hair on the pillow.

"Oh, Mrs. Briggs, you are wonderful," he whispered hotly against her ear giving Cora her own gooseflesh to contend with.

Sighing with satisfaction, Cora drew up one of her legs to rub against his. To her surprise, rather than feeling the smooth, muscled flesh of his leg, she toed the rough cotton of his storebought underwear.

"You're still in your briggans!" she exclaimed with disbelief.

"I was in such a hurry," Jedwin admitted as he raised his head. "I need to get up," he told her with a disappointed sigh.

"No!" Cora locked her legs around him and pressed him more closely against her.

Jedwin chuckled. "I'm not leaving the room, Mrs. Briggs."

Cora held to him stubbornly. "You helped me get rid of my nightdress," she said. "I'll help you get rid of these."

Holding him tightly inside her, Cora began skimming down his underwear with her feet and legs. This process involved a good deal of squirming and wiggling on her part. While pleasant, it was also somewhat funny. In minutes both were giggling.

When the briggans were tangled about his ankles, it became increasingly difficult for Cora to affect them in any way. He was quite a bit longer than she and even with him lying square upon her, his feet and ankles were beyond her reach.

The two began laughing in earnest as Cora squirmed and squiggled trying to reach the end of him without losing the middle. Jedwin tried to scrape them off with his own feet, but the french ribbed cuffs, meant to keep them from riding up, were also very effective in keeping them from riding down.

"This is not going to work," Jedwin told her, chuckling. "Let me loose."

Cora massaged his backside and rocked her pelvis against him. "You are not going anywhere, Jedwin Sparrow. Not until you've made me a happy woman."

"You're not a happy woman?"

"Well, maybe I'm happy," she admitted laughing. "But I'm not yet satisfied."

Jedwin grinned. "It will be my pleasure to satisfy you, Mrs. Briggs," he told her with feigned formality. "But right now I've got my feet shackled like a chain gang prisoner."

Cora pressed her breast against him and ran light kisses up the side of his neck, swirling her tongue in his ear. "Does that mean you are at my mercy?" she asked.

Jedwin met her lips with his own and their kiss was long and languid and luscious. "I've been at your mercy since the day that we met."

The briggans temporarily forgotten, the two shared a long, deep kiss that had them both tingling.

"Bend your knees," Cora said, suddenly drawing back from him.

"What?"

"Bend your knees."

When he did, his ankles were easily within Cora's grasp. She pulled off the confining underwear and tossed it off the bed.

"Oh this is much better," Jedwin told her as he braced himself against the footboard and pressed more deeply inside her.

He was full and erect again, and this time Cora felt only desire as her body melted against his.

"This feels so good," Jedwin whispered against her ear. "I can't even tell you what it is like."

He kissed her then, hotly, with new urgency. Using not just his lips and tongue, but his hands and hips and limbs. He kissed her with his total being.

"I love having you inside me," she told him.

"I promise to stay forever," he answered.

Slowly he began to move against her. Retreating and then advancing in a deliberate, languid pace.

"Oh yes, yes, that's so nice," Cora said, her eyes closed and her head back.

Jedwin continued, moving with a sensation so pleasurable it seemed decadent. Cora began to move against him. He moderated his pace to match hers.

As she became more animated, squirming and pleading with tiny moans in the back of her throat, Jedwin couldn't take his eyes from her. He watched her face, beautifully serene one moment and strained with desire the next. It was wondrous. The sight of her enjoying his body, enjoying his touch, inspired him to work harder to please her.

He drew out farther, almost to uncoupling then thrust again forcefully with a sensuous rocking of his hips. He watched Cora as she raised her hands from his body to clasp the metal bars of the headboard. Each movement released one of those breathy little moans from the back of her throat.

Jedwin watched her face and listened to her sighs, forcing his own thoughts from the hot, wet pressure of her dark recesses surrounding him. He slipped his hand between them to slide down the damp, heated flesh of her abdomen. Burgeoning from the hot, damp curls of her feminine mons was a rigid, aching bud of desire. He pressed this most secret peak of Cora's anatomy between his fingers and touched it sensually.

Her eyes opened to stare at him. Her expression was almost frantic with desire. Wrapping her legs tightly around him, she strained and stretched against him.

"Oh yes, Jedwin, sweet Jedwin, yes, oh yes."

He began to move more rapidly against her.

He feared to hurt her, but she seemed unconscious of any pain. She dug her heels into the mattress tick and met each thrust with one of her own. The bed frame banged against the wall in rough, loud rhythm. The blood roaring in his ears, Jedwin was beyond hearing it. But his ears functioned with perfect clarity when she spoke.

"Please, Jedwin, oh, please Jedwin, please . . . I need you!"

Bracing himself, he drove forcefully, determinedly inside her. Stronger and stronger. Deeper and deeper. Faster and faster. One hand still clinging between them to caress her, the other gripping her backside for control. He clenched his teeth together like a vise. The heat boiled up inside him. It threatened to explode.

"Cora," he moaned against her. "Now with me, sweetheart, now."

She clutched at him, coming straight off of the bed into his arms. Jedwin felt the muscles of her womanhood gripping and squeezing at him inside her.

"Cora!" he both screamed and whispered as the sweet flood of release and bondage flowed from him to her.

Chapter Fourteen

It was that awkward time of year. Too chilly to leave the windows open and too warm to light the stove. The church was closed and stuffy, and Jedwin pulled uncomfortably on his collar. Beside him, his mother, looking lovely as usual, was gracefully taking more than her share of the morning's compliments.

"You are looking so much better," Beulah Bowman told her. "I thought you were quite peaked just the other day."

"You were downright pale," Grace Panek insisted. "It was that awful tooth bothering you. Is it better?"

"Much." Amelia quickly changed the subject.

Jedwin politely answered any comments directed his way, but his thoughts were elsewhere.

Titus and Fanny Penny were seated in the pew just in front of him. Pretty little Maybelle turned around to look at Jedwin. She was wearing a dark blue dress with a pinafore of pale blue cotton, daintily embroidered with darker blue. Her silky white blond curls were tied up in a bright blue bow that was almost as large as her head. When Jedwin smiled at her, she put a finger in each nostril, raised her nose to resemble a snout and snorted like a pig.

From the corner of her eye, Fanny had caught sight of the exchange and gasped in horror. She scolded Maybelle in a hushed whisper before giving

Jedwin an apologetic look. Jedwin was biting his lip to keep from laughing out loud.

The church building was new, having been raised only the year before. The bright sturdy red brick outside contrasted rather unfavorably with the multicolored Venetian glass panes. The windows, purchased at a tremendous discount from Sears and Roebuck, were mismatched patterns, extras that the company had found it difficult to sell. Carlisle Bowman's brother-in-law had arranged for the mismatched set, and poor Carlisle had yet to hear the last of it. The window at the end of Jedwin's pew depicted a yellow and green torch with some sort of heraldic crest upon it. The next window up showed a Holland scene of red tulips and a blue and brown windmill.

When the crowd inside the church was finally settled, Opal Crenshaw struck up the processional on the fancy new upright piano. Song leader Willie Dix raised his arm and led the congregation in a rousing rendition of "Am I a Soldier of the Cross?" Reverend Bruder made his way from the back of the church where he'd been greeting to the front, taking his seat in the high-backed, silk-upholstered armchair to the right of the pulpit.

Jedwin loved to sing and allowed his melodious baritone to blend with the other voices of the congregation. His thoughts, however, were elsewhere.

In his mind he could still feel the touch and taste and smell of Cora Briggs. They'd slept wrapped in each other's arms until nearly dawn when they'd made love once more. A secret smile lit Jedwin's face. That last had been sweet and slow, with plenty of pauses for questions and experiments.

Again he'd whispered that he loved her and she'd covered his lips with two of her long slim fingers. He did love her, of that he was certain. However, it had been the height of idiocy to say so. There was no future for such a love. And Cora had known it. The look on her face had been sad. She didn't *want* his love. And there was nothing else that he could offer.

He glanced up to the front of the church. On the second pew, front right, sat the Bruders. Even from the back it was easy to pick out Tulsa May, her bright orange hair stood out in any crowd. The straw hat she was wearing was out of season and the long red ribbon that dangled down the back of it clashed with her hair like blood on a carrot.

A man couldn't choose where he found love, but he had the responsibility to choose whom he should marry. A hardworking, dutiful wife was what a man owed his family and his family name. A woman without moral blemish and above common suspicion was the admonition of God's law. It was also what would be expected by the community. It was what his father would have expected. He caught sight of his mother in the corner of his eye. He turned to her slightly and gave her a loving smile, which she returned. If he thought only of himself and his desires, he would ruin her life as well as his. The thought lay heavy on his heart.

The song ended, the crowd was seated, and a typical Sunday service began. The preacher took his place behind the pulpit and Maybelle Penny began to fidget.

The preacher was a tall, gangly man whose excessively long arms and legs made him appear clumsy. His carrot red hair was as vibrant as Tulsa May's. But instead of hiding it under a hat, he emphasized it with his long handlebar moustache of bright orange.

"I'm reading from the first book of Corinthians," the preacher boomed. "Chapter Five, first verse."

The preacher hesitated and cleared his throat as those in the congregation who could read quickly paged to the verse.

Raising his eyes, the preacher surveyed the crowd with high drama before he boomed out his chosen scripture. "It is reported commonly that there is fornication among you."

Jedwin's head jerked up from its casual glance at the Bible in his lap, his face suffused with color. Guiltily he glanced over at his mother, who seemed as embarrassed as he.

"The church at Corinth was not without wickedness," the preacher continued. "Among their members were some liars and thieves. There were drunkards and blasphemers. And"—he paused for drama—"there were adulterers and fornicators."

Jedwin struggled to keep his expression blank as he stared directly at the preacher. In his memory he could see again the pretty fall afternoon when the preacher stood in the middle of Mrs. Briggs's yard holding the incriminating tool apron.

"Like the Corinthians," he boomed as he walked to the front of the pulpit, closer to the congregation, "we have those in our congregation that are suffering the temptations of the flesh."

His mother squirmed nervously beside him, and Jedwin wondered guiltily if she suspected him.

"Carnal desire, brothers and sisters, has been with us since Eve lost Eden for the sons of Adam. Looking like angels but tempting like devils, fallen women, like King Ahab's Jezebel, have led many a weak man down that wide gate and broad way that leads to destruction."

"Reverend Bruder, may I interrupt you here?"

The entire congregation, including Jedwin and his mother, gasped in shock at the unexpected intrusion from the back of the church. Heads turned as each stared at the interloper.

"Brother Puser," the reverend said, recognizing Haywood standing at the last pew. "Since it's a rare occasion that you darken the church door, I'm sure you have good reason to disrupt our Sunday worship service."

Jedwin was even more sure than the preacher. Still reeling from guilt at the realization that the preacher was aware of his prospective sin, Jedwin somehow rose to his feet and hurried to Haywood's side.

"Conrad Ruggy brought his mother to me this morning," Haywood announced. "She died overnight from the diphtheria."

There were murmurs of sorrow throughout the congregation. Although the blacks were very separate both in their lives and their churches, Conrad was well-known and liked in the community. His mother—half black, half Chickasaw—claimed to be an Indian princess, and always held herself with such regal refinement that most believed it to be true.

"Miz Ruggy was old and weak," Haywood explained. "So it's not surprising that the sickness would take her so fast. But Conrad and his family are neither. They have all been exposed and many here have been exposed as well."

Like many in the congregation, Jedwin immediately saw himself accepting a cup of sour apple punch from Conrad's wife, Mattie Ruggy.

"This is, of course, terrible news," Reverend Bruder said. "But I see no call for breaking into the worship service."

"I believe in taking first things first, Reverend," Haywood answered. "Our young men ain't going to be caught in fornication or adultery if they can't draw a clean breath into their lungs."

Haywood directed his next words to the congregation.

"We need to refrain from large group meetings like this for the next week or so. Mrs. Sparrow and Mrs. Bowman and the others who've had the disease should be the only ones we let in or out. It's the only way we can keep this plague from running through our own families and hurting our children."

"But Mr. Puser—" The preacher never got to finish his sentence. Titus Penny jumped to his feet as if the pew were on fire and grabbed up little Maybelle.

"My family will be staying at home," he said. "I'll leave the store unlocked. If you all need something, just go in and get it and leave your money on the counter."

"Titus!" Reverend Bruder called to the young father, but the man was already through the church door, the rest of the congregation hurriedly following in his wake.

Finally, only the preacher and his family faced Haywood and Jedwin. Amelia was still sitting in shock in her pew.

"How dare you!" The reverend's face was florid with anger. "This is my church and *no one* gainsays my authority here."

"I did what I thought best," Haywood answered unapologetically. "I asked Conrad to go tell the blacks to break up their service. I thought you'd appreciate having me come to tell you in person."

"I don't appreciate this."

Haywood shrugged with unconcern. "You'll appreciate it even less if half your congregation turns up sick next week."

"The ways of the Lord are not ours to question," Bruder stated stiffly as he walked toward Puser.

Jedwin stepped in front of Haywood as if to defend the older man from the preacher's wrath. "You may know the ways of the Lord, Reverend Bruder. But Haywood knows the ways of contagion. If he says that we shouldn't be meeting in groups until the worst of this is over, I believe him."

"I do, too!" Amelia burst in. "Why, Mr. Puser lost his whole family to a plague. He's just trying to see that the same does not happen to any of us."

"Oh, you poor man." Jedwin heard the quiet, thoughtful voice of Tulsa May from the front of the room. She came hurriedly toward the group. "Of course he's concerned about us, Daddy," she said to the preacher. Reaching out a consoling hand toward Haywood, her expression was open and sincere. "Thank you so much, Mr. Puser," she said. Turning to Amelia, she added, "I've not had the diphtheria myself. But whatever I can do to help, I—"

Constance Bruder came up behind them. "For heaven's sake, Tulsa May! What on earth do you think that *you* could do?" Mrs. Bruder shook her head. "What's done is done," she told her husband with an expressive sigh before glancing to the rest of the small group. "We won't bother with any more meetings until you tell us it's safe. I'm sure Miss Foote at the school will be anxious to suspend classes, too."

There were nods of agreement.

"What about Miss Maimie?" she asked.

"Oh dear," Amelia said. "I can't believe I forgot about her for a moment." Turning to Haywood, she asked, "Does she know about Conrad's mother?"

"I doubt it," Haywood said. "But I would imagine the old gal will get the hint when nobody shows up for work this morning."

"Well, somebody has to go out there and speak with her," Constance Bruder declared. "For heaven's sake, how will she manage without servants?"

"That's what I could do," Tulsa May piped in. "I could go help Miss Maimie."

"What kind of help could you be?" her mother protested.

"Well, she'd certainly be better than nothing," Amelia declared. Giving Tulsa May a tolerant smile, she said, "Go get your things to stay a day or two, and James Edwin and I will drive you out there."

The young girl's eyes lit with pleasure and she took off toward the door at a run.

"Lightly!" her mother called after her. "I swanny," Mrs. Bruder said disapprovingly. "That girl's so cow-footed she sounds like a plow horse running through the house."

With the immediate problems concluded and the reverend's ruffled feathers smoothed, the group made their way out the door. In a low serious tone, Haywood was relating to the preacher how to best protect himself when calling on the sick or eulogizing the dead. Reverend Bruder listened with interest and thanked Puser for his concern. "Although," he said regretfully, "I was really counting on setting some sinner to boil this morning."

"Oh?" Jedwin asked, cautiously wiping his sweaty palms against his trousers.

Tulsa May came running around the house, her things packed in a gunny-sack poke hung over her shoulder.

"I'm ready!" she declared with youthful excitement.

Mrs. Bruder gestured at her daughter to hush, and the preacher continued as if the young girl had not arrived.

"After all this fuss about Cora Briggs's new fence, I went over there in the middle of the afternoon." He paused dramatically. "There was a man at her house."

Amelia and Constance gasped in horror.

"Who was it?" Amelia asked.

The preacher shook his head. "I didn't see. They were hiding out like Adam and Eve in the garden."

"Then how do you know there was a man?" Haywood asked.

"Somebody's been doing some pump repairs," he said. "There was a man's gray ticking mechanic's apron."

The ladies' eyes went wider.

"Maybe she hired somebody to fix it," Puser suggested.

"Then why were they hiding?" the preacher asked. The woman nodded in full agreement.

The preacher shook his head and sighed sadly. "I've gone back to her house twice since then, but she hasn't been home. I was really hoping to have a confessing fornicator or adulterer this morning."

"Don't you worry about it," Amelia consoled the minister. "When this diphtheria business is all done, we can take a closer look around us. We'll find the poor man that Jezebel has lured, I know we will." She patted the reverend's arm before turning her attention to her son. "James Edwin." Amelia held out her hand to be escorted to the buggy.

Jedwin's face was pale and his mouth was set in one thin line. "I can't go with you today, Mama," he said evenly. "I have work to do out at the farm."

"The farm?"

"Now son," the preacher interrupted. "Just because we've called off the service doesn't mean it isn't still the Lord's day. I won't have you working on Sunday."

Jedwin's brown eyes were as cold as glass.

"I am not your son, Reverend," he said quietly. "And I will work whenever I choose, following my own conscience if you please."

The preacher huffed in shock.

"But James Edwin?" Amelia asked, clearly horrified. "Who will drive me to Miss Maimie's?"

"Mama, you are perfectly capable of driving yourself," he answered tartly. He placed his hat on his head and offered a curt bow to the assembled group. "I can't imagine a more thorough waste of a beautiful Sunday afternoon than spending it with Miss Maimie."

Jedwin turned and walked away, leaving his mother to stare at his retreating back in disbelief.

The sewing parlor at the Briggs mansion was as dark and dreary as the mood within it. Miss Maimie sat straight-backed in a tufted chair, her feet raised on her ottoman. Amelia sat on the divan and Haywood Puser at her side looking distinctly ill at ease.

"I suppose one must take a day off for a death in the family," Miss Maimie said. "But you must tell Conrad that I will not allow them to remain in my employ if they do not return to work."

Amelia patted her hand comfortingly. "Mr. Puser believes that the Ruggys may come down with diphtheria themselves," she said. "You certainly cannot have them here if they are going to be ill."

Miss Maimie gave Haywood a look of disdain, but didn't reply.

Tulsa May entered the room bearing an elaborate pewter tea service which tottered precariously upon a tray. Holding her tongue firmly in one side of her mouth, she managed to set her burden on the marble-topped tea table before it clattered to the floor.

"Do you want milk and sugar, Miss Maimie?" Tulsa May asked the older woman enthusiastically.

Miss Maimie raised an eyebrow. "A *lady* drinks tea with only a dollop of cream," she said. With a smile she added, "But of course, you couldn't be expected to know that."

"No, I surely wouldn't," Tulsa May answered with an unaffected giggle as she gladly turned tea preparation over to Miss Amelia. "It sure is dark in here. With you never leaving the house, I suspect you hardly know when it is day or night."

Before Miss Maimie could answer, Tulsa May made her way to the long line of windows on the west wall and began raising the shades.

"Please!" Miss Maimie's scold stopped Tulsa May in mid-motion, but not before glorious yellow sunshine had flooded the room. "Young lady, the upholstery in this room is made of the finest silk plush. Sunlight will cause it to age and fade."

Tulsa May shrugged. "Yes, I guess it does the same to us, too," she said. "Let me find some old sheets or something to cover things up. It will be like a lady carrying a parasol."

As the carrot-headed flash swept noisily out of the room, Maimie turned to the woman beside her, eyes full of dismay. "My dear Amelia, you cannot actually expect me to allow this young person to *stay* at my house."

"Now, Miss Maimie," Amelia cajoled. "You said yourself that you will need help and she has volunteered."

"If someone stays with me, it should be yourself."

Amelia flushed with pleasure, wanting nothing more than to agree. Being Miss Maimie's companion would give her much opportunity for positively impressing the older woman.

"I cannot." Amelia was genuinely disappointed. "There are so few of us who can tend the sick, I really must do my part."

"What if *I* become sick?"

"Then I would certainly come and take care of you," Amelia assured her. "Tulsa May is a hardworking and friendly young girl; I'm sure you will have no problems with her."

"Hardworking? Friendly?" Maimie gave a dismissive wave. "What she is, is downright peculiar."

Amelia hastily glanced at Haywood, who looked ready to spit, and then hushed the older woman as Tulsa May breezed back into the room bearing an armload of linens.

"You cannot put sheets on my furniture," Miss Maimie snapped. "It will appear as if no one lives here."

Tulsa May grinned at her, unconcerned. "It's either sheets, Miss Maimie, or fading upholstery. I figured you would prefer sheets."

Miss Maimie's face turned red and her cheeks puffed out like a toad. "It would be infinitely simpler to pull down the shades!"

"But then the sun couldn't shine in," Tulsa May answered with youthful exuberance, heedless of Miss Maimie's fury. Placing a finger to her lips thoughtfully, Tulsa May gazed at the bare white windowsills. "What you need, Miss Maimie, is flower boxes. If you could see the blooms every day, why it would just cheer you right up."

"I don't want any flower boxes!"

"Of course you do," Tulsa May assured her.

"Window boxes, young lady," Miss Maimie began, her tone dripping with condescension, "are for poor people who have no gardens. I have some of the most beautiful gardens in the territory."

"Yes, you do, Miss Maimie. But you never go outside to see them. So it seems to me it's the same as not having them at all."

Haywood managed to cover his chuckle with a discreet cough.

"What seems to you—"

Haywood didn't allow her to finish. "Mrs. Sparrow, I'm sure that if you asked Jedwin, he'd spend an afternoon building some boxes for Miss Maimie. We don't want him in around the funeral parlor with this contagion."

"Oh yes!" Tulsa May exclaimed. "Get Jedwin to come out right away and build the flower boxes, then I can plant them while I'm still here."

Maimie's expression was stunned, her disbelief nearing apoplexy. "It's winter!"

Amelia hurriedly changed the subject. "Everyone is talking about changing the name of the town."

Miss Maimie momentarily continued to stare daggers at young Tulsa May. Since the girl seemed so unaware of the furor she had created, Miss Maimie reluctantly allowed herself to be led to a new topic. Her mood, however, was clearly dark. "Talking won't do a thing," she said. "If you want to have the name changed, you will have to write letters and circulate petitions."

"That's what I intend to do," Amelia assured her. "Of course, with the epidemic going on, I won't have much time—"

Miss Maimie waved her hand in a gesture of dismissal and gave Amelia a particularly friendly smile. "I do understand, Amelia," she said. "Not being able to follow through with an idea just comes natural to you, a heritage from your late father, no doubt. That farm would have been something to see if he had just managed to raise himself out of his lazy nature and work the place. With Moses Pratt for a father, believe me, dear Amelia, I could never hold your inpromptitude against you."

Amelia colored, but held her voice firm. "I have every intention of following through, Miss Maimie. But it will have to wait until the current crisis is past."

"I could write letters for you," Tulsa May suggested eagerly as she took a seat opposite Haywood. As they watched, however, Tulsa May's expression changed suddenly. "Of course, I really shouldn't," she said. "I don't want the town named Briggston. So it would be a type of lie to write letters suggesting it."

"What!" Both women were shocked.

"I don't think it's a very good name," she admitted with wide-eyed honesty.

Miss Maimie raised a disapproving eyebrow, her pleasant tone laced with an edge as hard and cold as steel. "What would you like to name the town, dear? Tulsa? Oh, I believe that is taken."

"You are not supposed to name things after people who are still alive," Tulsa May answered. "I think it must be a bad omen or something." She looked to Mr. Puser for support, but he only shrugged noncommittally. "I'm sure I read that somewhere," she said.

"Tulsa May," Amelia answered quietly. "We are not trying to name the town after someone alive. Trapper Briggs has been dead for many years, I'm sure."

The young girl shook her head. "Nobody in this town cares a thing for the old trapper," she said with a warm and unconcerned giggle. "I don't see any reason, in present company, not to be completely truthful about this. You, Mrs. Sparrow, want to name this town for Miss Maimie."

Haywood Puser held the reins with a look of disgust on his face.

"I just can't imagine what has gotten into James Edwin," Amelia Sparrow was saying as she sat beside him. "He has been escorting me to Miss Maimie's every Sunday since his father died. Why in the world would he make other plans today?"

"I tell you that boy of yours is just downright smart," Haywood said. "I wish I'd thought to make some other plans."

Amelia bristled. "No one begged you to drive us out."

"I'd been plenty happy to drive you both to Guthrie for a fall outing, but I'll tell you the truth, if I'da known what I was getting into today, I wouldn't have gone."

"Don't be silly," Amelia reproved him. "What have we gotten into?"

"I think Jedwin had it right, the biggest waste of a pretty Sunday afternoon I ever saw in my life."

Amelia Sparrow was in a much better mood than her escort. "I thought the time passed rather well, actually," she said. "It's not often that I have Miss Maimie all to myself. And I'm sure she appreciated the company. Days can be very long when you are alone."

Haywood's grin was wry. "Days can be very long when you spend them discussing how to change the name of a town."

Amelia smiled. "She does seem very pleased with the idea," she said proudly. "And it is the perfect time to be taking on a new and distinct discernment of our community."

He shook his head. "This community could use a doctor, a grain elevator, and a good clean saloon more than a distinct discernment."

"A saloon? Mr. Puser, really."

"Mellie," he said. "I don't care if you want to change the name of the town. Dead Dog ain't much of a name, I agree. But I suspect that when most of us think of the town, we just think of it as Town."

Amelia couldn't help but nod in agreement.

"But," Haywood continued. "If you are going to change the name, then that little Bruder gal is right. Think of a good name to give it."

"Briggston is a perfectly good name," Amelia said.

"Oh, yes," he agreed. "If your purpose is to suck up to that mean-spirited old crone, I guess it's about perfect."

"Miss Maimie is not mean-spirited," she insisted.

Haywood looked down at her with disapproval. "That old woman is as sour as that awful punch she serves." His jaw was set harshly. "I felt so sorry for that Tulsa May, I thought I was like to cry in sympathy."

Amelia sighed. "Well, yes, Miss Maimie is a bit uncomplimentary to poor Tulsa May. But surely you understand her motives. That girl is downright peculiar and just plainly ill-favored. Miss Maimie is only trying to encourage her to make the best of what little she has."

"There is plenty of room on God's earth for every kind of appearance and person." Haywood shook his head disdainfully. "That little gal seemed sweet enough and plenty smart. Those attributes will get a gal a lot farther than most people think."

Nodding, Amelia agreed. "She is a dear, isn't she? But she's so dreamy. Sometimes I think she doesn't even listen to what is being said around her."

Haywood shrugged. "Well, I hope she wasn't listening when that spiteful old peahen called her everything but snout face."

"Don't speak of Miss Maimie that way. She is the most important matron in our community."

"She's a bitter old witch who loves to berate people and make them feel bad about themselves," he said. "For heaven's sake, Mellie, she even does it to you."

"She only means to be helpful."

Haywood ignored her flimsy excuse. "She watches people and searches for their weak points. When she finds one she attacks."

Amelia shook her head at his fanciful description. "You make her sound like a ruthless pirate on the Spanish Main."

"I think I'd prefer spending my Sundays with a pirate," he replied.

Amelia giggled like a young girl and Haywood couldn't help but smile at her.

"I don't like the way she talks to you," he said.

"What on earth do you mean?" Amelia asked.

"She finds fault with your hair and your clothes and everything you say and do."

Amelia blushed self-consciously. "I am not a close relative of Miss Maimie's. I did not grow up with many of the advantages of society." Amelia folded her hands together nervously as if embarrassed about these admissions. "Miss Maimie tries to help me to mask my less than fortunate origins."

Haywood stared at the woman beside him in stunned disbelief. "Dammit,

Mellie, everybody in Dead Dog knows that you are the smartest and prettiest woman in this town."

His compliment was so unexpected that Amelia just stared at him in openmouthed amazement.

"Why . . . why . . . ah, thank you, Mr. Puser."

"Most of the men in this town, married or not, can't keep their eyes off you," he said. "I know I sure can't."

Amelia stared at him stupidly. Haywood Puser paying her compliments? Suddenly, she found herself very uncomfortable. As they made the turn up Main Street, she noted how deserted the town had become. She was inexplicably conscious of being alone with Haywood Puser. Desperately, she plunged back into their previous conversation, feeling safer with his displeasure than his admiration.

"Miss Maimie is of an age where speaking bluntly comes more natural." She was looking straight ahead and waited patiently for Haywood's next volley. When his silence continued, she turned to look at him. A broad grin was splashed across his face.

"What *are* you smiling at?" she asked curtly.

If possible his grin actually widened. He slipped the team's lines into his left hand and as casually as if he did so every day, put his right arm down on the buggy seatback and around Amelia Sparrow.

Her mouth dropping open in shock, Amelia immediately sat forward away from his touch. "Just what do you think you are doing, Mr. Puser?" she asked coldly.

Haywood raised his eyebrows wickedly. "Oh, just enjoying a nice Sunday buggy ride with a good-looking woman."

Chapter
Fifteen

"That pack of worthless, small-minded hypocrites!" Jedwin was furious.

He was pacing the length of the main room of the Pratt farmhouse. Cora sat watching him from a worn bedtick that she'd retrieved from the bottom of her wardrobe. The two of them had spent the better part of the afternoon carefully selecting the hay and sweet clover to stuff it. Deciding that meeting at Cora's house would be too dangerous, they thought Pratt farm seemed a perfect choice for their secret hideaway.

Jedwin was in no temper to test his handiwork this afternoon. He was like a bulldog with a bone, he just could not seem to let it go.

Cora, now half reclined on the makeshift bed, had her nose buried in Mrs. Millenbutter's book. Her serious concentration went unnoticed by Jedwin, who continued to pace irately. "Reverend Bruder called you a *Jezebel*." He slammed a fist into the flat of his hand angrily. "Luring weak men into sin." Fuming, he shook his head threateningly. "I'd like to *lure* that weak man into a dark alley and pound some sense into his brain."

"Don't worry about it," Cora said, looking up casually from her book. "Nothing anyone has to say about me bothers me a whit."

"Well, it bothers me," he declared sharply. "The man impugned your honor!"

Cora looked at the young man curiously and raised an eyebrow. She

174

considered pointing out that as a divorced woman, she no longer had honor.

"That preacher and his silly wife are ignorant, small-minded, and spiteful," he said. "You should hear the things they say about people."

"Everybody gossips," Cora told him. "I'm sure even the saints were guilty of it a time or two."

"Well, these are certainly not saints," he said. "They aren't even kind to their own daughter. The things they say about Tulsa May!"

Cora nodded. "Sometimes we are cruelest to those that we love."

Jedwin turned to stare at her, exasperated. "Why are you taking up for them?"

"Because I don't care about them, and I don't want them to ruin our day together."

"Nothing," Jedwin declared adamantly, "could ruin any time that I spend with you!"

Nodding hopefully at his words, Cora was immediately chagrined as he began to pace once more.

She sighed and sat up, laying her book aside. Her heart was full of sadness and longing. She had so wanted their idyll to last a while longer. Cora knew the realities would ultimately intrude. But she'd hoped for more time, just a little more time, giving her enough memories to last her forever.

"How dare those people think to judge you," Jedwin raved. "To judge us, to judge this . . . this happiness that we've found."

Cora closed her eyes. She couldn't allow him to continue to rant. The truth had to be faced. Sadly, she supposed that the truth had to be faced today.

"That's what they are supposed to do," she said calmly.

Jedwin turned to look at her. His expression was full of disbelief. "What?"

"That's what communities do, Jedwin," she told him. "They judge people who break the rules. We broke the rules."

"Rules?" Jedwin stepped closer to her. "I don't know what you mean."

"You know exactly what I mean," she said.

When he made no further comment, she sat up straighter and resolutely smoothed her hair back into place. Raising her chin with defiance, her words were spoken as coolly as if they were meaningless.

"*I* vowed to keep myself only unto Luther Briggs for as long as we both lived," she said. "And *you* have had lovemaking with me without benefit of wedlock. That's two rules we've broken."

Jedwin raised his hands to heaven and gave her a humorless grin. "Good Lord, Cora, your vows to Luther were over a long time ago," he said. "And what we've shared together"—he dropped down beside her on the bedtick and laid a hand possessively on her knee—"that is nothing that I am ashamed of."

"Maybe you *should* be ashamed," she said, moving her leg away from the warmth of his touch.

"Well, I'm not." He swallowed and then looked at her closely, a tender smile curving slightly at the edge of his lips. "What I've felt with you, Cora . . ." he began. "I guess some *would* call it sin. But it doesn't feel that way to me."

The sincerity of his declaration nearly disarmed Cora. Jedwin was so open, so honest. It would be easy to mislead him, deceive him, enjoy him. But she didn't want to hurt him. She would have to teach him to guard himself against her.

"Of course you don't think that it is sin. Does a thief think that it is wrong to steal?" she asked him. "Doesn't he tell himself that his victims have plenty and they won't miss what he takes?"

"I am no thief, Cora," he said self-righteously. "I didn't steal you from Luther."

"You are deliberately trying to misunderstand. You have talked yourself into believing that what we are doing is right, when we both know that it is wrong."

Jedwin hesitated. He'd attended church since he was still wearing nursery gowns. In his opinion his conscience was in perfect working order, but it didn't call him to question today.

"When I touch you, caress you," he said. "When I feel your hands on my body, Cora, I feel nothing but pleasure and joy, not even a prickle of remorse."

"But it is wrong."

Jedwin took her hand into his own and brought it to his lips. There was no jest in him now, only stark, cold fear. "Are you suggesting that we stop meeting each other?" he asked.

Cora looked at him for a long moment. That is what she should be suggesting, she knew. It was a wild folly to have let things go so far with him. But they had gone so far with her, too.

She swallowed the emotion that lodged so stubbornly in her throat. "No," she answered him in a whisper. "I'm not sending you away, Jedwin. I should, but I don't think that I can."

Jedwin felt her uncertainty in the trembling of her hand and the coolness of her flesh. "What are you saying?" he asked.

Cora looked distressed, and he squeezed her hand reassuringly.

"I'm saying, Jedwin, that I want your eyes wide open in this," she said.

He went very still for a moment. Perceiving insult, he released her hands and raised his chin obstinately. "Do you still think me an ignorant boy, Cora?" he asked quietly. "I may lack experience in romance, but I am no stranger to the truths in this world."

"You misunderstand me," she assured him hastily. Cora took his hand back in her own and stared at the strong tan knuckles that clutched her so securely. "It is those *truths of this world* that you must keep in mind. We are *not* lovers, Jedwin, only sinners."

He reeled back slightly as if she had slapped him. "I may be a sinner, Cora," he answered firmly. "But that does not mean that I am not in love with you."

She covered one side of her face with a hand, as if her head ached. "You must not be in love with me. That is why I invited you to my bed, so that you would realize that it is lust you feel and not love."

He took her chin in his hand and raised her face to his. Her eyes were bright, but her expression was calm.

"I don't care why you invited me to your bed," he said. "I am glad to be there. And Cora." He paused, offering her the faintest of smiles. "You may tell me what you believe. You may tell me how you think, what you know. You may tell me the craziest of your dreams." He leaned forward to place a gentle kiss on her lips. "You may not, however, tell me how to feel."

Cora pulled away from him. She rose to her feet and walked to the window. When she opened the shutter, the bright afternoon sun streamed down on her. It lit the shadows of her curves and hollows as if she herself were shining from heaven. Only her shoulders, bent in sorrow, belied the appearance. Jedwin leaned out a hand to grasp the hem of her skirt in his fingers. She turned to him.

"Just say to me, so that I will know for sure, that you know that what we are doing is wrong."

He gazed up into her troubled expression. "Why do you carry on with this?"

"Because it is important!" she snapped, becoming angry now. "I will not have a man who doesn't know the rules."

Releasing his hold on her dress, Jedwin scooted over to sit at her feet. He looked up at her, those intense brown eyes prying into the weary secrets she held locked inside her.

"Rules?" he said. "You're talking about rules again? Whose rules are these, Cora? Are these Reverend Bruder's rules?"

"They are *our* rules!" she said, her tone fiery with annoyance. "Civilization is based on rules, Jedwin. When the rules are broken, people get hurt. I want you to understand that. You must understand that. We have broken the rules and, therefore, people are going to be hurt."

Jedwin gazed at her, his heart in his eyes. "Cora," he said, "I hear what you are saying. I even agree with you mostly. But"—he reached out and took her hand in his own—"civilization is not in danger here. What we are doing, Cora, is beautiful. It is wonderful. Who will that hurt?"

"You," she answered quietly. "Maybe me."

He rose to his knees and drew her into his arms, pressing his face tightly against her abdomen as if the strength of his arms alone could protect her from all the dangers of the universe.

"Oh Cora," he whispered against her neck. "I will try my best never to hurt you."

"I know you will," she answered.

Taking his hand, she gestured for him to rise. Together they walked two short steps to the bedtick. Cora sat down gracefully and raised her arm to him.

"Lie with me, Jedwin," she pleaded. "Lie with me today, while we both still vow not to hurt the other."

Jedwin came down beside her. His touch was so gentle it was almost reverent as they kissed and caressed and dispensed with unneeded clothing. Deliberately they avoided any rush. Slowly, oh so slowly, they tasted of each other as if loitering could make their time stand still.

When Jedwin finally parted her legs she was more than ready. Still they lingered together, making the moment and the movement last as long as near forever. It was with something close to disappointment that the shuddering release flared through her body to ignite his.

Cora's fingers were stiff and cold as she slipped the clothespin onto the edge of the worn, gray length of patched cotton to keep it secured to the line. It was almost cold enough to freeze the wash, but she hoped that the bit of breeze that had picked up in the afternoon would be enough to dry the bedsheets.

"Good afternoon, Mrs. Briggs."

Her mind was so far away that it was no wonder she started at the greeting. Clad in somber black, the Reverend Philemon Bruder stood at the corner of the house.

Cora met his gaze directly. "Afternoon, Preacher. What brings you to this end of town?"

Bruder smiled, not unkindly, and walked toward her, his hands clasped behind his back. His face retained the unnatural pinkness of a fair-fleshed man who spent much of his time in the sunshine. And the wispy remains of his graying red hair and his bright orange moustache contrasted sharply with his complexion. "Just checking on one of my flock," he said.

Cora attached the last clothespin to the line, then turned to face him, hands on hips. "Am I a part of your flock?"

The preacher shrugged. "You once were. I suppose I should count you the lamb that went astray."

Folding her arms across her chest, Cora shook her head. "This 'lamb' didn't go *astray,* she was sent *away.*" Cora laughed. "As you well know, were I to show up at Sunday services, half the females of the congregation would keel over in apoplexy."

"Are you sure?"

"Aren't you?"

"Not at all. You have purposely kept yourself separate from your church. God's house is where you are supposed to come to in times of trouble."

Cora stared him down, chin high and uncowed. "I haven't parted ways with God, Reverend, just with the good people of Dead Dog."

The preacher's expression suggested that he wanted to argue further, but Cora was grateful that he let it drop.

"I've come to talk to you about some rumors spreading about you," he said.

"New rumors or the same old ones?"

"Brand-new ones," he said. "And if there is any truth to them at all . . . . well, I just won't have it."

Cora sighed heavily. The reckoning had come. "Why don't you have a seat, Reverend?" She indicated the empty washbench that sat in the afternoon sunlight. "Let me make us some tea."

The preacher agreed amiably and seated himself while Cora hurried to the kitchen.

As she poked new life into the fire, Cora tried to make a decision about what to do. If the preacher knew about Jedwin, she'd have to stop seeing him. If, however, he only *suspected* that there was a man, perhaps they could continue to get away with their little scandal for a while longer.

Cora prepared the tea service as she berated herself for such thoughts. If she were in her right mind, she should be planning to break it off with Jedwin, not hoping that she could outwit the town and continue.

She glanced out the back door at the reverend. She had left her copy of Mrs. Millenbutter's book on the bench and the preacher was perusing it casually. A good hostess would put the kettle on and return to her guest until the water boiled. Cora rudely lingered in the kitchen.

Not before the tea was steeping did Cora make her way out the back door, carrying the blue pot Amelia Sparrow had sent as a wedding gift in the middle of a plain cherrywood tray, surrounded by her best mismatched china.

"Here we are," Cora said with exaggerated cheeriness. The preacher didn't even look up. It was not until Cora stood at his side that he raised his eyes from the book.

"Oh, Cora." He came to his feet as if surprised to see her.

"Reverend, why don't you turn over that washtub?" she said, indicating the battered tin tub propped up to dry at the end of the bench.

The preacher immediately laid the book aside and placed the washtub with as much precision as if it were the pulpit in his sanctuary. Cora placed the tea tray on the makeshift table and seated herself opposite Reverend Bruder.

"Do you take sugar?"

"Just milk," he answered, refocusing his attention on the book.

"I'm sorry, I don't have any."

"What?" The preacher looked up at her, clearly preoccupied. "Oh, fine," he agreed before Cora had time to repeat herself. "This is very interesting reading. I've never even heard of Daisy Millenbutter."

Cora was momentarily surprised. "Oh, Mrs. Millenbutter gives wonderful advice. I am quite committed to her."

The reverend nodded. "When I picked it up, I thought it might be a new imitation of the writings of Mrs. Eddy, but it is quite different."

"You've read Mrs. Eddy?" Cora asked.

"Well, of course, and you?"

She nodded. "I found her fundamentals very uplifting, but the Eastern mystic element was somewhat unwieldy for me."

The preacher was looking at Cora as if he'd never seen her before. "I was not aware that you were a student of religion or philosophy."

"Only in a small way," she assured him, a grin teasing at the corner of her mouth. "At the Methodist Home it was either the study of philosophy or the fundamentals of hand washing."

Reverend Bruder laughed out loud. "And so you find Mrs. Millenbutter superior to Mrs. Eddy."

"No, not superior, just more suited to me. I have a great appreciation for fresh air and exercise. I suppose that blending my personal preferences in life with my philosophy for living was an easy choice."

He nodded approvingly. "So what aspect of Mrs. Millenbutter's philosophy was holding your attention this morning?"

"I was looking for a cure for diphtheria."

"Oh?"

"I heard that there is sickness in Low Town. I was hoping Mrs. Millenbutter could offer some worthwhile treatment."

"Does she?" he asked.

Cora sighed. "She recommends swabbing the affected area of the throat with lime juice."

The reverend shook his head. "In the big cities back East they give patients an antitoxin to cure them. I'd say we are just as likely to get some of that rare medicine as we are to find limes in the territory."

Cora agreed. "I was trying to decide what curative elements might be in the limes that we could find in some product we have here locally."

"A very good idea. What have you come up with?"

"Nothing yet," she admitted.

"Perhaps together we can think of something."

Cora nodded her willingness. "What do you know about limes, Reverend?"

"They are very aromatic," he said. "They have a distinct and pungent smell."

"And they are very sour," Cora added. "I can't imagine how horrible it would be to have it swabbed on one's throat."

"Not pleasant, I don't imagine," the preacher agreed.

"The juice of the lime stings very badly if you get it into a cut," she said.

The two sat quietly for a moment. "That's about all I know of limes," Cora said finally.

Reverend Bruder nodded. "All right. So now we must think of something that is readily available to us that smells to high heaven, tastes abominably sour, and stings in cuts."

The moments stretched on as Cora mentally inventoried the cupboards in her kitchen for the potential curative. She was near ready to give up, when she glanced at the reverend to see his eyes wide with surprise.

"What is it?" she asked.

"Whiskey."

"Whiskey!"

The reverend's face colored brightly and he looked away from Cora in embarrassment. "I have not always been a preacher, Mrs. Briggs," he said. He hesitated a long moment as if reluctant to speak. Taking a deep breath, he turned his eyes to Cora. "Once I was the most wretched of sinners. And I admit to having had a dismal familiarity with corn liquor."

"Reverend Bruder?"

"In my youth I was a drunkard," he said solemnly. "And I would be one yet, had my dear Constance, fine Christian woman that she is, not plucked me out of the depths of Satan's pit of despair and set me firmly on the road to redemption."

Cora was momentarily stunned into silence. With a nervous little cough, she managed to reclaim her voice. "I had no idea."

He shook his head. "None in town know," he said. "Since I accepted the call to preach, I've not said a word about my former life. We moved out here to the territory to leave that unfortunate past behind."

Cora felt drawn to alleviate the vulnerability in the formidable man beside her. "The past is truly past," she said, reaching over to gently pat his hand. "The fact that you have left your mistakes behind you says more for your character than if you'd been righteous all your life."

The preacher looked up at her. He nodded with more than a hint of admiration, feeling that she spoke as much for herself as for him. Rising to his feet, he gave her a modest bow of leave-taking. "May I take Mrs. Millenbutter's book to read?" he asked.

"Why, of course," she said. "You haven't finished your tea. Where are you off to?"

"Mort Humley's place."

"Mr. Humley's? Why?"

Reverend Bruder's bright moustache wiggled as his expression bloomed into a hearty grin. "I wouldn't be much of a shepherd," he said, "if I didn't know which of my flock has a corn-liquor still on his property."

Cora laughed out loud with wide-eyed surprise. She wondered, as she watched the reverend make his way to the street, when he would remember why he had come to visit her.

Cora made her way to Pratt farm nearly every day to see Jedwin. She worked beside him to get the oats into the barn. Gathering the shooks onto the wagon and safely stacking them out of the weather to wait for the threshing team to come through town. They worked and sweated and strained their backs and arms until they ached. It was the most pleasant task either could recall. They scampered in the fields and rolled in the haymow and took lunch together in the privacy of the old log homestead.

Jedwin looked the part of the contented farmer these days. The sun had browned his skin and his work clothes were gentle colors, not the somber grays and blacks of the mortuary. And in addition to his appearance and his clothes, a smile graced his face from morning until night and his laughter rang across the fields.

"I am so grateful for this time with you," Jedwin told her as he helped her spread the picnic cloth she'd brought for their luncheon.

Cora smiled, pleased. "It was a wonderful idea to meet here at the farm."

Jedwin's answering grin was hot and sensual. "The nights are just too short," he told her.

Cora raised her eyebrows in blushing challenge, feigning ignorance of his meaning. "But the nights are so romantic," she told him. "Have you forgotten about being romantic?"

Jedwin grabbed her wrist and bent his head over it in an elaborate kiss to her hand. "Romancing you, Mrs. Briggs," he claimed with comically exaggerated sincerity, "is all that I live for."

"Oh really? Well, what happened to poetry?" she asked as she handed him his dish of luncheon fare. "I haven't seen a passionate rhyme in weeks."

Shrugging, Jedwin sat quietly for a moment in contemplation, finally looking quite intently at the contents of his plate.

Setting it down, he dramatically smoothed a nonexistent moustache and thoroughly cleared his throat.

> "The fairest woman that e'er I've seen,
>   Feeds me nothing but beans and greens."

Cora huffed in feigned fury. "You'll see nothing but cornbread and water if you don't watch your step."

Jedwin held his hands before him as if warding her off in fear.

They ate their meal as companionably as lovers. Jedwin took an occasional bite from his plate, followed by one from hers. Cora quickly followed suit. Finally they exchanged plates, but quickly discovered it was not the contents of the other plate that lured them, but the person holding it.

As their stomachs filled they became more lethargic and serious.

"Have you given up work at the mortuary completely?" Cora asked him as she handed him a quarter piece of pecan pie.

"Nobody will let me near the place," he explained. "I've never had diphtheria, so Mama won't let me near the living and Haywood won't let me near the dead."

Cora's expression troubled momentarily. "Is the plague worsening?"

Jedwin shook his head. "I don't think they've had a death in a couple of days. That's very good. You know the preacher has my mother and the other nurses swabbing the throats of the sick with corn liquor."

"I know," Cora admitted with a giggle. "It was inadvertently Mrs. Millenbutter's idea."

The two laughed and talked about philosophy and friends and the reverend and finally the conversation reached the topic of the Methodist Home.

"It was not so bad at the Home," Cora confided to him. "It was just never home to me. I shared a room with nine girls. Nine girls whom I considered my friends, but I was still lonely. I hated it."

Jedwin's expression saddened. "You've been lonely here in Dead Dog, haven't you?"

Cora waved away his concern. "No more lonely than I've always been since Mama died. And since I've met you, I've not been lonely at all."

Jedwin's expression warmed into a smile. "Good."

Realizing the weight of her admission, Cora wanted to call the words back, to make him think he'd misunderstood.

"We've been so lucky," Cora said.

"Lucky to find each other."

"Lucky to be spared the diphtheria," she said. "A disease like that can devastate a town. It can wipe whole families off the face of the earth. I read in the Guthrie paper, the *State Capital*, that the sickness is running through both the territories like a wildfire."

Jedwin gazed at the woman across from him who was so desperately attempting to put distance between them. Jedwin would not dream of doing the same himself. Life was so sweet, so new, so precious to him now. Disease and death held no more fear for him than the potential separation from her. He reached for her and she came into his arms.

"I am learning so much about you, Cora," he said.

"What are you learning?"

"How fond you are of secrets."

Chapter Sixteen

Haywood heard the rustle of cook pots as he stepped into the doorway kitchen.

"Evening, Mellie," he said.

Amelia Sparrow glanced up and nodded silently.

"I heard you come in," he said. "How are things down in Low Town? Still looking better?"

"No new cases today," she answered. "And for all that I was sure it was foolishness, the reverend's whiskey cure seems to be helping."

Haywood nodded. "Whiskey is a good antiseptic. Maybe it really can work."

"I suspect the worst of it is over," she said. "In a day or two our lives will return to normal."

"Yes," he agreed, "I suppose so." He hesitated for a long moment, watching as with tired, slow-moving steps she puttered through the kitchen. "I just wanted to let you know, Mellie, that these past couple of weeks, working with you, well, it's given me a whole new perspective on Amelia Sparrow."

"Oh?" she said with disinterest.

Haywood chuckled lightly to himself and shook his head. "I used to think that you were the most spoiled, selfish woman on earth."

"What!" His words certainly captured Amelia's attention and she looked up at him sharply.

"You've really proved to me that isn't so," he said.

"I do not need to *prove* anything to you or anyone else," Amelia answered with cold fury. "I have worked with you to protect my son from contagion. Any mother would do the same."

"Maybe so," Haywood admitted casually. "But I don't think I would have enjoyed it as much with anyone else."

His grin was open and winning, but Amelia did not respond in kind.

Amelia raised her chin, attempting to recapture their former employer/employee relations. "As I said, Mr. Puser, the worst of this awful plague is past. I can assure you that there will be no need for you and I to fraternize so closely in the future."

Rather than accepting his setdown with good grace, Haywood laughed in Amelia's face.

She opened her mouth for a scathing retort; Haywood was saved, however, by the rapping of someone's knuckles at the front door. Shooting him a look of fury, Amelia stepped past Haywood into the hallway.

"Reverend Bruder," she said as she saw the preacher standing in the doorway. "What a pleasant surprise."

The wind was blustery, stirring Amelia's skirts wildly before she managed to close the door behind him. Taking off his thick wool coat and hat, he gave a slight bow of acknowledgment as she hung them on the halltree. "Miss Amelia, Mr. Puser."

"What brings you out this way?" Haywood asked, reaching a hand to grasp the reverend's.

The preacher straightened his wispy red hair and twisted his orange moustache into shape as he answered. "Just inquiring about the health of my community."

Amelia graciously led him into the formal parlor, Haywood following. The room was dark and continuously draped in mourning ribbons for the use of the families of deceased persons. The preacher had been in the room on countless less pleasant occasions.

"The whiskey cure seems to be working rather well," she assured him pleasantly. "We've been using little plugs of cottonwood spore twisted on a wire to keep the medicine against the throat for a longer time."

"Excellent idea," the preacher commended her. "And I am sure that the patients don't find it nearly as unpleasant as if we'd used limes."

"Limes?" both Amelia and Haywood asked in unison.

"That was the treatment originally recommended. But, with that out of the question, I improvised."

"Wherever did you hear about limes for a treatment?" Haywood asked.

Reverend Bruder smiled. "Why, from Mrs. Briggs."

"Miss Maimie?" Amelia was clearly surprised.

The reverend took a seat without waiting for it to be offered. "No, Cora Briggs."

If a thunderbolt had struck Amelia between the eyes she wouldn't have been more stunned. She seated herself quickly as if worried she might fall. "You've been visiting Cora Briggs?"

The preacher tutted. "I don't like the sound of that question. Mrs. Briggs is a member of my flock, I have not only a right, but an obligation to visit her."

"She hasn't set foot in church in eight years," Amelia protested.

He nodded in agreement. "She seems to feel that the ladies of the church would not welcome her."

"And we certainly would not!"

"Then she is totally correct in her perceptions."

The preacher's tone implied censure, and Amelia recognized that it was directed at her. Hastily she sought to assert her moral superiority. "Has Mrs. Briggs confessed with which men she is consorting?"

Reverend Bruder's face flushed slightly, uncomfortable with his own dereliction of duty. "We haven't gotten around to that discussion as yet. Our talks concern health and philosophy." As the two other occupants of the room stared at him, the reverend cleared his throat a little self-consciously. "I truly never got to know Mrs. Briggs adequately. I certainly never suspected such intellect. And I fear I have misjudged her. Once I regain her confidence, I will certainly want to counsel her about the wages of sin."

"Perhaps she could better explain it to you," Amelia suggested unkindly. "She's been *earning* those wages for some time."

"Mellie!" Haywood called her up sharply. Amelia gave him an exasperated look, but partial compliance.

The preacher glanced at Haywood in speculation.

"What on earth could that woman know about the care of the sick?" Amelia continued to protest.

"Apparently a good deal." He opened the book that he carried and handed it to her. Amelia had assumed that it was his Bible, but saw now that it was not.

"Mrs. Briggs has graciously allowed me to borrow her copy of Mrs. Millenbutter's very fine guidebook on health, posture, and spirituality. I am forced to admit, Mrs. Sparrow, that I have found it absolutely fascinating."

"It is a biblical work, Reverend?" Amelia asked.

"No, it's not *strictly* biblical; it relies a good deal on common sense. I believe that by following many of the instructions in this book, we can more likely protect the health of the people of this community."

Haywood reached out for the book and Amelia handed it to him. As for Amelia, her interest was not even piqued. She was absolutely certain that nothing that Cora Briggs had to offer could be of any value.

"I thought, Reverend, that as a minister of the gospel, your concerns would be more for our souls, especially the sinful ones, than for our bodies."

"My concern is for both, Mrs. Sparrow. God gives us our health and life as well as our spiritual being."

"Then certainly such concerns should be left for God," she said.

The preacher leaned back in his chair and stubbornly folded his hands across his chest. "I believe he is supposed to 'help those who help themselves.'"

Haywood nodded as he perused the book. "Certainly none of this would hurt anyone, Preacher," he said. "Fresh air, hygiene, deep breathing, and good posture, at least nothing in her prescription is inherently deadly."

"That's what I felt," the reverend said and then added with a chuckle, "Actually, what I've *felt* is a good deal better. I've been taking a long constitutional every morning and working on my posture exercises in the privacy of my own parsonage. I highly recommend it."

Reverend Bruder rose to his feet, taking a deep breath. He raised his hands over his head in a full body stretch. This had the effect of making his coattails rise almost to his belt. Both Haywood and Amelia stared at him as if he'd lost his mind.

"Ahhh . . ." he said as he slowly brought his arms back to his sides. "I truly believe I have never felt so good in all my life. Well, I must be on my way."

"Your book, Reverend." Haywood held the book out to the preacher. He reached out in a fatherly gesture and managed to pat affectionately both the book and Haywood's hand. "You may borrow it for the day," he said. "Mrs. Briggs gave me permission to loan it about town. I'm giving everybody a day to look it over. But don't worry. At my request, Titus Penny has contacted the company and requested a hundred copies for sale in his store. They should be arriving on the train within a few weeks."

Jedwin pulled the team to the barn area behind the Briggs mansion. The old flatbed hearse was loaded with lumber and paint, a great pile of topsoil, and baskets of flower bulbs. Jedwin's work apron lay spread across the top. Jumping to the ground, he began to unhitch the horses. Leaving them in their collars, he tied them to a convenient hitching post within reach of both the water trough and the tall grass left standing around the edge of the barn.

"Good morning." He heard the call from behind him and turned to see Tulsa May making her way toward him from the back door of the house. Her work dress was cheap calico of a nondescript brown, but somehow it suited her more than her usual fashionably colored attire.

"A good day to you, Miss Tulsa May," he called back to her. "I'm surprised to see you here."

Tulsa May looked puzzled. "Why? You knew that I was staying with Miss Maimie."

He nodded. "I just expected you would be out for your morning exercise, like just about everybody else in this town."

She giggled happily, her gap-toothed smile making her appear almost attractive. "Isn't it a sight on this earth?" she said. "I saw with my own eyes Lily Auslander, who is as broad as Mama's old milk cow, taking baby steps down Main Street with a bag of butter beans on her head!"

Jedwin laughed at the image. "Wait until you see Carlisle Bowman tossing Indian clubs."

Cheerfully the two swapped stories of the latest craze that had swept through Dead Dog.

"Papa wants Mother to start a special Saturday afternoon meeting for young ladies," she told him. "He wants her to call it Prayers and Posture."

Jedwin raised an eyebrow. "I would imagine you will be expected to attend."

Tulsa May smiled with exaggerated brightness. "Only if the sun continues to rise in the east and set in the west."

Jedwin shook his head. "Well, at least it will keep you busy after you get these flower boxes planted."

"I'm so glad that you could get free to come and build them."

"I understand Miss Maimie is not exactly thrilled about this addition to her house."

Tulsa May waved away his concern. "It will do her good. Aggravation is a wonderful medicine," she said. "It keeps her mind active."

"Is that your prescription for the lady?"

With a delighted sigh, she nodded. "I told Conrad and Mattie to take all the time they need to recover and get their affairs in order. I find Miss Maimie a very enlightening challenge."

"I'm sure she finds you equally as interesting."

"Not interesting. As I said before, aggravating."

With Tulsa May's help, Jedwin began unloading the lumber from the wagon. "Haywood said you want boxes for every window on the ground floor."

She nodded. "Eighteen windows in all," she said. "But the front windows are in sections of three. I think you could just make long boxes there."

Jedwin agreed. Slipping his work apron over his head, he bent forward slightly, crisscrossing the strings at the back of his waist before tying them in front. He looked up to see Tulsa May staring at him, an unusual expression upon her face.

"What is it?"

She started slightly, as if being caught, and then gave a hasty shake of her head. "Nothing, nothing," she insisted.

Jedwin sensed a strange unease, but didn't question her further. "I'll start here in the back," he said. "By the time I get to the front, I will have made all possible mistakes and will be putting my perfected product up for company."

Tulsa May nodded vaguely and then seemed to deliberately pull herself out of her musing. "That seems like a perfect plan to me," she said with a determined cheerfulness.

"I hope that all this hammering doesn't upset Miss Maimie."

This time Tulsa May's laugh was genuine. "Oh, I guarantee that it will. Honestly, I can hardly wait. It will keep her busy assaulting your character for the entire day."

Jedwin chuckled as Tulsa May began to peruse the load in the hearse. "I see you even brought me some of your own dirt," she said.

Jedwin clutched his heart as if wounded. "*That,* young woman, is not *dirt.* It is my own personal blend of compost-mulched topsoil."

"Oh, then excuse me, sir," Tulsa May said to him with a respectful curtsy to the dirt pile. "What did you bring me to plant?" she asked.

"As much as I could," he answered. "I swear, Tulsa May, you are about the only person in the world that I know who would take it into her head to plant flower boxes at the beginning of winter."

She nodded in agreement. "Anyone can plant flowers in springtime. I prefer a real challenge."

"Well, I nearly brought you some immortelles to stick into the ground," Jedwin said. "But I thought the better of it."

Tulsa May was attempting to pry open the lid of a bushel basket with her fingernails. Jedwin helpfully pulled a screwdriver from his apron and popped the top off the basket. "Most of these are jonquils," he told her. "They are about the hardiest flower I know and they'll bloom most any time of year. I've heard stories about them coming up through the snow. But I can't say that I've actually seen that myself."

Tulsa May nodded. "What are these?" she asked, holding up a very round ball-like bulb.

"Those are tulips. I don't have much luck with tulips myself."

"So you gave them to *me* to try?"

He chuckled. "Well, my bad luck with them comes from the moles and gophers. I put these bulbs in the ground and those varmints seem to think they are playtoys. They will dig them out and roll them down their runs. When spring comes my tulip bed is barren, but I have the occasional tulip popping up in the yard, through the carriage-house floor, or right in the middle of the street!"

Jedwin shook his head as Tulsa May laughed at his exaggerated dismay.

"I figured that up in these flower boxes, the gophers wouldn't be able to get to them. But," he said dramatically, "the first time I come out here and see little ladders made of twigs leaning up against these flower boxes, I'm giving up tulips completely!"

Jedwin worked most of the morning, cheerfully hammering together the flower boxes. Tulsa May helped as much as she was allowed. Miss Maimie set up a constant complaint about the noise and had the young girl scurrying to and fro in attempts to placate her.

Tulsa May clearly wanted to work with Jedwin and she quickly showed an aptitude for painting. Her carpentry talents, however, were limited. Midway through the chore Jedwin heard her howl and raced to her side. She'd managed to catch the side of her thumb between the hammer and the nail head, raising a dark blood blister.

Tulsa May was trying to shake the pain out when Jedwin reached her. He grabbed her hand and began blowing forcefully on the injured thumb. As she quieted, he began to stroke her fingers and palm, urging circulation rather than swelling the area. After a moment he realized that the service he was performing was intimate in nature. He glanced up at Tulsa May to see her grimacing in pain, but in no way embarrassed by his closeness. Jedwin also felt no shame. There was nothing of man and woman in his touch. Only the comfort of brother for sister. He released her hand.

"Are you okay?"

Tulsa May nodded, holding her thumb in her own mouth for a couple of seconds before shaking it once more. "I'm fine," she insisted. "Mercy sakes, I'm so clumsy, you'd think I'd be completely callused over by now."

Jedwin looked at her a long moment. The penny brown eyes and the gap-toothed grin were so familiar and so endearing.

She was giggling over her own clumsiness. "I was just trying to put a little bit of *myself* into these flower boxes."

His smile warm and genuine, Jedwin leaned forward to tousle her carrot-colored curls. She was just a little girl. Had he ever really planned to marry her? "I really like you, Tulsa May. I've always thought you'd make somebody a good wife. Now I'm sure that one of these days some lucky fellow is going to fall head over heels in love with you."

She looked at him curiously for a moment before giving him a laughing reply. "He'd best not fall 'head over heels,' Jedwin. I think one clumsy person per couple is enough."

The rest of the afternoon's work passed without event. Tulsa May worked on the planting while Jedwin finished the box building on his own.

She shoveled the compost-mulched topsoil into Miss Maimie's wheelbarrow and was quickly filling the flower boxes beneath the window with it. "What's this?" she asked, holding up a coarse grain sack.

"It's Epsom salts," Jedwin told her. "Put a little dab in with each bulb you plant and it will make your leaves greener and your flowers brighter."

Tulsa May looked at him skeptically and then shrugged. "You are the expert."

Jedwin hesitated for a moment before nodding. "Yes, ma'am, I guess that I am."

Cheerfully, he continued his work sawing, hammering, and nailing. Tulsa May shoveled the dirt, planted bulbs, prattled incessantly about the future of the Briggs mansion flower boxes, and took occasional breaks to answer the shrill call of Miss Maimie from the house.

Finally they were finished.

"These boxes look really good against the windows," she said.

"I hope you don't expect Miss Maimie to agree with you."

Tulsa May giggled. "Even if she did, she'd never say so. I just want to brighten up her life a little. Sometimes I think she looks at life through spectacles made of gloom."

Jedwin nodded. "Why are you so kind to her? I can't say that I've ever heard her say a nice word about anybody."

Tulsa May shrugged. "I guess when it comes to Miss Maimie, I'm luckier than most."

The look of stunned disbelief on Jedwin's face was so comical, Tulsa May laughed out loud. "It's true," she insisted. "I have an advantage."

"I can't imagine what it might be."

She furrowed her brow in concentration as she sought the right words for explanation. "Most people find Miss Maimie's criticism hard to take, because they are not used to falling short of the standard. They go through life, generally living up to expectations. When Miss Maimie is critical, they are so surprised and hurt, it never occurs to them to question her right to make judgments.

"For myself," Tulsa May said. "I haven't lived up to anybody's standard since the day I was born. My parents wanted a boy. I wasn't. If I was a girl, I should be pretty. I wasn't. If I was not pretty, I should be graceful. I wasn't. If I was not graceful, I should be talented. I wasn't. If I was not talented, I should be sensible. I wasn't."

"You have some wonderful qualities, Tulsa May," Jedwin protested.

"I know that," she agreed. "But I wouldn't have if I hadn't questioned the standard that I was being asked to live up to." Tulsa May blew out a little puff of air as if the call had been close. "I sometimes look at Miss Foote at the school, and I see what could have happened to me. If I believed what other people think about me to be true, why I wouldn't think much of myself at all. I'd just be a shadow of a person, not ever deserving of happiness."

Tulsa May looked at Jedwin, her eyes shining with intelligence and empathy. "But I *questioned* their opinions," she told him quietly. "I *ignored* their judgments and decided that *God* made me the person that I am. It wasn't Miss Maimie's decision." She shrugged cheerfully. "Anyway, it's hard to hold *her* up as the example of contentment."

Jedwin chuckled, agreeing. "So you think we should just be ourselves?"

"I think we should each choose our own standards and rules. Your mother has chosen to live by Miss Maimie's rules. But you can choose to live however you please."

Jedwin reached a soiled hand to raise Tulsa May's chin. "How did you get to be so wise?"

Tulsa May shrugged offhandedly and her eyes sparkled with humor. "I guess it was contemplating philosophy when I should have been learning where to put the demitasse spoons."

The two laughed together for a moment, then Tulsa May spoke again. This time her tone was more serious. "So what are you going to do about Mrs. Briggs?"

Jedwin's hand stilled. "I don't know what you mean."

Tulsa May patted his arm. "Nobody knows," she assured him quickly. "At least I don't think that they do. I figured it out on my own."

Jedwin's maple brown eyes glittered with coldness. "I don't know what you think that you are talking—"

"Mr. Panek told me about the leather pump pieces that you bought," Tulsa May interrupted. "And that apron . . . well, it's exactly like the one my father described seeing at Mrs. Briggs's house."

Jedwin hesitated. "Mrs. Briggs and I are friends."

Tulsa May's mouth widened to a broad gap-toothed grin. "That's what I thought."

Her obvious amusement angered Jedwin. "I don't care what your thoughts or assumptions might be. I will not hear a word against her."

Tulsa May's expression reflected her incredulity. "A word against her?" The young girl laughed with delight. "Why would I say a word against the only other person in this town who cares as little for Miss Maimie's opinion as I do?"

Jedwin couldn't quite believe what he was hearing. He sat staring at her until she flicked a trowel full of personally blended compost-mulched topsoil his way.

Jerking backward, Jedwin sat on his heels and brushed the dirt from the bib of his apron.

"I've always admired Mrs. Briggs," Tulsa May told him. "Though, truth to tell, I don't think I've ever shared even a word with her. But I always thought it was pretty special how she stayed right here in town and didn't so much as flinch, let alone bow her head, before your mother and Miss Maimie."

"Mrs. Briggs has tried to make the best of a bad situation," Jedwin said.

"I know. Even Papa admires her for that. I heard him tell Mama just yesterday that it takes two to break up a marriage."

"Your father's right. Although it certainly took him a while to come around to that conclusion."

Tulsa May grinned. "Papa's recent conversion to spiritually based exercise helped him reached that conclusion, I suspect."

Jedwin nodded in rueful agreement.

"So, do you love her?" she asked.

"What?"

"I said, do you love her?"

Looking back at his work, Jedwin began digging and planting, his jaw set tightly. "Tulsa May, you are a very bright girl, but there are things in this world that you just don't understand."

"You think I'm too young to understand about love?"

"No, not love, per se," Jedwin admitted. "I think you are too young to understand some of the problems that love can cause."

Tulsa May nodded sagely. "I'm sure you're right. I don't understand all of the problems. I just understand that you've seemed happier and freer the last few weeks than I've ever seen you before." She shrugged innocently. "I just thought that might mean you are in love."

Jedwin's long-suffering expression slowly melted to chagrin as he shook his head at the young woman.

"Miss Bruder, those bright brown eyes of yours see entirely too much."

Tulsa May's grin broadened. "Then you do love her?"

With a deep sigh, Jedwin nodded. "Yes, I love her."

Tulsa May sighed wistfully and her eyes looked dreamy. "I'm so happy for you. Of all the adults in town, I like you the best."

"Thank you." Jedwin gave the young girl a look of concern. "You do understand that this is not some fairy tale where everyone lives happily ever after."

Tulsa May's eyes popped open in surprise. "Why not?"

Jedwin wiped his brow on his sleeve and gazed off into the distance. "Real life just doesn't work out that way."

"Doesn't she love you?"

"Yes," Jedwin admitted. "I think that she does."

"Then what's the problem?"

Jedwin turned his eyes to Tulsa May, his mouth drawn into one thin line. "Mrs. Briggs is a divorced woman," he said.

Tulsa May waved away his concern. "Well, that's certainly easy enough to fix."

"How?" Jedwin asked.

"Why, you can marry her."

Chapter
Seventeen

Cora hummed quietly as she stirred the gravy, feeling warm and smug and pleased to have Jedwin Sparrow at her house for supper. Looking up, she almost absently gave him a smile of pleasure before she caught sight of his face. Abruptly she stopped stirring.

"What is it?" she asked.

"I've been doing a lot of thinking," Jedwin began.

"You've made a decision about the farm." Admiration shone in her eyes.

Jedwin nodded. "I'm moving out there. I think if I can spend the winter making some major improvements on the grounds, come next spring it will be ready for a real crop."

Wiping her hands on her apron, Cora looked thoughtful. "You are really giving up the undertaking business completely?"

Jedwin nodded. He reached for her hand and gestured for her to take a seat beside him. "I'm not giving it up. I never chose it. I've always hated embalming," he said quietly. "I guess that's no secret to you."

She gave him a small smile of agreement.

"For years I tried to please my father by following in his footsteps." Jedwin shook his head. "But I couldn't. And Mama wasn't much help. She pushed me even harder than he did."

"Why did she do that?" Cora asked.

"She was scared, I guess," he answered. "You know, I think until the day he died Mama wasn't sure that he would keep us."

"Keep you?"

Jedwin nodded. "Mama was no great catch as a girl. Although she was young and pretty, my grandpa was far from prosperous. I don't think anyone expected her to marry well. Mama was ambitious and smart. And she set out to capture a man who could support her. My father could."

"And she captured him," Cora said.

Jedwin nodded. "I don't think she was ever even quite sure how she'd done it, and she worried all her life that her good fortune might just walk out of her life as easily as he'd walked in."

"Did your mother tell you that?"

Jedwin laughed humorlessly. "Not likely," he said. "I doubt if she would even admit it to herself. But I'm sure that's what she thought."

Taking her smaller hand in his own, Jedwin caressed her fingers, more for his comfort than her pleasure.

"She and my father never loved each other. Mama did tell me that. Of course, she didn't have to. It was very obvious."

"Did they argue?"

"Never," Jedwin answered. "Not a cross word was ever spoken between them." A wry grin warmed his face. "But then, they rarely ever spoke at all. The only things they ever talked about were the business and, of course, me. It was all they had in common."

Cora nodded. "The only things that they both loved?"

"I guess that's true," he said. "But I'm not sure that Mama understood that. I think that she was always afraid that if I failed him as a son, he would turn us out."

"Oh, surely not."

"Certainly he wouldn't have," Jedwin agreed. "Certainly he didn't. And I was a big disappointment to him in the business."

"You just didn't have the talent for it," Cora insisted.

"I just didn't have the stomach for it," Jedwin said more plainly. "I hate working with dead bodies. They are like empty discarded packages of people I once knew. And as for embalming procedures." Jedwin shook his head. "I get light-headed when I cut my own finger. Can you imagine me opening up a body to examine the organs for cause of death?"

"Oh, Jedwin." Cora reached out a hand and caressed the long straight jawline that was smooth and freshly shaven.

"I remember the morning that my father died," he told her quietly. "There was no one else to take care of the body. I knew that I would have to do it."

His intense brown eyes took on a wary, faraway glow.

Cora saw the pain in his eyes and squeezed his hand tightly.

"I dropped down on my knees beside that table." He looked straight at her, so openly, so honestly. "I'd never prayed in that room before or since, but I prayed that day. I knew that I had to prepare my father's body. And I begged God for the strength to do it."

Cora brought his hand to her lips and kissed him tenderly.

He looked up at her now, the intensity of his eyes almost pulling her within him, now that she knew its source.

"With a great deal of help from heaven, I managed to do justice to my father," he said. "More than justice," he admitted. "When I'd placed him in the casket and rolled him into the front parlor, I made a decision."

Jedwin lowered his eyes momentarily and then raised them again to hers. "I fixed up the room until it was perfect. Exactly as he would have done it himself," he said. "Then I told him that I loved him. And I swore I would never prepare another body again as long as I lived."

"Oh, Jedwin," Cora whispered.

The tears were running in rivulets down the side of her face. And Jedwin tried to tenderly erase them with his thumbs.

"I have kept my promise, Cora," he said. "And now I'm making another. I'm giving the business to Mama and I'm going back to the farm. It is where I've always wanted to be, and I do not intend to deprive myself any longer."

Cora was in his arms, holding him tightly. He feathered light gentle kisses in her hair. There was no passion in them, only tenderness. Her poor, brave, honorable Jedwin, she loved him so much. She felt so safe and warm in his arms. Would that it could last forever.

"What is that smell?" he asked suddenly.

Cora pulled from his grasp in momentary confusion as she sniffed the air.

"The gravy!" she cried as she jumped from his arms and ran to the stove.

The steaming white sauce had solidified in the bottom of the skillet and was now a large, very deeply browned gravy-cake.

"Oh no!" Cora exclaimed in dismay.

Jedwin laughed out loud. "It's all right, Cora. Your cooking is not the thing that attracts me most."

*   *   *

Cora awakened slowly, squinting at the faint glow of the lamp beside the bed. Jedwin sat beside her, fully awake. They'd given up on the gravy hours before. She smiled up at him. His chest was bare, as was the rest of him, she suspected. He'd propped a catalog on his knee and was using it as a writing desk for the paper and pen he was using.

"What are you doing?" she asked, her voice gravelly with sleep.

His smile warmed her as he bent down and laid a tiny kiss on the end of her nose. "I'm writing you a poem, Mrs. Briggs," he said. "Isn't that what swains are supposed to do?"

She grinned back at him and yawned, raising her arms high above her head and allowing the sheet to drop from her bared bosom to her waist.

Smiling invitingly at the man beside her, she laid her head against his naked chest. "I think we've gotten past the romance, Jedwin," she said.

"Oh no!" he insisted with feigned disapproval. "We will never be past the romance."

Cora smiled against the firm flesh that covered the muscled young abdomen. Lazily she began twirling the blond hair that grew there.

"Honestly, Jedwin," she said with exaggerated sincerity. "I do prefer having loving with you to listening to your poetry."

His smile turned into a naughty grin. "Honesty does not become you, Cora. Keep lying to me, it makes me feel better."

She laughed. "Oh well then," she said. "I much prefer your clever little rhymes to all those terrible, nasty things you do to me."

His grin broadened. "Terrible, nasty things?" he asked. "Why, Mrs. Briggs, you taught me everything that I know."

She punched him playfully and would have gladly progressed to a spirited wrestling match, but he stopped her.

"I want you to hear my latest effort," he insisted. "Now sit still and listen. Maybe you will hear something important."

"Oh all right," Cora agreed. Sitting up in the middle of the bed, she threw off the quilted covers and turned to sit cross-legged before him, naked.

Jedwin allowed himself a casual perusal of the woman before him. "You are trying to distract me, Mrs. Briggs," he accused.

"Yes," she admitted.

He shook his head firmly and grabbed the cotton bedsheet to drape around her modestly.

"First, listen to my poem," he said. "Then we can celebrate with our bodies."

Cora's expression was teasingly stubborn, but she nodded.

Looking down at the words he'd written, Jedwin bit his lip nervously and looked back at her. Immediately she sensed that this was not another "swain as dumb as a boar hog." A flicker of fear ran through her and she wanted suddenly to stop him, to not allow him to say the words.

Jedwin cleared his throat and began to speak.

> "I love you more, Cora
> Than many would dare.
> You have given life purpose.
> Of your past, I don't care.
> We broke the rules
> When I came to your bed.
> Now, I want to atone.
> I want us to wed."

As he finished, he raised his eyes to look into hers. It was a question. It was a proposal.

A lump of sorrow formed in the back of Cora's throat and she pulled the worn bedsheet more tightly around her. Oh, how she loved him. But she must be cruel.

"Don't be foolish, Jedwin. I will never marry you," she snapped.

Jedwin paled slightly, but swallowed his disappointment. He hadn't expected this to be easy. He had approached it wrong, he knew. He should have kept it more serious.

"I don't need a poem to say that I love you, Cora," he told her. "I do love you. I've told you that already."

Cora shook her head. "It's lust," she said. "You love my body, Jedwin."

He reached out and grabbed her. "Don't try to make it coarse and common," he said. "I love *you*, Cora. I love *you*, and I think I can tell the difference."

She pulled out of his grasp. "Don't love me, Jedwin," she said. "You will only be hurt."

Wrapping the sheet more closely around her, she rose from the bed and hurried behind the dressing screen.

"What are you doing?" he asked.

"I'm getting dressed," she answered. "And you should, too."

"Cora, it's the middle of the night."

"Oh." There was a sneer in her voice. "I suppose that you were hoping for a little morning romp. Well, I am completely out of the mood. Just pull on your pants and go."

Jedwin was across the room in an instant. Jerking up the hinged screen in his hands, he threw it violently against the wall. "Don't hide from me, Cora. We are going to talk about this."

Clad in her muslin drawers, with one arm in her pleated chemise, which dangled around her neck only partially concealing her, Cora was furious.

"Not unless *I* say we are going to talk!" she yelled at him. "You are not my father or my husband. You are just the man I have loving with and that gives you no rights at all."

"Not even the right to love you?"

They stood staring at each other in silence. Both were breathing heavily and both faces flushed with emotion. Both were hurting.

Jedwin regained his balance first. Gently reaching to her, he helped her get her right arm into the camisole and gently smoothed the material down her body, covering her from his sight.

The tenderness in his touch brought tears to her eyes, but she fought them.

"You mustn't love me, Jedwin," she whispered.

"Why not?" he asked. "And don't tell me it's because you don't love me, because I already know that you do."

Covering her face with her hands, she let the threatened tears erupt. "I've tried, Jedwin," she told him. "I've tried not to love you and not to show that I love you."

He wrapped his arms around her loosely, comfortingly, and pulled her back to the bed. Seating himself, he brought her into his arms and rocked her like a baby, cooing quietly with nonsensical words.

"I know you feel that you are a bad woman," he said. "This town has painted you as some kind of wicked sinner and you've begun to believe them."

"No, no, I haven't," she insisted.

"Then what else?" he asked. "All that talk about sin and rules. Good Lord, Cora, you talk more like an ax murderer than a divorcée."

"You don't understand."

"You're right," Jedwin admitted. "I don't understand. I admit we've broken the rules. But I want to marry you."

Cora dug her hands through her hair and shook her head.

"You cannot marry me and you shouldn't love me."

"Why do you keep saying that?"

"Because it's true, I know. I've already been through this once."

"Been through what?"

"This! This . . . this . . . when a man falls in love with the wrong woman."

Jedwin grabbed her chin and raised it to look at her. Her hair was in wild disarray.

"Tell me." He whispered the words, but they still had the ring of command. "Tell me about Luther."

"I thought you didn't care about Luther," she challenged.

"I don't. But I care about you. I care about every breath you've ever taken, every tear you've ever shed, every moment that you've spent without me. Some of those moments were spent with Luther Briggs. Tell me, Cora."

She looked up at him, unsure. "I never talk about it. I rarely ever think about it."

"Then tell it quickly and be done," he said.

She sighed heavily, biting her lip as she raised her tear-streaked face. "Luther Briggs never loved me," she said without emotion. "When he married me he was in love with another woman."

Jedwin's brow furrowed. Somehow he found it difficult to believe that any man could not be in love with Cora.

"Are you sure?"

She chuckled humorlessly. "Oh yes, very sure. He told me so himself."

"And you married him anyway?"

"I was already married to him. He didn't tell me until our marriage was already over."

"Then why did he marry you?"

"To please Miss Maimie." Her tone was no longer sad, it was angry. "Isn't that why everyone in this town does what they do? To please Miss Maimie."

Jedwin shook his head in disbelief. "A man doesn't marry a woman to please his mother."

Cora raised a skeptical eyebrow. "I thought you were planning to marry Tulsa May Bruder?"

He flushed lightly. "But I'm not marrying her now, I'm marrying you."

"Jedwin, Tulsa May Bruder *is* the woman that you should marry."

"Not if I don't love her."

"Then you *should* love her. That's why I wanted to be your mistress, so you would see that I am not fit for your love. Tulsa May or someone like her would deserve you."

"Tulsa May would suit my mother and this town just fine. But she wouldn't suit me." He held on to her tightly. "You say Luther loved another. Would you have me marry Tulsa May and do the same?"

"That's what I'm trying to avoid!"

"You could avoid it by marrying me."

The fight went out of Cora and she lay limply against him. "I can't let you marry me, Jedwin," she said.

"Why not?"

"Because I love you and I want you to be happy. You could never be happy with me."

"I am happy with you."

"You are now. Now, no one knows. But they will know, Jedwin, and they will disapprove."

"I don't care about that."

"Yes you do, Jedwin. You need friendship, you need approval. It's something that you've always craved. Why else have you tried so hard to please your mother, to please your father? If you marry me, Jedwin, no one will be pleased. You will be an outcast."

"But I will have you," he whispered.

"It won't be enough."

"It will be enough for me," he said.

But she knew that it wasn't.

The morning sunlight was shining through the windows of the tiny upstairs study where Amelia took care of her book work. She was humming.

The dress she wore was a pale blue organdy that hadn't been out of her closet in ten years. She'd had a difficult time lacing her corset tight enough to wear it, but the effect was worth the effort. She felt ten years younger. She felt giddy. Although she attempted to keep her mind on her work, time after time her thoughts strayed to Haywood Puser. It had been so long since a man had paid court to her. And she was sure she had never been paid court to by a man like Haywood Puser.

"Haywood." She said the name aloud to hear it on her lips. She liked the sound of it. She liked it very much.

With a tittering little laugh, she wondered if a trip to a regular dentist could have been as enlightening as having a tooth pulled by Mr. Puser. She definitely doubted it.

Seating herself dutifully at her desk, she sorted the piles of papers before her into separate stacks of receivables, payables, and receipts. Allowing herself to be distracted, she gazed almost sightlessly for several minutes out the front window at the cold gray day. Winter was clearly upon them now, but she had never felt warmer.

With a grudging sigh, she pulled out the ledger and began her painstaking paperwork. As she carefully recorded the numbers in the appropriate columns, her mind continued to mull the events of the previous evening.

She had allowed him to eat supper with her. He'd teased her foot under the table. They'd talked business and the weather and the future. And for dessert he had kissed her breathless.

"Let me stay the night, Mellie," he whispered hotly against her neck.

"Absolutely not!" she said, with mock chagrin that he had even asked. "Mr. Puser, you forget yourself."

He'd grinned down at her. "Mellie honey, you make me forget myself."

A wide, blushing smile spread across Amelia's face in remembrance as she recorded the next item in her register.

The movement of her pencil stopped abruptly. She stared at a small receipt. Her face paled and a bitter, angry cold seeped into her veins.

"Oh please, no," she whispered with quiet desperation.

Slowly, she rose to her feet. As she looked out on the cold winter day, her world seemed now almost as bleak as death itself. She felt old. She felt very old and foolish.

Picking up the paper, she calmly carried it out of the room. Walking slowly and deliberately Amelia made her way down the stairs. Her face was blank of expression. Her head was held high with forced pride. She listened to her own footfalls on the stairways as if they were sounding a dirge.

She heard him before she saw him. He was whistling. *Whistling*. A happy man, whistling in celebration of his latest conquest.

Amelia's jaw hardened as she stepped into the embalming room. He was straightening up one of the cupboards. His back was to her as he squatted precariously, whistling his cheerful tune.

She stood watching him for a moment. Silently, solemnly watching as she measured each breath in her chest as if it were her last. From the corner of her eye she caught sight of the broom and she reached for it. Holding it in her hands as if it were a foreign object, she stared at it sightlessly for a moment, before her gaze turned once again to the man who had deceived her.

Fury gave her strength. She raised the broom high above her in a dangerous arc and brought the tightly knitted lengths of straw forcefully upon Haywood Puser's head.

"What the—" he cried, startled.

The force of the blow knocked him to the floor and he lay there momentarily staring at Amelia with stunned disbelief. When she raised the broom to hit him again, he sprang into action.

"Dammit, Mellie, what's the matter with you!" he yelled as he rolled to the left, scrambling to his knees.

"You liar!" she screamed. "You low-down, scheming womanizer!" She punctuated her words with wild swipes of the broom to his head and shoulders.

Haywood managed to get his arm up to ward off the worst of the blows, but he still felt the brunt of her fury.

"What is this about?" he asked her, completely confused and becoming downright angry. "Are you *crazy*?"

"I must be!" Amelia screamed back at him. "To allow a carouser like you to kiss me."

"Carouser?" Haywood shook his head. "Good Lord, Mellie, are you going to always take on so about a little kissing? You enjoyed it as much as I did."

With a furious cry, Amelia raised the broom to strike again, but this time, Haywood grabbed it. With little effort he pulled it out of her grasp and threw it across the room, where it clattered loudly in the silence between them.

"Have you taken leave of your senses?"

"I've just got them back," she assured him. "The moment I saw this!" she said, slapping the crumpled piece of paper into his hand. "Now try to deny what is written there in black and white."

Haywood was totally flabbergasted. With a good deal of curiosity he looked down at the paper in his hand.

"What is it?" he asked.

"You *know* what it is!" Amelia's voice was loud enough to be considered a screech.

"I know *what* it is, Mellie," he said with the last of his patience. Quickly looking over the handwritten notice, he brought his gaze back to hers. "It's a bill of sale for some pump part," he said, "a foot valve."

"*I've* got no broken pump!" she spat furiously.

Haywood shrugged. "Maybe it's a mistake."

"It's a mistake, all right," she said. "And *you* made it. I want you out of here by this afternoon."

She turned her back on him, intending to make a haughty exit. Haywood stared at her for only a minute before reaching out to grab her arm.

"Don't you touch me, you . . . you . . . libertine."

Haywood dropped her arm immediately and his eyes widened in surprise. "Libertine? Good God, Mellie, I just kissed you, dammit. And I must say you don't have a very high opinion of yourself."

With a strangled sound of fury, Amelia turned to him and raised her fist like a drunken cowboy in a saloon fight. Haywood caught it easily and held it, along with her other arm, firmly to her side.

"I don't know what is going on here, Mellie," he said. "But I intend to find out."

"Why don't you just admit it?" she said coldly, her face only inches from his. "Last night you were sweet-talking me and kissing me. But you've been spending most of your time with that big-bosomed divorcée!"

Haywood was so taken aback at her words that he immediately released her.

Taking full advantage, Amelia rushed out of the room and up the stairs. Tears were rolling down her cheeks by the time she made it to her bedroom door. She ignored them as resolutely as she did the pain that had lodged deep inside her.

Letting herself inside her room, she threw herself across the bed and bawled like a young girl with a broken heart.

She hated him! She hated everyone. She hated her father and Big Jim and Haywood. She hated Miss Maimie. None of them had ever loved her. No one could love her. She could never be loved. Her tears gathered in a soggy pool on the lace bedspread beneath her. Only James Edwin loved her, she decided, and that was because it was his duty.

Her intent to wallow in her misery was short-lived for the door to her room burst open and banged loudly against the wall.

With a startled gasp, Amelia sat up immediately. "How dare you!" she accused furiously. "You will leave this room immediately."

"I will leave, Mellie, when I've had my say." As he walked farther into the room, Amelia hurried to her feet. She certainly couldn't be lying on the bed with a man in her room. And she would not allow herself to be at a disadvantage with this womanizer.

She wanted to keep her distance, but Haywood snaked an arm around her waist and pulled her close to him.

"Let me go," she ordered immediately. The smell, the feel, the warmth of him was already too familiar.

"Mellie Sparrow, you are the most disagreeable woman I have ever met in my life," he said quietly. "And if I had any sense at all, I'd let you stew in your own juices for the rest of your life."

His mouth, only inches from hers, seemed suddenly warm and tempting. In her unerring memory she could almost feel the tickle of his beard on her cheeks and throat. It was her own desire that frightened her as she pressed herself more firmly against the wall to get away from him.

"Do you really think that with all the misery you put me through, I'd still pursue you if I had another woman on the side?" He shook his head doubtfully. "Listen, gal, let me tell you right now, you have greatly overestimated your charms."

"Oh!"

"Now don't go getting all insulted," he said, reaching out to catch the hand that she raised with the intent to slap him. "I'm just a man who believes in one woman at a time. Since my wife died, there have been a few, Mellie, I admit it. But never two at once. At my age, I've got neither the time nor the constitution for it."

"You fixed her pump," Amelia insisted, her voice rough and scratchy from the tears she'd shed.

"Whose pump?"

"Cora Briggs's pump," she snapped. "Reverend Bruder said a man had been there and was working on her pump. Now I've got a bill of sale for the parts."

Haywood raised a curious eyebrow.

"If that's not enough," Amelia added, her lip trembling with the revelations, "the preacher said the man had a gray ticking mechanic's apron. I made one like that for James Edwin for his birthday three years ago. It's hanging on the inside of the basement door. That is, *if* you put it back where you found it."

She pushed against him ineffectively, but Haywood felt the strength of her anger. "You borrowed my son's apron," she accused. "And you bought parts in his name to fix a pump for your little lightskirt, your fancy piece, your . . . your divorced woman!"

Haywood stepped back from her and looked into her tear-stained face long and thoughtfully. "Well, I'll be damned." He chuckled lightly.

"What are you laughing about?" Amelia was hoarse with fury.

Haywood looked down into her eyes and raised a wary eyebrow. "Well, Mellie," he said. "I could tell you, but I doubt you would find it as amusing as I do."

Leaning forward then, not touching her anywhere but on her lips, he kissed her, slowly, languidly, totally unconcerned for the complaints she uttered against his mouth.

"Mellie honey," he said as he stepped away from her. "I've never been within ten feet of Cora Briggs. We haven't even shared so much as a lingering howdy-do. I'd like for you to believe that, but if you don't, well—"

He turned to leave and Amelia watched him walk out of the room, her heart weighed with a heaviness of sorrow. He sounded so sincere. Could she believe him? She wanted to believe him. But what about the evidence? Amelia ran out to the hallway.

"If you didn't do it, then who did?" she asked him from the top of the stairs.

He looked back at her thoughtfully, as if considering his reply. "You look right pretty in that little blue dress, Mellie," he said.

Momentarily distracted, Amelia looked down at the brightly colored dress she'd donned this morning. The dress she'd donned for Haywood Puser, the new man in her life.

The new man that she trusted.

As Haywood turned once again to go, the cobwebs dissolved in Amelia's mind and suddenly she saw everything clearly.

"James Edwin," she whispered in disbelief.

With the cold weather fixing to set in, Cora was determined to empty the ash bin on the stove. Several times she'd thought to ask Jedwin to do it, but when he was around she could never remember. Now she was glad. It was best not to get any more dependent on him than she already was. Besides, a lone woman "getting her ashes hauled" by a handsome young single man was becoming a bawdy cliché.

Sliding a wooden crate under the floor skirting of the stove, she carefully covered the surrounding area with an old sheet. If she actually dropped the pan, the sheet wouldn't be much help. But if she only spilled a bit of ashes, it would be a lifesaver.

The room wasn't just chilly, it was downright cold. She'd let the fire go out last night and hadn't lit it all day. She wanted the coals good and dead. She could not risk a fire. Carefully easing the pan out of its grooves, she found it difficult to keep her mind on her task.

Jedwin Sparrow had asked her to marry him. He wanted to live out on his grandfather's farm and raise wheat, oats, and flowers, and have her to be his wife, his partner, his helpmate. Tears pooled in Cora's eyes. There was nothing that she wanted more.

It was the life that she had always envisioned for herself when she'd lived in the Methodist Home. And if she were free to choose, he was the man she wanted to share it with. But it could never be.

Gently, Cora set the nearly overflowing ash pan into the crate.

It was strange that she rarely blamed Luther for her problems. He was certainly not blameless. He was weak and disloyal and a liar. She should still hate him. But she realized that she didn't. He had broken the rules of society, deliberately, knowingly. And like most culprits he'd assumed that no one would ever suffer for it but himself.

Jedwin wanted to believe the same.

She had tried desperately to make him understand. To make him see the truth as it really was. But he would not. Perhaps he *could* not. Maybe a person had to live through disaster before fully understanding.

Cora Briggs *had* lived through it. She had done nothing wrong in her marriage to Luther. Waking each morning with a smile on her face, she had only one ambition: to make a peaceful, happy home for her husband. She had done everything in her power to be a good, loyal, and dutiful wife. It was all she had wanted. In those cold, lonely days with Pa and later in the pristine politeness of the good Methodists, she had longed for only one thing—a home.

She had worked hard for her home, and if life were fair, she should have lived happily ever after. But life was never fair. She'd learned by experience that the rain sometimes fell harder on the just. When rules were bent the innocent as well as the guilty were punished.

In memory she could see him again. Standing so tall and handsome next to the door, his black hair slicked down with sweet-smelling pomade and his form as handsome as any man she'd ever seen.

"I never meant to hurt you," Luther had told her sorrowfully on that last day of their life together. "I really thought that it would work." He shook his head in disbelief at the misery that had come to pass. "You would never know about her, and she would never know about you. And my mother would be happy and none would be the wiser.''

"But I am wiser," Cora had answered, her voice as cold as any territory winter. She hadn't slept in days and her eyes were red and swollen from hours of tears. "I am wiser now than I ever wanted to be. I would not wish such wisdom on another person."

"Oh Cory." His eyes pleaded for forgiveness, but it wasn't in her then.

"Get away from me, Luther," she said. "Leave this house today. Leave and go to *her*."

"I am so sorry, Cory," he whispered.

"You should be," she said, giving no quarter. "Now go to the woman you should have never left and try to make up to her for what you have done." Cora looked away and bravely raised her chin to face the loneliness of her future. "Your children have the only chance of happiness in this," she said quietly. "I won't take that away from them."

He'd walked away then. Leaving her with a house of her own, a shiny new bicycle, and a reputation she didn't deserve but could never live long enough to overcome.

Cora sighed as she covered the crate of ashes with a damp towel to keep them from scattering in the wind. Her heart was as heavy as the fully loaded crate.

Was Luther happy now? It was a question she rarely asked herself. In truth, she hoped that he was. He had given up his fortune, his home, his heritage, even his mother, for the woman that he loved. You could almost admire a man for that.

She did. And she admired Jedwin who was willing to do the same. But it was too big a sacrifice and she was not going to allow him to throw his life away on a disastrous marriage. She loved him too much.

Dragging the heavy crate to the doorway, Cora stopped to pull on her coat and scarf. She was hot from her labors and hated the warm weight of the coat, but stepping outside, damp, in the cold air was simply asking for trouble. And although the diphtheria was no longer a threat, Cora couldn't risk even a head cold. She was a woman alone, she reminded herself. There was no one to care for her, not now, not ever.

The air was crisp and cold as she stepped outside with only a light wind blowing a chill through her clothes. She could taste the moisture in the air and predicted that there would be snow before morning. The scent of the afternoon was flavored with wood smoke as the chimneys of each house added a bit of gray to the sky.

Cora made her way to the shed where she retrieved her shovel and the wheelbarrow. The latter was burdened with a wheel as creaky as hundred-year-old bones and a large rust hole in one corner of the barrow, but it would hold a crate of ashes, Cora was sure.

She hadn't been able to convince Jedwin that it would ruin him to marry her, so she had to think of some way to discourage Jedwin from *wanting* to marry her.

It was too late for the usual discouragements, she admitted to herself. He already knew she was a regular for bathing. She hid no horrible flaws beneath her clothing. And he didn't care that she wasn't the best cook in town. He said that he loved her hair, although it was frequently untidy. And he'd described her backside as generous rather than broad.

Cora shook her head thoughtfully. If women spent such an amount of their time working on ways to draw men to them, then surely there must be equally effective ways of pushing them away.

She loaded the crate of ashes on the wheelbarrow, stopping to scoop out a bucketful that she left near the door. If it did snow tonight, she'd sprinkle them on her back step.

Her thoughts still far away, Cora rolled the crate of ashes out to her big prized pecan. She'd lay a thin circle of ashes around the base of the tree. Ashes were an old Indian remedy for keeping the bugs off nut trees. While fancy solutions could now be purchased for insect control, ashes were not only cheaper but better.

What could she do to drive Jedwin away? she wondered. She could claim not to love him. But he'd already said that he knew that she did. She could act shrewish and difficult. But with *his* mother, Cora thought wryly, he was probably used to that.

When her circle of ashes was spread neatly and evenly beneath the tree, Cora propped her shovel once more against the side of the wheelbarrow and started back across the yard.

The rest of the ash pan contents would be sprinkled upon the garden. This was a cautious and careful procedure. A shovelful of ashes poured over a straight line, downwind. A few ashes could add lime to the soil, enriching it and protecting it from insects. Too many ashes would kill the ground, making it unfit to grow even the sturdiest of weeds. She smiled to herself. Mrs. Millenbutter would have described it as balance.

There must be a simple, certain way to get a man out of your life, she thought. Men were always leaving women. Half the songs written said as much. What did those women do to send those men away? Suddenly, as if the answer had been swimming around in her head, a tune came to her lips.

> "Jaimie had sworn that he loved her.
> 'Til he'd found out that she was untrue.
> Now he's happily wed to another.
> And thinks of her never, would you?"

Cora stopped the careful dusting of the garden to contemplate the words. "'Til he found out that she was untrue." That was it. That was the secret. No man, not even a man who claimed to love, would stay by a woman who had betrayed him.

Could she make him believe that she *had* betrayed him? It wouldn't be easy. He might look for a scheme, a plot to outwit him. A strange frightening feeling came over her. She swallowed nervously and set the shovel point down in the dirt, her arms no longer strong enough to hold it upright. If she truly wanted to send Jedwin away, she must do more than try to make him *think* she betrayed him.

She must betray him.

The image of Titus Penny came immediately to her mind. She could see him again sitting at his desk. His smile leering and suggestive. That stringy brown hair and that annoyingly overwaxed moustache did not spark desire in her breast. "That big old bed of mine down on the corner can get mighty cold of a night," he'd said so smugly.

Cora ran a glove-covered hand through her hair, only to discover it was trembling too much to straighten her errant locks.

"I can't do it," she whispered aloud.

It was the only way, the only sure way to let Jedwin go. The words of the song haunted her. 'Now he's happily wed to another, and thinks of her never, would you?'

That's what Cora wanted for him. Happily wed to Tulsa May Bruder and thinking of her never, ever. No lingering tender longings that would cheat his wife. No tempting daydreams of what might have been or what could be again.

Could she do it? Could she betray Jedwin with Titus Penny? She swallowed nausea in the back of her throat. She had learned a long time ago that she could do whatever she had to.

Cora raised her chin and spoke the words aloud, determinedly, defiantly. "You've had two men already. One more shouldn't make much difference."

Chapter
Eighteen

"Could I speak with you in the family parlor, please?"

Jedwin looked up from the basin where he was washing up to see his mother in the mirror behind him. Her question was spoken in such a way as to suggest a command rather than a request.

It was as good a time as any, Jedwin decided as he wiped his face with a towel and retrieved his shirt from the back of a chair. He wanted to talk to her, too.

Following her downstairs, he could feel the tension in the air. His mother was angry. He regretted that. He'd hoped that he could explain the new directions he'd decided for his life without much fuss from her. He was, however, ready to take on her arguments whatever they might be.

They stepped into the parlor. Amelia walked to the center of the room before turning to look at him.

"Why don't you sit, Mama," Jedwin said politely.

Her eyes were as hard as flint. "No thank you, James Edwin, I believe I choose to stand."

"Very well," he answered, moving over to the fireplace where he could at least lean on the mantel. It was the height of bad manners for a gentleman to sit while a lady stood, and Jedwin was not willing to give his mother that advantage. "I have been wanting to speak with you."

"Oh, you have?" Amelia clasped her hands together, and raised her chin purposefully. "Well, I've wanted to speak with you also. But you are away from the house so much these days, I hardly know your comings and goings."

"You've been busy yourself," Jedwin pointed out. "With the epidemic scare and running to and from Low Town, you've certainly kept on the move."

"I was out doing my Christian duty," she said with cool self-righteousness. "I know my duty and I do it without complaint."

Did she? Jedwin wondered, but kept his doubts to himself.

"And while I was busy ministering to the sick," his mother said, "how exactly were you occupying yourself?"

"I've been working at the farm. I managed to get all the oats in the barn and have started some improvements on the place."

Assuming his statement was merely an alibi, Amelia disregarded it. "I'm sure that was a novelty," she said lightly. "Pursuing some useful endeavor."

Jedwin's eyes widened at the insult but chose to ignore it. "I realize that a huge burden was placed on yourself and Haywood. But I would remind you, Mama, that you forbade my help."

Amelia's mood was combative. "Would it have done any good to have you help us?" she asked.

It was a clear cut and the wound of Jedwin's pride was sharp, but he bore it. She spoke the truth. He had had no intention of helping them in the embalming room, even if they had asked. There were things in his life that he could not, would not, do. But, he told himself sternly, there were others that he could. And it was time that he start doing things of which he was capable and stop mourning those he was not.

"I've made some decisions about my life," he said. "I intend to make some changes that will, to some extent, affect you."

Jedwin turned to pace the room, gathering his words with careful prudence. His mother would not be pleased with his decision to farm, but he was sure that he could convince her to accept it as inevitable.

Had he glanced up at her, he would have seen Amelia's dark look. She raised her eyebrows and commented tartly, "I hope your decisions include mending your evil ways."

Jedwin turned to stare at her, his expression masked. "Whatever do you mean, Mama?"

Amelia raised her chin and spoke sternly. "I believe you know exactly what I mean, James Edwin."

Looking at his mother's rigid features, a trickle of apprehension flowed through him. "You will have to speak plainly," he said softly. "I cannot read your mind."

"No you cannot," she agreed shrewishly. "But I am sure that you know it!" Amelia Sparrow folded her arms across her chest and stared at her son with daggers in her eyes. "I would never have thought," she said, raising her voice to a high decibel, "that after all the Christian principles and social responsibilities that have been taught to you in this house, that I would be forced to speak about a subject so abhorrent to me."

Jedwin stared in silence as his mother gathered her sanctimonious outrage around her like a cloak.

"I cannot in this world believe that a son of mine, a young gentleman with the best advantages and of the highest moral example, would sink to consorting with a female of the worst sort."

Jedwin's eyes narrowed and he felt the anger rising like burning gall in his throat. So she knew. Momentarily he wondered who had told her, but it didn't really matter. He had wanted to wait until he and Cora were wed, but it was not to be. "Cora Briggs is not a 'female of the worst sort,'" he said flatly.

Amelia's eyes sparkled with the fire of fury. "My heavens!" she said with sardonic mockery. "What sort is she then, James Edwin?"

Jedwin held his temper, but only barely. "She is *my* sort, Mama."

"You admit it?" Amelia nearly spat the words at him before laying a hand on her chest as if she had been stabbed. "Have you no shame?"

Jedwin's brown eyes were as dark as midnight and colder than the worst mid-winter as he scanned his mother. "There is nothing to be ashamed of. You know nothing about Cora, or about what she deserves," he said. "She is a divorcée, Mama, not a murderess."

"The way you defend *Cora*," Amelia replied, "clearly says that she is more than just a divorcée. She is your mistress!"

Jedwin opened his mouth to reply, but closed it abruptly. He stared at his mother stonily. His silence was condemning.

"You don't deny it," Amelia accused.

"It is none of your concern," Jedwin answered calmly.

"I am your mother!"

"If I were not already aware of that, the fact that you tell me so daily would lead me to that conclusion."

"I've sacrificed my whole life for you."

He shrugged with deliberate unconcern. "You've told me that often enough.

But in honesty, what you mean is that you expect me to sacrifice *my* life for you."

Amelia's mouth dropped open in disbelief, stung to the core. Without conscious thought she raised her hand and brought it forcefully across his face. Blood splattered from his broken lip onto his crisp white shirt. Amelia stared at the bright red stain with horror.

Jedwin's hand came up to his bleeding lip. His jaw trembled in anger. He quickly stepped away from her, crossing the room to turn his back on her and gather his temper.

Amelia was silent with disbelief at her own actions. Words of apology sprang to her lips. She choked them back. Tears gathered in her eyes, but she would not relent and allow them to flow. She bit her own lip painfully as she stared at the straight, strong back that was turned against her. He was her son. He had always done what she wished. But this was new, this was different.

She took several long, deep breaths before she attempted to speak. "I am not unaware," she began in quiet, but clipped tones, "that many young men will have occasion to sow some wild oats."

At the sound of the term, so reminiscent of his own words, Jedwin was stung. He turned to his mother.

"It is not 'wild oats,' Mama," he declared forcefully. "I love Cora Briggs. I intend to marry her."

Bringing her hand to her throat in shock, Amelia paled visibly. "You can't mean it?"

Jedwin's gaze held steady. "I do mean it, Mama. So I would suggest that you hold back any scurrilous statements you wish to make concerning my intended."

"Your intended." The words slipped through Amelia's lips with whispered disbelief. "You have asked her to marry you?"

"Yes, I have."

Amelia could only stare at her son. "You don't know what you are doing."

Jedwin bristled. "I know exactly what I am doing, Mama. I am a grown man and do not need you to lead me around like a trained bear."

"How dare you?"

"How dare I? This is me, Mama, James Edwin. You don't have to resort to pretense in front of me, do you? We both know the truth here. Am I the only one who will admit it?"

"I have been a good mother to you—" Amelia began in defense.

"I have not disputed that," Jedwin interrupted. "But you have tried to make me live my life as you saw fit."

"I've tried to lead you to do what's best."

"I should be the one to know what is best for me."

"You are just a boy."

"I am a man."

"Oh yes," Amelia scoffed. "Now that you've writhed in sin with some harlot you think you are a man."

"I have *known* I was a man since the day my father died," Jedwin told her evenly. "Do you remember when my father died?"

"Of course I remember!"

"Sometimes I think that you don't. You've conveniently forgotten those first months. You've forgotten how you leaned on me, how you needed me. You've forgotten how frightened and scared and weak you felt facing the world. You've forgotten the floods of tears you shed on my shirtfront."

His voice was cool and his temper was calm. "I have not forgotten. But when you became strong again, I was happy for you. I love you, Mama. I wanted you to be yourself again. So, I've let you play your little games. I've listened to your unending advice. And I've tried to do those things that you've wanted. That is at an end," he said. "I love Cora Briggs and I am going to marry her. If you don't like that, I am sorry, but I will not be changing my mind."

Tears ran down Amelia's cheeks as she shook her head. "She will drag you down," she told him. "No one in this town will ever accept you. How can you run a business if the community disapproves of your marriage?"

"I don't intend to run a business," Jedwin replied calmly. "I am giving the mortuary to you. It was you who earned it, after all. I'm going to farm. It won't matter what people think of a lowly farmer."

"James Edwin, I beg you. Don't throw your life away. Cora Briggs is not worthy of you. You should have a wife of your own, not another man's leavings. You deserve more than this woman."

Jedwin stared at his mother silently for a moment before an unexpected smile began to twitch at the corner of his mouth. "What an irony," he said to her with the lightest of humorless chuckles.

Amelia stared in amazed horror at her son's amusement.

"What can you find to laugh about?" she questioned him in astonishment.

"This is truly the funniest thing," he said, shaking his head and laughing ruefully. "You and Cora are in exact agreement."

*   *   *

The snow fell from the sky in huge flakes the size of twenty-dollar gold pieces. Fortunately, the ground was still warm enough to melt them on contact. For that reason, Cora did not slow her step as she hurried to the Penny Grocery and Dry Goods.

She did not usually walk to town, much preferring the modern haste afforded by her Hawthorne Safety with the duplex drop-frame. Today, however, she didn't ride because she didn't wish to dress in her usual bicycling costume. Wearing her rusty brown walking skirt with her pale peach blouse, she thought she looked her best. And her best was exactly what was required.

She had agonized over her decision until late into the night. In her head she knew that it was the perfect plan and the answer to her problem. Her heart, however, cringed from the terrible finality of it. She had decided at last to let her head rule. It was following her heart that had gotten her into this mess.

Reaching the front of the store, she casually mounted the two block steps. Surreptitiously she glanced through the oval window of the door to see who was inside. She wasn't sure she could face a soul this morning. And she was positive that she couldn't face either Jedwin or his mother.

Luck was with her. The store was warm, quiet, and empty. A snappy orange fire crackled in the big potbellied stove in the corner and there was no one but Titus in sight.

Quickly straightening her collar and brushing down her skirt, Cora stepped inside.

At the jingle of the bell over the door, Titus looked up. Seeing her, he nodded before glancing guiltily around the store.

"It's pretty cold out there this morning," he commented.

Nodding vaguely, Cora removed her coat and hung it on one of the hooks in the corner. Her reflection in the small mirror above the hooks startled her. Her color was high, her cheeks bright as cherries. And her eyes glittered with a strange emotion that looked like fear. It was merely the cold, she told herself.

As she walked across the room, Titus motioned to her to follow him into the back. She obeyed without comment. But soon found the crowded back room seemed especially so this morning. Cora attempted to keep her distance from Titus among the boxes and crates. At the same time, she urged herself to approach him and get it over with.

She had thought about the visit, planned what she might say, over and over again. She hadn't thought that it would be easy, but she hadn't imagined how difficult it was going to be.

"I see that you've survived the diphtheria without trouble," Titus said conversationally.

Cora glanced up and nodded vaguely. "Yes, and you too," she said.

The silence between them lengthened. Cora tried to rally her nerve but time and again it failed her.

Titus made his way over to his work area and seated himself in the chair. Casually he leaned back and put his feet up on the desk.

Cora felt his eyes on her. It made her feel queasy. If she couldn't bear for him to look at her, how was she going to allow him to touch her? With hell-bent determination, she turned to look at him.

Titus clasped his hands behind his head in a casual pose and smiled with pleasure. "I've got some wonderful news for you, Cora honey," he said.

"News?" she asked.

"Yes, ma'am," he answered, lowering the timbre of his voice. His grin was impudently familiar. "I was worried, as I'm sure you were too, that with the store shut down for so long, those pecans you brought me would rot in the box."

Cora stared at him for a moment, uncomprehending. She had completely forgotten about the cash crop that was to get her through the winter.

"The pecans," she said stupidly.

"That's right, Cora honey," he told her eagerly. "Well, don't you worry your pretty head about it a minute longer. What is left of them are still looking fresh and fine. And"—he chuckled lightly at his own expense—"truth to tell, you were exactly right, you know. They sold very well."

"I'm glad," Cora answered absently.

"Yes, ma'am," he said, grinning as he motioned her to come closer. "I'm going to be able to do right fair by you this year."

"That's good," Cora answered, sounding completely uninterested.

His expression puzzled, Titus sat straight in his chair and leaned forward, looking at her closely. "Are you all right, Cora honey?"

Cora didn't feel all right. She felt sick and scared and frightened. "I'm fine," she told Titus, forcing a less than impressive smile to her face.

Titus continued to look at her curiously for a moment, before he shrugged. "Well, I think I can safely assure you that you've got enough money to keep you in flour and meal for the winter."

"That's nice," she answered woodenly. Turning from his gaze, stifling in the warmth and closeness of his hovering nearness, Cora wandered idly around the storeroom looking at everything and not looking at anything.

Titus watched her and began to fidget as the tension of the room became palpable.

"I hear Preacher Bruder is taking up your exercise regimen," he said.

Cora returned to him and nodded absently.

Titus smiled. "He's got my Fanny walking and deep breathing already. She says she might even take up gymnastics after the baby comes."

"I'm sure it will be good for her," Cora replied.

Titus laughed lightly. "And getting the preacher interested in all this nonsense has been pretty good for you."

"What?"

"I know the good reverend had got a bee in his backside about your getting your fence painted and your pump fixed."

Embarrassment stained Cora's cheeks. "I have a right to a painted fence and a working pump," she snapped.

Titus held up his hands as if to ward her off. "I ain't saying you don't, honey," he said with a smug grin. "I think a pretty woman like you is entitled to whatever she can get for herself."

Cora paled and fought the nausea that threatened her. She turned to him with her chin raised defiantly. "You are exactly right, Titus," she said.

Penny started slightly at the use of his given name, but recovered quickly. "Did you come here for a reason, Cora honey? You got some trouble or something, well, I cain't stand down the preacher, but I'd do what I could."

Cora's expression softened slightly. He wasn't lying. She knew that he would do what he could for her. He could be a kind and decent man. But he could also be a pompous, weak-minded skirt-chaser. And that was the Titus Penny that she needed to see today.

"Your wife hasn't had the baby yet," she commented with studied nonchalance as she came to stand in front of him and leaned forward to prop her elbows on the desk.

He looked at her strangely, as if taken aback both by the question and her unexpected approach. "Why no," he said, puzzled.

Her bravado faltered and her lip began to tremble. For the sake of her pride, she gave her back to him. It appeared a coy gesture, but was truly one of self-preservation. She walked away from him. She wanted to keep walking, but she could not. She had come this far. She was this close. She had to do it. She had to do it for Jedwin.

Cora turned to Titus again. A whole room separated them. More, a whole world separated them. "Is your bed still cold and lonely?" she asked him quietly, controlling the tremor in her voice.

Cora saw his eyes widen in shock. Titus coughed as if choking on his own reply. He looked at her skeptically, as if not quite believing.

"What are you up to, Cora Briggs?"

Raising her chin high, Cora stiffened her back and walked toward him. "I'm asking you if you're needing a woman in your bed, Titus."

She saw the perspiration bead on his upper lip. He rose to his feet and, putting one hand on his hip, postured like a bantam rooster.

"I might be," he answered her with an overblown assurance that wasn't quite made credible.

Cora swallowed bravely and gave him what she hoped was a winsome smile. "Why don't you come over to my house this evening and we'll see if we can warm each other up and end some of this loneliness."

Titus took a step forward and tripped over something nonexistent. Nervously he righted himself, pretending that his clumsiness hadn't happened.

Cora waited, watching him. Listening for his answer, but not ready for it. Never ready for it. His answer, whether yes or no, would be a humiliation that she could never outlive.

Titus continued to look at her warily. "How much?" he asked finally.

"How much what?" Cora was puzzled by his question.

He gave her a worldly-wise look that didn't quite ring true. "How much is this 'warming up' you're offering going to cost me, Cora honey?"

Paling visibly, Cora felt as if she'd been slapped. She hadn't anticipated the question and the insult of it cut.

Stubbornly she planted a welcome smile on her face. "Let's just say I'm like the pickles in your barrel," she told him. "The first sampling is free."

She turned to walk away from him, her heart pounding like a drum. She had done it. She had finally become the cheap tramp Maimie Briggs had made her out to be.

When she reached the doorway, she turned back to Titus. His worldly bravado was all gone and he stared at her with near disbelief. Another minute, Cora thought, and his tongue would be hanging out.

"Don't show up until it gets dark," she told him with pragmatic concern. "And come to the back door."

Titus nodded speechlessly. Cora made her way outside, her legs feeling like rubber, barely capable of holding her up. She was doing the right thing, she assured herself. Jedwin would find out her perfidy soon enough and he would go on and live the normal life he deserved.

The stinging at the back of her eyes became tears and she pulled the brim of her hat low as she hurried back to her house. She *was* doing the right thing, she reminded herself. She loved him. Enough lives had been ruined. She would see that his was not.

Chapter
Nineteen

The snow fell more heavily, but it was her own tears that obscured her vision. Cora didn't see the man sitting on her front porch until she had stepped through the gate.

"Jedwin!" Her exclamation was a near shout of surprise. "What are you doing waiting on the front porch? Someone will see you."

Jedwin rose lazily to his feet. "Maybe I'm hoping that somebody does." He looked handsome and welcoming in his dark coat, sprinkled with snowflakes, the bulk of which had collected in his hat brim. Then as the woman he waited for came closer, his expression changed suddenly.

Cora lowered her eyes and tried to step past him, but it was too late. Jedwin pulled her into his arms and raised her chin to look at her.

"You've been crying," he said. It was not a question, but his tone intimated one.

Jerking her chin out of his hands, Cora tried to move away. "It's nothing."

Jedwin wouldn't free her, but rather wrapped his arms more protectively around her. "It is something," he insisted quietly. "Any tear you shed is more precious to me than diamonds."

Cora chuckled bravely. "You *are* becoming a poet, Jedwin, after all."

"Love can bring the poetry out of a man," he said.

She struggled within his grasp and he immediately released her. "I don't want to hear that, Jedwin."

"I know," he answered quietly. "Both the women in my life are crying today."

Cora looked up.

"And," he continued, "both are crying because I love you."

"You *told* your mother?" Cora's words were whispered in disbelief.

Jedwin merely nodded. "I can't prevent my mother's tears," he said. "But I will wipe away yours, Cora."

"Please, just go, Jedwin," she pleaded. "Someone will see you."

He shook his head. "It doesn't matter. I love you, Cora." Whether it is what you wanted or not, you are my woman. And I don't go anywhere anymore, without you."

"Don't talk that way, Jedwin," Cora insisted.

But Jedwin leaned toward her, gently touching his lips to her own. Then slipping his arm behind her legs he lifted her to his chest.

"What are you doing?" Cora protested as Jedwin carried her into her house.

"I'm going to take you upstairs and dry those tears in your eyes," he answered.

"Jedwin, this is foolish. Your mother will forgive you and you can still go back," she said as he stepped across the threshold with her in his arms.

"Cora," he told her, looking down at her warmly. "You should know by now that I don't want to go back. I only want to go forward. And that only if I can go there with you."

He took the steps easily and a little hurriedly, as if he could not wait to lay her on her bed. And he didn't. Crossing the bedroom with unseemly haste, he laid her in the middle of the bed and immediately joined her and hugged her to him.

"Jedwin, please."

He grinned down at her. "Do you remember the first time I came to visit?"

"It is something we should forget," Cora told him firmly.

"I'd like that, too." He laughed easily, unconcerned. "You should have knocked some sense into me that night," he said. "A mighty blow to the side of my head and orders to get myself out of your house. That's what I deserved," he said. "But you didn't, did you, Cora?"

"I should have!"

"But you didn't. You decided to teach me a lesson instead."

Cora squirmed under him, attempting to avoid the tenderness of this conversation.

"You decided to teach me about romance. I think I've been a very enthusiastic student." He placed a tiny kiss on the end of her nose.

Still struggling, Cora deliberately tried to take offense at his words. "Is that what you want to hear, Jedwin? What a debonair swain you have become?"

His grin was wicked. "You may save your praise for later, sweetheart," he told her. "Today, I am going to be the teacher."

"What?"

Jedwin raised himself up on his knees and knelt before her on the bed. "I intend to teach you how to say that you love me."

"I do not *want* to love you!" she declared adamantly.

He nodded. "I know, Cora," he said. "But you do. And I'm going to help you to say it. In fact, you won't be able to stop yourself."

Cora looked clearly skeptical, but Jedwin was unconcerned. He began undoing the buttons of his coat. "I know it's a little chilly in here, but you needn't be so bundled up."

Cora's coat, still slightly damp from melted snowflakes, was much too warm for inside the house. Sitting up, she tried to move away. Jedwin was kneeling on her skirt.

"Let me up," she said to him.

"No," Jedwin answered easily.

Raising her eyes to look at him, Cora was confused. "Let me up," she ordered more frantically. "I need to take my coat off."

Jedwin's grin was absolutely wicked. "I'm sorry, ma'am," he told her with feigned humility. "I can't let you up today until you tell me that you love me. I can help you with your wrap, however."

"Jedwin!" Cora complained. Her face was screwed up in stern disapproval.

"We just undo these buttons here," Jedwin told her. "And we peel this cloak off your back like skin off a potato."

"I am not a potato," Cora insisted with the force of her remaining dignity.

"No, ma'am," Jedwin agreed. "Potato wouldn't describe you at all. Why, you are sweet as ripe peaches," he said as he pulled the damp wool away from her bosom. "And you're as warm and smooth as breakfast grits on a winter morning." His hand ran the length of her back as he freed her from her coat.

Casually he tossed it on the floor beside the bed. Cora moved as if to rise again, but once more Jedwin stayed her.

"Now, Miss Peach Grits, where do you think you are going?"

"Let me up, Jedwin," Cora said but not quite as insistently as before.

Jedwin threw his own coat on the floor with hers. Leaning forward, he worried the buttons on the front of her pale peach blouse.

She slapped at his hands. "Stop it!"

He gave her a teasing wink. "Miss Peach Grits, I swear that your name doesn't tell the whole story about you."

He'd managed to open her blouse and was systematically releasing the hooks on the front of her corset. "There is definitely a sour-persimmon aspect of your nature," Jedwin assured her. "And a hard shell around your heart that's more formidable than those native pecans of yours."

With a good deal of skill he managed to pull open her corset. Her chemise was thin and nearly translucent, but he still saw it as a nuisance and smoothed it hurriedly up to her neck, baring her to the waist.

Cora's breath caught in her throat as he casually lifted one breast in his hand, assessing it thoughtfully. "You may taste as sweet as peaches," he told her. "But these are looking a bit more like melons, I'd say."

Before she had time to comment, Jedwin opened his mouth against her. There was only sweet pleasure in his touch and the most dangerous threat was his teeth teasing across her swollen nipple.

Cora buried her hands in his hair, reveling in the warmth, the tenderness, of having him in her arms again.

Just one more time, she vowed silently to herself. *Just one more time and she would set him free forever.*

She arched her back, offering her bosom, but then he pulled his face up to her own. She wanted to taste his lips.

Pulling back from her, Jedwin soothed the low moan in her throat. "Yes, sweet Peach Grits," he whispered. "We'll get to that, we'll get to all of it."

On his knees, he slowly released the buttons on his shirt. His eyes were almost black with intensity as he slowly removed the shirt from his body. The fasteners on his gray-ribbed undershirt was disengaged just as easily and it followed the rest of the discarded clothing to the pile at the side of the bed.

The snowy afternoon was gray, but the light in the bedroom was perfectly good. "Look at me," Jedwin whispered.

Cora's brown eyes met his much richer ones.

Slowly, his fingers worked along the pin of his belt buckle. He slipped it from its notch with one long brown finger. But his eyes never left Cora.

Her mouth went unexpectedly dry as she watched him. Loosening the buckle, he began to lazily draw the belt through the loops of his trousers. Slowly, so slowly, the length of leather in his hand grew longer and longer.

Cora held her breath as he pulled it finally from the last loop and held the smooth brown cowhide in his hand. To her own surprise, she reached out to touch the supple leather. It was still warm, warm from the heat of his body.

"Nice belt," Cora said, trying for a light tone. Her voice cracked slightly.

Jedwin leaned forward, his bare chest brushing against her own as he looped the belt over the top of the headboard.

"I've heard it said this is how some of the Cherokees marry."

Her eyes widened, then suddenly appeared haunted.

"Yes," she told him. "That is the way."

"Listen to me, Cora." He raised her face to look at him, softly pulling her thoughts from some strange place she'd allowed them to go. "Let you and God witness," he said, "that I've hung my belt here above you. I'll never hang it on another woman's bed."

He brought his hand to her cheek and caressed her softly. "I would make vows to you in a church with a ring," he said. "But you won't let me. So this is my vow. I will never love another as long as we live. In my mind, from this moment until forever, I am your husband."

"No, Jedwin—"

"I can't take it back, Cora," he said with two fingers against her lips. "You've won me."

He kissed her then, sweetly, lovingly, with all his being. His lips tasted her lightly, deeply, and then lightly again. His hands ranged over the naked flesh of her arms and breasts. His legs fidgeted restlessly against her skirts, eager to find a more intimate embrace.

She clung to him. Eagerly she accepted his kisses and urged him to take more.

He wanted to oblige her, but felt he needed her to say she loved him. The feeling was too precious not to share. Disengaging himself, he kneeled before her once more.

"I am going to please you," he told her. "That is another vow I make to you. No man has ever *wanted* to please you as I do." His voice drifted off into a whisper.

Cora's breath caught in her throat as she looked into the intensity of his gaze. A tense ball of flame seemed to tighten a pulse inside her and she clenched her thighs to resist the ache that his words provoked.

"I want to hear you say that you love me," he told her quietly. "I know that you do, but still I want to hear you say it." His voice lowered into a husky whisper. "I am going to kiss you in a thousand ways. I will find places to put my lips that no man has ever touched and I'll make you my own. I'll give you such pleasure you will dream only of me for the rest of your life. And you will tell me you love me," he said. "I know that you will."

He moved closer, gently caressing the soft down of her cheek.

"I want to be more than your lover," he told her. "Let me prove to you that I am all you long for. I will be your home, your family, those things that come so easy to others and have been so hard for you to find."

Cora trembled in anticipation. Her nipples were hard and high as if on their own they would reach out to find his hand, his lips.

Slowly, so very slowly, he disengaged her skirts from the constraints with which he had held her. Smoothly, as if bringing up the curtain on opening night of the nickel theater, he raised her skirts all the way to her waist. Her flimsy cotton drawers were her last barrier against him. Easily stripping them down off her legs and casting them away, he sat looking at her, naked before him.

Trembling under his gaze, Cora drew up her knees trying to hide herself behind their slim perfection. Jedwin paused, but only a moment, then leisurely, tentatively he touched her. Placing a firm brown hand on each knee, he tenderly parted her thighs—wide, and then wider still—until she was completely open to him and her secrets were his.

Removing his hands he sat back slightly, reverently accepting the vision as Cora's position remained unaltered. She felt too vulnerable, she wanted to cover herself, to pull her legs together, to flee from his hot gaze. But she stayed open and honest before him. She was truly his. Her breath came in halting little gasps as she felt her womanhood melting before his eyes.

Still watching her intently, Jedwin's hand dropped to his own lap drawing her eyes to him.

"Do you want to touch me?" he asked her. "Do you want to touch your husband's body?"

He ran his fingers along his extended length, outlining it against his trousers for Cora's gaze. "It's only for you, Cora. All of me is all for you."

Her eyes widened and her hands trembled with the desire to stroke him.

"Let me show you how it can be between us," he said. "Let me prove that we can have more of a marriage than those who are more conventionally wed. This is our marriage bed, Cora. I know in my heart that no other has ever or will ever be husband to you but me."

Cora's whole body quivered on the brink and she knew that he was right. She felt that if he were even to reach toward her, she would explode in a thousand hot pieces.

And she craved that explosion.

"Jedwin . . ." His name was a plea for mercy, and a whine of pain.

"It's all for you," he reiterated, stroking himself casually before her.

Cora could take no more. She reached for what he offered and brought it to the haven that it sought. She was eager, squirming, desperate.

Jedwin set his jaw painfully and held back his own pleasure. She urged him to hurry to please her.

"It's for you, Cora," he whispered as he struggled to maintain his control. "All of me is for you, however you want."

Steady, rhythmically, he rode her. Calm and silent as he listened to her tiny cries of need.

She must admit she loved him, he reminded himself. The words themselves had the power to break down walls of fear and shame. He knew she must say the words. He must make her say them.

"Oh, Jedwin, please," she begged. She dug her fingernails into the thick fleshy muscles of his buttocks. The pain of it felt like pleasure to Jedwin as he followed her lead. He would do whatever she wanted. He would be for her, whatever she wanted him to be.

"Please! Please!" she sobbed as she met each thrust with all the strength in her body. "I need you, Jedwin. I need you."

"And I need you, Cora," he told her evenly, his eyes closed tightly against the tormenting, beautiful sight of her desire. "I will always be here with you. I will always be the man that you want me to be."

"Jedwin, please! Oh Jedwin," she pleaded.

"I love you, Cora," he answered. "I love you."

Her head flailed against the pillow and her teeth clenched in desire close to pain.

"Jedwin!" she cried. "Oh Jedwin, I love you, Jedwin. I love you."

As if heavy chains upon him had snapped, Jedwin's eyes opened wide and he slammed deep into her body with near brutal force.

"Cora?" His breath was short with exertion.

She opened her eyes and looked at him. "I love you, Jedwin."

Jedwin awoke slowly. The room was now fully dark and he was naked and alone on Cora's bed. Cora. He looked up in the dim light of the evening and could make out just the outline of his belt still hanging from the bedstead. If spirit and soul and promises were anything, then he was, in truth, Cora's husband.

He smiled a warm, lazy smile and stretched. His muscles ached from exertion. There was no more pleasant form of weariness. She loved him. And she had finally said so. It had been like a dam breaking in their hearts. Nothing, no community censure, could stop them now. The onrush of love was too swift and strong for even the most determined ill-wisher.

Closing his eyes, he smelled the first faint odors of supper drifting up from the stairs. Then an unexpected sound. Someone was knocking on the kitchen door. Jedwin was immediately alert. He could hear the murmur of voices in the kitchen below. He could not hear what was being said.

"Titus!" Cora was genuinely surprised by the rapping on the back door. The past few hours had been close to heaven. She loved Jedwin and Jedwin loved her. That was all that existed in the world. She was his, for better or worse. And both were ready to face that.

Cora had forgotten, however, that worse had been invited to show up on her doorstep that very evening.

"Come in," she said, seeing his guilty glance toward the road as if fearful that someone might notice his clandestine visit.

Cora took the corn bread off the fire. With a deep breath, she considered how she would get out of this ill-considered plan of hers. And how she would get out of it quickly. What could have come over her to embroil herself in such a scheme?

"Titus, I—"

"No, Cora," he said as he raised his hand halting her. "I must speak first."

"But I—"

"I've been thinking about you all afternoon," he interrupted, fiddling nervously with his hat.

"Yes, well, I—"

"I can't do it," he said simply.

Cora opened her mouth to speak and then shut it abruptly.

"This is all my fault," Titus said, as he began to pace the narrow confines of the kitchen. "I know that I have led you to believe—"

He stopped and turned to her. Pulling worriedly on his waxy moustache, his expression was one of shame. "I've been looking your way for a long time." He did not seem at all proud of the fact. "And I've made no secret of it to you.

You are a fine-looking woman, Cora honey. Having you here, just on the other end of my street, sleeping alone at night . . ." He blushed with embarrassment. "It's been like a temptation to me, like a fantasy."

Titus looked at her for a moment and then allowed his gaze to stray away from her. Surveying the kitchen without curiosity, he could not meet her eyes.

"I'd be doing bookwork in the house and worrying about the future, the business," he began quietly. "Maybelle would be having a little set-to, screaming and stamping her sweet baby foot. Fanny would be furious with her behavior and mad at me 'cause she thinks I've made Maybelle a brat."

He paused for a long moment, then gained the courage to give her a sideways glance. "I'd just sort of let my mind wander, Cora honey. I'd imagine that I'd walk up the street and knock on your door. You'd be all pretty and flushed, like you are after one of your bicycle rides. You'd invite me in and it would be all peaceful and quiet and . . . and . . . and I'd be visiting you."

"Titus, please," Cora tried to interrupt.

"No, honey, let me finish," he said. "This afternoon when you made your offer." He chuckled without humor. "Well, if you'd had a feather on you, you could have knocked me over with it."

"I was too hasty," Cora told him.

"I snapped up the chance fast enough," he continued. "But all afternoon I've been thinking and thinking. Good Lord, Cora, I sure couldn't think of anything else."

He turned to her then. His eyes were warm and worried, almost sorrowful. "You are a damn fine woman. Any man in this town would feel honored to have you look in his direction," he said. "But I can't do it."

"That's fine, Titus," Cora told him gratefully. "I understand."

He resumed his pacing. "You're too good about it, Cora, and I owe you an explanation at the very least."

"You don't owe me anything," she insisted.

"I do," he declared. "And the simple fact is that I . . . well . . . I love Fanny."

The admission disturbed Titus so much, he actually covered his face in shame after uttering the words. "For all the troubles we have and spats we get into," he told Cora quietly, solemnly, "I truly wouldn't have no other wife. I think I wouldn't want to live without her."

He swallowed his grief and pride as he turned to Cora. "And if I were to take a mistress, sure as there is sunrise, sooner or later she would know. It would hurt her so much," he whispered.

He raised his chin and shrugged off his naked emotion with assurance. "Oh, she would stay with me. I'd never have to worry about her taking Maybelle and heading on her way. Her folks raised her up to believe in duty. She believes a woman stays with her husband even if he beats her twice a week."

"Yes," Cora agreed, thinking of Mrs. Penny's unswerving disapproval of her. "I know that she does."

"But, I don't want her with me because of loyalty to some vow she's taken in church. I want her with me because she wants to be."

His eyes had misted over with tears and Cora reached a hand out to touch his arm. "Please Titus," she said. "Let's not speak of this another moment. I do understand and I admire you. Go home to your wife."

"I'm so sorry, Cora honey," he said, his brow furrowed in genuine concern. "I want to help however I can."

"You always have helped me," Cora told him.

"I know the kind of woman you really are," he said. "And you wouldn't have come to me unless things were getting pretty bad."

Titus patted the feminine hand that lay so comfortably against his arm. "Do you not have money to make it through the winter? I could give you a loan, off the books of course, to get you by."

"She's already got all the help she's going to need."

The words coming from the parlor startled them both and they sprang apart guiltily. Titus's eyes widened in shock as Jedwin Sparrow stepped into the kitchen, barefoot and wearing only hastily buttoned trousers. He was much taller, and his presence seemed to cramp the small room.

"Jedwin?" Titus uttered his friend's name with near disbelief.

Nodding sternly at the other man, Jedwin walked to Cora's side and wrapped his arm loosely around her waist before laying a tiny kiss on her temple.

"That supper sure smells mighty good," he told her, before turning his attention back to Titus.

"I guess you didn't know about me and Cora," he said, only a glimmer of anger shining beneath the surface.

"I . . . why I had no idea, Jedwin, I swear," Titus assured him hastily.

Jedwin nodded understanding. "Cora invited you here to bring me to my senses, no doubt."

"To bring you to your senses?" Titus asked, his tone very puzzled.

"I'm going to marry her, Titus," he said firmly. "And she's been trying everything under the sun to convince me that she's not fit to be my wife."

He looked down at Cora with a shake of his head. "If I don't miss my guess," he said, reaching down to take Cora's chin between his fingers and raise it up so he could look into her eyes. "Taking a new lover—my friend Titus here—was supposed to make me realize that you could never be a faithful wife to me."

His eyes as wide as saucers, Titus Penny continued to stare at the couple before him.

Jedwin turned his attention back to the man. "It just goes to show you how little my Cora knows about men," Jedwin said to him. He turned back to Cora, grinning.

"You throw another fellow into the fray," he told her, "and it just makes a man more determined than ever to have you for his own."

He turned his attention back to Titus. "Isn't that right?"

Titus cleared his throat and nodded nervously. "You have nothing whatsoever to be jealous about," he assured Jedwin hurriedly. "I am a very married man and nothing, absolutely nothing, has ever happened between Mrs. Briggs and myself."

Jedwin's grin was victorious. "I know," he said. "You love Fanny." Turning to the woman beside him, his grin widened. "And Cora loves me and she's going to marry me one of these days."

"I wish you both well," Titus told them as he moved hastily toward the back door.

"I hope to see you at the wedding," Jedwin said with apparent unconcern.

"Well, I'm not sure—"

Jedwin's smile would have melted butter. "Of course you will be there," he said evenly. "Fanny will never hear about any of your petty triflings with my Cora. And I certainly won't be mentioning your visit here tonight, so there is no reason why we can't all be friends."

Titus opened his mouth to speak and then changed his mind and swallowed. With a polite doff of his hat, he said, "Ma'am, I look forward to that happy day and would be very pleased to attend the ceremony."

Cora was about to assure him that that was unnecessary, but Jedwin continued. "And the rest of your lovely family will be in attendance also, I hope?"

"Why, yes, yes, of course."

"Good, good." Jedwin was nodding at him in approval.

Titus had his hand on the doorknob with great hopes of scurrying out of harm's way. Jedwin, however, had one more blow to deliver.

"Oh, and Titus," he said.

The other man turned back to face him, worriedly.

"I know that your wife will be more than willing to welcome my new bride into the community."

Chapter
Twenty

Cora stared at Titus Penny's departing back as he retreated down the snow-covered road before she turned to the man beside her. "I can't believe that you told him that we are going to be married."

Jedwin shrugged. "I can't believe that you told him to come here tonight."

Flushing, Cora turned back to the stove. "This corn bread is not going to be fit to eat," she said. "Half cooked, then allowed to cool, and then cooked again."

"Don't try to distract me, Cora," Jedwin said. "It's pretty low to be willing to sleep with another man in order to get away from me."

Cora didn't answer. She couldn't face him.

"I wouldn't have," she said finally. "Not after—"

"Not after this afternoon," he finished for her.

She nodded.

"I know that," he said. "You have promised yourself to me and I haven't a worry that you would be unfaithful." He leaned up against the cold side of the stove and looked closely at her.

"But I would like to know what happened to your *rules,* Cora," he said.

She looked up at him, mute.

"Remember?" he said. "The framework of civilization, the protection of society, the preservation of morals. The rules you are so intent on not breaking. Those don't apply to Titus?"

"Of course they do," she said, feeling oddly out of control.

"But you didn't care if he committed adultery, ruined his life, hurt his pregnant wife and child?" he said.

"Of course I care," she insisted, turning to him angrily. "But I care about other things, too."

"What other things?"

"I care about you."

Jedwin nodded. "I know that you do. You were going to sacrifice yourself, Titus, Fanny, even little Maybelle because of me."

"I didn't think about them," she admitted remorsefully. "I have nothing at all against them, but I didn't think about them at all."

"Of course you did," Jedwin said. "You've never done a thoughtless cruelty in all your life."

Frustrated, he grabbed her arm and pulled her away from her continued attempts to finish cooking dinner. "You knew that there would be pain and anguish and hurt. But you were willing to let it happen."

Cora stared at him, guilt lining her features. She had no defense against the truth.

"Why were you willing to let it happen?" he asked. "You were willing to ruin my life and yours and theirs for this foolish sense of obedience you cling to."

"I wasn't going to ruin *your* life," she insisted.

"It would have been ruined, Cora," he answered evenly. "If I believed you capable of such treachery, if I thought you left me for another man, my life would have been ruined. I wouldn't want to live. I'm not sure I would be able to do so."

Cora shook her head, trying desperately not to believe him.

"Why would you have done such a thing?" he asked. "I know you are sensitive to other people's pain. Why did you plan to do that?"

She turned her head to look at him. Her face was lined with misery. "I don't know," she said.

"You do know."

"No."

"Tell me, Cora. You've already said it upstairs, let me hear it in the kitchen without my lips upon you."

"Because . . . because I love you," she said.

Jedwin nodded. "And love is more important than the rules, isn't it, Cora?"
She was silent for a moment considering the words as if for the first time.
"Isn't it?"

"Yes!" she said, then, "No!" She shook her head. "I don't know!"

He reached for her then. Gently enfolding her in his arms, he held her close.
Her tears nearly unmanned him, but his only chance to really win her, to win
her forever, was to fight now and give no quarter.

"I don't know," she sobbed quietly against his shirt.

"Oh Cora," he whispered lovingly against the top of her head. "Don't cry,
sweetheart. Of course you don't know," he said. "You can't know. It was a
trick question."

She pulled back from him, her eyes bright with tears. "A trick question?"

He nodded. There was no amusement in his eyes, only sincerity. "The rules
can be more important than love," he said. "And *love* can be more important
than the rules."

Pulling her against him once more, he tried to make her understand. "You
are right about needing the rules," he said. "We need the Ten Commandments.
We need the laws of the land. Without them," he admitted, "we'd just be the
most crazed of animals, killing each other for want of a soup bone."

He brought a strong masculine knuckle to her chin and raised her face to
look at her. "And the customs of our society are all very important, too."

She nodded only slightly.

Holding her head in his hands, Jedwin gazed down into her eyes. "But
sometimes, rules don't help to uplift us, they only restrain us."

"That doesn't mean we can ignore them," she said, her voice hoarse with
tears.

"No," he agreed. "We can't ignore them. There has to be a balance."

"A balance?" Her brown eyes were bright with tears and wide with
curiosity.

"A give-and-take, an evenhandedness of judgment, there has to be an
apportionment of grace. It's so in nature, it must be so in civilization, too."

"There can be no give-and-take in right and wrong," Cora told him.

"There is leverage of the spirit," he said. "What would Mrs. Millenbutter
say?"

"Mrs. Millenbutter?"

"Yes," he answered. "When you throw that Lewis wand in the air, how do
you know it will return to your hand?"

"Gravity."

"Yes, gravity," he said. "It's a balance of nature. Up is too high and down is too low. You must find the wand and the wand must find your hand, which is in between the two."

Cora's expression was puzzled.

"And what about walking with that bag of marbles on your head? Is that just a practice of young belles ready for their coming out, or is it a lesson in keeping yourself in perspective?"

"I suppose it's both," Cora admitted.

"Didn't you tell me that Mrs. Millenbutter says that the physical, mental, and the spiritual are equal parts of the same whole? That if one is not developed as well as the others, existence ceases to be in harmony and all aspects of your life will suffer?"

"Well, yes," Cora admitted. "I can see that there must be balance in all that we say and do, but the rules we choose to live by are not open to being bandied about and obeyed as we choose."

"Yes, but in balance," he said. "Divorce *is* an evil to be avoided. A man and wife *should* be committed to their marriage vows and that *should* offer protection and provision for families and children. It is a well-intended rule that I'm sure serves good purpose most of the time," he said. "But, with us, with our love and the balance of our lives it serves no good purpose at all."

"Jedwin, I believe you," Cora said. "I have never felt myself to be some evil sinner. I was blameless in my divorce, but the fact is that I am divorced and society says I must pay a penalty."

He shook his head in disagreement. "You have suffered long enough for the mistake of marrying Luther Briggs. Heaven knows, even the worst of criminals can finally pay his debts to society. I love you and I want to marry you. And I think that your debt to this community, to Miss Maimie, to my mother, to our church, is paid in full."

"But you shouldn't have to pay."

"I won't have to, unless you refuse to marry me," he said.

Her head held high and her back straight, Amelia Sparrow stepped into the foyer through her own front door and quietly closed it behind her. With slow, casual grace, she removed her hat and coat and hung them carefully upon the hall tree. Calmly she walked down the hallway to the family parlor. Stepping inside, she systematically made a thorough perusal of the furnishings of the room. Her survey stopped at a small, delicately hand-painted Bohemian glass vase. Picking it up, Amelia admired the lovely blue and gold flowers so painstakingly reproduced by the artist for only a moment before hurling the pretty piece at the nearest wall.

The sound of shattering glass was as satisfying as releasing a long-held breath. Amelia sighed. With the beginnings of a smile forming on her lips, she snatched up a tiny bisque figurine and hurled it after the vase.

It was with a genuine grin that Amelia reached for a stunning piece of imported majolica. She did not, however, have the opportunity to throw it.

"What the hell is going on here, Mellie!"

Amelia turned to stare at Haywood Puser, who looked very annoyed as he came racing through the door.

Without answering she raised her arm to throw the fancy pottery, but Haywood grabbed her hand and none too gently returned the bric-a-brac to its usual place.

"Stop it, right now," he ordered.

"This is my house, Mr. Puser," Amelia snapped, grateful to have a human target for her anger. "And I will tear it down to dust and splinters if I so choose."

Haywood folded his arms across his chest and surveyed her skeptically. "You go right ahead, Mellie," he told her. "But I'm sure not going to be volunteering to help you pick up the pieces."

With little enthusiasm, Amelia glanced at the mess of shattered glass that littered the floor. The sight of it dampened her pleasure in the sport a good deal.

"Well, at least bring me the broom and dustpan," she told him, not the least bit kindly.

He immediately fetched as he was bid and after hurrying back to her side, proved himself a liar by squatting down beside her to help pick up the largest of the glass pieces.

"Is there any reason for this assault on the crockery?" Haywood asked her. "Or are you just practicing for the skillet throw at the next Fourth of July Picnic?"

Amelia gave him a freezing look. "I have just had tea with Miss Maimie."

Haywood raised an eyebrow. "*Our* Miss Maimie? *Dear* Miss Maimie? The *sainted* Miss Maimie?"

"Oh, do hush!" Amelia sounded extremely vexed.

Haywood allowed his sarcasm to lighten as easily as the furrows disappeared from his brows. "Well, are you going to tell me what happened?" he asked. "Or are you just going to stay in a pout all afternoon?"

"I do not pout!"

Amelia's declaration was made with such conviction that the sight of her sulkily protruding lower lip spurred Haywood to an out-and-out chuckle.

"As you say, Mellie," he answered.

Resisting the urge to throttle him Amelia stood up and began to pace. "They know about James Edwin," she said.

Haywood continued to sweep the broken glass for a moment. "Who knows?"

"Miss Maimie knows!" she answered, slapping her fist impotently against her thigh. "And Fanny Penny and Constance Bruder and probably the whole town! He is telling people," Amelia said. She raised her hands to heaven in disbelief. "He's told Titus Penny that he intends to marry her."

Haywood managed to get the last of the broken glass into the dustpan and covered it protectively with the broom.

"So he's going to marry her," he said. "Isn't that something?"

"It's something, all right," Amelia countered. "It's a nightmare." She paced the length of the room once more in agitation before seating herself in her sewing rocker and covering her face with her hands. "How will I ever hold my head up in this town?"

"Oh, for heaven's sake, Mellie," Haywood said. "It can't be as bad as all that."

"It certainly can be," she insisted. "It's even worse! Miss Maimie told me not to think that it is all my fault, just because my *bad blood* has finally shown itself."

Haywood whistled with appreciation.

"Constance Bruder said that James Edwin may no longer be welcomed in the church."

"That don't seem quite Christian. I have my doubts the reverend would agree with that."

"And Fanny Penny said that this scandal is the most horrible crisis Dead Dog has ever faced."

Haywood laughed out loud.

"How dare you find humor in this!" Amelia's words were almost a screech. "This is the worst thing that has ever happened to me!"

Shaking his head in disapproval, Haywood pointed a finger at her. "Now there you set off on the wrong foot again, Mellie," he said. "This is not the 'worst thing that has ever happened to' *you*, because it ain't happening to you, at all."

"Of course it's happening to me."

"It's happening to Jedwin and Miz Briggs," he told her with firm conviction.

"My son's life is like my own," Amelia declared self-righteously.

"It damn well is not."

"Do not curse at me, Mr. Puser!"

"I will curse at you if I think you need it. And right now, you are sure needing something to shake some sense into you."

"If you had any sense, you'd realize what this means."

"I know exactly what it means," he said, his voice now raised almost as loudly as her own. "It means Miss Maimie has got another way to push and prod and make you feel bad about yourself. She doesn't really need a new way, of course. She's been managing to keep your confidence cut down to a nub for a good while now. And Miz Bruder, well, it's her husband's job to get sinners to repent. If they ain't no sinners around, well, I'd say he'd be pretty nigh worthless to the community. And as for Fanny Penny, I'm thinking it's high time that Titus took that wife of his in hand. She's been snubbing half the folks in this town. And those folks are the very ones buying her husband's goods and keeping her in beans and gravy." He crossed his arms obstinately. "That woman's got a right snippy, prideful attitude. I think that a one-by-four used with some precision on her backside would cure her of that affliction permanently."

"Of course," Amelia accused, flailing her hands in the air. "Beating would be your answer for everything!"

"Not everything," Haywood assured her. "But there's been more than one time when I've thought it might do you a world of good."

"How dare you!" Amelia rose to her feet with the obvious intention of slapping Puser's face. Haywood easily grasped her hands in his.

"Now don't go starting something you cain't finish, Mellie," he said. "I said I've thought of it. I'm sure we can both bear witness that I ain't never laid a hand to you in anger." Then with a wicked glance toward her, he added, "Though I have let it linger there for pleasure a time or two."

A furious "Oh!" escaped Amelia's lips but she was too upset to argue.

"Now Mellie, I'm sure that Miz Briggs ain't that bad. Even the preacher seems to be revising his opinion of her. Jedwin is a right smart fellow. He wouldn't love her if she was all that folks have said she is."

"You don't understand," she complained with more than a hint of anger in her voice. She dropped to the divan, burying her face in her handkerchief. "It makes no difference if she is a saint. I am losing my son."

"Oh Mellie, Mellie." Haywood chuckled as he shook his head, his mind searching for the right words, the right way to make her understand.

"This control you have on Jedwin," he began quietly. "This need to be a part of every aspect of life, Mellie, it's like a bad tooth."

"What?"

"Do you remember your bad tooth?" he asked.

"Of course I do," Amelia snapped. "It bothered me forever. I was in constant pain."

"That's right," Haywood said. "But you didn't want me to pull that tooth."

"Well, of course not," Amelia answered, clearly puzzled. "Nobody wants the pain of having a tooth pulled. And nobody wants to lose any of their teeth. What does this have to do with James Edwin?"

"Mellie," he said. "I'm thinking that your need to run Jedwin's life, to be the most important person in the world to him, well Mellie, I'm thinking it's like that abscessed tooth."

"Whatever do you mean?"

"I mean that part of your loving of Jedwin has gone rotten," he said. "You've hovered and bullied and managed for him until you've made a sore place in his heart."

"That's the most foolish thing I've ever heard." With a haughty jerk of her chin, Amelia moved to rise from the divan.

"It's the most truth you've heard in a long time, woman, so I'd suggest that you listen," he said. "You've been trying to smother that young man and keep him tied to your apron strings since long before I met you. It's a credit to Jedwin's character that he's managed to retain the gumption that he has. You would have turned him into a sniveling sissy lisping, 'yes mama, no mama' until his gray beard was dusting the floor."

"How can you say that? You know I love my son," Amelia insisted.

"Yes, Mellie, you do," Haywood agreed. "And if you want to keep him, you are going to have to let him go."

"What?"

"Trying to run his life is a bad tooth festering and causing you both pain. Pull that bad tooth, Mellie," he said. "Pull it now and get it over with. It will fall out one of these days anyway; you can't hold him forever."

He raised her chin and planted a tender, consoling kiss on her forehead. "We aren't perfect, Mellie," he said. "Nor is anything about us. Sometimes we have to give up a little of what we have in order to keep the rest of it. If you give Jedwin his life and his freedom, you will have a loving son for life."

"Haywood," she whispered. "I'm so scared."

He looked at her tear-brightened blue eyes for only a moment before he seated himself on the divan and wrapped his arms around her.

Chapter
Twenty-one

"Excuse me!" Jedwin was shocked as he stood on the threshold of the family parlor and saw his mother on the divan kissing Haywood Puser.

"James Edwin!" Amelia screeched in horror. She tried to jump to her feet so quickly that she stumbled and landed very soundly on Haywood's lap.

"What is going on here, Haywood?" Jedwin was clearly puzzled by the unexpected scene.

Amelia righted herself and stood up in dishabille, but head held high, in the center of the room. Haywood rose to his feet, his face flushed. He cleared his throat with the intention of smoothing over the situation. Amelia, however, had other plans.

"Jedwin, I swear it is not what you think," she assured him with hastily gathered dignity. "My business with Mr. Puser is . . . well, it is strictly business."

Jedwin's eyebrow was raised in amusement. *"Business?"* he asked. "Exactly what kind of business were you two planning?"

"Now Jedwin," Haywood began, clearly ready to defend the delicate honor of Mrs. Sparrow.

Amelia interrupted him. "James Edwin Sparrow," she snapped with fury born of discomfiture. "I am a grown woman and in my own home. If I choose to allow a gentleman to kiss me, it is no concern of yours."

Jedwin was slightly taken back. Shrewdly, he assessed the situation and kept the grin that itched at the corner of his mouth under control as he spoke to his mother in a calm and civilized manner.

"Mama, Mr. Puser is a friend of mine, as you know. And I have always liked him." Jedwin paused to send a chillingly calculated look toward the subject under discussion.

Again Puser opened his mouth to speak.

"You are probably not aware of this, Mama," Jedwin continued quietly. "But Haywood has a reputation with ladies. A reputation that I believe to be totally deserved." Jedwin cleared his throat primly. "My father has been dead for some time," he said. "And I can certainly understand that you might find some interest in another man. However, I will not allow him to do damage to your heart or your honor."

Amelia's nostrils flared in fury. "My heart and my honor, young man, are my own," she replied shrewishly. "I will do with them as I wish."

"But Mama—" Jedwin began.

"If I choose to entertain a gentleman in my parlor," she told him angrily, "then I will do so. It is *my* business and none of your own!" Amelia, standing hands on hips in the middle of the room, stamped her foot in such a way as to signal the onslaught of a tantrum.

To the total amazement of both Amelia and Haywood, this brought a guffaw of laughter from Jedwin Sparrow's throat.

Both started at the sound and turned to stare at young Jedwin in disbelief.

"What on earth is so funny?" Amelia questioned threateningly.

Her anger seem to tickle him even further. In all the years since his father had died, Amelia had shown absolutely no interest in love, or marriage, or even gentlemen friends. Jedwin had worried that his forty-three-year-old mother may have thought she was far past all of that. Apparently he was wrong.

"Stop laughing!" Amelia was nearly beside herself.

Nearly choking, Jedwin held up a hand in surrender as he tried to contain his laughter. "I'm sorry, I'm sorry," he managed. "I swear, Mama, Haywood, I couldn't be happier. I've been wanting to see you two get together for years. Now, I walk in on you, prepared for another battle of wills on living my own life and I find that you've already begun to live yours."

Amelia swallowed her embarrassment and raised her chin in defiance. "Mr. Puser and I have become friends," she said. As if suddenly realizing the correlation her son had drawn, she hastily cast off any sense of similarity in their situations. "There is nothing sullied or illicit about our relationship," she stated haughtily.

Jedwin nodded. "I feel the same about myself and Mrs. Briggs, Mama. We love each other and there is nothing for me to be ashamed about in that."

She shook her head. "It is not the same."

"It *is* the same. But I don't think we should be surprised that we behave in the same manner. You did raise me to be the man that I am, to go after the things that I want, just as you have."

"I didn't raise you to create a scandal in this community," Amelia countered in a condemning whisper. "Mr. Puser and I have both been widowed and are free to seek a new association. Mrs. Briggs is *divorced;* clearly she should not be considered eligible for a fine young man like you."

"Scandals pretty much create themselves, Mama. I consider her very eligible and I'm the only one who needs to be concerned." Jedwin shook his head. "People who like to believe the worst, always will. I don't like to believe the worst. Not about Mrs. Briggs, not about you, not even about Haywood here." He glanced at the older man. "Mama, I probably know this fellow a bit better than you. I know that he's a sweet-talker to the ladies, a bit of a rounder, and he has led his share of lonely widows off the straight and narrow."

"Oh!" Amelia was mortified as she glanced over with sudden uncertainty at Haywood beside her. Determinedly, she sleeked back her disheveled hair and nervously wiped her damp palms on her skirt.

Jedwin ignored Haywood's glare. "That's what I know about him, Mama, and if I was one to believe the worst, I'd be busting his jaw right now. But I'm not about to hit him, 'cause I think the galloot is probably in love with you."

Haywood cleared his throat nervously and gave Jedwin a cautious look. "I'd best go to my cottage. I suspect you and Mellie got things to say to each other."

"No, stay. You are nearly family to me, Haywood. What I'm here to say is about family, about our family." Jedwin's expression was sober as he looked hopefully at his mother.

Amelia's stern demeanor seemed near collapse and Haywood instinctively took her hand.

"I want you two to be happy," he told them quietly. "Can't you try to want the same for me?"

Amelia raised her chin stubbornly as she pulled away from Haywood.

Standing on her own, head high and shoulders straight, she looked through
Jedwin as if she couldn't see him and refused to answer.

Her son waited a very long moment before sorrowfully, reluctantly, he
nodded, accepting his mother's choice.

"I just came to pack up my clothes," he told Haywood with cordiality that
didn't match the solemnity of his expression.

"You are moving in with her?" Amelia's voice was little above a whisper.

Jedwin looked into his mother's eyes and knew that the wonderful decisions
he'd made in the last few days were going to hurt her deeply. "I'm moving out
to the farm," he answered evenly. "Cora and I won't be living together until
we are duly married."

"She is going to wed you then?" Haywood asked.

Jedwin nodded. "Yes, I think so."

"Soon?" his mother asked.

Jedwin shrugged. "I've spoken to Reverend Bruder. He was a little
surprised, but I think he's warming up to the idea. He'll come around." Jedwin
paused wistfully, hoping that the same could be said for the woman in front
of him. "I want you to be at my wedding, Mama."

An uncomfortable silence lingered in the parlor. It was not going to be easy,
Jedwin thought. But nothing worth having ever was. Reluctantly, he took his
leave.

"The mortuary belongs to you, Mama," Jedwin told them from the
doorway. "I'm having a lawyer in Guthrie draw up the papers." With only a
ghost of a smile, he warned Haywood, "She is really your boss now."

The cloying quiet of the parlor was made more so by the sound of Jedwin's
step on the stair. Amelia's eyes dropped to the fine Turkish carpet at her feet
as she bit her lip to hold back the tears that welled in her eyes. A painful sob
filled her throat, but she held it back as stubbornly as she had any attempt at
reconciliation. Her lips were trembling as she turned to Haywood.

"Hold me," she whispered.

And he did.

Jedwin found packing simple. The numerous dark, solemn suits that hung
in his wardrobe were left right where they were. He had no intention of taking
his funeral garb with him. He was a farmer now, he needed one good suit for
Sunday and plenty of sturdy work clothes for the rest of his life.

His mood was mixed. Part joyful, part frightened for the unknown future
ahead of him and the hurt he'd seen in his mother's eyes. Change was never

easy. Whether it was the move from childhood to adulthood or from life to death, hopes were shattered, routines were disrupted, plans were reshaped and dreams were altered. But change was inevitable and important. The adult world made childhood a pleasured memory and death gave life value and urgency.

As Jedwin crammed the last of his work shirts into his gripsack, he heard the sound of wagon wheels coming down the street. It was not at all an unusual sound, but for some reason it captured his attention. With a modicum of interest he glanced out the window.

A well-kept farmer's wagon was slowly making its way toward the mortuary. It was driven by a young man wearing a brown flop hat; a younger boy sat stiffly by his side. It was only as they got closer that Jedwin noticed the long, covered length of a body in the back of the wagon.

Setting his gripsack by the door, Jedwin hurried down the stairs.

"We've got a body coming to the front door," he called toward the parlor as he made his way across the foyer. He heard movement behind him and knew that Haywood and his mother were following him.

He was waiting when the wagon stopped on the street, directly in front of the door. Haywood and Amelia hurried off the porch to join him.

The young man called a halt to the horses and set the brake. He could not have been a day over sixteen. He was a good-looking farm boy with thick black hair and exceptionally bright blue eyes. Something about the boy and those eyes struck Jedwin as familiar.

The younger boy was about eight, Jedwin speculated. He, too, had thick black hair, but his features were different. The high cheekbones and narrow eyes suggested an Indian heritage. The short hair and farmer's clothing suggested a white man's life. The young boy's expression was totally blank, but from the flush in his cheeks and the redness of his eyes it was clear he'd been crying.

"Can I help you?" Jedwin said, reaching up to help the younger boy from the wagon. The boy gratefully took his hand.

"Are you the undertaker in this town?" the older boy asked.

"Yes, I am," Jedwin answered, forgetting he'd just resigned. "I'm Jedwin Sparrow," he said. "Who are you two?"

"This is my brother Arthel," the older boy answered. "And folks call me Greasy." There was a slight hesitation in his voice before he glanced back at the body in the wagon. "We've brung our daddy for burial."

Jedwin glanced thoughtfully at the body in the back of the wagon. "How did it happen?" he asked him in the gentle, comforting tone that he had always used with grieving families.

"Diphtheria," the boy answered, his chin raised bravely high. "Arthel here got it first," he said, indicating his younger brother. "And Mama was taking care of him when she came down with it." The older boy's lip trembled and Arthel's stony expression crumbled into unwanted tears. "We was set to burying her when we realized that Pa had taken sick, too."

"You've lost both your parents?" Jedwin asked, reaching out to lay a comforting hand on the younger one's shoulder.

Greasy nodded. "Pa knew he was dying," he explained. "So he told us to come here to Dead Dog. He said he had family here that would take care of us."

The young man's desperate attempt to be brave was painful. "I thought maybe some of his family would nurse him back to health." His words stumbled slightly at this recognition of his lost hope. "But he died on the road last night."

Haywood came forward and grasped the halter of the horse firmly. Nodding to the boys, he said, "I'll take your father around back." The youngsters watched as he began walking the wagon away. It was clear that a burden had been lifted off their shoulders.

"Come inside," Jedwin told the two. Turning back to the house, he saw his mother. Her eyes were as full as his own.

"I bet you boys are hungry," she said to them with all the maternal warmth that any woman could muster.

"No, ma'am," the eldest assured her quickly. "We ate this morning."

"Well," Amelia answered, unswayed. "A bit of cider and a piece of pone will warm you up at least. Come on into the kitchen."

Jedwin followed his mother and the boys through the house. Familiar with grief, he produced a quiet, unassuming stream of conversation about normal everyday events: the weather, crops, and politics.

Amelia quickly contributed an appealing array of food and drink to the kitchen table. Despite earlier protests to the contrary, both boys ate heartily. The older watched the younger with both pride and worry. As if wanting to insure that nothing ever hurt the child again.

Jedwin felt a surge of admiration for the boy. He remembered his own father's death, those hard, heavy first days when the world was such a lonely place and the weight of it had been placed squarely on his shoulders.

"Greasy's a pretty unusual name," Jedwin said to the older boy. "I suspect it was earned rather than given."

The boy smiled slightly. It was a warm and easy smile. "Mama started calling me that," he answered with a nod. "I like to build gadgets and motors and such. I guess I manage to get a lot of grease on me."

Little Arthel laughed lightly, his childish voice high-pitched and giggly. "He don't build 'em," the younger boy declared. "He takes 'em apart and half the time they won't never work again."

Greasy gave his younger brother a look of menace that was so typical of feigned brotherly rivalry that both Jedwin and his mother felt sighs of relief drifting through them.

"I believe I've got a bit of apple cobbler up in this pie safe," Amelia told the boys. "You think you could manage a little bit of sweet after your pone?"

When the boys answered enthusiastically, Jedwin made his way to the door, quietly leaving the boys in her care.

He made it through the embalming room and out the back door to the wagon just in time to help Haywood carry in the body.

"Ain't that a sight," Haywood said to him with a gesture toward the house. "Are those two going to be all right?" he asked.

Jedwin nodded affirmatively. "I think they are taking it about as well as can be expected," he said. "Losing both your parents and being suddenly alone . . ." He didn't need to finish the thought.

Haywood nodded. "And especially rough on the older one. He'll be wanting to take care of his brother and raise him up when he ain't even been half raised himself."

Jedwin couldn't help but agree.

"Let's get this body inside," Haywood suggested as the two returned their thoughts to the business at hand.

Jedwin took the shoulders and Haywood the knees as they lifted the man across the bed of the wagon onto a sturdy wooden plank. It was not an easy task. He was a good-sized man and already in rigor mortis. But the two of them brought him inside.

"You'd best not be in here," Haywood told Jedwin as he began to gather the equipment for embalming.

Nodding absently, Jedwin realized almost with surprise where he was. He hated the embalming room. Usually, just thinking about walking inside it caused the back of his throat to burn. Today, as he looked around him, it was just a room.

"I don't feel the least bit ill," he told Haywood in wonderment.

Even the odor of the room, although certainly not pleasant, no longer seemed to hold the horrible gagging smell he hated so much.

Haywood glanced at him curiously, but didn't pursue the subject. "The boy says it's diphtheria," he told Jedwin. "Just 'cause you didn't catch it when it came through town, don't mean you couldn't get it still."

Still slightly stunned, Jedwin hesitated for a moment before nodding in agreement. "All right," he said. "You take care of the father, Haywood, and I'll see what I can do for the boys. I hope the man still does have family here in town."

As if in a measure of respect, Jedwin glanced down at the dead stranger's face.

The man's bright blue eyes stared back at him from unclosed eyelids; he was no stranger. Jedwin stared at a face he hadn't seen in years, but which was as familiar to him as if he'd seen it yesterday.

"Oh my God!" he whispered to himself.

Without a word of explanation, Jedwin left the room, closing the door behind him with quiet care. He paced the hallway alone for several moments. Facts and questions were bombarding him at such a rapid velocity that he couldn't quite manage to think.

Finally, he stopped his frantic pacing and took a long cleansing breath. Swallowing, he raised his head resolutely and stepped to the door of the kitchen.

"Greasy," he said gently. The young boy looked up from a dish of his mother's best cinnamon-and-apple cobbler. He had to be at least fourteen, Jedwin was sure.

"Could you come with me for a moment."

The older boy rose to his feet and followed.

"How old are you, Greasy?" he asked calmly.

"Sixteen in the spring," the young man answered.

Jedwin nodded.

He led the way through the hall and into the formal front parlor. The boy looked around with curiosity at the formal fancy furnishing of the room shrouded with crepe of black, white, and purple, but brimming with the lightness of numerous vases of brightly colored dried flowers.

"This is where we will be laying your father out," Jedwin told him.

The boy nodded mutely.

"I'll be contacting the preacher this afternoon," he continued. "He will help us to decide what day and time to have the funeral."

Again the boy indicated agreement with silence.

"I, of course, want to do whatever I can to help."

"That's real nice of you, Mr. Sparrow," the boy answered politely.

"Greasy," Jedwin asked in a quiet, almost hesitant tone. "Could you tell me your real name, your full name?"

The handsome young man with the startlingly familiar blue eyes looked up at him.

"Oh, why yes, sir," he answered, not realizing he hadn't done so already. "It's Luther Harlan Briggs, sir, just like my pa."

Chapter Twenty-two

The long, shiny black rig pulled up directly in front of the house. The isinglass shades were drawn down as usual and in the bright light of the afternoon sun it was easy to read the words SPARROW MORTUARY in gold letters above the windows.

Jedwin set the hand brake and tied the lines to it before he stepped to the ground. He pulled off his hat and ran a young, strong hand through his thinning blond hair. Routinely he checked the cleanliness of his fingernails, the straightness of his tie. It was another condolence call, but it was so much more. He adjusted his coat more primly and stepped to the porch of Cora Briggs's little cottage.

When he reached the front door, he took one deep cleansing breath for courage before knocking. She opened the door almost immediately.

"Jedwin," she said in surprise. Since he'd told her that he would be moving out to the farm today, she hadn't expected to see him before sundown. "Don't you look splendid," she told him with pride as she noted the fine tailoring of his best black mourning coat. "Did you come to take tea with me?"

Her smile was so open, it hurt Jedwin to look at it. He shook his head.

Cora glanced beyond him, and saw the funeral coach bold as brass in front of her house in the middle of the day.

"You're parked right in front of the house," she said with confusion. "I thought we'd decided to be very discreet until after the wedding."

"Cora—" he began, slowly removing his hat and holding it in his hand as a sign of respect. "I'm afraid I'm bringing you some bad news."

"Bad news?" Cora repeated his words with a strange tremor in her voice.

Jedwin looked into her eyes, wishing what he had to say would mean nothing to her, knowing that the past is never truly gone, only buried like the dead, beneath the surface we live upon. "Luther Briggs has passed away, Cora," he said. "His body is at the mortuary."

Cora's eyes widened in surprise and she shook her head in disbelief.

"It's true," Jedwin told her gently. "He died of the diphtheria last night. His sons brought him in this morning."

He watched as those plain, ordinary brown eyes that he had grown to love, welled up with tears.

"Oh Jedwin," she whispered.

"I love you, Cora," he told her.

"I love you, too," she said. The tears began to flow down her cheeks as she stepped forward and into his waiting arms.

The cabriolet stopped directly in front of the main entrance to Miss Maimie's big, white house. Greasy Briggs pulled the team to a halt expertly, before hopping down to assist Mrs. Sparrow.

His brother Arthel scrambled down on his own and was already hurrying up the steps to the porch. The youngster was full of curiosity and jumpy with eagerness.

"Thank you for driving, Luther," Amelia told the young man, offering her arm to him as if he were her escort. "I can drive myself, of course. But I rarely do. I feel such difficult skills are better left to the gentlemen."

Her words were meant as a bolster to the brave adult facade that the young man was desperately trying to hold in place.

"You're very welcome, ma'am," Greasy assured her. Stopping to stare at the huge three-story mansion, he allowed his eyes to travel the distance of the porch and the flow of the lawns. "This is a mighty fine house."

"Yes," Amelia agreed. "It is lovely. This is where your father grew up, you know."

Greasy whistled impressively. "It sure beats our little place in Muskogee," he said.

"And this street," Amelia told him, indicating the worn dirt track they had just come up. "It's Luther Street," she said. "Named for your father."

Greasy turned back to look at the road behind him as if hoping to find something that would somehow make his father closer.

"What a place!" Arthel told them as he came running from the far end of the porch. "It's like a palace or something. Are we gonna live here forever?" he asked.

Both Amelia and Greasy ignored the younger boy's comment. Her mind was still reeling from the events that had transpired. His mind was purposely blank. Not anticipating anything would, he hoped, keep him from being disappointed.

"Go ahead," Amelia urged Greasy, pointing at the large brass knocker above the doorknob.

He raised it and rapped sharply three times. Ill at ease, the three waited on the porch for a very long couple of minutes before the door opened.

"Mrs. Sparrow!" The thrilled youthful voice was that of Tulsa May Bruder, looking especially pitiful in a worn brown work dress and a soiled apron. "Hello," she added shyly to the two boys that she didn't know.

"Good afternoon, Tulsa May," Amelia said, in a clipped businesslike tone. "I need to speak to Miss Maimie, if you please."

"Come on in," she answered with easy countrified manners, as she opened the door widely and waved them inside. "I just fixed some tea for Miss Maimie in her sewing room. You want some too, Mrs. Sparrow?"

"No dear, that's not necessary," Amelia answered as she methodically removed her black lace gloves and deposited them carefully in her handbag. Turning to the Briggs boys, she offered a bright smile of comfort. "Let me go up and speak to her," she told them. Amelia patted Greasy comfortingly on his strong, broad, young shoulder. "Perhaps Tulsa May can get you some buttermilk or something."

"Surely, Mrs. Sparrow," Tulsa May answered easily as she watched the dignified older woman hurry up the stairs.

Bringing her attention back to the two handsome young boys standing with her in the foyer, Tulsa May gave them a warm and welcoming gap-toothed grin. "Come on into the kitchen with me," she said. "I can find something to eat if you want."

"I'm starved!" the young one told her gratefully.

"Arthel!" Greasy reprimanded his brother sharply. "All we've been doing all day is eating," he told Tulsa May. "I'm sure we don't need a thing."

Tulsa May grinned at Arthel and nodded at his brother. "Well, come into the kitchen anyway," she told them. "I swear it's the only room in this house where you can sit down and make yourself comfortable. The whole place is just too fancy for normal living."

The two dutifully followed her, gazing around at the fancy furnishings in silent agreement.

"My name's Tulsa May," she told them. "I'm just helping out here for a few weeks until Mrs. Ruggy is a bit more like herself."

The handsome older boy smiled at her politely. "The runt's name is Arthel," he said. "And I'm called Greasy."

"Miss Maimie?" Amelia's voice sounded tentative as she knocked lightly before opening the door to the sewing room. "Afternoon, Miss Maimie."

The old woman looked up from her tea and waved her in. "Back already, are you?" Maimie asked. "You are doing the right thing, Amelia. If you side with that boy and his woman's perfidy against this town, it will surely go against you."

Amelia nodded absently. "I've not come about that, Miss Maimie. I'm afraid I've got some bad news."

Miss Maimie screwed up her face rather unattractively. "Bad news, eh? I know what that means, more business for the gravediggers." The old woman shook her head and then snapped sharply. "It better not be Mattie Ruggy," she said. "I need that old woman to run this place. That red-haired preacher's girl is as stupid as she is ugly!"

"No, no," Amelia said quietly. "It's not Mattie." Moving closer to the older woman, she dropped down on her knees beside her chair and picked up the pale, gnarled hand that lay against the lap quilt. "It's Luther, Miss Maimie."

"Luther?" Miss Maimie looked at her momentarily with incomprehension before her aged eyes widened in disbelief. "My Luther? My son?"

The old woman's cool, spiteful mask crumbled before Amelia's eyes. Reaching out, she wrapped her arms around the woman's neck and allowed her tears to fall upon her shoulder and her sobbing to be muted against her body.

Cora sat in Jedwin's lap in the sewing rocker. She had cried a little, but mostly she had just held on to Jedwin and allowed herself to be consoled. They rocked together slowly as Jedwin thoughtlessly hummed.

"While the train rolled onward,
A husband sat in tears,
Thinking of the happiness,
Of just a few short years.
For baby's face brings picture of
A cherished hope that's dead,
But baby's cries can't waken her,
In the baggage coach ahead."

The sad, mournful tune somehow offered comfort to both of them.

"He was not a bad man," Cora told Jedwin finally. "He was only a weak one."

Jedwin continued to rock her gently "He must have been a very weak one," he said with a moment of hesitation. "I've met his sons."

Cora nodded. "Sons," she said with a light sigh, and gave Jedwin a ghost of a smile. "The second one was a boy also. I never knew."

"Yes, he looks to be about eight years old."

"That sounds about   "

"He looks a bit more Indian   the older one," Jedwin said. "The older one is a ringer for   "

Cora nodded. "That's nice.

Jedwin's hands were steady but   his heart   was trembling. "It was eight years ago when you were   were   statement rather than a question.

"Yes," Cora answered. She hesitated   ven   all this time, she did not wish to make explanations, as   she   wanted to protect those who were truly innocent. "The baby was already on the way. That's why   hurried through the divorce proceedings."

"Why didn't he marry her when the first boy was born?" Jedwin asked. "That was years before he met you. Were they separated? Did he not know about the boy?"

Cora shrugged and gave a humorless grin. "He did marry her," she said.

"What?"

Cora smiled tightly and reached over with a gentle finger to close his jaw. "He married her Cherokee fashion," she explained.

Jedwin looked at her closely with both concern and surprise.

Cora gently caressed his temples. "I guess it must be something like when you hung your belt on the bedstead," she told him. "The law doesn't recognize it, but the parties involved know vows when they've made them."

"Luther Briggs was married to another woman?" Jedwin was clearly appalled.

"Yes," Cora answered. "I didn't know about it, of course, not at first. Though Miss Maimie kept dropping hints. I'm sure that woman thinks I'm the stupidest female in the territories. I trusted Luther completely. I never worried at all."

"Because you loved each other?"

The question gave her pause. "No," Cora said. "Luther and I, well, I don't think we ever loved each other." She raised her eyes to meet his, with honesty. "But we were married. I'd been brought up to believe that was reason enough to give my trust."

Jedwin nodded. "Do you think she trusted him, too?" he asked.

"It wasn't the same. Although the Cherokees are basically monogamous," Cora explained. "Occasionally a man will have two wives. Apparently it's even more common when the man is white."

"So, she knew about you, but you didn't know about her."

"No, I didn't know about her. Not until the very end."

"But Miss Maimie knew."

Cora's jaw was set in anger. "It was Miss Maimie's idea!"

"What?"

Cora repeated her words. "She didn't approve of Luther's Indian wife," she said. "She was ashamed that Luther had married her and she didn't want anyone to know."

"And no one did," he said.

"That's right. Luther kept his little family in Muskogee and always came home alone. His life in Muskogee was far enough away that nobody in Dead Dog was the wiser."

"But that wasn't enough," Jedwin said, prompting her.

"No. After a time, Miss Maimie decided she needed grandchildren," Cora said. "Luther tried to convince her to accept the one she already had."

"I can imagine Miss Maimie's reaction," Jedwin said.

Cora nodded.

"So Luther married you to please her," he said.

"He tried to avoid it as long as he could," she said. "But it seemed Miss Maimie actually owned all of Luther's companies, all the land, the investments; everything had been left in her name instead of his. She'd held those reins for years and when she wanted grandchildren, she decided to tighten them up." Cora sighed sadly. "She told him that if he didn't marry a decent white woman within six months' time, he'd be a pauper."

"So he married you."

"Yes." Cora nodded. "When he came to the Methodist Home, he was almost desperate for a bride. He'd defied his mother almost to the last minute, and then he saw everything he'd worked for all his life, everything that he needed to support his family, slipping away from him. He asked me to marry him almost immediately. I knew nothing about Cherokee wives or his finances or even his mother. I just saw a handsome young man who was going to take me away from my lonely orphan life and love and cherish me till death do us part."

Cora's tone held a hint of bitterness for her youthful fantasy. Jedwin pulled her more closely in his arms and hugged her tightly.

"He wasn't really committed to living with me or the marriage at first," she said. "His plan was simply to bring me to Dead Dog and leave me with his mother. He wanted to continue to pursue his life in Muskogee with his *real* wife and child."

"But that didn't work," Jedwin said.

"It probably would have," Cora told him. "I never suspected a thing. I was so happy, especially after he built me my own little house away from Miss Maimie."

She sighed, glancing around at the familiar walls that were the legacy that Luther Briggs had left her.

"Building this house really angered Miss Maimie. Maybe it hurt her, I don't know. I only know she wanted to hurt me. It was Miss Maimie herself who told me about everything, the wife, the child, Luther's continued unfaithfulness," she said. "And you know Miss Maimie. She told it in the most horrible, sordid, disheartening way possible. Somehow, even though she was the one who was honest with me, I could never quite forgive her for that." Cora sighed almost apologetically before continuing her story.

"The next time Luther came home, I confronted him immediately. He should have left me then. That would at least have given me some shreds of honor to live with. But he told me that he was going to give her up. That he would be a faithful and dutiful husband to me. And I wanted to believe him. So I let him stay."

"But he didn't keep his promises," Jedwin surmised.

"He tried," Cora admitted. "For the next several months he spent nearly all his time with me. He really tried to make our life a real marriage," she said. "I truly believe that. But, he loved *her*. It was as simple as that."

Jedwin nodded, understanding.

"When he found out she was carrying a child, he just couldn't stay away any longer."

She raised her eyes to Jedwin's. There was no bitterness in them now, only understanding.

"He gave it all up," she said. "Me, his mother, his business, his heritage. He threw it all away for a woman that he loved. I've tried to hate him, Jedwin. But I can do nothing but admire him for that."

Jedwin looked down into the eyes of the woman that he loved. Cora had kept Luther's secret—for Luther, for his children, for Miss Maimie, for the town. She'd shouldered the blame and shame of sins that were not her own. And she had done it because despite the rules of the society and the conventions of the community, she knew it was the right thing to do. Jedwin found he couldn't help but admire *her* for that.

"I love you, Cora," he whispered. He ran a gentle hand along her cheek. "I can't even grieve for Luther Briggs. He's with the woman he loves, and I am with mine."

She swallowed bravely and gave him a tiny smile. "I am truly free to marry now, Jedwin."

His eyes widened as a smile twitched at the corner of his mouth and he feigned shock, squeezing her close. "Absolutely not! You are *my* wife and I have no intention of ever letting you go."

"How?" Miss Maimie asked through the tears. "How did my son die?"

Amelia had held the older woman in her arms through the quaking sorrow of loss. "It was the diphtheria," she answered quietly.

"Diphtheria?" she said, her voice strangely distant. "Just like here. A plague on the people."

"No one knows the whys of disease," Amelia told her soothingly as she dried the tears from the old woman's cheeks with her own handkerchief. Outliving one's child must be the cruelest pain on earth, Amelia thought. "Only God knows why he calls some home and leaves others here to ripe old age," she whispered.

Maimie nodded at the sage words. "God's mysteries are beyond my understanding. To take Harlan from me in the prime of life and now dear Luther in my old age, I don't know that I can bear it."

Tears fell from Amelia's own eyes as she hugged Miss Maimie's thin frame to her.

"It's been bad then, in Muskogee?" the old woman asked.

Amelia shook her head. "I don't really know. All I know is what the boys told me."

"The boys?"

Hesitating for only a moment, Amelia smoothed back Maimie's wispy hair. "Luther's sons," she answered. "They brought his body back to Dead Dog for burial."

Maimie appeared momentarily confused before her expression hardened into one more familiar to Amelia than the vulnerability she'd shown so far.

"That squaw had better not have come to my door expecting charity!"

The vehemence of the old woman's words startled Amelia momentarily. "Squaw? You mean the boys' mother?"

Miss Maimie raised her chin haughtily. "I suppose she thinks I will pay her off to keep quiet."

"The woman is dead," Amelia assured Maimie hastily, patting her hand as if trying to revive sense in her.

"She's dead, too?"

"Yes." Amelia took a deep breath before telling her the whole story.

Maimie stared at Amelia for a long minute, as if assessing her words.

"So he sent his little half-breed no-names to me?" she asked coldly. "Well, I'm not about to have a pair of blanket-wrapped savages sitting on my front porch."

Amelia's mouth dropped open in shock, and she rose to her feet, stepping back from Maimie as if fearful of contagion.

"Miss Maimie," Amelia said, clearly striving to keep in control. "You are not yourself right now. I can understand that you were unhappy with his liaison with this Indian woman. But what he may or may not have done in his life is past now. Death is the final forgiveness." Amelia forced a hopeful smile to her lips. "You have two grandsons who need you."

Maimie raised her chin haughtily. "That's what that squaw wanted," she said bitterly. "Luther thought she loved him, but I knew she just wanted my money, my position, my social standing. She had those foul little half-breeds to try to steal my legacy, to steal a long tradition of noble family from me."

"Miss Maimie, you're not thinking straight," Amelia told her, her confusion rapidly turning to distaste.

"Mine is the finest heritage in the territory," Maimie said. "Perhaps the finest in the entire country. We were the princes of the South before the war, you know. Princes! I would never allow the blood of that greatness to flow through the children of a common native woman."

Amelia tried valiantly to hold on to her temper. Up to now allowing Miss Maimie to pretend to an aristocracy and nobility that was pure fantasy had been a harmless game. But rejecting her son's children based on such a blatant falsehood was beyond Amelia's understanding.

"That blood does flow through their veins, Miss Maimie," Amelia said sternly. "You should see the boys. Both favor Luther. And the eldest could be him in his youth almost exactly."

"It's not true!" the old woman cried. "I know in my heart that it could never be true."

"It is true," Amelia insisted. "Let me bring them upstairs so you can meet them. You'll see that they are Luther's sons. They are the legacy that he's left for you. They are your grandchildren."

The old woman waved away her words. "You would have me acknowledge them?" Miss Maimie shook her head. "I hoped for more from you, Amelia. As a mother yourself, a mother of a boy who is as wayward as my Luther, you should see that I can make no bargains with propriety. If I acknowledge those . . . those *children,* why it would be as good as saying that such illicit alliances are acceptable. Propriety and decency and civilization would be sacrificed. Don't you see that? And what about my Luther? If I bring his half-caste issue into my care, he will never learn that he cannot thwart my wishes."

"Maimie, Luther is dead," Amelia told her. "He can never have his way or learn anything more, not ever."

Maimie started slightly at the words, as if she'd forgotten about the death of her son. Momentarily her bright blue eyes welled up with tears and her face revealed the pain that tore at her heart. But she whisked it away with a defiant glance. "I will never acknowledge those children, not to my dying day. I do not blame them for being born. But they are the unlawful, immoral product of a union that could never be sanctioned."

"They are orphans, Miss Maimie," Amelia pleaded. "They need you."

She shook her head with finality. "I cannot, with good conscience, foist these interlopers on my community. Send them to one of those Indian schools. That's where they belong."

Amelia stood staring at the old woman in the chair before her. Shaking her head, she found it so difficult to believe that any mother, grieving for the loss of her son, could deny or withhold the comfort of her grandchildren. But the evidence of such a lack of loving sat right before her. Turning, she made her way to the door. Numbly, she tried to decide what she would say to the boys.

How she would explain a grandmother who was so wrapped in her own self-righteousness that she cared more for the rules of society than for her own flesh and blood?

At the door, she hesitated, turning back to the old woman. "Miss Maimie," she said, "you've meant a lot of things to me in my life. When I was a young girl, I was terrified of you. You never hesitated to berate me, to make me feel worthless, to remind me that I was less than nothing to you. When I was older I admired you. You were the town of Dead Dog. Your favor made or destroyed a person's life. You had power that no other man or woman in this town ever possessed. No one would ever cross you. I wanted to please you. I wanted to be seen with you. Sometimes I was so jealous, I almost hated you. Sometimes life looked so hopeless I wanted to give up because of you."

Amelia sighed heavily as if a giant burden had just been lifted from her shoulders, and she was free for the first time in memory.

"Miss Maimie," she said, "most of my life, I've wanted to *be* you."

As she turned to go, there was only pity left in Amelia's tone. "You are a bitter, lonely old woman. Who pushed her own son away from her years ago. Your son apparently forgave you; he wanted to give you another chance. Two more young lives to share in and take joy from. Most of us have to live eternally with our mistakes. But you were offered a chance to make amends, to try again, to make it right, to truly love."

Amelia shook her head sadly. "And you've repeated the same mistake you made before. You've put what was more acceptable to you before what was best for your child."

Looking back at the lonely old woman in the sewing rocker, Amelia knew that she would never be in this room again, that never again would she have the desire to visit Miss Maimie.

"I used to want to be you," she said. "I used to daydream about it. Plan how to make it happen. Struggle to imitate you. But I will never be you, Miss Maimie. I intend to make a point of that."

Chapter
Twenty-three

Cora still lay quietly in Jedwin's arms in the parlor rocker when they heard the tapping on the door. Curiously, Cora hurried to the window. Her eyes widened and she turned back to Jedwin.

"It's your mother," she whispered.

Jedwin was as surprised as Cora and started to the door. She stopped him. "This is my house, Jedwin," she told him as she tried to repair the damage her hair had suffered with the repositioning of a few hairpins. "I will greet any guests we have."

Her chin raised defiantly, Cora opened the door.

"Good afternoon," she said, greeting Amelia with exaggerated politeness.

"Good afternoon, Mrs. Briggs." Glancing past the young woman, she added, "Jedwin."

The two women stood facing each other at the threshold of the cottage.

"May I come in?" Amelia asked.

"Please," Cora answered, holding out her hand in welcome.

Stepping inside the Briggs cottage was something that Amelia Sparrow had never done. But she didn't waste time looking around. She kept her eyes only on the young couple before her. She watched her son protectively slip his arm around the young woman's waist. Biting her lip, she swallowed the wave of loneliness that suddenly seized her.

"May I sit?" Amelia asked.

"Please do," Cora answered stiffly, offering her the divan. "Do you want tea?"

"Tea? No," she answered, then changing her mind, "Yes, Mrs. Briggs, I would love to take tea with you."

Amelia sat straight-backed and perfectly poised as she twisted nervously at her gloves. She couldn't even raise her eyes to look at her son, who was sitting across the room from her, almost as uncomfortable as she was.

"The tea will only take a moment," Cora said, returning to the room. She seated herself near Jedwin and glanced at him, silently begging for his strength.

Amelia cleared her throat nervously as she searched for a neutral topic of conversation. "I drove myself from the Bruders' parsonage," she began finally. "It has been such a long while since I've handled a team." She rubbed her elbows meaningfully. "I'd forgotten what a strain it can be."

"Someone surely could have driven you," Jedwin said.

"I wanted to drive myself," Amelia assured him quickly. "I think that perhaps I don't spend enough time in my own company, depending upon myself, thinking my troubles through."

Cora observed Mrs. Sparrow closely, before giving a hasty glance toward Jedwin. "I know just what you mean," she said. "My bicycle gives me the same sense of independence. Mrs. Millenbutter believes that physical exertion can help clear the mind."

Amelia nodded. "Mrs. Millenbutter? Oh yes, the reverend seems very high on her theories."

"There are ways to build up the strength in your arms," Cora told her. "So that you will have no problem controlling your own team."

Nodding, Amelia managed a deliberate interest in the subject. She posed enough viable questions to keep the conversation pleasant and continuous until Cora returned to the kitchen to make the tea.

Without Cora in the room, Amelia's bright blue eyes drifted to brown ones belonging to her son.

"What are you doing here, Mama?" he asked with quiet curiosity.

"I've just come from Miss Maimie's," she began finally.

"Oh?" Cora said quietly as she carried the tea tray into the room.

"How did she take the news?" Jedwin asked.

Amelia raised eyes to her son and then let them drift over to the woman that he loved. "She took it in a way that no one but Miss Maimie would."

Jedwin and Cora exchanged glances, but Amelia did not comment on that further.

Gracefully, displaying the etiquette she had learned at the Methodist Home, Cora poured tea for Jedwin's mother from the teapot Amelia had given her as a wedding gift.

Accepting the cup and saucer offered, Amelia nodded with both recognition and approval.

Cora's almost imperceptible sigh was one of relief and she looked at Amelia Sparrow with a new sense of hopefulness.

"Where are Luther's boys?" Jedwin asked.

"At Reverend Bruder's house," Amelia answered.

Jedwin raised his eyebrow in surprise and exchanged a glance with Cora.

"It was Tulsa May's idea," Amelia explained. "When she realized the boys had lost their parents and had no home, she immediately offered her own. It would have been absolutely un-Christian for the reverend and Constance to renege on such an invitation. So I suspect the boys will be there until young Greasy has had time to sort out what he wants to do."

"Maimie will have nothing to do with them?" Cora's question really didn't require an answer. They all already knew.

"No," Amelia said. "It seems that acknowledging her own grandchildren would be a great breach of social etiquette."

The young people nodded silently.

The silence lingered in the tiny little cottage. Again, Amelia cleared her throat.

"It seems, Mrs. Briggs," she said, "that I owe you a rather overdue apology." Determinedly Amelia raised her eyes to Cora's. Her sincerity was visible and genuine. "I have sorely abused you and spoken unkindly against you on too many occasions to even be remembered."

"You didn't know the truth," Cora said evenly.

"Ignorance is no excuse. I was purposely spiteful and vicious about your problems with Luther. And with only modest encouragement from Miss Maimie, I systematically made it my business to ruin your name in this town. For that I am truly sorry."

"Apology accepted."

Amelia looked almost startled at the ease with which she was forgiven. She had yet to feel like it was deserved.

"If these last eight years of abuse were not enough," she continued, "I spoke unkindly about you to my son, who loves you very much. I made unreasonable demands, cruel threats, and . . . and shed guilt-provoking tears."

Amelia's eyes went to Jedwin at this last.

"I've always said that I've done everything to bring my son happiness," she told them. "But when he found that happiness, I tried to take it from him."

"You don't have to ask for my forgiveness, Mama," Jedwin said. "You know you always have it."

She lowered her eyes to her lap in shame, attempting to hide the tears that gathered in her eyes. Swallowing bravely, she raised her gaze once again to the young couple before her.

"I know that it may be too late," she said. "You are probably thinking that now that Cora is technically a widow and that the story will come out and she will be vindicated through the whole town, I have nothing but my own gain to achieve here. I'm sure there is some truth to that. But I wanted to openly tell you both that I am sorry. I was wrong, all wrong, completely wrong from the beginning. Perhaps you can never forget what I have done, I will understand if you feel that way. But I'm hoping . . . praying . . . begging, I suppose, that you will not shut me out of your lives together."

Jedwin wanted to assure her that such a thing would never happen, but he turned instead to Cora. The decision was hers.

Cora looked back at him for a long moment, before a warm and loving smile came to her lips.

"I have no family of my own, Mrs. Sparrow. Of course we want you in our lives. All children need a grandmother."

The relief on Amelia's face was visible as she dabbed at the corners of her eyes with a handkerchief.

"You are quite right," she said. "Being a grandmother would certainly give me a chance to be the kind of parent I've always wanted to be."

Jedwin grinned at her. "Maybe one of our children will grow up to love the mortuary business."

The laughter was a little strained, but it was genuine.

"About the mortuary, Jedwin," Amelia said. "Your father truly did leave that to you. He loved you and wanted to leave you all that he'd achieved in his life."

"Mama—" Jedwin began.

Amelia held up her hand to interrupt him. "It is not the life for you. That is plain as the sun coming up in the morning. But I can't allow you just to hand it back to me as if it is nothing. It is a very profitable business, and I've some money of my own. I believe, given long-term installments, that I will be able to buy you out."

"Now Mama—"

"Thank you, Mrs. Sparrow," Cora piped in. "We certainly will need some money to get the farm back into shape. Jedwin is hoping to start a commercial floriculture venture. It would be the first in the state. A bit of capital could help him get the business off to a good start."

Jedwin looked at his future wife and raised an eyebrow, but he did not gainsay her.

"I'm sure," Cora told Amelia cheerfully, "that your son can work out some very fair arrangements. He is the most kind, honest, trustworthy man I have ever known. You can be very proud of yourself for raising him right."

It was nearing dark when Amelia left the cottage. The tea had been very nice, and she and Cora were now on a first-name basis. When talking of the wedding, the young couple had suggested a simple service with just themselves and Reverend Bruder. Amelia had dissuaded them.

"Just leave the details to me," she told them. "This will be the biggest, most beautiful church wedding that Dead Dog has ever seen."

Her mind full of wedding details, she had just set the team to a trot when she saw Haywood Puser waiting for her at the end of the fence.

"Oh! Haywood, you frightened me," she said, pulling up. "What are you doing here?"

"Waiting for you, Mellie," he answered. "I came to see if Mrs. Briggs had scratched your eyes out and you'd have to be led home."

Amelia smiled brightly and shook her head. Without invitation, Haywood climbed onto the seat beside her.

"Cora and I are not yet the best of friends, but I think that someday maybe we could be. And that's a good thing for a mother and daughter-in-law."

Haywood grinned. "It's not a bad thing for sons and mothers, either."

With very improper familiarity, he wrapped his arm around her as the horses pulled the buggy at a leisurely pace.

"I went over to the preacher's about the funeral."

"When is it?"

"Tomorrow. We decided just to get it over with for the sake of them kids. They need to get their grieving done and get on with their lives."

Amelia nodded. "How are the boys?"

"They seem to be doing okay," he said. "That little Tulsa May has taken those two on with the same kind of enthusiasm for the project as building those flower boxes for Miss Maimie. And the boys themselves have already managed to win over Constance."

"Really?" Amelia was almost giddy with delight.

"I suspect the reverend will be coming around soon. He already told me that a childhood sorrow such as this had turned many a man to the cloth. And that little Arthel took to juggling the reverend's new Indian clubs like he was a professional."

Amelia's eyes widened with exaggerated glee and they laughed together easily.

Haywood gave her a little squeeze and Amelia pulled away with a look of censure. "Mr. Puser!"

His grin didn't appear particularly apologetic.

"I've decided to buy the mortuary from Jedwin," she said, changing the subject.

"Now that's a damn good idea, Mellie," he said. "It will get this burden off that boy's back once and for all, and give him a little money for his farming to boot."

Amelia smiled at him. "I'm glad that you approve," she said. "Of course, Mr. Puser, I will be keeping you on. You don't have to worry about your job, I assure you."

Haywood shrugged. "Oh, I ain't worried," he said. "They's plenty of jobs on down the line. I'll just be heading out to see what I can find."

"What?"

"I said I'd be heading out."

"Why?" Amelia asked, almost dumbfounded.

" 'Cause it's your funeral parlor now. I've always worked for Jedwin, you know."

Amelia's expression hardened. "You won't work for a woman?" she asked, fury glistening self-righteously in her eyes.

"Oh, I don't mind working for a woman, Mellie," he assured her easily. "I just mind working for you."

Amelia's mouth opened in shock and she found herself too stunned to speak. A million thoughts ran through her head, none of them particularly happy.

"Where will you go?" she asked finally.

"Oh, I don't know," Haywood said. "Place don't matter much. I've got this idea to own my own mortuary."

"To own your own mortuary?" Amelia was stunned. "I didn't realize you had the money to start your own business."

"Oh, a man don't always need money," he said. "Lotsa men got themselves a business without putting up a penny."

Amelia shook her head. "I don't know how."

"It's simple, really," Haywood told her. "I just need to find me a widow woman that's got her own mortuary business. I marry up with her and I got my own business, no cash, no carry."

Amelia pulled the horses to an abrupt stop in the middle of the street and gaped at him. She stood staring at Haywood in the center of town.

He grinned at her.

After a moment she grinned back.

Chapter
Twenty-four

"With this ring, I thee wed."

Cora looked down at the wide gold band that was being slipped on her finger as she listened to Jedwin's words. Glancing up, she caught his eyes and they smiled a sweet private smile all their own before looking toward the good reverend.

"By the authority vested in me," Reverend Bruder bellowed to the crowd, "by this church and the Territory of Oklahoma, I pronounce these two, man and wife. What God has joined together, let not man put asunder."

Bringing his eyes back to the young couple, the preacher was all smiles. "You can kiss her now, son," he said, as if the two were in need of his permission.

Jedwin pulled Mrs. Cora Sparrow into his arms and brought his lips down to hers. The kiss was warm and sweet and welcome, as if the gentle touch of lips truly did seal the vows they made for all time.

As the kiss lingered, matrons began to titter behind their fans and a couple of the younger men began to applaud in appreciation.

The two pulled apart, flushed. With a prideful grin of satisfaction, Jedwin offered his arm to his new bride and gave a slight nod to Opal Crenshaw at the piano. The cheerful, smiling woman struck up a rousing rendition of "Happy the

Home When God Is There" as Jedwin and Cora marched up the aisle and out of the church, the reverend following behind them.

Stopping on the steps, Jedwin took the opportunity to kiss his wife on the end of the nose. "I love you," he managed to whisper before the entire community of Dead Dog began pouring out of the church door to offer congratulations.

"We think so much of this young man," Grace Panek told Cora. "Osgold and I are just so happy he has found you."

"Jedwin." Carlisle Bowman shook his hand and then offered a polite nod to Cora. "You have my best wishes, ma'am."

Nora Dix exclaimed delightedly over the fashionableness of Cora's dress, while her teenage daughter, Emma, fairly drooled at the pale confection of peachy-beige satin and lace.

Holding Lily Auslander firmly at her side, as if for protection, Constance Bruder almost too cheerfully invited Cora to attend the Ladies' Tuesday Meeting when she returned from the honeymoon trip.

"We are studying the Book of Job," Mrs. Bruder told her hopefully. "And we devote a half hour every meeting to deep breathing and exercise."

As the crowd began to spill out onto the church lawn, Jedwin and Cora were swept along with them. Children were beginning to run wild with freedom after the confinement of the wedding service. Amelia, with the help of Beulah Bowman, began dishing out cups of sweet cider to the guests and urging the newly married couple to come and cut the cake.

At the urging of his wife, Kirby Maitland brought out a chair for Fanny Penny.

"For heaven's sake, Fanny," Mrs. Maitland scolded. "That little boy of yours is barely two weeks old. You should never have left your bed so soon."

Fanny just smiled. She looked strong and healthy and prettier than she had in a long time. Titus had claimed he needed to be escorted by the prettiest woman in Dead Dog and Fanny was just as insistent that she be at his side.

Amelia finally managed to lure Jedwin and Cora to the cake table.

"You cut the cake and feed it to her," Amelia directed.

"What?" Jedwin did not seem particularly disposed to the idea.

"It's a symbol," his mother insisted.

With a shrug, Jedwin cut a small piece of the fancy cake made of fine-milled flour and offered it to Cora.

"It's wonderful," Cora complimented her new mother-in-law and gladly watched the older woman preen with delight.

As the youngsters began running forward to snitch pieces, the women served up the plates and Cora and Jedwin once again braved the crowd.

"Watch me, Miz Cora," Tulsa May called out from the lawn at the side of the church. "I'm learning the wand." The young girl twirled the shiny new Lewis wand with some skill. Cora offered a splash of genuine applause and an admonition to keep practicing.

Mort Humley sidled up to Jedwin and stuck an elbow in his ribs. "You need a tot of corn liquor for your weddin' night?" he asked in a cautious whisper. "It's guaranteed to warm up the coolest of new brides."

Jedwin grinned and patted the older man on the shoulder. "No, thanks, Mort. I think I can warm things up on my own."

Young Arthel was showing Ross Crenshaw's boys how to throw the Indian clubs as little Maybelle Penny stamped her foot and demanded attention. "Me! Me! Give them to me!" she screeched in fury at the boys nearly twice her size.

"I hope we can get out of here soon," Jedwin whispered warmly in Cora's ear. "That hotel in Guthrie is looking like paradise to me about now."

Cora nodded and opened her mouth to voice her agreement when the sound of a buggy on the road drew her attention. A fancy black phaeton, slightly out of fashion but splendidly dressed out, pulled up in the church yard. Conrad Ruggy sat on the driver's seat in his Sunday best and high hat. Behind him, as regally bedecked as a queen, was Mrs. Maimie Briggs.

A hush fell over the crowd and each person looked at another to take the lead. Osgold Panek looked to Titus Penny. Titus looked to Carlisle Bowman. Carlisle looked to Reverend Bruder. But it was Jedwin Sparrow, his wife on his arm, who walked out to Miss Maimie's rig.

"Good afternoon," he said politely. "It was nice of you to come, Miss Maimie. You do know my wife?"

Cora nodded to the older woman, but it was Miss Maimie who offered her hand. "I wish you the very best, Mrs. Sparrow. I've brought you a wedding gift. Conrad . . ."

At her gesture, Ruggy stepped down from the buggy and retrieved a sterling silver tray from the seat beside him. With a smile and a wink he handed it to Cora.

"My husband brought this piece to me from Saint Louis," Miss Maimie explained. "I meant someday to give it to your mother, Jedwin. But I think I'd rather that you had it."

Cora looked down at the fancy piece of scrolled silver and thought how much better it would look in Amelia's home than in her own.

"Thank you very much, Miss Maimie." She showed no sign that she'd seen through the spiteful woman's machinations. "Won't you get down and have a bite of our wedding cake?"

As Jedwin helped the frail old woman to the ground, Fanny hurriedly gave up her chair. Seated among the standing company, Miss Maimie quickly regained her color and the haughty lilt to her chin.

"What a lovely little boy, Fanny," she said sweetly. "And don't worry, I'm sure that you will regain most of your figure eventually."

Slowly, as if doing a penance, each member of the community came to pay their respects and take turn with Miss Maimie's spiteful tongue. But somehow her barbs seemed less sharp than remembered.

When Miss Maimie espied young Tulsa May, it was on the tip of her tongue to call the girl over for a reminder of her unacceptable dowdiness. What stilled her tongue was the young boy laughing at her side. Miss Maimie's heart caught in her throat as she saw the sleek black hair, the bright broad smile, and the vivid blue eyes she thought to never see again. "Luther!" she whispered under her breath.

A crash of breaking glass kept her exclamation unheard.

"Maybelle!" Titus Penny's voice was a loud gust of surprise as he stared at his young daughter, Indian club in hand, standing among the colorful broken glass that had once been a Dutch windmill.

Cora came out from behind the dressing screen in a new pink calico nightdress that she'd never worn before. She stood silently at the end of the bed, waiting for Jedwin to notice.

The lamp beside him, Jedwin lay in the bed, scribbling on a piece of paper. Minutes went by and he didn't raise his head. Cora got tired of waiting. She cleared her throat loudly.

Jedwin raised his head to look at her.

She smiled and gave him a graceful curtsy in her new attire.

"Pretty," he said, before returning immediately to his writing.

"I bought it readymade in that fancy emporium in Guthrie."

He glanced up again and grinned. "Kind of a waste of money, I suppose. I'm just going to take it right off you."

As Cora's mouth dropped open, Jedwin turned his attention once more to the paper in his hand. She stood there staring at him in disbelief.

"You seem mighty busy tonight," she said, a hint of pique in her voice.

Jedwin didn't even glance up. "I've wasted a whole week honeymooning with you. I'm a working farmer now, I've got to keep my mind on my business."

"You '*wasted* a whole week honeymooning'?"

Jedwin didn't answer.

"Is this how it's going to be?" she demanded.

Jedwin looked up again. "What?"

"Marriage!" she screeched. "Is this how it's going to be? You just do what you please and ignore me like I'm a piece of the furniture until you get me into bed."

Jedwin gave her a long-suffering look of patience. "You're my wife now, Cora," he said simply. "Wives are not like women you sow wild oats with. You can't expect me to continue to treat you like a fast fancy woman."

"I don't expect you to treat me like a stranger. I won't stand for it!"

"I'm afraid you don't have any choice," Jedwin said, with a gesture toward his belt that still hung around the top of the bedstead, a visible symbol of promises made, as sacred to him as the ring on her finger.

"Don't worry," he told her. "I know my duty as a husband and I'll do what's required to get you with child at the earliest possible opportunity."

"Duty!" Frantically she struggled to control the anger that seethed within her.

"Yes, duty, Cora," Jedwin said calmly. "That is what marriage is about after all. What else could you want?"

"Love!" Cora screamed.

"Of course I love you," he said. "Surely you'd never question that."

"But . . . but . . ." She was speechless with exasperation.

"Ah!" Jedwin said, raising his finger as if suddenly having an idea. "I suppose you are talking about romance."

Cora didn't answer, but strived only to keep her temper in check.

He shook his head disdainfully. "Cora, Cora, Cora," he said. "Romance and marriage simply do not mix."

She snapped. Grabbing the pillow on her side of the bed she raised it over her head. With a scream of blood lust worthy of an Indian on the warpath, she brought it down with all the force in her body on Jedwin's head.

One on-target hit was not sufficient and she raised the pillow again and again, pounding him into the bed. Jedwin finally managed to wrestle the pillow away from her and toss it onto the floor. They struggled together for several moments. She on top first, then he, then she again. More than once they nearly fell off the bed, but managed somehow not to. Cora's fury gave her strength and for most of the fight she had the upper hand. But finally her arms began to ache and her strength began to fade. It was only moments before the natural physical superiority of the male finally overcame her most valiant efforts.

He held her down full-length on the bed, his body on top of hers. Both her hands were grasped in one of his and he held them high above her against the headboard. She could feel them pressing against the leather of the belt that hung there.

In Jedwin's other hand, he still gripped the piece of paper he had so diligently been writing upon when the fracas had begun.

He brought the paper up before his eyes and in the pale yellow light of the coal-oil lamp he quietly read to her what was written upon it.

> "A man searches for happiness
> The whole of his life.
> But he won't ever find it
> Until he takes him a wife.
> A woman to help him
> Be the man he can be.
> To love and to cherish
> For eternity.
> I have found such a woman.
> Her name, it is Cora
> For happily ever after
> I will always adore her."

His grip loosened on her hands and she wrapped her arms around him. She looked deeply into those intensely brown eyes that she loved and saw his heart.

"Jedwin," she whispered.

"Yes, my love."

"Stick to farming. You'll never make it as a poet."

From the *Prattville Populist*,
Prattville, Oklahoma
June 17, 1914

CITY'S FIRST HOSPITAL TO
OPEN ON LUTHER STREET

Citizens and community leaders gathered Saturday night to celebrate the opening of the new Millenbutter Memorial Hospital. The gleaming new facility, slated to open July 1, was made possible through renovation of the Briggs mansion, former home of Mrs. Harlan (Maimie) Briggs, late of this city. The building, part of the estate willed to local businessman Luther H. Briggs, proprietor of Briggs's Bicycle Shop and Auto-Mobile Garage, has remained empty since the death of Mrs. Briggs four years ago. Citing high property taxes on such a large area in the center of town, Mr. Briggs, on behalf of his brother and himself, requested that the property be turned over to the city of Prattville for public use.

It was Mrs. Haywood (Amelia Pratt) Puser, daughter of city founder, Moses Pratt, who conceived of the idea of a hospital for the citizens of the community. With the help of society matrons Mrs. Titus (Fanny) Penny and Mrs. James E. (Cora) Sparrow, a suitable physician was found to take charge of the facility.

Odysseus Parker Foote, M.D., nephew of Miss Prudence Foote, long-time Prattville educator, is a recent graduate of the George Washington University School of Medicine in Saint Louis, Missouri. Dr. Foote was on hand for the dedication ceremonies.

The First Baptist Church Young Ladies Choir made the occasion festive with a snappy rendition of "Put On Your Old Gray Bonnet." Mayor Clyde Avery gave a speech concerning the growth and future concerns of the city. And Reverend Philemon Bruder spoke of the Lord's blessing on the hospital and all the sick and afflicted that are to be cared for within.

After the dedication, a box supper auction was held to raise money for purchase of the most modern of medical equipment and tools. More than two hundred gaily decorated items were auctioned for sale, totaling more than ninety dollars in donations. The most expensive price was paid by Mr. Jedwin Sparrow of Cimarron Ornamental Flower Farms. Six dollars bought the woven wicker basket trimmed in bright blue ribbon fashioned by Mrs. Sparrow. The Sparrows' second son, five-year-old Jimmy Trey, commented to this reporter that he was sure the basket contained the "same old bean patties, cooked greens, and celery hearts." The young man suggested that, unlike his father, he would have picked a basket sure to contain fried chicken.

T. M. Bruder
Special Reporter to the *Populist*